THE BOMBER JACKET

K.M. KING

WILD INK PUBLISHING, LLC

A Wild Ink Publishing Publishing Original

wild-ink-publishing.com

ISBN: 978-1-958531-79-2 (Paperback)
978-1-958531-80-8 (ebook

ONE

PART 1: 1997

"THREE FIVE SIX POINT six. Three five six point five. Three five six point four." Beth mouthed the mileage markers as they blipped by the passenger window in a green blur, keeping time with her right foot on the floorboard of the car.

"Do you have your passport, Susie Q?"

"Yes, Grandpa," Beth replied. "It's right here, same place it's been since we left the house." She patted the thin, black passport purse hanging around her neck. "My ticket too."

After three and a half years of attending college part-time, she had finally accumulated enough credits to be a junior, and more than enough funds in her bank account for this very ticket to Scotland. Her first choice had been England, the country of her literary heroes—William Shakespeare, Lord Byron, and Jane Austen among them. But she had gotten enough signs to encourage the switch and ignore her grandparents' objections, particularly those unnerving dreams.

A slight smell of old leather had drifted up when she patted her purse. She sniffed appreciatively, never tiring of the scent or feel of her vintage RAF bomber jacket. Her grandfather Henry's aftershave, with its hint of pine trees and burnt wood, also hung in the car's confined space. A gift from a long-lost friend in 1941. Her bomber jacket had been a gift to herself. Her grandmother Naomi called it "an ugly thing from a war that everyone wants to forget."

Henry's thumbs kept beat with the steady kathunk, kathunk, kathunk of the tires on the road's seams, driving eastward on the Pennsylvania Turnpike in his habitually careful way, five miles under the posted speed limit, oblivious to the glaring drivers who zoomed past.

"Now, what time is your flight again?"

"Grandpa, we've got plenty of time." Beth's boot kept tapping as she stared into the steel gray January afternoon, trying to focus on the mile signs instead of the anxiety his question raised. "My flight doesn't leave until three fifty-five. We only need to be at the airport an hour before boarding. It's just two-fifteen, and we're nearly at the river."

The car hit a bump, sending the taste of shellfish and lard into her throat. She'd requested only yogurt and granola, but Naomi had shamed her into having homemade crab cakes, French fries, and coleslaw.

"I've gone to all this trouble to make your favorite dinner, and you're not even going to eat it?"

"You've never even flown..." Henry's voice interrupted thoughts of Naomi's shuttered face and stiff goodbye embrace. "...and you've got to change planes in New York..."

"Grandpa, I'll be fine." Beth put as much assurance as she could into her voice.

Henry nodded. "I don't doubt you can take care of yourself, Pumpkin. You've had to do too much of that over the years. You're even paying your own way through college. It's not how I wanted it."

"Oh, don't go getting all sentimental on me now; you'll turn me into a blubbering idiot," she countered with a joke, needing her grandfather to be his usual calm, unruffled self.

"It's just that there's no one to meet you in London, Beth. You'll have to get to your hotel and later the train station..."

"It's okay, Grandpa, really. I got all the details I needed from school. I know the taxi fare to the hotel, which is already booked for my two-night stay. I've already bought the train ticket for Sunday's trip to Edinburgh. It's the *Flying Scotsman*. Isn't that a cool name for a train?"

Her grandfather muttered, "I knew a flying Scotsman, once," before he grew suddenly silent. Relieved by the quiet, Beth scanned the slate-colored, seamless clouds for precipitation. As they neared the Susquehanna River, the overhanging hills cast the car into a gloomy shadow. When Henry said several times that morning that "it smelled like snow," Beth regretted turning down a friend's offer for the forty-five-minute ride from Carlisle to the Harrisburg Airport. She knew her grandfather hated driving in bad weather.

At least he didn't seem to mind the chill in only his cardigan sweater, but Beth was glad for her wool-lined leather coat.

"You can wear history, lovey!" The owner of the vintage clothing shop told her in October when she saw Beth admiring it. "World War II. Royal Air Force. It's the real deal and a bargain for the price I'm asking. Try it on."

At four-hundred and twenty-five dollars, it was no bargain, but the six-month temp job as a road crew flagger had bulked up her bank account.

"It looks great with your brunette ponytail," the shop owner gushed. "And for a tall, lanky girl like you, finding the right coat must be hard. This one fits like it was custom-made."

True enough, Beth instantly felt at home in the jacket. It was more than the right fit though. Something about it gave her a sense of presence.

When she got home that Saturday afternoon to the faded Victorian house on Pitt Street where she had been raised by her grandparents, Naomi was in the huge kitchen, doing her Saturday baking. She had just pulled a pumpkin pie from the oven when Beth walked in.

"Hi, Grandma."

Catching the sight of Beth in her vintage coat, Naomi gasped, the pie tumbling from her hands to land with a crack of splintered glass and orange splatter on the spotless, washed-out linoleum floor. Her deeply wrinkled face was as white as her starched apron.

After a moment of shocked silence, Beth took several hurried steps toward her grandmother, "Nana! Nana, are you..."

"No, absolutely not!" Naomi thrust one trembling hand forward as if to ward off an attacker. "Where did you get that... thing? Henry said he... I told you a thousand times to stay out of the garage attic."

"I never go up there! It's locked, anyway!"

Naomi pulled a ladder-back chair away from the huge farmhouse table, and sat down, shaking, taking shallow breaths. "Answer me. Where'd you. Get. That. Thing."

Beth tried to keep the alarm from her voice. "*Wear It Again, Sam*—the vintage clothing shop on High Street," she said, stepping closer.

"*Why* in the hell did you buy such an ugly thing?" Naomi's voice was still shaky.

Beth decided to avoid yet another endless, useless match of wills and simply said, "I've always wanted one."

"You'll take it back this very minute!"

As usual, her grandfather tried to intervene, but his "Now Naomi, it's only a jacket," had sent her grandmother stomping out. But her grandmother's over-the-top reaction wasn't the most unsettling occurrence of the day, for that night she had the first of many intense dreams that slowly changed everything.

"Only a couple minutes now."

Her grandfather's voice interrupted Beth's reverie once again, and she realized they were crossing the Susquehanna River where massive chunks of ice floated by in silent elegance.

Beth had a sudden image of her grandparents' life without her: Henry sitting alone in the cozy TV room, flipping between the History Channel and Turner Classic Movies. Naomi was in the spotless kitchen concocting some high-cholesterol dinner that her grandfather wasn't supposed to eat.

Her stomach suddenly clenched. "Grandpa, you'll remember to take your heart medicine, won't you?"

After a moment, Henry said in a stern voice, "History's important you know, Beth. There's lots of history where you're going."

Beth tried to follow his train of thought. "Yes, I've been reading lots of Scottish history ever since I changed my study-abroad destination."

"I'm not talking about ancient history," Henry replied. "Though I guess at your age, any history seems ancient."

Beth laughed. She had grown up watching Henry's favorite television shows and movies, many of them focused on World War II.

"You're going to places that are important to *your* history." He said it so softly, Beth barely heard him. She had been pointing to the exit for the airport.

"My history? You mean *your* history. Your war years and all." Not that she ever pressed her grandfather about his war experiences. Even when she was younger, she understood this was something too painful for a casual chat.

"Goddammit, it's snowing!"

Her grandfather's rare profanity was a sure sign of his unspoken worry. She could see several light flakes.

"Grandpa, just drop me at the terminal. At the unloading point. I don't want you to get caught on the highway in a storm."

"Goddammit!" Henry muttered again, as he pulled up to the luggage drop-off point. Beth's heart lurched at the sadness on her grandfather's face. It took all her willpower to hold back tears as she unbuckled her seatbelt and grabbed the backpack at her feet. "Pull the trunk release, Grandpa."

She had already hoisted the two huge suitcases onto the sidewalk by the time her grandfather walked to the back of the car.

A man behind her said, "Skycap? Ma'am? Can I take your bags?"

Henry nodded to the uniformed baggage handler. After pressing a bill into the man's hand, he slammed the trunk lid with undue force. At an alarming speed, the flurries became thick, heavy flakes landing on Beth's hair, kissing her cheeks as they fluttered by.

"You should have a hat on, Beth." Her grandfather's voice was as gritty as sandpaper. "Come on, let's get you out of the weather."

"Please, Grandpa, you'll just make it harder for me if you come in and wait. Plus, you can't park the car here. I'll worry about you driving home if the snow gets worse." Beth felt her voice shaking. In her twenty-two years, she'd rarely been away overnight from her grandparents. Perhaps she had sensed her grandfather was terrified he'd lose her as he'd lost her mother; or maybe she had dreaded asking her cold, forbidding grandmother for permission to do ordinary things girls her age did.

Henry clenched and unclenched his hands. "What if your flight is canceled?"

"I'm sure it won't be. And if it is, I'll call. I promise."

When had he gotten so frail-looking?

"It's not right to let you go off across the ocean without someone to wave goodbye."

"Oh, Grandpa, I'll be fine. Really." Beth threw her arms around him, all the joy of the journey draining away with unexpected worry. He returned her embrace with a rib-cracking bear hug. She heard his breath catch as he stepped away, moisture gathering at the corners of his eyes. Reaching into his shirt pocket, he took out a folded sheet of paper and handed it to her.

"What is it?" She took the paper, confused.

"Put it away someplace safe. It's a list of places to go see in Scotland. Places you *need* to see, Susanna Elizabeth."

She was unnerved by his intensity, by his fervor. What was that he had said earlier about places important to *her* history? She tucked the strange words away. No time now. "Sure, Grandpa, sure," she said, thrusting the list into her jeans pocket, out of the dampness of the falling snow.

The skycap cleared his throat. "Which airline, ma'am?"

"American Airlines," Henry answered for her.

Beth kissed her grandfather's wrinkled cheek. "I love you, PopPop." She whispered the childhood endearment in his ear. "Please take good care of yourself while I'm gone."

Her grandfather surprised her by gripping her shoulders and looking her straight in the eye. "No matter what you learn, remember I thought I was doing the right thing. For everyone. Don't forget that, Pumpkin. Please don't forget that."

"What, forget what?" Beth replied, startled and confused.

"Coming, ma'am?" the skycap interjected, distracting Beth.

"Bye, Grandpa," she said, fighting to keep her composure as she followed the baggage handler out of the biting cold into the terminal. Once inside, Beth turned to wave. Her grandfather stared at her forlornly. When he blew her a kiss, Beth managed to blow one in return, then hurried after the skycap, her eyes blurry.

With her bags checked through, Beth was free to roam JFK airport during her three-hour layover. But the distraction of shops and people-watching soon wore off. She found a quiet corner to sip a cup of Earl Grey and examine her grandfather's list near a neon sign displaying today's date and time: January 2, 7:09 p.m.

The items seemed to be in no particular order: Edinburgh. Drem Aerodrome. Traprain Law. Holyrood.

She knew Edinburgh was the capital of Scotland. After all, she was going to the University of Edinburgh. Holyrood was a palace in Edinburgh. Skye was an island to the west on the must-see list in her tour book. Stirling was the site of a famous castle and the Wallace Monument. The others she hadn't heard of.

Thinking of her ultimate destination, she recalled the first Sunday of November, the day she'd made her impulsive decision to switch schools and countries for her semester abroad. And what a day it was. First, a minister from the Church of Scotland preached at their Presbyterian Church. She was enthralled by the soft burr of his accent and the smattering of Scottish words that slipped into his sermon—*wee lassies, aye, kirk, burn*.

That afternoon, curled up with the Sunday paper, she came across an article encouraging tourists to visit Scotland year-round, not just during the famous Edinburgh Arts Festival in August which culminated in a massed performance of hundreds of bagpipers. How strange to encounter Scotland twice in one day.

That evening she joined her grandfather halfway through a television show about Mary, Queen of Scots. When pictures of Holyrood Palace in Edinburgh appeared on the screen, a sudden, uncontrollable shiver ran through her body.

She must have made some kind of noise, because Henry looked at her oddly and said, "Ducky, are you okay? Are you cold? You're shivering!" He draped her grandmother's crocheted, striped afghan over her shoulders.

"Thanks, Grandpa, thanks. I'm not cold, but this feels good, though. It's just... well, weird. Today we had that Scottish preacher from Edinburgh. Boy, I loved his accent, didn't you? And then this afternoon I came across an article about Edinburgh and now this show..."

An idea was percolating in Beth's mind. "Maybe it's a sign."

"A sign?" Her grandfather stared at her. "What kind of... sign?"

"Well, three things, in one day, about Edinburgh. And when I was investigating opportunities for study abroad, the University of Edinburgh was an option, but I brushed it off 'cause I'm a British Literature major and wanted to go to England, but maybe..."

"But maybe what, Pumpkin?"

Beth stood, suddenly excited. "Yeah, that's what I'll do! Tomorrow I'll ask my counselor if there's a way to change schools."

"It's not like you to be impulsive." Her grandfather frowned at her in the oddest way.

"No, it's not," she agreed, wondering at his look. "But it's fun to do something on a whim, and Scottish universities have a great reputation. I can still visit England, in the summer before I come home. Cool! I'm really excited now. I'm going to go make some notes about what I'll need to ask the counselor."

"Will they let you change so late in the game?" Her grandfather took a sip from his cup of tea. He liked something warm in the evening.

Beth put her hands on her hips and grinned. "I'll come up with this story that I've just discovered I have Scottish ancestors and I want to do some family research."

Her grandfather began coughing violently, the teacup in his hand rattling. She grabbed the cup and saucer and put them on the end table. "Are you all right?" she said in alarm, patting him firmly on the back.

"Yes... yes... I'm... I'm... fine," he said between coughs that rattled his whole body.

"Here, stand up and walk around. That might help." She pulled him to his feet. "Let's go out to the kitchen," she said, leading him toward the back of the house. She tried not to panic, knowing his history of heart attacks.

Henry's coughing had brought Naomi to the kitchen doorway. "What's wrong?" Her brows came together in a concerned crease.

"Tea... went... down the... wrong... hatch," Henry got out between coughs.

"Do you want more tea? I'll go get your cup," Beth offered, but he shook his head. He had stopped coughing, but still breathed unsteadily. "Why don't you sit down?" she asked.

"No, I'm better standing for a minute," he said. "I'm fine, really."

"Okay. You gave me a scare. Did I startle you with my news?"

"What news?" Naomi asked, still frowning.

"I've just been telling Grandpa. I'm thinking of switching schools and going to the University of Edinburgh. In Scotland."

Naomi crossed her arms, "Oh, no good can come of this. You tell her, Henry; tell her it's a bad idea."

Henry did not reply but stared at Beth with a look she couldn't interpret. Beth had been surprised. He always supported her ideas, often taking her side against Naomi's frequent protests.

"Well, I'm sorry my idea doesn't excite you, but I'm going to see how to make it happen."

But the "signs" from that day weren't the only reason she decided to spend the semester in Scotland. It was also the dream she'd had earlier that morning, a version of the same, yet ever-expanding dream she'd been having every night since she bought the bomber jacket. Alone in her room, she'd flipped to the back of her journal where she recorded details about THE DREAM, as she called it.

Sunday, October 19, 1996, 6:07 a.m.

I had the most peculiar dream last night. It seemed to consist only of smells.

There's engine oil, a smell I know from helping Grandpa work on the car. It's a smell that feels thick. My head felt thick, too, weighted down, and my thoughts felt thick, like I was trying to swim up from the bottom of a pool of molasses, sticky heaviness pulling me down into forgetfulness.

Yet there's something I must remember, but it's lost in all the cloying smells that are stealing my breath.

I was drowning in a pool of engine oil. No, no, not drowning, there is air. And, yes, I'm breathing, but the breathing feels muffled, confined. And there's another smell—the sharp, bitter odor of cold metal, a smell I can almost taste. Then the sweet, musty smell of leather and slightly damp wool, like my bomber jacket.

There's something else. Another odor. In the dream, I was sweating. Now, sitting here writing in my journal, I know what it was... the smell of fear.

Taking a sip of her now-tepid tea, she could still recall waking up from that dream in a pitch-black room, her heart pounding. For a minute she couldn't think of where she was until the illuminated dial of her bedside clock caught her eye, 3:53. Her face, neck, and armpits were drenched with sweat. Shivering, she curled under the blankets but lay awake for a long time.

Until the remnants of fear faded away.

Beth stared out the huge glass airport window into the dark night blinking with the lights of landing and taxiing airplanes. How vivid that first dream was and how unnerving that she dreamt it every night for a week. The same smells, the same sensations. Then a week later it changed. Her journal entry spelled it out.

Oct. 26, 1996, Monday, 6:05 a.m.

Last night was the 8th night in a row that I had THE DREAM. There is always the smell of engine oil, old leather, and damp wool. And the bitter taste of cold metal. Not long ago I began to have a sensation of muffled breathing, as if someone had a hand over my mouth and nose or I was wearing a scarf. And there's the constant knot of fear in the pit of my stomach.

But last night something new happened. I heard something. There's been that occasional thumping noise in the background but now it's a constant, low roar that seems to take up the empty space, so the dream feels full.

Two days later she had written,

THE DREAM is growing, widening, expanding. As if at first, I was in a tight cocoon limited to smells, tastes, and then sounds. Now there is a sense of being in a place—a confined space, a contained space. There is a sense of an inside and an outside, and I'm on the inside. And that constant, low roar seems to be coming from the inside.

Then in another two days, something both alarming and exciting happened in THE DREAM. She had heard a voice next to her ears. Muffled, crackly. But distinctly a man's voice.

Soon the dream began to contain a sensation of movement. Next came a feeling that she was holding onto something in front of her as she was seated. Night after night some fog in her brain seemed to be lifting. She was more... aware—no, hyperaware. Though she couldn't see anything, all her other senses were now engaged: smell, taste, touch, hearing.

And every night she awoke, sitting straight up, the clock reading 3:53. Then right before the Scottish minister's visit, she had THE DREAM that changed everything. She turned to that journal entry and read it slowly.

Saturday, November 1, 1996, 3:53 a.m.
It's always 3:53 when I wake up from THE DREAM. But tonight I had to write right away. I'm wide awake, sitting here in the middle of the night with my bedside light on, and it feels like my bed is an island surrounded by a dark sea. Tonight THE DREAM changed completely.

I felt as if I were wearing my bomber jacket in THE DREAM. It was keeping me warm. It was comforting. And I heard a voice—my voice. I AM the person in the dream, I mean, I'm not, but it's like I am. I'm experiencing what the person in the dream is experiencing, the smells, tastes, sensations, sounds, and feelings. So, it feels like I am the person.

I heard my voice. Responding to that crackly voice next to my ears.

"Roger that. Mission accomplished. On target for home."

I said it—I mean, he said it, with a Scottish accent.

I'm the pilot. And I'm Scottish.

TWO

I SHOULD GET UP and stretch my legs before I go to sleep, Beth thought as the flight attendants on the British Airways plane moved through the cabin, distributing soft wool blankets in a deep blue plaid and tiny pillows covered by crisp, starched cotton.

The disadvantage of the window seat meant disturbing the passengers in the aisle, something she had already done twice for a trip to the tiny airborne bathroom. Hopefully, she wouldn't need it after a rare indulgence in a glass of red wine. She had thought it would settle some jitters that had lingered in the lower reaches of her stomach ever since lunch, but it had only made her head fuzzy.

Beth looked at the passengers to her right, a middle-aged couple she had learned from friendly chit-chat were from Connecticut heading to visit their daughter in London. They had settled down to sleep as soon as the supper trays were taken away. Beth saw the woman's chest rise and fall rhythmically, amusingly in sync with her husband's gentle snoring, which Beth found comforting. It reminded her of her grandfather whenever he fell asleep after dinner sitting in his chair watching the news.

Just then, the passenger in front of her reclined so far back he felt like a threatening intruder in her private air space. "So much for getting up," Beth muttered to herself, now hemmed in on all sides.

Wishing her glare penetrated through the seat into the passenger's brain, Beth spread the blanket over her lap and stuffed the pillow between her headrest and the window to her left. She zipped her bomber jacket, the comforting leather smell mixing with the lingering odor of roast beef and mashed potatoes, and folded her arms, tucking her hands underneath her armpits. As the cabin lights dimmed, she rested her head against the pillow.

She closed her eyes and let the sounds sink in. The cabin was quiet except for a few soft conversations and an occasional whine of a fussy child. There was a sense of muted airlessness that made any sound shrink to the size of the airborne life raft in which they were seated. She noticed the hissing sound of air from the overhead vent and the roar of the engines, which earlier had been part of the white noise of this confined space, distinguishable only if it changed pitch in accelerating or decelerating.

The window's cold dampness penetrated her mind as she became aware of her forehead leaning against it. She opened her eyes and stared out at the reflection of the wing lights on thick clouds. She had imagined that traveling so much nearer the stars would be like flying among them. But the stars were as invisible as the ocean, which remained a vaguely menacing presence miles below, especially after the crash-landing instructions only she seemed to pay attention to.

Beth thought of the thinness of the air on the other side of the window, outside the pressurized cabin, and the frigid temperatures at 26,000 feet. Shivering at the thought of the cold, she nestled deeper into her coat and tucked the blanket more firmly around her jean-clad legs.

Exhausted from the day that had started before six and a restless sleep last night, Beth tried to will herself to sleep, but sleep was an unwelcoming host. After several minutes she gave up and stared out the oval window, which looked like an eye fighting sleep, with its blind pulled halfway down. The deep, dark night was the black pupil staring back at her, and the blinking red light at the wing tip was the red, angry iris pulsing with blood.

Beth sank into the forward motion of the plane, a barely perceptible sensation as the plane streaked across the night sky at six hundred miles an hour. Toward England.

Going home. Aye, we're headed home. Another night near spent. Another night survived.

The chill of the plane penetrated the leather and wool of the jacket. It was never warm at the height they flew. The only warmth came from the fear in the pit of one's stomach. Fear that shrank the further back across the channel they flew, the nearer the aerodrome they got, but as that fear shrank, the sense of cold increased.

The crew was quiet; they always were on the return trip. The nervous chatter that accompanied the trip out was stilled by exhaustion, hunger, and the anticipation of getting home.

Somewhere below was the water. He could not see it, only sense it. It was always there, a kind of being, churning, roiling, on a cold night. Like his stomach.

His stomach always gripped on the way back. On the way there he was calm, focused, steady, even when the flak was exploding around them. But on the way back, that's when the fear swept over him. That's when the odds began to play in his mind.

How many missions now? Each one done made the possibility of not coming back higher. Would Lady Luck hold? He didn't trust her. Just when you thought she was on your side, she'd bugger you. Couldn't afford to get cocky. Always had to be wary on the way back. His eyes constantly darted between the fuel gauge, the altimeter, and the speedometer. And ahead. To the right. To the left. His ears constantly listened for a change in the sound of the engine, for a warning sputter, or a hint of a cough.

They depended on him, the men. To get them home.

The plane hit an air pocket and dipped. The sting of acid rose to his throat. Thickening clouds warned of turbulence. *"Look sharp, we're heading up to get out of this cloud cover. It might—"*

"—get a wee bit rough." Beth blinked as the intercom crackled off above her.

She felt the plane accelerate as it began to climb, and she sat up straight.

To her right, the couple slept on. She looked up to see the fasten seat belt sign lit. The look of confusion on her face must have caught the attention of a passing flight attendant.

"Not to worry, miss. The pilot says there's some turbulence ahead," the young woman said in a quiet, comforting British accent. Beth remembered the pilot's introduction over the intercom. A Scot. Michael MacDermot. "Might get a wee bit rough in spots," he had said about the flight, "but mostly a quiet night ye'll have."

Had she been dreaming? She would swear she hadn't closed her eyes. Maybe she had been hypnotized by the sameness of the view, the blinking light on the wing of the plane. If she had been asleep, it couldn't have been for long.

She realized with a start this was the first dream she'd had since early November—since that night she realized she was dreaming about the pilot who'd once worn her jacket. The dreams had stopped suddenly after that night. Though she was happier for better sleep, she supposed. And it gave her one less thing to worry Henry with—she'd never have told Naomi, who'd tell her she wouldn't have bad dreams if she stopped eating sweets at bedtime. Still, she had felt oddly bereft. As if a friend had suddenly departed without saying goodbye.

As she thought about what she just dreamt, assuming it was a dream, she realized it was different in many ways. She played it over in her head, analyzing. The pilot had seemed so real—no longer a sensation, but now embodied, though she could not see him—wait. She gasped. Of course, she could not see him. She was viewing the world from *his* eyes: noticing the dark and the threatening clouds trimmed in moonlight, feeling the unseen ocean below.

And, also for the first time, she had heard his thoughts.

She shivered, unable to shake the deep, penetrating, bone-chilling cold filling the cabin of the bomber. Seeking warmth, she turned up the wool collar of her jacket, hunkered down into her seat, and pulled the blanket up to her neck. Closing her eyes, she tried to imagine herself back into THE DREAM.

"See you again soon." She whispered a promise.

Aye, said a voice that seemed to float back to her across the night sky. *Aye, soon.*

On Sunday morning, Beth woke up in a panic in the tiny room of the low-budget London guest house. Worn out from her whirlwind tour of the city, her mind still drugged from jet lag, she had overslept. Scrambling into her jeans and Shippensburg University sweatshirt she had laid out the night before, she jammed her feet into her brown leather boots and shoved her pajamas and cosmetic bag into her suitcase.

Forget the plan to walk the seven blocks to Kings Cross Station. Instead, she hailed a taxi with some difficulty on the crowded London street and mouthed a silent *thank you* to her grandfather for his thoughtful Christmas gift of lightweight luggage on wheels. Once at the station, she made a hasty stop to check her bags and hurried to the platform where the Flying Scotsman was boarding.

Her heart was still pounding wildly as she searched for an empty seat in the third-class, six-passenger compartments. She hadn't bought a first-class ticket because it was too expensive, which meant she did not have a reserved seat. After walking through several cars, she saw a group of older women getting settled in a compartment and mentally counted them.

One. Two. Three.

"Excuse me, I'm sorry, but is there room for one more?" she asked, a bit out of breath.

"Oh dearie, you look a wee bit frazzled," the woman closest to the open sliding door replied in an obvious Scottish accent. "Aye, we're only the three of us, and you can have the window seat if ye'd like. Moira, give the lassie the view."

"Oh, no, really," Beth shook her head rapidly. "I don't want to take anyone's seat."

"Think nothing of it, dearie. We've seen the Anglish countryside before. And I'm guessin' ye're a student? An American?"

Beth had discovered how quickly her accent and attire gave her away, in spite of the bomber jacket. Or maybe because of it. "Yes, ma'am. Heading to Edinburgh for a semester."

"Oh, aye? 'Tis a marvelous place, is Edinburrah."

Beth made a mental note of the proper pronunciation of Scotland's capital city.

As the ladies moved to the places nearest the door, Beth sat in the first available window seat, which faced the rear of the train. Once everyone was settled, the lady seated cattycorner from her nodded at the backpack Beth held on her lap and said, "Ye can put your sack up in the overhead bin if ye want," she said helpfully. "And maybe your wrap."

"Oh, no thanks." Beth smiled back, her pulse beginning to settle down now that she was safely on the train. "There are things I'll want."

"Well, then, there's plenty of space on the floor; ye can set it down there so it's in reach."

Beth nodded, smiling at the gentle, grandmotherly concern of the woman. She had a flash of envy, wishing her grandmother was like that. So much for her looking similar to Naomi. That's where it ended.

Before long, two other passengers claimed the remaining seats in the compartment—the other window seat and the one next to her.

Within minutes the train was underway. When she had booked her nonrefundable ticket in November, she discovered that the famous train had been leaving at ten o'clock in the morning from the number ten platform at King's Cross Station since 1862. Facing a seven-hour trip, she was prepared for a long day. Taking her journal and her tour book from her backpack, she set it on the floor against the wall and relaxed.

The view out the window caught her eye, and she watched the landscape gradually change from city to suburbs to countryside. The gently rocking motion of the coach, the rhythmic thunk of the wheels, and the warmth of her leather coat began to lull her into a hypnotized state. Her journal and tour book lay ignored on her lap.

Less than an hour outbound, the sunny London morning faded into a dank, cold English winter day laden with rain. She watched the drops on the window being stretched into long thin rivulets by the speed of the train. The stormy day filled the compartment with a low diffuse light that made reading possible but created a sense of muted isolation. The man next to her and the woman in the other window seat were silently absorbed in their newspapers.

Beth inconspicuously eyed the three Scottish women. Their low-spoken, lighthearted chatter about who was meeting them at the train station filled her with piercing homesickness, recalling the forsaken look on her grandfather's face as she left him at the airport.

I have no one to greet me in Edinburgh. No one to even know if I do arrive.

The smell of leather seats, damp clothing, flowery perfume, and a vague mechanical odor that Beth associated with trains permeated the enclosed compartment, giving it a musty heaviness. Occasionally, a welcome rush of fresh air blew in as her fellow passengers came and went at stops or made a trip to the Water Closet, or WC as it said on the door, which Beth thought was an amusing name for a bathroom.

Blinking herself awake, she picked up her journal. Noting her time of departure from London and her expected arrival time in Edinburgh, she spent the next thirty minutes jotting down the details of yesterday's visits to Buckingham Palace and the British Museum. She read over her entries from the previous two days, describing tours of Westminster Abbey, the Houses of Parliament, the Tower of London, and London Bridge; rides on the ubiquitous red double-decker tour buses; and a frigid walk through St. James Park.

Then she mused in words about the exciting days ahead: her arrival in Edinburgh late in the afternoon, finding a taxi to the college where she had arranged an after-hours arrival, being shown to her dorm room, and finally, meeting her roommate, a totally unknown entity. Orientation beginning Tuesday and then classes next week.

Writing herself out, she lost herself in her recently purchased tour book, reading in detail about the buildings, architecture, history, and heroes of the country she'd call home for the next five months. Using a yellow highlighter from her inside jacket pocket, she marked things she particularly wanted to see. Stirling Castle. The Isle of Skye. J. M. Barrie's Birthplace.

From time to time she looked around, noting the changing passengers and the forward movement of her watch as the train hurtled her toward Scotland. She assuaged her hunger with a granola bar and sips from her plastic water bottle.

It was easy to lose track of time, sitting in the rear-facing seat, entranced by the slightly dizzying sensation of watching the scenery zip by as she traveled backward at a high speed, nearly hypnotized by the sound of the rattling wheels. Only the conversation of the other passengers or the occasional call of the conductor recalled her to the present as he walked along the passageway between compartments. She found her eyes growing heavy, and her head occasionally bobbed in a sudden lapse into sleep. Blinking after one such occasion, she glanced out the window and was startled to see another train next to hers, traveling at the same speed in the same direction on a parallel track.

Beth stared into a compartment full of people who were laughing, smiling, and conversing. Two men in uniform played cards. At the window, a woman in a perky black hat with a mesh veil smiled as she leaned toward a man seated across from her.

Beth gawked rudely but unabashedly at the cozy scene across the span of mere feet. She felt for a moment as if she were sitting in the compartment with them. The woman was lovely with thick, rich chestnut hair that fell in waves to her shoulders. Her face was softly rounded, full, and alive with a smile. She had luscious red lipstick, startling against her pale face. The man had sharp, angular features with high cheekbones. A hint of a Norseman. Stoic, yet with an air of watchful happiness, he looked intensely at the woman. The tableau was warmly inviting, yet somehow odd. Almost like a scene from an old movie she'd watched with her grandfather.

The sound of the compartment door sliding drew her attention from the window. Only she and two of the three Scottish women remained of the original passengers who had filled the compartment when it left London. A young bearded man in a stylish tweed golf hat and a trendy windbreaker with an L.L. Bean insignia entered the compartment.

Looking back out the window, she was astonished to find the other train gone. She leaned against the glass, peering back down the track to see if her train had pulled ahead of the other, but there was no sight of it. Perhaps it had sped in front of them. She quickly switched to the forward-facing seat and gazing ahead, saw nothing. Then, looking across to where the other train had been seconds before, she realized that there were no rails there, no track running parallel to the one on which her train clattered north.

Beth closed her eyes, disoriented. There had been something off about those passengers. The woman's hat was very... old-fashioned. Come to think of it, the man seated across from the lovely woman had also been in some kind of uniform—blue, double-breasted, with silver buttons and a belt. She had noticed a pair of wings above his left pocket. He was holding a blue uniform hat with a black leather lip on his lap. And in the overhead compartment, she had glimpsed... she strained her memory. Was it? Could it be? Yes, a sheepskin-lined bomber jacket.

Her eyes flew open in alarm, an odd sensation creeping along her spine. She stared out at the rain-splattered English countryside. The mist hung low over the distant rolling hills. There was a timelessness about them. They had probably looked the same ten, twenty, or fifty years ago. Had the train been there, or had she imagined it? Had she fallen asleep for a few minutes? Her head felt light; her stomach woozy. She had rushed out of her hotel room without grabbing even a roll, and how long ago had she eaten that granola bar?

Since her experience on her flight over, THE DREAM had resumed on a nightly basis. There was more dimension and depth to it compared to November when the dreams had started. It was also more exhausting, as every night she felt the palpable relief of crossing the English Channel and finally bumping down onto a grass landing strip.

She stared through the rain-streaked glass as if the landing strip were out there in that green landscape. In last night's dream, he left the cockpit. That was new. Very new. Not only that, someone had met him. Slapped him on the back. A man, dressed in overalls.

The new passenger had taken the seat across from her. She sensed he had gotten up and down several times, taking off his jacket, and putting it in the overhead compartment. Beth squeezed her eyes shut, willing herself back onto the landing strip. There was a hint of dawn when they touched down. Someone waited there in addition to the mechanic in overalls. Someone important. Someone who made the pilot's heart beat wildly with anticipation.

Beth heard a muttered oath and felt a sudden cloudburst of papers come raining down on her head and lap. She jerked as if someone had touched her with a live wire. Looking up, she saw the young man with the tweed hat standing over her, holding an open leather briefcase. He had an apologetic smile on his face.

"Oh, aye, I'm so sorry, I'm a bumbling idgit."

The mild Scottish burr in his voice threw her mind into chaos. It was the same accent as the bomber pilot. She blinked, and struggled to remember where she was. A train. Bound for Scotland. She looked back out the window. Not dawn. Late afternoon. Rain. Rolling hills. She looked over at the two women passengers. They were watching with amusement.

"I really am a clumsy bamstick."

"A what?"

"Oh, sorry. When I'm a bit befuddled, I forget myself and slip into Scots."

She stared up at him. His accent was decidedly less Scottish now.

"Oh, bamstick. It's my grandmother's favorite word. It means a stupid, foolish person."

"Bamstick." She said it softly, letting the sound of it roll off her tongue.

The man flung his briefcase on the empty seat beside him. Startled, Beth slammed her hands on the papers, pressing them to her thighs as he leaned forward, hands extended. The man slowly sat back and gripped the armrests, his face now arranged in a carefully neutral expression.

"Sorry, sorry," he said and flung his hands in a gesture of surrender.

Beth felt the blush rise from deep within her. She looked back down at the papers on her lap and noticed neat, handwritten notes on yellow legal-size tablet paper and photocopies of what appeared to be old documents.

"Are these numbered?"

"What?"

She arranged the yellow pages so they faced in the same direction and set aside photocopied documents on the seat beside her as she came across them. Beth picked up one of the note pages and looked closer at it.

"Oh, I see. Here, a page number, at the bottom." She began arranging the pages in numerical order. Something made her look up. The man sat with his head tilted slightly to the left, resting on his open palm, his elbow propped on the armrest. Was that amusement in his face?

He had begun to smile—a strong, easy smile that made her lips twitch. She took in his athletic build and his relaxed manner. He had a neatly trimmed beard, high cheekbones, and a ruddy complexion. His thick, bushy eyebrows topped deep-set, dark brown eyes, and brown, thick, wavy hair touched the collar of his shirt. He was dressed in khakis and a thick, cable-knit sweater in a rich hue of green.

Disconcerted to be caught staring, she glanced down at the yellow tablet paper on her lap. The odd list of names caught her eye. "Fairey Battle 240?" she said, reading out loud, and with a quick glance up at him, continued the list. "Bristol Blenheim Two and Four, 231. Armstrong Whitworth Whitley 169. Vickers Wellington 160. Handly Page Hamden 140."

Looking up, she asked, "Fairey Battle. What? Tinkerbell and Captain Hook?"

The man folded his arms, smiling more broadly. "J.M. Barrie was born in Scotland."

"I know. His house is a national historic site. Near the town of Dundee. Is that where I'll find two hundred and forty fairy battles?" She resumed arranging the papers.

"No. It's a type of aircraft. World War II."

She paused, motionless, and looked up at him. "Do you know a lot about the war?"

He smiled. "That's my line of work."

"War?"

"No, no, history."

"Really. Are you a teacher?"

"I'm a professor at the University of Edinburgh."

"A professor? You don't look old enough to be a professor." When she saw his shrug, she stammered, "Oh, I'm sorry, I..."

"No. I'm brand-spankin' new, as you'd say in the States. Just started in the autumn term."

Once again, she realized how quickly her accent gave her away, though she thought he now sounded more American than Scots.

"I'm sorry," he said. "I'll just get these papers out of your way." He stretched out his hands, and they hung in the air, apparently waiting for her to pass them to him. She found herself staring at his neat, trimmed nails and long, lean fingers.

"Oh, I..." She was momentarily distracted by her observations. "I was thinking. Sorry, I got distracted. You know, traveling on a train, you know, it makes you..."

"Philosophic?"

"Yes, I guess that's what I mean. Why do you think that is?" Beth said as she handed him the sorted, organized tablet papers. She saw that the two women were unabashedly eavesdropping. Suddenly, Beth didn't feel awkward addressing them.

"Would you say," she said to the woman in the tan slacks, who had first greeted her when she came into the compartment, "that train travel makes you philosophic?"

"Ye're travelin' alone, aye?" the woman replied.

"Yes."

"Well, then, when you're travelin' all alone, especially a great distance, sitting and starin' out the window, watching the fields and the towns fly by, it gets ye ta thinkin' about a lot of things. The past, maybe. The future, maybe. Yes, I'd agree with ye."

"Nay," her companion, a woman named Moira countered. "It jest gives ye sa ore behouchie and makes ye carnaptous."

"A be what with a car what?" Beth said.

"Behouchie," the professor replied. "Means your backside. Carnaptous is cranky, irritable." He sounded very professorial and she said so.

The women burst into laughter. Beth felt mottled spots of embarrassment on her face and looked across to the man. He stuck out his hand. "I'm Robbie, by the way. Robert McLeod."

Beth shook his hand. "Nice to meet you."

He continued to hold her hand and Beth realized she hadn't introduced herself. "Beth. Schmidt. Susanna Elizabeth Schmidt, actually. Beth for short. My grandfather sometimes calls me Susie Q." This time she turned a vivid red. "I don't know why I said that."

Robbie chuckled. "It's cute, though. My grandfather would just call me little shait."

Robbie stood and shook hands with the other two passengers. They exchanged introductions and Robbie returned to his seat. Following his lead, Beth did the same. The women introduced themselves in turn as Dorie McLeash and Moira Givler.

In the middle of introductions, Beth's stomach rumbled. Her cheeks flamed again.

Dorie winked at her. "That's the problem with travel, lassie. In addition to a sore behouchie, it jest makes a body hungry. Here." She fumbled in her carryall bag. "Have a Scotch pie. It's well past lunchtime, ya nae."

Moira laughed. "Dorie here canna think unless her tummy's full. I dinna think the wee American girl knows what you're offerin' her, Dorie."

Beth looked at the pastry. "It looks good. Smells good too, but I don't want to take your lunch. I need a walk, so I think I'll find the dining car."

"I'd be glad ta share. But if ye prefer, the club car tis a bit further along the front."

Beth sat back down and handed Robbie the photocopies which had been sitting on the seat next to her. "These look interesting."

His eyes brightened. "You like history? World War II military history?"

"Under the right circumstances, I do."

"And what might be the right circumstances?"

"If I weren't so hungry and..."

"And?"

Dorie chimed in, "And maybe if there's a fine Scots laddie who'd be a tellin' the story."

Beth laughed, as did the others. "Yes, perhaps," she said, pleased she maintained her composure. "It's still a few hours to Edinburgh, right?" She made sure to pronounce it the Scottish way... Edinburrah.

"About an hour and a half," he smiled back.

"Well, I've got a lot of questions, actually, about World War II, and if you've got time to answer them..."

He nodded and replied, "Are you heading to Edinburgh, too?"

"Yes."

"Looking up your ancestors?"

"No," she replied.

"You're not Scottish?" he asked. "Probably Irish. You've got a wee bit of an odd combination. Elizabeth is a good English name. But Schmidt is German, or maybe—" He broke into a wide, knowing smile. "Pennsylvania Dutch."

"What?" Her face lit up now. "How would you know about the Pennsylvania Dutch?"

"I spent two years in the States when I was a teenager. My father's company sent us to Philadelphia. Bucks County, actually. I've been through the Amish country, Lancaster County."

"Well, I'm from Carlisle, in Cumberland County, but my grandfather was born in Lancaster County."

"Carlisle." He smiled brightly. "Another solid English name."

"My grandmother is from York County," Beth added.

"Is that so? Well, you're traveling through Yorkshire right this moment." He watched as Beth turned to look out the window at the gently rolling farmland. "We're in the Borders Region. Northern England. Be in southern Scotland soon."

"Oh, yes, I've been reading about it. Lovely villages and old abbey ruins. Like Melrose."

Robbie grinned. "That's where my heart is buried."

Beth blinked in surprise, as the women laughed. "I beg your pardon?"

"My father was a closet Scots historian. He named me Robert Bruce."

Awareness dawned. "Ah. Robert the Bruce. That's right. I read it in the guidebook. From the Wars of Scottish Independence. Early 1300s. His heart is buried at Melrose Abbey. I get it! Let me guess, you have a brother named William Wallace?"

Robbie laughed a warm laugh that put her at ease. "No. Just a younger sister, Caitlin. She's twenty-two. Have you any sisters or brothers?"

Beth shook her head. "No. It's just me and my grandparents. They raised me. My mother died shortly after I was born. She was a single parent, and I never knew my father." She said it like a recitation, an explanation she had given all through her growing-up years.

"I see."

Thankfully he made none of the typical noises of sympathy, shock, or surprise.

"This is actually the first time I've been away from them."

"Oh, aye. On a wee vacation?"

"School, actually. Edinburgh University, as a matter of fact."

"Really?" His eyes widened. "What a coincidence. What are you studying?"

"British Literature."

She smiled broadly at his look of astonishment. "I know. My grandmother thinks it's ludicrous for an American girl to be majoring in British Literature. 'Why don't you take something practical, like nursing,' she always said. Ugh. I hate needles. 'Or at least study your own literature,' as though America was unrelated to Britain."

"Why Scotland? Cambridge or Oxford would be more the choice for British Literature."

Beth hesitated for a moment, trying to come up with a logical-sounding reason, and settled on, "I know Edinburgh University has a great reputation, and it's very welcoming to foreign students."

"Yes, there are over seven thousand of them each year."

Beth's stomach rumbled again.

Robbie smiled. "I'm keeping you from lunch. May I show you the way?"

"Am I likely to get lost?"

Dorie and Moira burst out laughing. "Ye're not makin' too many points here, laddie."

Beth tried not to laugh, but did anyway, seeing the chagrined look on Robbie's face. "I'd be delighted if you'd show me the way, Dr. McLeod."

"Robbie."

"Robbie, but I feel really strange calling a professor by his first name."

"Are you taking any history courses?" he asked.

"Well, I'm taking two literature classes and an overview of Scottish culture and history. It didn't seem like much—three classes—but that's what they recommended for visiting students. I've been preparing by reading Bonnie Prince Charlie and the Jacobite Rebellion, as well as exploring some of Sir Walter Scott's novels."

Robbie's nod seemed to imply approval. "You'll find the University system here quite different from the States, so you'll be glad you limited it to three. Four is the usual load for typical students. I know that history class you're talking about. It's a survey class intended for non-majors, and I don't teach it. So, I'm not your professor, so no big deal. Call me Robbie."

Beth thought he used a lot of American slang for a Scottish professor, and said so.

"I spent last year—ninety-five to ninety-six—doing a postdoctoral course at Duke University on the influence of Scotland and Scots on America."

"Ah, that explains it," she said as she grabbed her backpack and followed him out the door and through several cars toward the front of the train. The rain had stopped, clearing up the view of the heather-covered moors they were traveling through.

When they got to the club car, he took the seat across from her at a vacant table, which was covered by a starched, white tablecloth. Cloth napkins, silverware, and glasses completed the place settings. *In a train*, she mused. *Feels a little bit like something from an old movie.* The phantom train flashed through her mind.

She ordered a tossed salad with balsamic vinaigrette dressing and a pot of tea, and he ordered a tuna sandwich and a lager. She ate her salad with enthusiasm and then, still hungry, ordered cream scones—warm currant scones served with clotted crème and strawberry jam.

They chatted as they ate, and she learned that he enjoyed all time periods of history, from ancient ruins to the Twentieth Century.. She said she liked movies from the thirties and forties and vintage clothing, which prompted him to ask about her jacket. "It's authentic, isn't it? RAF bomber jacket. Someone's souvenir?"

"No, I bought it in a vintage clothing store near home. I needed a warm jacket last fall for an outdoor job, and this fit, and I liked the way it felt."

"Was your grandfather in the war?"

"Yes, actually, he was in England. With the Air Force."

"Was he a pilot?" Robbie asked, sipping his lager.

"No, he was a mechanic. He never really says a lot about it."

"No, they don't."

"*They* don't?"

"The vets. The guys who fought. My grandfather was in the Navy. Saw some pretty rough action, I think. Never talked about it, though, until near the end of his life."

"The grandfather who called you a little shait?" Robbie nodded, smiling affectionately. Beth continued. "My grandfather sometimes talked about the pilots. How he admired them. Their courage."

"Do you know what unit he was attached to?"

"You know, that's funny. He never said. But I never asked. Guess he thought it wouldn't mean anything to me. You know, all those unit numbers and divisions and whatnot."

"Do you know where he was stationed?"

"He never said exactly where. He did give me a list of things to see." Beth retrieved her journal from her backpack and took out the list her grandfather had given her. "He didn't say much about them. Just said something about them being places I need to see. It was odd. 'Cause they're all here in Scotland."

"What's on your list?"

"Well, Edin... burrah." She smiled at him shyly as she practiced her accent.

He beamed. "Verra good. We'll have ye speakin' like a Scot yet. What else?"

"Well, there are some places in Edinburgh... the Royal Mile. Holyrood. Then he listed Drem Aerodrome. What's an Aerodrome?"

"An airfield. Airbase."

"Ah."

"It's not there anymore."

Disappointment sunk in. Beth frowned. "Not there?"

"No, there's a bit of a museum nearby now with some old airplanes and such, but Drem itself is just an overgrown stretch of land, with some shops nearby. A shame, really." He took another sip of his amber colored beverage.

"Why would he want me to visit there?"

"Maybe he was stationed there. It was very active in the war, though I don't believe there were any American airmen there."

"He never said anything about being stationed in Scotland. He would have said so, once he knew I was coming, wouldn't he?" She frowned at her own question.

"What else is on the list?"

"There are some other places. I'm not sure what they all are yet. Traprain Law. The Wallace Monument. I just read about that in my tour book. Skye. Skye sounds beautiful."

"A very fascinating list."

"Why?"

"Well, Traprain Law is a volcanic plateau between Edinburgh and Drem. Stirling is a prime tourist site. Even in the War. Skye is an island in the Inner Hebrides and, as you said, just lovely, and very romantic."

Beth wrinkled her brow, wondering not for the first time why her grandfather would want her to see all these particular places. And what had he meant by that odd statement, being part of *her* history?

"Are you meeting some people, then, when you get to Edinburgh?" Robbie asked.

She shook her head. "Why?"

"It's just, well, there's a week till the term starts, and I could show you around the city. Maybe even out to Drem, if you want to go."

"Really?" She was suddenly cautious. It must have shown on her face, for he said, "I'm safe. Got good references." She smiled faintly.

"Where are you housed for the term? In a dormitory?"

"Yes, Polloch."

"You might find a native like myself helpful in getting around and showing you the sights, helping you get settled," he said in an encouraging voice.

Beth found his offer attractive, but she had only just met him. Her habitual shyness with men kicked in. "I'm used to finding my own way," she replied, trying to sound grateful.

"I'm sure you are."

'I'm sure'? "What's that supposed to mean?"

"Ach, nae, don't get so defensive," he replied, his accent suddenly more pronounced. "I meant only that American girls are all so independent."

"Really?" Beth had no intention of telling him that she wasn't like other American girls, at least the ones he apparently knew. But neither did she want him to know how disorienting, exhausting, and unnerving most of her trip had been so far.

But something about him seemed calm and grounded, and she found the idea of his company appealing. *However,* she thought to herself, *he is a professor, young as he is, and it just doesn't seem quite right.* She replied, a little more bluntly than she intended, "No, thanks. I'll be fine."

By his sudden stillness, she knew she had offended him, but couldn't figure out why. Surely, he was only being polite. "No, really," she tried again, "I appreciate it, I do," now stumbling over her words in a hurry to mitigate her rudeness. "Honest. But... I just..."

"Need some time on your own to get settled?"

She nodded. Though it was the truth, it wasn't what she was going to say.

"Fine. Really." He crossed his legs, smiling slightly. "I'm sure you'll meet lots of other Americans here, as well as others from all over the world. Edinburgh is very popular for visiting students. I'll probably be seeing you about the campus. It's not as big as it seems. But," he clasped his hands and stretched his arms. "You will let me get you to the university? We can share a taxi. I can help you with your luggage. Did you have it checked?"

She hated to think of the expense of another taxi, but after all her recent traveling and the exhausting days in London, she was more than ready to treat herself to the luxury of a hired cab.

"Oh, that would be lovely. I'd appreciate your help with it."

He smiled his warm, easygoing smile again.

"Least a Scot can do for a visiting American."

THREE

·

SNUG IN HIS NEW lightweight, weatherproof running gear with its reflective vest—a Christmas gift from his mother—Robbie jogged his way through the empty predawn streets around Edinburgh University.

After a night of pub crawling with his flatmate Andrew, he was tempted to skip his habitual morning run and whacked the snooze alarm more than once when it began ringing at six. But Robbie prided himself on staying in shape. In the dark, cold winter months, he ran, switching to cycling once warmer weather and longer days arrived in this city just north of the fifty-fifth parallel. Though the longest night of the year was almost a month ago, the sun still wouldn't be peeking over the horizon until nearly eight-thirty.

He paced himself for a slow, steady five-mile run, choosing well-lit, straighter streets, saving the twisting, turning, hilly roads beyond the campus for his warm-weather biking. Not that anything in Edinburgh was flat. Halfway through his run, he turned off Dalkeith Road and headed down Old Church Lane. As he jogged through the Pollack Halls area, his turnaround point, he thought about Beth. It'd been six days since he'd seen her, telling her to feel free to look him up at his office as he helped her get her bags from the taxi at her dorm.

He'd expected to run into her on campus but hadn't seen her in the Student Center, near the library, nor around the College of Humanities and Social Sciences where most of her classes would be held. He was a bit disappointed.

Different, that girl, he ruminated, his thoughts keeping pace with his feet. *Sort of old-fashioned. Kind of unusual for an American girl, an odd combination of maturity and naiveté*, recalling their relaxed conversation and her sudden wariness at his offer to show her around. *She's interested in history.*

That made him smile.

As usual, during his run, his thoughts flowed organically, and the thought of Beth and history took him to memories of his year at Duke and merged into his application process for the position at Edinburgh University and his astonishment at landing the position, which brought him around to thoughts of his father.

Wish the old man would be excited about my job. After all those years of dragging the family to every historical site in the U.K. and on the continent, you'd think he'd be pleased I took up history. Robbie jogged in place for a moment to let a car go by. *But, noooo, that's not good enough for my father, who apparently expected me to become an engineer and join Grandpa's firm. No matter that Grandpa died of a heart attack from overwork at the age of fifty-five.*

As he crossed Nicolson Street, Robbie recalled his father's words with bitterness. *"I brought you up to appreciate your Scottish heritage, not to make a fool of yourself over it."*

Returning to the main campus, he stopped at a newsstand to pick up his Sunday morning entertainment—the *New York Times*, the *London Herald*, and *The Scotsman*—to accompany a pot of coffee. Insisting on good coffee was another American habit he had picked up in his recent year in the States. He could barely drink the brackish instant swill so many Scots took for coffee. For background to his newspapering, he always tuned his radio to a BBC station that played the latest American hits by bands like Smashing Pumpkins, the Cranberries, and Oasis.

By early afternoon, he had showered, trimmed his beard, and made himself and Andrew a hearty brunch of eggs, potato scones, beans, fried tomatoes, and black pudding, a Scottish culinary preference that no amount of time in America could break him of. Walking to the window of his fourth-floor flat, he spotted a rare sunny January sky. He suddenly longed to be out in the daylight before the demands of the semester and the typical dreary, dark Scottish winter encompassed his days.

"Andrew," he called to his flatmate who, as usual on a Sunday, was in his bedroom frantically throwing together lecture notes for the week. "Want to get some sun?"

"Sun?" Andrew shouted back in his thick British-accent. "What's that? It doesn't exist in this bleak northern climate. Besides, classes start tomorrow. I've got to pull together my lecture on early Mesopotamian culture."

"Aren't you using the same lecture as opening day in the fall?" Robbie teased, walking toward his flatmate's room. "Wearing your Indiana Jones hat and hawking the joys of archeology? Weren't all the lassies queuing up for your office hours?"

"Funny, old man. Nothing wrong with a bit of flair in teaching, I say," Andrew countered as Robbie reached the doorway. "I use Indiana Jones as Hollywood's stereotype of an archeologist. Such a misunderstood profession." Andrew looked up from his desk, which was piled high with textbooks and papers.

Robbie leaned against the door jam. "Talk about Hollywood, there's no end in sight of the drama of Clinton and Monica Lewinsky. It's all over the newspapers."

"Those Americans, never able to be discreet," Andrew shrugged. "Besides, you teach British history, not colonial history, so you don't have to bring it up in class tomorrow."

"America's not a colony anymore, you imperialist Sassenach. That's Gaelic for Outlander, by the way. And I teach Scottish history. Remember the other country on this island?" Robbie threw back a good-humored insult.

"Oh, blow it out your arse, you ignorant highlander," Andrew returned genially. "Scottish history is so nouveau. So boringly contemporary. Now in ancient Persia..."

"Oh stuff it, you prat. You're just pissed that the Americans were able to kick your King George the Third out of their continent."

"Bugger off," Andrew replied civilly. "Besides, he's your King George the Third, too."

"Go play with your ziggurats. I'm going to get some rays." Robbie stretched.

"Rays? Such vulgar American slang. You've been undeniably corrupted by that postdoctoral year. And, of course, you're already prepared for tomorrow. You always were a bit of a show-off at Oxford, always trying to be at the head of the class."

"I didn't have to sleep till noon. You Normans never could hold your liquor."

"Yeah, and you Celts couldn't hold your land," Andrew shot back and then, in a change of tone, added, "Could you pick up some crisps and soda on your way back? I'll spot you for it."

"No problem. See you in a bit."

An hour later, Robbie was wandering around what was left of the Abbey of Holyrood, located at one end of the Royal Mile, which stretched between Edinburgh Castle and Holyrood Palace. The abbey had once been a stunning cathedral until numerous religiously motivated attacks since the sixteenth century had repeatedly damaged it until the roof collapsed in 1768.

Robbie had a lifetime membership to Historic Scotland, the state-run organization that oversaw the site and others throughout the country. It was another thoughtful gift from his mother, allowing him to visit the magnificent ruin whenever he wanted to. He enjoyed staring out the vacant arched windows, imagining the lives of the Stuart Kings who had lived in the attached palace, still a royal residence and home to the Queen's annual visit to Scotland.

After a saunter through the garden, sighing that the day had once again become overcast, he followed the meandering path to the front of the abbey, which faced the steep volcanic hill called Arthur's Seat. Mentally rehearsing tomorrow's lecture, he nearly overlooked the girl with long, brown hair in a vintage bomber jacket, sitting on a bench facing the abbey in the darkening day. Her gloved hands were clutched in front of her, her head tilted, as if listening to something.

"Beth!" he said, surprised at his delight.

The American girl looked up at him with cloudy, confused eyes.

"It's Robbie—from the train. Robert McLeod."

"Oh, yes," Beth replied, blinking rapidly, then jumped up, as if caught doing something she shouldn't be.

"I'm sorry. Did I interrupt some deep thoughts? You seem distracted."

"Sorry. A lot on my mind."

"Are you having trouble settling in?" He looked at her more closely. She looked tired, he thought, and a bit wan. Her attitude was distant. He knew from experience how difficult an adjustment to another country could be, even one where your native language is spoken.

"It's hard to explain."

Robbie smiled encouragingly, trying to overlook her lack of welcome. He thought they had made a connection when they'd met. "Now, come on. You're a literature major. You've studied the great writers. You can explain."

Beth frowned. "I don't see the point."

"You know all the words."

"You've lost me, Professor McLeod." There was a defensive edge to her voice.

"You can quote Shakespeare and Byron and Tennyson, can't you? And, Robbie. Please. Remember, I'm not your professor."

"That's true." A slow smile eased the tension on her face.

"Which part is true?"

"That I can quote the classical writers. And that I'm not in your history class."

"Well, talking about history, want to know why the Abbey was built here?" he said, gesturing at the ruins in front of them.

"I'm sure you'll tell me, Prof—Robbie, whether I want to hear it or not," she replied, but her voice was encouraging.

"Aye, so here it is. In 1127 while King David the First was hunting in the forests to the east of Edinburgh, he was thrown from his horse after it had been startled by a hart."

"A heart? Like in a valentine?"

"No, no." Robbie laughed. "A hart. A deer."

"Oh, okay." She nodded.

"Mind you, there are variations of the story."

"Naturally." Beth smiled.

Robbie smiled inwardly. *Now she's more like the relaxed girl on the train.*

She tilted her head slightly as she added, "I'm sure you'll tell me those, too."

Robbie nodded. "Naturally. What else would a history professor do?" He continued. "The king was saved from being gored by the charging animal when it was startled, either by the appearance of a holy cross descending from the skies or by sunlight glittering off a crucifix that suddenly appeared between the hart's antlers, as the king attempted to grasp them."

"This is history? Sounds a bit like C.S. Lewis."

"Aye. But history's interspersed with people's private miracles."

She grew suddenly somber again and didn't respond at first. When she did, he had to lean in to catch her words. "But the shadow of the past still looms large in this place."

"Yes, and the shadows of the world. Can you hear that jet overhead?" he replied, trying to coax another smile out of her.

She recited in a singsong voice, "And moving through a mirror clear, that hangs before her all the year, shadows of the world appear. There she sees the highway nearby, winding down to Camelot. And sometimes thro' the mirror blue, the Knights come riding two and two. She hath no loyal Knight and true..."

"You know your Tennyson. The Lady of Shallot. *She hath no loyal Knight and true.* Hath you a loyal Knight and true?" He said it in jest, but realized he wanted to know.

She frowned at him, stiffening. "Are you asking me if I have a boyfriend?"

Robbie threw up his hands. "None of my business." Why was she being so prickly?

"Then why do you ask?" she shot back.

He couldn't understand why he was detecting walls. She had been so friendly and warm on the train. What was he doing wrong? He worked to keep the irritation out of his voice. "So I know if I'm to be professorial or a welcoming Scottish laddie."

Beth's face conveyed wariness. "History lessons would be welcome."

"Professorial, then? How about a friend who is slightly professorial?"

When she didn't reply, he tried to change the subject. "What I'd like to know is what you see when you look at these ancient walls? You were staring at them so intently, a wee bit ago."

"It's not seeing so much as..." She stopped. He sensed a sudden withdrawal behind her own walls and wondered at her history. To his surprise, she stood up and started walking rapidly along the path toward the exit.

"Wait. Where are you going?" He hurried after her and caught her arm, exasperated at her behavior. "What is it? What's got you so upset? Did I say something wrong?"

She halted, staring at him until he dropped his hand, but she said nothing. In frustration he broke the silence, maybe a little too fiercely. "Tell me!"

Her eyes narrowed at him. "You wouldn't understand."

He grunted in annoyance. "I'm an intelligent person. I'm capable of understanding."

She sighed deeply, and then said softly, "Standing in the shadows of this ruin, you can feel the weight of history. It'd be easy to get lost... in time. To hear..." She turned away from him, staring off into the distance.

"Hear what?" He took her arm and turned her gently back to face him. She kept her eyes glued on the vacant arched windows behind them but pulled her arm away and stuck her hands in her pockets. In spite of her wool-lined bomber jacket, she looked cold.

"Echoes." She nearly whispered the word.

"You hear echoes? Voices echoing?"

"No, the echoes of voices. From the past."

Robbie looked around. The day had gone from cloudy to wintry in the last ten minutes, with a chill wind picking up. He and Beth were the only people in sight, and he heard no one talking, no one walking. Being alone here, on such a day could certainly fire the imagination. But he wanted to lighten her darkening mood. "What voices? Mary Queen of Scots? She lived here, you know. A lot of people say the place is haunted."

She took her hands from her pockets. In one was a colorful wool ski cap, which she twisted in her hands, and then put on her head. She looked at him, frowned, and said in a tone that seemed to be questioning her own certainty, "His voice."

"Whose? King David's?" She was not responding to his attempts at levity. He grew uncomfortable with her silent, serious gaze but sensed she was gauging his trustworthiness. He asked, hesitantly, "Whose voice?"

At last, in a whisper, she said, "His," and patted the bomber jacket.

Robbie felt a chill that had nothing to do with the rising wind. He wasn't sure he really wanted to understand. "You heard *his* voice? What do you mean?"

She patted her coat again, watching him warily.

He responded slowly, tentatively, "The airman who owned your jacket?"

When she nodded, he went on, "Do you know whose jacket it was? I thought you said you bought it in a vintage store."

"I did buy it at a vintage store... back in Carlisle, the Carlisle in Pennsylvania."

"Was there some identification with it? Do you know who he was?"

She shook her head. "No. Not completely... yet."

"Not completely. Yet?" He knew he sounded incredulous, but she made it sound like the guy was going to stop by and introduce himself.

"I know he was a bomber pilot. I know his first name is Colin."

Robbie's research instincts kicked in, overtaking his mounting concern at her bizarre statements. History was a safer approach. "That's a good clue. Colin is a fairly common name, but how many bomber pilots named Colin could there be? We could do some research."

He was relieved to see her face light up. This was better. They could connect safely in the realm of history. She probably just had a very active imagination.

"So how would I find him?" she asked.

The eagerness in her voice was charming. He didn't find a lot of girls interested in historical research. *Yet she's saying she hears this pilot's voice, or the echo of his voice here, at Holyrood.* There was something unsettling about it all. *And how did she know his first name?*

"I have a friend," Robbie offered. "He works for the Imperial War Museum. He can look up records. And then there's the Scottish War

Memorial just up the Royal Mile in Edinburgh Castle. We can look there, too."

"When? Now?"

Robbie laughed to stave off his concern at her ferocity. "Now? Before we get something warm to drink?" He felt both pulled and put off by her intensity.

She sighed, looking a bit deflated. "Yes, I'm sorry, it's just that..."

He asked, wary of her answer, "Tell me. You said you heard an echo of his voice. Here?"

She looked at him with her hazel eyes, watching, wary. He worked hard to keep any judgment from his gaze, any emotion that would scare her off.

Research, Robbie, you're doing research, he warned himself.

"Yes, I heard... I thought I heard... his voice... here." Her tone was hesitant, cautious.

"Was he alone?"

"No."

"Who was he with?"

Beth stuck her hands back in her pockets and looked away. "A woman."

"Do you know *her* name?"

At his tone, she grimaced back at him, tilting her head, and crossing her arms defiantly. "No." She exhaled the word, like a breath, then added more fiercely, "But I know something about her."

"What?" He was becoming intrigued, in spite of his better judgment. He made the tone of his voice more curious, more encouraging.

"She's not Scottish."

That piece of information was a surprise. "How do you know that?"

"Because she doesn't have a Scottish accent."

"So, you could hear her, too? Like they were having a conversation?"

"Yes, I did. Just a piece of a conversation."

"Back there, a little while ago," he asked. "When you were sitting on the bench?"

"Yes."

"Was she English?"

"No." He heard her reluctance to say more. She looked at the gravel path, then the barren trees, then at him. "American."

A warning sounded in the back of his head. "American?"

She nodded, watching him. He said, carefully, "Maybe it's just..."

"Just what?" She stood up straight, glaring now.

"Maybe you're just..."

"I'm just what!" Her defensiveness was bristling.

"Well, wishing. Projecting."

An eyebrow raised slowly. "So, the dreams are just projections?"

"She hath no loyal Knight and true," Robbie said, then cringed internally at his lack of sensitivity. *But wait, she said, what? "Dreams?"*

"Because I have no love interest in my life, I project it into my dreams?" She answered his previous question in a way that unnerved him.

"What dreams?" He was confused. "I thought we were talking about hearing voices." He stopped, hating the way that sounded. Like she was...

"You think I'm hallucinating?"

"No, no. I'm trying to get what you're saying."

Her eyes were no longer distant, just cold. Unfriendly. Challenging.

"I have these dreams. About him."

"Dreams?" *This has really gotten beyond weird*, he thought. Yet she had seemed so grounded, so serious, so focused when he had met her on the train. "How often do you have these dreams?"

"Ah, well, from time to time. I've had them more often here in Scotland. But today, here, I heard the woman say..." She turned and started walking away again, this time even more rapidly. He had to jog to catch up with her.

"Wait. Don't go," he said, keeping pace with her.

"You think I'm mad. Insane." She marched on, jaw set.

"I didn't say that. Stop!" When she didn't, he softened his voice. "Please. Just tell me about the dreams."

She halted suddenly but didn't look at him. "I can't."

"Why not?" He had an urge to shake her.

"I've never... you're the first... person I've told about this. About him. I'm half afraid... that... if I talk about it... I'll... lose him."

All his instincts told him to say goodbye politely and walk away. This was not someone to get involved with. Too intense. Too obsessed. But he couldn't walk away now; he was intrigued by her story. And by her. Carefully he said, "I need to ask you something."

"You think I'm out of my mind."

"Have you ever or are you doing anything?"

"Doing anything?"

"Drugs. Especially hallucinogens."

"You're joking!"

He could tell she was truly offended, but he went on. "No. Of course not. You're a college student. You're an American..."

"Oh, so all American college students are dope addicts," she said waspishly.

He grunted with frustration, tapping his foot. "Don't be ridiculous. But people experiment. Lots of college students, everywhere."

"I don't experiment. I never have. I've only ever had an occasional glass of wine."

"Not even whiskey since you've been in Scotland?" But his levity wasn't returned.

"It's not a drug-induced hallucination," she stated flatly.

"Aye. I believe you." Well, he believed she wasn't using drugs. His Celtic ancestors would have believed it was the spirit of someone not yet ready to leave the earthly realm. He mentally shook his head at such superstition.

She interrupted his internal dialogue. "Then what do you believe I heard?"

Robbie frowned, looked at the distant hill he had climbed many times, then back at this odd American girl. "You are taken with the idea."

"With what idea?"

"The pilot. It's very romantic. Here you are in Scotland. He's Scottish, you say."

"It's not romantic. It's not. I have no romantic feelings for him. It's not like that at all. Oh, this sounds so stupid. It's all too real. The images, the sounds, the smells."

"You smell things in your dream?" Robbie felt he was really getting beyond his depth. But she didn't seem unbalanced.

"Fuel. Metal. Cordite." She listed each thing with such conviction. "And he's afraid..."

"Here, sit down on this bench." He indicated one nearby.

She ignored him. "It's too real, you see. Too realistic. It's not romanticized. No hazy pictures. No dreamy scenes. It's as though I'm seeing it all..."

"All what?"

She was angry now. "No!"

Robbie put his hands on her shoulders and gripped them. "I *will* believe you. Aye. Honest. I know, really, how strong a connection you can feel to the past. I'm a historian."

She relaxed slightly under his grip. "Yes, you study history, but I'm..."

"You're what?"

"I'm living it."

FOUR

FOUR DAYS LATER ON a sleety Thursday afternoon, Robbie ran into Beth on campus—literally.

He was crossing Bristo Square near the Student Center, with his windbreaker hood tossed over his head, carrying a cup of take-out coffee. Momentarily glancing toward a group of laughing students, he ran head-on into someone.

"Oh, I'm sorry. I'm such a clumsy bamstick," an apologetic American female voice said. Robbie was concentrating on not dropping his coffee and didn't look up, but instantly recognized her voice.

"Beth!" He was delighted to see her again, in spite of that unsettling conversation at Holyrood, which had been cut short by a sudden, intense snow squall. She had sprinted away through the swirling flakes, calling over her shoulder, "I really have to go." Though he could have easily caught up with her, it was apparent she was done talking to him.

Now here she was, dressed casually in her bomber jacket, jeans, and boots, easy to pick out as an American. European students seemed to have a more sophisticated fashion sense, he thought to himself, but he had always been attracted to the relaxed manners and style of Americans.

"Oh, Professor McLeod, hello." A cautious greeting.

He replied evenly, "Bamstick? You're getting the lingo down."

She smiled, more warmly now, and said in a poor imitation of a Scottish accent, "Aye, I might be a wee American lassie, but I'm a quick learner."

Robbie laughed, noticing her lack of headgear, "Beth, you should have a hat on in this miserable weather."

"You sound like my grandfather." The warmth left her face as she walked away.

Robbie groaned inwardly, "Wait a second, about your grandfather..."

She turned to face him. Her head and jacket were accumulating tiny white shards of ice. He flattened his voice. "I'd be happy to take you to some of the places on his list. Traprain Law and Drem are only an hour from here."

Her face lit up, so he added, "Let's go grab some coffee in the Student Center. Talk there out of the weather."

Looking slightly alarmed, she shook her head and nodded at his carry-out cup. "I'm fine. Besides, you already have your coffee."

"Okay. Well, then, how about going to Traprain Law and Drem this Saturday?"

"Can't," she shrugged. "Signed up for a tour of the history museum."

"Well, then, next Saturday?"

Beth bit her lip, chewing it thoughtfully. "Yes, that works," she said in a tentative voice.

"Great." He was relieved to get a commitment, even if it felt like he had drug it out of her. "How about I pick you up at your dorm at 10 a.m.?"

She shook her head slowly. "Why don't we... ah... meet somewhere."

"Okay, if you prefer," Robbie agreed, to save an argument.. "How about the café on Nicolson Street? The Celtic Cow?"

"Sure. That'd be great. See you then."

She walked off before he could say another word.

That afternoon he called his friend at the Imperial War Museum in London and asked him to research World War II bomber pilots with the first name of Colin and try to narrow them down to those who were native Scots. He wasn't sure if he should encourage Beth's somewhat unnerving obsession, but maybe he could offer a more rational, reasoned approach to her search.

The following Tuesday, his friend emailed the results.

Although he was seeing Beth in four days, Robbie knew she'd want to see these results right away. After looking up her number in the student directory, he made three attempts to contact her, leaving his number on her answering machine, but she did not respond.

Finally, early Wednesday evening, Robbie decided to visit her dorm. He used his privilege as a faculty member to obtain her room number. Though he could have waited until their date on Saturday, he was eager to share the information. To convince her he could be helpful.

No, not date, he reminded himself severely. *She would definitely object to that. It's just a local history tour. Yeah, why am I persisting? Am I just a free ride for her? But I'm the one who offered,* he grunted.

This girl ran hot and cold, aye, but maybe that's exactly why he was so... intrigued. And there's something unique about her. A bit naïve, old fashioned, but bright and passionate about what she liked. She doesn't pretend to be anyone other than who she is.

Striding up the dorm stairs, he recalled the fall orientation lecture on professional conduct. He and Andrew had arrived late and were forced to sit in the front row of the large hall. A thin, strident, bespectacled woman, dressed in a severe black suit, was brandishing her laser pointer like a sword. She constantly glared at them throughout her slide presentation, as she warned in excruciating detail of the hidden landmines of faculty-student relationships.

When Robbie received a particularly piercing glare, he was tempted to stand up and yell, "Kaboom," but refrained, considering he was at the beginning of the arduous path to tenure.

Going to Beth's room was one of the prohibitions on the slide titled, "Crossing the Danger Zone." It proved to be a warning he should have heeded. Beth's door was opened by a stunning, blonde Swedish girl who happened to be in his History of Ancient Scotland lecture.

"Oh, Professor McLeod? How nice to see you," Anja said in her heavily accented English, with an expectant lift of her waxed eyebrows. "What ken I do fer you?"

"Does Beth live here? Beth Schmidt?" he stammered, flustered at being caught in a clear breach of professional behavior.

"She does! Bett, a gentleman to see yew!" she called over her shoulder. Then with a wink at Robbie and a conspiratorial smile, she said, "Oh, think I check the mail, yah?" He stood to one side as she walked past him out of the room.

"Hello, Professor!"

Robbie turned back to see Beth at the door, dressed in grey sweatpants and a maroon Shippensburg University sweatshirt. She had a wary look on her face. "This is a surprise," she added in a tentative voice, and after a moment, opened the door wider. "Come in."

"Ah, thanks," he replied, fervently regretting his impulsive visit. When she shut the door, closing them in the small room furnished with two single beds, two desks, two built-in closets, and a small, plush chair, he felt suddenly claustrophobic.

"Would you like a soft drink? I even have some Iron Bru," she said, referring to the intensely sweet orange soft drink that was Scotland's best-selling nonalcoholic beverage. "Or coffee? I can make some. Anja provided these lovely amenities." She nodded to a coffee pot on top of the mini refrigerator and waved at the chair. "Have a seat."

He stood with his back almost touching the door, watching her puzzled expression. Probably shouldn't risk any additional breach of professional conduct. Still, he was pleased that she was warming up. He wondered again if helping her pinpoint the original owner of her bomber jacket was the right thing to do.

"I have something for you," he finally said and thrust a piece of folded computer paper into her hand. "You won't believe what my friend James found."

He watched as she unfolded the paper. "He wasn't able to sort out Scottish pilots from the others, but he did come up with a list of pilots with the name of Colin. My mate was thorough. He even included anyone whose middle name was Colin, just in case he went by his middle name. A very common practice here in the U.K."

Beth looked down at the paper, her long hair shielding her expression.

He continued, speaking rapidly. "I know it's a rather long list, with twenty-seven. But it's a start. If you want, we can make a formal request for a copy of each record. Costs a little, since you're not a relative."

When he paused for breath, she looked up. He was stunned by her expression. Her face was pale, her eyes wide and unfocused, her breath suspended.

"Beth?" he asked, concerned, taking a half-step toward her. She blinked several times, then shook her head as if to clear her thoughts, folded the paper, and stuffed it in the pocket of her sweatshirt. To his astonishment, she reached past him to open the door.

"Ah, thanks, Robbie. I have to be somewhere. I'll see you Saturday." Her voice was clipped, almost as if she couldn't catch her breath.

He stared at her, his head spinning at her sudden change of mood. His usual glib tongue failed him. Managing to mumble, "Yeah," he left the dormitory as quickly as he could.

As he scampered back to his office, a passing student called in a jovial voice, "Are ye runnin' to something or from something, Professor McLeod?"

Good question, Robbie thought, merely nodding an acknowledgment of the student's jibe. He thought about his interactions with Beth. They seemed to have a pattern. She was often slightly startled at first as if pulled out of some deep place. Then came a smile and a welcoming demeanor, which gave him an odd wrench in his stomach, followed by a bit of bantering. Finally, when he overstepped some inexplicable, invisible boundary, she would suddenly retreat into wariness or retreat physically.

He contemplated this pattern until by Saturday morning waiting outside the coffee shop on Nicholson Street, he had figured out a "safe" approach. He would be strictly "professorial"—friendly, but not friends.

"Nice car," Beth said, once again friendly and smiling, when he helped her into the passenger seat of the Austin Healy.

"It's my roommate's. Andrew's."

"Expensive, isn't it?" Beth replied as they headed east out of Edinburgh into the bright day. The morning was the typical unpredictable Scottish weather: sunny with scarcely a cloud in sight, but conceivably raining some kilometers away.

"Uh-huh," he replied, his attention on the traffic.

"What does your roommate do for a living that he can afford a car like this?"

"He's a professor, like me. Ancient history, though. Mesopotamia. Persia."

"Wow, I didn't realize being a college professor paid so well."

Robbie snorted. "Andrew comes from the upper crust of English society. His family probably earned their money on the backs of the peasants centuries ago."

"You don't much like your roommate, then?" Her tone was charmingly innocent.

He chuckled. "Oh, no. We're great mates. Met at Cambridge."

"So... you don't own a car?"

He sighed. "Doesn't fit in the budget yet, not with the massive school loans." But fortunately for me, Andrew is not just thoroughly rich, coming from some ancient stock of English landed gentry; he's also thoroughly generous with his material possessions."

"Lucky you."

He heard the smile in her voice and relaxed. It was going to be a good day. "Let me tell you about Traprain Law," he said in his best professorial tone.

"Could I stop you?" Beth replied with a chuckle, which relaxed Robbie even more. He launched into his explanation.

"Laws are volcanic hills formed three hundred and twenty million years ago and eventually worn down to rocky promontories. They stand out starkly against the flat farmland in the area known as East Lothian that runs from Edinburgh along the Firth of Forth and to the North Sea. At one time they served as prehistoric hill forts."

He continued talking, filling the hour-long drive with details about the geography and history of the surrounding countryside. After some time, she interrupted his discourse. "You're very good at presenting what could be boring information in an entertaining and amusing way."

"I'm flattered," he grunted, then added as an afterthought, "I *guess* that was a compliment. Actually, I earned my way through much of college by being a tour guide for the wives and kids of rich American golfers."

At Traprain Law he helped her over the wooden stile at the car park and led the way up the steeply ascending, narrow dirt path. He pointed out various birds as they climbed—jackdaws, green woodpeckers, wrens, finches, crows—laughing at her amused comment, "So you know more than just history."

Thirty minutes later, as they reached the top, Robbie caught Beth's hand and helped her up onto the plateau. Her ungloved fingers were cold in his warm ones, but she pulled her hand away the moment she was safely on the level surface, then caught her breath when she took in the vista.

After a moment, she turned in a full circle, slowly, like a figurine on a music box dancing to a melody he could not hear, taking in the sky above and the earth below.

The land spread out like a patchwork quilt on a Scottish bed: the roads were the ribbons connecting the squares of faded green, winter brown, and washed-out yellow; the farm buildings were the knots at the intersections of each square. In the distance to the north, another plateau broke the flat fertile farmland, looking like a frosted cake with a sprinkling of icing sugar.

Robbie stood silently, observing. What caught his eye weren't the low, pale wisps of cloud that scurried across the sky toward them, nor the undulating surface of this plateau, pockmarked with a hundred rabbit warrens, nor the car speeding past on the country road below. It was Beth that captivated him.

He observed the way the wind blew the strands of her long, straight, brown hair into her face; noticed how she kept her hands tucked inside the pockets of the faded bomber jacket; saw the manner in which her eyes took in the stunning sight before her, a sight he had seen many times. But he'd never seen a young woman so enthralled with this ancient Scottish countryside.

───────⋈───────

The climb to the top of the plateau had been exhilarating and exhausting, though Robbie didn't seem to be winded at all. Now that she had caught her breath, Beth looked at the lovely view, musing that everything on this piece of grass-covered rock was reduced to three colors—grass green, earth brown, and mist gray. The air was damp from the gauzy clouds, which seemed close enough to touch. Impulsively, she reached up to see if she could, then put her hand down, concerned Robbie would think she was being silly.

She continued to look at the vista before her, trying to ignore his observing eyes and his amused smile. He stood, one hand in his windbreaker pocket, the other smoothing his beard.

As Beth stood in the silence of the deserted plateau, she began to hear the sounds that only stillness brought out: birds twittering in the grass, wind sighing through patches of bracken, her heart drumming in her chest. She closed her eyes. Without visual stimuli, her heartbeat seemed louder, deeper, as if it came from a cavernous space within the earth, penetrating her feet, rising through her legs, filling her chest, entering her arteries, and at last sounding in her ears.

She understood then why ancient peoples felt mountains and hills and heights were sacred places, dwellings of the spirits. Opening her eyes, she noticed a shallow pool of water caught in a circle of concave rocks. Could she see within it the reflection of the past, present, and future, as some ancient Druid princess might have done, standing right here?

At that moment, she sensed the bomber pilot.

If she looked out of the corner of her eye, he was there, in the way that you can see some stars only by looking at them obliquely. When she felt the blast of chill air that came with the thickening clouds, Beth wasn't sure who said, "The sky looks a wee bit threatening."

"I love the way the weather changes so quickly here." A female voice sounded dreamy. *"At home, it's a long time in coming. You know hours ahead that it's going to rain or snow."*

"Well, it's what they say about Scottish weather." The man's voice, her pilot's voice, seemed to come from inside her own head. *"Wait a wee minute, and it'll change."*

"Oh, yes." The girl laughed, but shivered slightly in the dress that he thought wasn't warm enough for a Scottish summer day, even in the lowlands, then smiled the brilliant smile that made her face glow, the smile

that penetrated his heart like a long, thin blade, with a pain so real he put his palm against his chest.

She stepped closer and put a hand over his, saying, "Colin, what is it?" Her voice, filled with concern, wrapped itself around his mind like warm arms, the way her arms felt when they danced, that one time he had allowed himself that delicious agony.

"What is it?" the woman repeated when he didn't answer.

Beth sensed his inability to respond as instead, he looked ahead, out over the farmland that lay like a quilt of green and brown and yellow below the ancient plateau.

"Tell me what you see," the girl said in her charming American accent.

"I see a storm coming. You're likely to get wet if we stay. We'd best be going."

The wind sighed. Or was it the girl?

"I'm used to wet weather, Beth. I've got my rain slicker on. It's waterproof."

Beth blinked, confused, disoriented.

"Are you all right? You're verra pale, all of a sudden." She heard the soft Scots accent, but this one with an American overlay; felt a hand on her arm, pulling her back from the edge of the cliff. She didn't know when she had gotten so close.

"Vertigo," Colin warned. "It can come on suddenly."

Beth turned. Robbie stood there looking at her, his face a study of concern. She looked over his shoulder, but the flat, undulating highland was empty, just dried grass stirring, tiny birds flitting, and misty clouds descending. She felt a cold quiver move through her body that had nothing to do with the chilly February day. It was becoming alarmingly easy to lose herself in that other place, to drop into that other time in just the blink of an eye.

"The ware started en finished hair o' this area o' Scotland," the gray-haired male guide's Scottish accent was so thick, Beth had to strain to catch each word, interpret each phrase. They were at the Museum of Flight on the former East Fortune Airbase not far from Traprain Law.

"The fairst plane shot dune in th' war was a Junker 88, t'was shot dune by a fighter fraim Drem. I remember I was a wee boy, hidin' in the cella' wit me aunt in Haddintin when the Jerries let go thay bombs. Thay dropped two land mines on Traprain Law t'as well."

Beth tapped one foot impatiently. The guide went on and on, supplying far more historical facts and personal anecdotes than she was interested in. She managed to ask him about Drem when he came up for air.

"Drem t'is wair the 603 Squadron was stationed fer a beet, but it's nair but an overgron field en a few tumble down buildins," the guide said. Then he went on with his spiel about the last battle of the war which took place over the Firth of Forth.

"A Jerrie U-boot got through the antisoobmarin nettin' at the mooth o' the Fairth and it sourficed aftair the saise fire agreemint t'was signed. Seems his rajio t'wasn't cooperatin'. Wane it sourficed, it faired ouf a volley of torpadoes and the locals thoug' t'was fairworks a celebratin' the en' o' the wahr."

It took Beth about two minutes to digest what the guide said and when she realized it was a funny story, it was too late to laugh without appearing "a bit taiched in th' haid."

———— ⋈ ————

"I had hoped there would be more of an airbase remaining," she said to Robbie as they explored the museum on their own.

"The biggest draw here is the Concorde," he answered.

"I don't want the 1990s; I want the 1940s," she replied, knowing she sounded petty and regretting it when a flash of hurt feelings crossed Robbie's face. She hadn't been sure she wanted to spend more time with him, after that conversation at Holyrood. She had been too forthcoming, too revealing, and was sure he had thought she was "mental" as the Scots kids would say. Yet there was something about him that made her want to take him into her confidence, ask him to help sort out this increasingly unnerving ability to hear the bomber pilot's thoughts.

That day at Holyrood was the first time she had clearly heard the bomber pilot's voice outside her dreams, and the first time she had sensed him while she was awake. Not only that, listening in on a snippet of conversation in which an American girl called him "Colin" and then was interrupted suddenly by the friendly Scots professor she had met on the train.

At any other time, she would have been delighted to see Robbie, but she had been so disoriented and overwhelmed by her "waking dream," as she came to call it. And just earlier this morning to sense Colin's presence at the top of Traprain Law. And that American girl again.

She had a difficult time paying attention despite Robbie's enthusiastic explanations of the endless exhibits at the Museum of Flight. Robbie was apparently a museum-a-holic; he read every sign, then relayed the meaning of each exhibit, layering her resistant mind with facts. She liked museums and history, but this wasn't what she expected of this visit, especially after her second waking dream. Her mind and heart were still back on that ancient plateau.

Over an hour later, she roused herself to joke, "That sign says exit," but he'd been oblivious to her growing impatience. Beth was exhausted and disgruntled by the time they left.

Even though the day was growing grayer, it felt good to be outside. The cornflower-blue doors, set between narrow eight-paned windows, contrasted jarringly with the ugly, faded-brown, one-story cement buildings. But the only evidence of the former East Fortune Airbase was one tumble-down hangar and several deserted barracks.

She was anxious to move on. To Drem. Colin's presence had appeared on Traprain Law, but not at East Fortune. If he had visited Traprain Law, maybe he had been stationed at Drem.

Robbie must have felt her impatience. "Shall we move along to our next stop?"

On the drive from the Museum of Flight to Drem, she was lost in thought. When Robbie came to her dorm room earlier in the week, she had been shocked but pleased to see him. He was, after all, a genuinely likable guy.

"A gentleman to see you," Anja had said with her Scandinavian accent. Beth couldn't imagine any gentleman coming to visit. She hadn't talked to a single guy in any of her lectures, preferring to sit in the front row where she could hear the professor. She was older than many of the students in her classes and felt out of place. Even in the small, weekly tutorials of ten to fifteen students, she kept to herself, talking only about the assigned reading, too uncertain to strike up a conversation. The other students, especially the other Americans, probably found her stuck up.

Robbie had seemed extremely pleased with himself when he handed her a piece of paper and explained the reason for his visit, but Beth quickly lost track of what he was saying when she looked at the list. Her vision went fuzzy, realizing that *one* of these names typed in New Times Roman must be *her Colin*. Touching that piece of paper made Colin real.

Her lungs felt as if someone had squeezed all the air out, and her trembling legs were near collapsing. She couldn't put together a coherent thought. All she could manage to do was thank him for the info and open the door for him. He had looked stunned and more than a little hurt. Yes, she had been abrupt, but he was just helping her with research.

"I'm sorry the Museum wasn't what you hoped for." The apology in Robbie's voice brought her back to the present. She hated that he was apologizing.

"No, it's not that at all, Robbie. You're being great. It's just... well, it wasn't on my grandfather's list, and I didn't want to waste any of our day going somewhere my grandfather hadn't suggested... oh, not that you don't have good ideas... I mean..." She mentally kicked herself for sounding so ungrateful.

"Aye, it's fine Beth. Really. I'm enjoying this. It's been years since I've been to Traprain, and the Museum of Flight is just that, a museum. I kind of get carried away in museums."

Beth snorted.

"Aye, you noticed, did you? Well, maybe Drem will be a wee bit more authentic, but I believe there's not much left other than a field. Some say they're planning some restoration, but it hasn't begun yet."

"Yes, fine."

"It's not likely your bomber pilot was stationed at Drem."

"Why's that?" It was interesting that Robbie called him *her* bomber pilot, when she thought of Colin the same way.

"Well, there were no bombers that flew out of Drem. Just coastal defense. He would have had to be stationed further south in England when the bombing began in earnest. And, honestly, though they call it a bomber jacket, it's really a flight jacket. Unless he was here for training. There was a training school at one time, but I don't remember the years. We should have asked the guide. I can do some more research... that is... I mean, if you want me to."

She noticed he had gone from eager to cautious, as if afraid to offend her. Why would he think doing research would offend her? "Your help is really great, Robbie. What I would like, I think, I mean, if you could show me where to do some research on my own... not that I don't want your help, it's just..."

"I know. It's different when you discover the information yourself. It means more."

She nodded. "I'm not a historian. I mean, for God's sake, you went to Cambridge and Oxford." She said the names as if they were holy. "It'd be a great skill to learn, but I don't want to use up your time. You're busy..."

"'Tis no problem at all, really. It would be more fun... ah, educational... if I taught you how to do the research rather than do it myself for you. And really, it's no bother."

She thought she heard him say under his breath, "Not at all."

After a moment he said, "I wonder why Drem was on your grandfather's list?"

Beth frowned. "He didn't say anything about why places were on his list, just they were things I should see. He said it rather oddly. Like it was important, but I can't imagine why."

"If your grandfather was an airplane mechanic, he'd have been with the U.S. Forces, and they were also stationed in England. "

Beth thought for a moment.

"He never talked much about the war. Actually, after I bought the jacket, I thought he might object to seeing me wearing it. But it was my grandmother who hated it. Said I looked stupid in it and I had wasted my money. She was angrier than I'd ever seen her that day I came home with it on."

"Did she lose someone in the war?"

"Yes. Her brother and sister. Her brother in the South Pacific.

"Her sister?"

"Gretchen. I never did know how. In the Blitz I think."

"In the Blitz! She was killed in England?" He ran his hand along the bottom of his beard.

"Yes. Weird."

"Was she a nurse?" Robbie asked.

She shrugged almost apologetically. "I don't really know. My grandparents never talk about that time. You understand."

"Aye, it makes sense. Many of that generation lost so many they loved in many horrid ways."

"Yes, yes, exactly," she said, then lapsed into thought. Was this what he meant when he said "I thought I was doing the right thing. For everyone"? *Had he done something horrible in the war? Wait, that's impossible. He was just a mechanic.*

She supposed being in the UK could give her a natural opening to finally approach her grandfather on the war, especially since one of the places on his list was a military airport. But telling him about her dreams and her search for the bomber pilot was out of the question.

She had known that her dreams would seem bizarre to other people, that she might be thought unstable if they knew how many nights the dreams occurred, or how many days were occupied with thoughts of Colin. Robbie's response at Holyrood simply confirmed it.

Beth was relieved he hadn't asked her again about them. She wanted to convince Robbie this was historical research, not an emotion-laden quest driven by weird dreams. No sense in making him think she was loopier than he already believed.

As if he read her mind, Robbie interrupted the silence hesitantly, "Those dreams? Have you had any more?"

She continued to stare out the passenger window at the cold February day. "No," she murmured. "It was just a quirk, I think." She added conviction to her voice, choosing what might put him at ease. "Letting my imagination run away with me. I think I was overstressed. A lot to take in. Dorm life. A new country. Like you said."

"I see." He sounded relieved. "Well, dreams can be unsettling. A semester abroad is very disorienting. Best to put it in the realm of academic research."

"Of course," she said, trying to make her voice bright and agreeable. If she was going to use Robbie's help, she needed to hide the increasing connection she was feeling to Colin.

Drem was exactly as the tour guide described: an overgrown airfield with a few deserted structures. On the edge of the airfield, the Fenton Barns Retail Village occupied many renovated wartime buildings, including some hangars.

The moment she stepped onto the airfield, she began to feel a sensation like vertigo, even stronger than at Traprain Law. *But I'm not standing on the edge of a cliff. Maybe this vertigo is some reaction to his presence. Or maybe it's the upheaval of time.*

Beth realized she would have to walk these fields, explore these buildings, and visit the nearby villages on her own. With Robbie and his probing eyes, she would not be able to experience Colin's presence or hear his voice.

"Shall we walk around?" Beth started at Robbie's voice. A sudden onslaught of driving rain sent them scurrying to the car, eliminating the need for an excuse. Beth giggled, feeling an unexpected sense of release. She *would* find a way to come back on her own and explore this new connection to Colin. The day had been a grand success. "Well, I guess that ends our visit," she said. "Another day maybe?" She smiled brightly, suddenly giddy with happiness, and was rewarded by an equally brilliant smile from Robbie.

"Ah, you Americans. Put off by a little bit of rain. 'Tis a fair Scottish day."

Beth laughed exuberantly, looking out at the rain moving across the field in sheets. "Well then, let's have some Scottish fare—a cup of Scotch broth, tea, and a scone." She felt, more than saw, Robbie's warm, enveloping smile.

"Aye, a lovely idea," he replied. "Let's go to Haddington. I'm pretty sure there's a tea shop on the square."

"Excellent," Beth enthused, unspeakably grateful that he didn't suggest the nearby villages of Guillane or Dirleton, where, according to the tour guide at East Fortune, many of the Drem crew members had been housed and entertained during the war.

She stretched her arms, resting her hand momentarily on Robbie's shoulder, and said in an authentically reproduced British accent, "On, James. Take the lady of the manor to tea."

FIVE

As he dropped Beth off near her dorm late that afternoon, she was surprised when Robbie said in an offhand manner, "I know this great little Indian restaurant, a wee bit dressy, but great food. How about if we go next Saturday night?"

Before she could respond, he added, "We can talk about the next steps in researching your bomber pilot's history."

Relieved that he wasn't asking her for a date, she agreed. "How about if I meet you there," she suggested. "Could be a bit awkward, you coming to the dorm."

"Oh, aye," he said. "It feels so unchivalrous, though."

"Well, she *hath no loyal Knight and true*. I'm capable of getting to the restaurant."

"I've never said you weren't capable," he replied and gave her the address and a time. Beth had a suspicious feeling he fancied himself a knight and her a damsel in distress. And to her surprise and frustration, the upcoming non-date was an unexpected distraction. She spent most her of time between classes reading, as each of her courses had a list of twenty to thirty assigned books. She now understood the term used in British universities—*reading* a subject. Though it wasn't expected that students read everything on the list, Beth was making a valiant effort.

In her spare time, she skimmed her expanding dream journal and did research on RAF Bomber Command because in a newer dream she had discovered the plane he piloted, when Colin said, "Don't worry, fellas, this old Lanc will see us safely home."

Since her journey across the Atlantic in January, she had been dreaming about the bomber pilot nightly and thinking of him daily, often in the middle of a lecture or tutorial. But the dreams continued to be limited to the cockpit of the plane or the grassy airstrip where he landed at dawn. The experience at Traprain Law reinforced the unnerving but exhilarating realization that if she went to places he had apparently visited, she might have a "waking dream."

But this week she found herself spending lots of time fretting about what to wear Saturday, like some giddy schoolgirl. She finally decided her usual attire of jeans, sweatshirt, and bomber jacket would be out of place at a nice restaurant. One of two dressy outfits she brought along would have to do.

Another circumstance also distracted her: a disconcerting change in her dreams. They shrank to snippets of previous ones, as if she were playing one of her grandfather's old Tommy Dorsey records and the needle stuck, continuously repeating one phrase of a song. Morning after morning she wrote "another repeat" in the section of her journal reserved for THE DREAM.

To her surprise, on Saturday evening as she was getting dressed for her evening out, Anja was still lounging on her bed, paging through a magazine. Normally she'd be with her boyfriend, a graduate student who had a private flat in town.

"Bett," she said in her heavily accented English, "Hew look nice. Hew have date, no? Let me help hew with look."

Over Beth's protests, Anja whipped out some jewelry and a delicate cardigan to complement Beth's attire—a flowy black, mid-calf skirt, her sleek, just-polished, leather boots, and a simple white blouse. Anja's chunky necklace, heavy bracelet, and pink, lacy sweater added charm and sophistication, Beth thought, when she gazed in the mirror on the back of her closet door.

"Is he hunk, no?" Anja's tinkling laughter lilted as she fiddled with the necklace.

Beth looked away, trying not to let Anja unnerve her. "It's not a date, but yes he's nice-looking. I guess."

"Hew guess?"

"We're just friends. He's helping with some history research. Besides, he's older and..."

"Ahye! Older man, Bett? Oh, hew sly von! Who would guess?"

"No, no." Beth protested. "He's a professor and..."

Anja's shriek of delight made Beth blush. "Ah, ya, hew *are* sly von. Eeets Professor McClot, no? All the girls luv heem. Gut way to have gut marks. He likes yew. Come to room!"

"No! No!" Beth saw her face grow redder in the mirror. "I met him on the train in January on my way from London. I... he's not... I'm not in any of his classes. It's not like that."

Anja nodded knowingly. "Ya, ya, vhatever, Bett. Hew just have gut time!"

"Thank you, Anja, for the jewelry and the sweater," Beth said, feeling unusually grateful toward her roommate. From the day Beth arrived, Anja had been casually indifferent and frequently absent, derailing Beth's image of a chummy college dorm experience. On the nights Anja stayed in the dorm, she lounged on her bed, reading Swedish-language magazines and listening to loud music on her headset, but rarely conversing. Beth found it more comfortable to spend the evenings at the library.

Anja picked up a strand of Beth's long, straight hair and said, "Ja, ja. Hew need to cut hair, Bett. So not style, so sixties. Hippie luk." She shook her head in disgust.

"I like my hair long," she said, somewhat defiantly.

"Ja, ja," Anja appraised Beth's face with a keen look. "But luk like waif. Short hair hew be...ah...classee."

Beth shrugged, picking up her long, hooded woolen cloak, a recent and expensive impulse buy. It was a gorgeous loden green and wonderfully warm. Anja eyed the cloak and nodded. "Bett rumantic type. Ja. Color purrfict for hew." She waved and winked as Beth opened the door. "See hew Sunday. Vill be wit Micah, tuunight, ja. Room ist all fer yew."

Beth rolled her eyes at Anja's hints. She expected Beth's evening to end up like her own, in bed with some handsome guy. Not that Robbie wasn't handsome, Beth thought when she saw him walking across busy Princess Street toward the restaurant, where she stood out front waiting.

Eating in fancy restaurants was something she did only on her birthday, a treat from her grandfather, who delighted in taking her to a different place each year. Her grandmother thought the indulgence "a criminal waste of money" and refused to go along, which actually made the evenings more pleasant. Naomi's way of acknowledging Beth's birthday was to make one of Beth's favorite breakfasts or give her a new hand-crocheted scarf or hat.

As Robbie got closer, she saw he was dressed in black slacks, a camel-colored cashmere sweater, a black dress shirt, a tartan tie, and a black pea coat. Oh... wow. Dashing.

"Will I do?" he asked at her appraisal, opening the door for her.

"You look... very nice," stammered Beth. "I was worried I wouldn't be dressy enough."

He helped her off with her wrap and gave it to the coat check girl. "That's a smashing outfit. Quite becoming. With your cloak, you could be a character from Dickens."

Beth was sure she turned a bright shade of pink. Robbie just grinned.

The restaurant was classy. Starched white tablecloths and napkins, heavily polished silverware, and a small red lamp in an elaborate bronze holder graced the table. Bronze light sconces on the wall cast a soft glow on the red brocade wallpaper and white paneling. Tall palm fronds and bronze statuary added to the exotic air.

There were a number of women in beautiful silk saris and men in what she called Nehru jackets. But there were also men in suits, women in dress slacks, and even the occasional man in a jacket and expensive-looking jeans.

Dinner was wonderful. Robbie suggested a mild curry dish that was sweet yet tangy. The creamy cucumber yogurt sauce on her salad made a delicious contrast to the main course, as did the slices of a juicy orange, and the crisp, semi-dry white wine that Robbie ordered.

Robbie asked about Beth's impressions of Scotland, and what did and did not meet her expectations. They laughed about ideas one got about another country from movies and TV.

At the end of their leisurely dinner, Beth nursed the last of a second glass of wine when their conversation hit a temporary lull. Her head was verging on fuzziness. "So, tell me about your father. He must be very successful."

Robbie picked up his spoon and made designs on the tablecloth, a frown on his face.

Beth looked at him in surprise. She had not known him to be at a loss for words. "Your father makes you sigh?"

"Is it so obvious? Hey, your glass is about empty. More wine?"

"No, no, really," Beth said vigorously, which made Robbie laugh. "I'm not really much of a drinker. My head's already a bit light."

Robbie put the spoon down and leaned his elbows on the table, resting his bearded chin on his folded hands. "So, it's easy to get you a wee bit intoxicated?" He twitched his eyebrow and stroked his chin, smoothing his beard in an exaggerated gesture. His very deep, brown eyes had a penetrating, intelligent gleam to them.

"Yes," she nearly snorted. "I'm easy to get tipsy, but I'm not easy."

"Aye," He said with a dramatic sigh, "I would have figured as much." Then he smiled, signaling the waiter. "How about coffee?"

"No, really, but maybe tea."

"Tea? You've really taken to the Scottish tea and scones bit, then?"

Beth sat up a bit taller, stretching slightly. "My grandfather is a tea drinker, so I grew up drinking it, except Friday nights."

"Oh?"

"Yes. You see, one Friday night a month my grandfather and I have a standing date to watch old movies." Beth sighed fondly. "He drinks some bitter-tasting ale, something dark and malty he learned to like when he was stationed in Britain during the war. He makes hot chocolate and popcorn for me."

"What kind of old movies?"

"Oh, whatever we can get on the classic movie channel or from the video store. Black and white movies from the thirties and forties.

Comedies. Dramas. War movies. Documentaries on the History Channel."

"Seems like odd fare for a twenty-something girl."

"It's our special date." Beth felt moisture pool at the corner of her eyes.

"It can be hard to be so far from home," Robbie said in a soft, gentle voice, his face going serious as he reached across the table and put his hand over hers. Beth felt the comfort, and then something else, some unexpected longing, some undesired attraction. Something she'd only felt once before, the first summer she'd been a flagger on the road crew two years ago.

"Thank you." Her smile wavered. But she withdrew her hand and clasped it to the other in her lap, trembling a little. She wasn't blind, Robbie's behavior brimmed with attraction to her, but it was too much to believe. Plus, physical interaction was just so... new. Almost uncomfortably new. At the question in Robbie's eyes, she looked down, fiddling with her napkin. Finally, he prodded, "So, your Friday nights with your Grandfather?"

Beth looked back at Robbie. "I think he did it initially when I was in junior high to rescue me from my grandmother's attempt to teach me womanly arts."

Robbie laughed out loud, leaning back in his chair. "Now you *do* sound like some Dickens novel," he said.

"Well, my grandmother tried her best to teach me to knit and crochet on Friday nights, once I turned eleven. For nearly a year, we tormented each other, I with my total ineptitude to remember whether it was 'knit two, purl one,' or knit one, purl two,' and she with her total lack of patience with my clumsiness."

Just then the waiter came to the table. "Coffee, sir?" he asked in lilting, Indian-accented English.

Robbie nodded. "Yes, for me, with cream and sugar, tea for the lady."

When the waiter left, Beth said, "Tell me about your father. He's an engineer, you say? In Tain, where you're from?"

"Not Tain, Edinburgh. Has an apartment here. Goes home on weekends."

"Really?" Beth said, trying to imagine such a life. "That must be difficult for your mother. But he gets to see you here, right?"

"No, actually, no."

"You don't?"

Robbie made a face. "No, we don't see eye-to-eye."

"You don't see eye-to-eye or aye-to-aye," Beth joked, giving that latter phrase an exaggerated accent.

"You're very droll," Robbie chuckled.

"But you don't see him at all? Really?" She was more serious now.

"We encounter each other occasionally in Edinburgh and at the holidays at home. Let me tell you a story, and maybe it'll explain our relationship."

Beth nodded. Robbie told such wonderful stories.

"I was a first-year student at the University of St. Andrews..."

"I thought you went to Cambridge and Oxford."

"I did. Transferred to Cambridge in my junior year. Did my graduate work at Oxford."

"Oh, right. Sorry, go on," Beth nodded encouragingly.

Robbie continued. "Over the Christmas holiday, I'd decided to tell my father that I was switching to history from engineering. The science and math classes had been torture, as they had in prep school, but the history classes made my brain come alive."

Beth smiled. "I'm a dolt at math. I can sympathize."

Robbie launched into an apparent simulation of his father's voice. "*I shoulda sent you to the public school in the States like I wanted to, where you'd have gotten a decent education.*"

"Public school is what we call private school here in the U.K.," Robbie said, in an aside, then returned to his story, continuing in his father's voice, "*But your mother insisted. Said you should experience life as an ordinary American. Even the schools in Australia were better than those American schools.*"

"You lived in Australia, too?" Beth interrupted, surprised and envious.

Robbie nodded but didn't break his story. *"And what did you get for your American education? Why you had to make up for it in that preparatory school? It woulda been cheaper to send you to one in the States."*

"I pointed out that I'd been accepted at St. Andrews, but he said he practically had to grovel for them to hold a place in the engineering school, promising I'd prove myself in first year."

"Well, Da," I said, *"maybe engineering isn't the best choice."*

"What the hell are you speaking of, boy? Look what it's got you. Travel to places you'd have never been if your father had been something else, like a broke historian."

"But, Da, you love history. Why you named me for..."

"Robert the Bruce and Robbie Burns both. Aye. A proud heritage we Scots have. But you can't get rich on heritage unless you own a castle and make it into some damn tourist site. We McLeods made our own way in the world. There are no lords to hand you down a peerage."

Fascinated, Beth leaned forward as Robbie's story unfolded, resting her forearms on the table.

"I argued that there were lots of jobs to be had in history, and he replied, *'If you want a job with the National Trust, volunteer to clean bird shait off St. Kilda's over your summer holidays.'* So I went back after break and dutifully tried to get excited about the math and science classes that were the prerequisites for acceptance into the engineering school."

"But it didn't work, did it?" Beth interjected sympathetically.

He paused as the waiter brought their after-dinner beverages. Robbie took a sip of his coffee then replied to her question. "As always, it was history that enthralled me. And it was my father's fault. Hadn't he used every school holiday to take us all over Europe, visiting everything from prehistoric burial mounds on Orkney to Winston Churchill's tomb in Westminster Abbey, the cave paintings in France to Hitler's lair on top of a mountain in Berchtesgaden?"

Beth listened to Robbie tick off places she had only seen in books and said, "Oh, I'd love to go back to Westminster Abbey."

"It's impressive, no matter how old you are. We'll go sometime."

Beth rather liked the sound of him making casual plans for them.

"My classmates, in whatever part of the world we were living," Robbie continued, "would be at the beach or mountains or a city for holidays, but my family would be trudging across battlegrounds, climbing over cathedral ruins, and learning about life in colonial settlements." He paused for another sip of his coffee. "This is probably boring."

"Oh, no!" Beth replied enthusiastically. "It's better than a movie. Or a novel."

Robbie chuckled. "Glad to be entertaining," he said, then went on with his story.

"Later that year, in April, my father was driving me back to school on the last Sunday of my spring holiday, a trip of about six hours. I decided to use that time to convince him of the value of a history degree."

"Oh," Beth shook her head. "Six hours to fret about the conversation."

"Fret I did. Thing was, I had already spoken to my advisor and switched my concentration to history for my second year. I figured the car would be the safest place to bring up the subject. The ride was quiet, except for when my father was doing his usual traveling history lesson as we went through, near, or by various historical sites. It was like being on a family vacation again, except we didn't stop."

Beth laughed sympathetically. "But think what you learned growing up."

"Aye, that's true," Robbie snorted. "But look where it got me. It wasn't until we were an hour from the university that I finally took a deep breath and marched onto the battlefield. I decided on an all-out frontal attack. We had left the A9 and were headed east on local roads to St. Andrews. The road was busy with Sunday drivers, but that didn't slow my father down."

"*Da*, I said, and my voice was aggravatingly wavering. I distinctly remember twisting my Philadelphia Phillies cap in my hands. My father hated that hat, and I wore it just to annoy him. "*Da*, I said, *I've made a decision about school, and there's no talking me out of it. And it's your fault anyway. You're the one who made me fall in love with history, I mean all those trips to Culloden and Glencoe and the Orkney Islands.* I could feel his eyes boring into me, so I stopped rambling and got right to the meat of it. I told him I'd switched my major to history."

Robbie stared into his coffee cup. For a moment he seemed lost in memory. Then blinking, he smiled wryly. "I have to tell you, the silence in the car fell like a death sentence. I tried to breathe, reminding myself that I was twenty, old enough to make up my own mind. I awaited my father's reaction. Anger. Fury. A storm of protest. But there was only silence."

"Oh." Beth shuddered. "I know all about that. That's my grandmother's favorite weapon. Silence, cold enough to freeze your bones."

Robbie chuckled. "You do understand then. So, I glanced out of the corner of my eye to gauge my father's facial expression. It was as chiseled and cold as the Callanish standing stones on the Isle of Lewis. I'll take you there sometime. My father stared straight ahead, continuing to weave in and out of traffic, passing the slower drivers, and keeping his BMW in top gear."

"For the next forty-five minutes, my father said nothing." Robbie shook his head at the memory. "The silent treatment is my father's preferred punishment, and it can go on for days. But he always shows his immediate anger by driving at ridiculous speeds."

Beth gave him a sad, sympathetic smile. "Oh, Robbie, it must have been awful."

"It wasn't until we reached the outskirts of St. Andrews that my father spoke. *So you're saying,* my father said in his most sarcastic voice, *that you're giving your heart to history.*"

"*Aye,* I replied, struggling to control my words in the face of my father's sarcasm."

"*Well then, perhaps you'd be a bit more faint of heart if the coins were not flowing.*"

"I told him I didn't understand what he meant. He replied, *What I mean, Robbie, is that if you're so in love with history, maybe you need to find a way to make it pay for you.*"

"I said that of course, I'll be looking for teaching jobs and maybe work with The Trust or Historic Scotland."

"I don't mean when you finish your studies. I mean now, my father said."

"We had pulled into the parking lot which served the dormitory complex. Dusk was setting in. My father was already pulling suitcases out of the boot, that's the trunk, by the time I grabbed my coat from the back seat."

Beth loved the pictures Robbie painted with his words; the scene was so vivid, she felt as if she had been riding along with him in the car and was standing next to him by the trunk. *He could be a writer, too,* she thought, admiring his easy way with words.

"I told him I would prove that history was a good choice, that I could get a good job. His answer was to tell me that he wasn't going to contribute anything more for my education costs after the end of my first year, and I was lucky the Scots pay the college tuition for their students, so I'd only need to come up with funds for housing, meals, books, and transportation, plus any entertainment I chose to indulge in."

Beth could hear the growing thickness of his voice. The story was surely painful to tell and difficult to relive. She felt a new tenderness toward him, recognizing some hidden place of vulnerability, and knew an unexpected longing to comfort him.

"The last thing he said was, *I brought you up to be glad of your Scottish heritage, not to make a fool of yourself over it.* Then gave me one last cold look, walked around the side of the car and got in, slamming the door like an exclamation point, and pulled off, leaving me and my suitcases in the car park."

With a deep sigh, Robbie swallowed the rest of his coffee and signaled the waiter. "I'll have a dram of Glenlivet," he said. When Beth shook her head at his look, he said, "And the tab."

While Robbie waited silently for his whiskey, Beth wondered about her own parents. What might they have thought about her choice to go abroad for a semester and to pursue a degree in British Literature? According to Henry, Suzanna had studied art and anthropology in college. But those were useless thoughts, as she'd never met either of them. Both died when she was an infant.

Beth waited quietly for Robbie to go on. After a sip of his whiskey, he smiled wearily, "So, that's the story."

"And what happened after that?" Beth asked softly, leaning across the table.

"My mother says he had the same conflict with his own father about a career, but in that case, Grandda won. I never met Grandda. He died before I was born. Working too hard, my mother says. Building up that engineering firm with his brother Clement, the firm my father eventually took over after Clement died."

Robbie made a grunting noise. "My father thought I'd come around, but I didn't. I worked really hard to put myself through school, giving tours to rich Americans who came over for golf. My buddies who'd be doing the caddying would say, *Hey, if your wife or kids are bored, I've got a friend that does these personalized tours.* I wasn't one for caddying or golf. It was my grandfather's game, and my father's. Not mine. I prefer a pick-up game of football or rugby, or biking, or hiking up Ben Nevis, or hill walking in the mountains west of Tain."

"When I won a partial scholarship to Cambridge, he didn't even congratulate me. Just made some stupid remark like, *A scholar would have earned a full ride.*"

"You must be brilliant to have won a scholarship to Cambridge," interjected Beth.

Robbie shrugged. "I've had to work hard and study hard. I liked living in the States. Wouldn't mind going back again to teach for a while. European history. Put on the Scots brogue, and the students would believe anything I said."

They laughed for a bit before Robbie said, "Listen to me blathering on and on." A slight flush tinged his cheeks, but it could have been the whiskey, she thought.

"Do you see your father in town, ever?"

"You'd think we'd run into each other, but we move in different circles. It's helped at times being his son, to get some clients and contacts with the Trust. He is a donor. I've friends who work for the Trust and for Historic Scotland, and they send clients my way. But then, my father wouldn't know the staff. He'd only hobnob with the moneyed crowd. The crowd my mother always hated. She'd rather share tea from a crockery pot at the kitchen table."

Robbie swallowed the last of his whiskey.

"I live in the same town as my father. He's here five days a week. But we never see each other. He's never forgiven me for proving him wrong. My summer tour business is picking up again, now that I'm back from my year at Duke, and of course it's my first year as a professor. When I do go home for some of the holidays, it's really to see my mother and sister Caitlin. My father and I just talk about the weather or politics or sports. He never asks about my schooling. Or even my job here at the university."

Beth heard the hurt beneath Robbie's bitterness and thought of her grandmother's often cold indifference. *We have something in common,* she mused.

Robbie grimaced. "So, good lord, I've told you my whole life story. Let's get out of here. How about a walk? Put that new Scottish cloak to a test, aye?"

"How'd you know it was new?"

"Didn't think you brought it from the States."

When she tried to pay for her share of dinner, protesting that he hadn't even let her chip in for gas the previous weekend, he said she could get their next meal. They walked around the crowded streets of downtown Edinburgh for nearly an hour, Robbie tucking Beth's arm in the crook of his in an old-fashioned gesture that she found very touching. She finally had to say, "Robbie, I'm nearly frozen."

He took her to another restaurant, where he ordered her hot chocolate laced with Drambuie, and he had another shot of whiskey. They shared a piece of Dundee cake and spent another hour talking about history, politics, and the state of the world.

When he put her in a cab after midnight, he squeezed her hand. "Thank you, Beth."

"For what?" she asked, clueless as to what he would be grateful for.

"For listening. You are a natural listener. I can talk on and on about Scottish history or American history, but I don't...well...not so much about my own."

Nodding, Beth gave him an appreciative smile.

After the taxi pulled away, she realized that they had not once discussed the bomber pilot.

Six

"You were unusually quiet today."

Beth, putting on her bomber jacket at the conclusion of the Survey of Scottish History and Culture tutorial, looked in surprise at the boy standing next to her.

"Sorry?"

"Usually you have so much good stuff to say. You seem to know it so well." The boy had an accent she couldn't place. It sounded American, but not quite.

"Oh, hey. I'm Iain."

She studied the hand he had thrust out, then, blushing, quickly put out her own to complete the handshake. "Yes, ah, sorry. I was daydreaming." *Fretting because I hadn't had a dream about Colin since last Thursday, and I've been wondering if spending time with Robbie was the cause*, she added silently.

"That doesn't seem like you. I mean, you're really right on top of the discussion. And I notice you sit right up front in the lecture, too."

Beth frowned. He had noticed her?

"You're Miss Schmidt."

Beth looked at him, puzzled, but only for a second. Their professor called everyone by their proper names. "And you're Mr. Frasier."

The boy nodded. "It's Iain, unless you're a prof." He had a head full of blonde, flyaway hair and intensely-blue eyes that went well with a blue parka and tailored jeans. "You're American."

She nodded. "You're not?"

"Well, yes, North American, but you southern neighbors hog the American name."

It took her a second to realize what he meant. "Oh, you're Canadian." That explained the accent. "Where from?"

He opened his parka to reveal a Toronto Maple Leafs sweatshirt.

"Yes, I see. Toronto."

"And you?"

"Pennsylvania. Carlisle. Not too far from Gettysburg."

"I've been there!" He smiled a somewhat toothy grin revealing slightly crooked teeth. "It was cool, but I liked the nighttime ghost tour better than the daytime stuff. I'm not really into battlefields or history too much. Except if they're on a video game."

"If you don't like history, why are you taking this class?"

"Pretty much required for visiting students. Thought I ought to know about my heritage."

"So, you're Scottish?" They were following the other students out. "Oh, yes, I should have figured with a name like Iain Frasier."

"Yes... way back. Family got booted out after Bonnie Prince Charlie lost at Culloden."

Beth was awed. "You can trace your family history that far back? Wow, that's so cool."

Iain shrugged. "My immediate family's not so much into it, but I've got a cousin who's in a well-known Canadian pipe band. Wears the kilt and sporran and the whole thing."

He held the door for her. "Thought it'd be cool to spend part of my junior year in Scotland, and the parents were all for it. Willing to dish out the money. I'm having a great time."

They stood to one side of the door in the hallway, and the conversation suddenly lagged. She wondered why he had talked to her. She was about to say she had to get to the library when Iain started, "I was wondering..." and they were interrupted by a familiar voice.

"Beth, how are you?"

She looked away from Iain to see Robbie standing in front of her, smiling warmly. Beth felt suddenly awkward. "Ah, I'm fine. And you, Ro... Professor McLeod?"

"I'm great, Miss Schmidt." He said her formal name with a slightly sarcastic Scottish accent. "May I speak to you a minute?" He took her by the elbow. "Excuse us a moment, young man," he said offhandedly to Iain and walked her to the other side of the hallway.

Beth pointedly pulled her arm away and watched the smile leave Robbie's face. "Oh, I'm sorry. I... that was stupid. I didn't mean to commandeer you, but I wanted to talk to you privately."

Beth made a gesture at the students passing by. "This isn't so private."

Robbie looked across the wide hallway to Iain staring at them. "Is he a friend?" Robbie's voice had an odd edge to it.

"A classmate."

"I see." His gaze was still leveled at Iain.

"You wanted to talk to me?" she prompted.

"Yes, yes. Sorry. It's just, well, I realized that we didn't make any plans at dinner to visit another of your grandfather's recommendations. I was wondering if you'd want to take a spin to Stirling and the William Wallace monument, this Saturday?" he asked enthusiastically.

When Beth didn't reply, he added in a less enthusiastic voice, "It's on your list."

Beth's immediate reaction was delight, but an image of a young man in a leather jacket scrambling out of a bomber on a cold morning got in the way. She said somberly, trying to convince herself, "I do want to visit the places on my grandfather's list."

Her uncertainty must have come across to Robbie because he said in a more serious tone, "Yes, and getting you off campus. That's good for your mental health." Then he added in a teasing voice, "And having lunch. One has to eat."

"Yes, one has to," Beth intoned, wondering at his statement about her mental health and trying to erase the pleasant memories of their recent dinner together. Robbie was leaning against the wall, arms crossed, wearing a puzzled frown. He was clearly confused by her hesitation.

With a sigh, she nodded and said cautiously, "Sure. It'd be very thoughtful of you. But you'll let me pay for lunch and the admission."

"I have a membership, so the admission is already free. If you insist, you can pay for your own lunch, but you don't have to pay for mine. After all, I'm earning money at this institution, and you're dishing it out."

Beth's uncertainty increased at his offhanded reminder of their unequal status. She replied flatly, "You're right. Look, I have to go. Ah, how about if we meet like we did when we went to Traprain Law." She started to walk away, but his hand stopped her.

"I was also wondering... well." To Beth's surprise, Robbie looked nervous. "Well, how about if we take in a movie Friday night?"

She was speechless. What was this? Saturday was a kind gesture, a ride to a historical site. A movie was a date. "A war documentary?" Beth asked, knowing she was being ridiculous.

Robbie snorted. "No. I like to take one night off from history. A movie. Like made in Hollywood. Not Holyrood." He laughed at his own joke.

Beth sighed inwardly. *So, a date, then. And last week's dinner wasn't?* A voice taunted her. Yet the thought of another Friday night alone in her room was almost unbearable. *Besides, it isn't a date; he's only being kind. He's a professor. He wouldn't date a student,* she shouted back to the objections in her head.

"That's very nice of you," she said, voicing some of her thoughts. "It certainly beats spending Friday night in the dorm."

Robbie looked startled, then laughed ruefully. "Beth, you're good for me. You constantly bring me down to earth. I'll meet you in front of the movie theater on Leith Street at half six."

"Right-oh," Beth blushed, realizing she had sounded rather rude. "See you then." She walked back to a frowning Iain who was watching the whole time.

"Who's that?" Iain asked, watching Robbie stroll toward the exit. "You called him professor?"

"Yes, Professor McLeod. He teaches history. He's... ah... helping me with... research."

"Oh, I see."

Beth didn't like Iain's tone. She replied, "Well, I have to go and…"

"Wait, no, I wanted to ask you something."

Beth tried not to sigh. He probably wanted her study notes.

"I was wondering if you'd want to go out Friday. Get a drink."

Absent-mindedly, she shook her head. Was she hearing this right? "Out?"

"Yeah. You can tell me about the U.S.; I can tell you about Canada."

"But you've been to America."

"Only a couple places. Have you been to Canada?"

"No. I haven't been anywhere. Except Scotland. And London."

"So, great. We'll have an educational discussion," he said innocently at first but spoiled it with a smirk.

Beth snorted, about to say yes just because he was so amusing. She had a sense Iain was majoring in fun, rather than focusing on his courses. Then he added, "Besides, I bet you need to get out more."

Beth bristled at his insinuation. "What do you mean?"

"It's just I can tell you're a serious student. A scholar, my mother would say. What she wishes I was. You're away from home. It can be lonely. I noticed you kind of keep to yourself."

Beth was unnerved both by his insight and the fact he had been observing her without her noticing. And how could this be that two guys were asking her out for the same night? This just didn't happen in her life. She'd only ever dated one guy, Jason, and that was as platonic a relationship as possible.

"I… I… well, I can't. I mean I have something I'm doing Friday night."

At his disappointed look, she wavered. Iain had a very appealing nature. Younger, but the first student who made any effort to reach out to her. Hesitantly, she said, "But maybe another night?"

Iain perked up. "Great. Saturday?"

Beth nearly rolled her eyes. "Ah… I'm going on a trip on Saturday and don't know when I'll be back."

"Well then, Sunday."

Sunday was the night she wrote her grandfather at her favorite campus building, the Law and Europa Library which overlooked a cobblestone courtyard surrounded by a quadrangle of medieval-looking stone buildings.

But making excuses for three nights in a row would probably send an "I'm not really interested" signal, and the fact was, she *was* interested. She could write her grandfather Sunday afternoon.

At her hesitation, Ian asked, "What? You don't go to bars on Sundays? You're a religious type?"

"No, no," Beth couldn't help laughing at his conclusion. "It's fine, I can go out Sunday."

"Whew, I was beginning to think you were giving me the brush-off."

Beth was startled by the obvious relief in Iain's voice. She replied, "No, no, really, I'm just... I don't usually go to pubs. I mean, back in the States, a lot of the college students I hung around with were underage."

Iain looked at her blankly. "Are you opposed to drinking?"

"Ah, no, it's just I don't do very much of it."

"No problem. I'll show you how. It's easy to learn."

Beth shook her head in amusement.

Iain added encouragingly, "You'll have a great time. I promise. Can I come by your room Sunday night and get you? Are you in Pollock Hall? I am too."

They made arrangements, and Iain said as he left, "See you Sunday, if not before. Maybe I'll see you in the dining hall."

Beth nodded, bemused. She thought it was going to be a typical quiet weekend, and now she had the entire weekend booked. She must be dreaming. That thought brought her up short.

Because she wasn't dreaming the dreams that mattered.

Three days later the biting February air nibbled at Beth's cheeks as she made her way through the jostling Friday night crowds on Leith Street.

She spotted Robbie before he saw her. He stood beneath the movie marquee in a tweed golf cap, his heavy woolen pea coat, a tartan scarf, corduroy slacks, and western boots. His beard added to the sophisticated look. She wondered if someone had told him a beard would make him look like a professor, just as someone had once told Abraham Lincoln that growing a beard would make him look more like a president. She thought Robbie looked distinguished, though he'd hate that descriptor. "That's a word for my father," she could hear him say.

The rowdy teenagers laughing and pushing at each other in front of the cinema formed a barrier of noise and bodies. She stood curbside, shouting Robbie's name, but he didn't hear her. A sense of distance and isolation seeped into her mind, and for a moment she thought of going back to the dorm. *What am I doing here in this country so far from my family, meeting a professor, of all things, for a date?*

No, it's not a date, she reminded herself harshly for the umpteenth time. *Especially not today. It's Valentine's Day. Maybe his sweetheart is too far away to take out tonight.*

A sudden feeling of dislocation overcame her. The buzz of the marquee lights filled her head, and a disorienting sensation of moving through time and space jarred her sense of reality. Last night's dream, the first about Colin in more than a week, reappeared before her eyes.

Colin was away from the airfield, and it was evening. He was surrounded by laughter and raised voices. In a crowd. The people weren't distinct, but she sensed them. She knew that he was looking for someone. That he was anticipating, yet nervous. A night not unlike tonight. Feelings not unlike hers.

"Beth? Beth!"

Beth blinked. Robbie stood in front of her with a puzzled smile.

"You look like you were a thousand miles away. Didn't you hear me calling?"

She shook her head gently; any movement intensified the vertigo.

Robbie took her arm, for which she was grateful, and said, "Come on, we'll miss the opening. I've got tickets already. It's nearly sold out."

The smell of buttered popcorn on a rush of overheated air made Beth's stomach rumble loud enough for Robbie to hear.

He chuckled. "Well, something to tide us over a wee bit. How about a snack?"

She nodded. She hadn't eaten supper. She had spent the afternoon watching an old documentary on World War II in the library's media center and had rushed to shower and change and hop the student shuttle bus, all while last night's dream played over and over in her head.

Robbie made his way to the concession stand while Beth stood at the edge of the lobby assessing him dispassionately. He *was* nice-looking. Not drop-dead handsome, but very easy to look at with brown, thick, wavy hair that he wore long enough to touch the collar of his shirt and his full face with its high cheekbones and fair skin and neatly trimmed beard. She was often tempted to reach up and brush his thick, bushy eyebrows into order.

Then there were his deep brown eyes, curious and bright like a bird's, even when he put on his reading glasses. His easy smile always brought a response from other people, who seemed to warm instantly to his attentive, friendly manner. He had a self-confident but not arrogant manner, which she appreciated; and she admired his strong, athletic build that she had learned came from his daily morning jogs.

He was not only easy to look at, but also easy to be with. He never made her feel stupid or awkward, even being a world apart in sophistication and experience.

He motioned with his head from across the lobby for her to join him and they went into the theater. Finding it full, they settled in seats down front, surrounded by jabbering teenagers.

"By the way," she nearly shouted over the noise, "what are we seeing? I assume it's not an art film with the crowd that's here tonight."

Robbie laughed. "I'm sorry. I thought I said. It's a new release with Pierce Brosnan. An action-adventure, disaster-type movie. *Dante's Peak.* I like an escapist movie now and then, and this is set in the States, so I thought you might appreciate it."

"Who wouldn't appreciate Pierce Brosnan?" she asked rhetorically, which made Robbie laugh. Disaster movies were not her favorite genre, but she was relieved he hadn't picked a romantic comedy. That would have been embarrassing on this day set aside for lovers. She munched the heavily buttered popcorn, sipped a Diet Coke, and lost herself in the movie.

As always, Beth sat silently in her seat after the film ended, watching the credits, oblivious to the commotion around her. A touch on her hand startled her and brought her attention to Robbie, who sat looking at her with a bemused expression.

"You really lose yourself in the movie, don't you?" He said with an undertone of teasing.

She sighed and shrugged. "Well, this movie was diverting. Not like some that I really get lost in. I just like to read the credits. Gives me time to... ah... come back. The same thing happens when I read. I feel like..." She stopped. She sounded odd.

"Like you're really there," he ventured.

"Yes," she agreed. "I've always loved stories. My grandpa read to me at bedtime when I was a little tyke."

"Your grandpa?" he said as they stood. He helped her find her hat and scarf, which had slipped to the floor. "Isn't that a grandma thing?"

She made a disparaging noise. "Well, maybe it is, but my grandmother isn't the stereotypical grandmother. Maybe because she had to be more of a mother..." Beth's voice faded as she turned to follow Robbie out of the theater.

He held the door for her, "Let's get something to eat. We can go to the Black Bull. It's nearby. Too chilly to walk much further."

"I thought you Scots all had ice water in your veins," she teased.

Robbie hooted at her suggestion, shivering when a blast of cold air hit them. "I despise this sleety rain," he said, pulling the collar of his coat up around his neck and tucking her arm in the crook of his.

"Showery rain. Sleety rain. I love the way the weathergirl on the radio describes the forecast. Gale force winds in the west. Winds fresh from the east. But brighter in the north with some sunshine as well."

"That's amusing, is it?" Robbie asked, smiling.

She nodded. "It's just so flowery for the weather. Makes it seem so much less harsh." He chuckled at her description.

The pub was a short walk. Inside it was smoky, dim, and crowded, but deliciously warm and dry. Robbie took Beth's hand and led her into a far corner where he found two tall stools at a bar table that a group of college-aged boys was just vacating. Beth felt a moment of panic, wondering if Iain might be among them.

"Hey, professor," one said, giving Beth the once-over. She felt heat rise on her cheeks at his keen interest and disengaged her hand. "Out on the town?"

"Looks like it, Mr. McMaster. Thanks for the table," Robbie replied, ignoring their obvious curiosity and their attempt to wrangle an introduction. "Better get back to your dorm and prepare for Monday's lecture. I'll be sure to call on you."

"Sure thing, Dr. McLeod," the boy named McMaster said in a knowing voice.

Beth tried not to look embarrassed. After the young men left, Robbie said, "That's the problem with a small city like Edinburgh. You run into your students everywhere. It's hard to have a private life. What do you want to drink?" He was practically shouting to be heard over the din of the crowd and the throbbing rock-and-roll emanating from the nearby jukebox.

Beth never knew what to drink in a bar. Out of desperation, she said, "A rum and coke."

Robbie nodded and headed to the bar. Beth took off her jacket and looked around. The pub was paneled with dark wood and festooned with brass fixtures. Cigarette smoke hung heavily in the air. Beth wished they would ban smoking in bars. She hated the way her clothes and hair smelled the next morning.

Above the front door was the tavern's signature Black Bull's head with flashing red eyes. Black and white photos of rock-and-roll legends covered the walls. Around the corner was an alcove with a pool table and some gaming machines.

As she sat there, Beth again felt the pull of last night's dream in which Colin had walked into a room from the cold, winter night. The smoky, noisy atmosphere of this room was similar, but the music was all wrong. It should be Tommy Dorsey and Benny Goodman. Music her grandfather played on his record player. Old, scratchy 33s and 78s that Naomi said were rubbish.

Something told her, sitting here in this smoky, crowded, overheated bar, that her grandfather would have been more comfortable out on a Friday night at her age than she was. But if he did hang out at bars in his youth, it was surely before he and Naomi were married, for Beth was unable to imagine her grandmother in a pub or tavern.

By the time Robbie came back with their drinks, her head had begun to ache from the pounding music. To hear anything Robbie said, she had to lean very close to him across the small table, a position that created a heightened sense of intimacy. It sent her pulse into an uncomfortable erratic rhythm and the unexpected reaction gave her pause for thought. She felt oddly breathless and confused.

"I ordered a plate of fish and chips; hope that's okay with you." Robbie said, casually dropping his free hand over the one she had laid on the table.

Beth looked up. Robbie's face was only six inches from hers. His nose was slightly crooked. Without thinking, she took her other hand from around her drink, and reached out, gently running her forefinger down the ridge of his nose. His eyes grew intense, the brown of his irises almost black in the dim light.

"I broke it in a biking accident." He took her raised hand and slid it by his lips, kissing her fingertips with the lightest touch.

Beth sat back with a sudden jerk, pulling her hand away and knocking her drink over.

"I'll get a towel," Robbie jumped up. He returned with several napkins. As he mopped up the spill, Beth held her glass up in both hands, her face flame-red. Jason's words fluttered back to her from a Friday night two years ago.

"Don't worry; you're gonna blow some guy away someday. He'll fall head over heels in love with you." Robbie? Was this happening?

Robbie didn't say a word as he took the nearly empty glass from her back to the bar. A few moments later, he returned carrying a creamy-looking drink and a basket of fish and chips.

"There's a table in the back where they're playing pool. It's a little bit quieter. Why don't you grab my beer and follow me?"

As they settled at a table in a far corner, he said, almost to himself, "You are a strange creature, Susanna Elizabeth Schmidt." He took a forkful of the crunchy fish. "Careful, it's hot."

"I... I didn't... I wasn't trying to... flirt," she said, finally getting the words out, swallowing compulsively as he stared at her intensely, his fork paused on its way to the next bite. She felt stupid as she realized how provocative her gesture had been.

"Why don't you go by Susanna?" His voice was light.

"It was my mother's name, and for some reason, my grandmother didn't like it. How did you know my whole name?"

"You introduced yourself on the train. I think Beth suits you. Susanna doesn't."

He tried to take her hand again.

"Don't." Beth drew back. "I said I wasn't trying to flirt."

"No, I don't think you were. I don't think you know how to." He looked at her with a serious smile. "You really are just so... refreshing."

"Refreshing?" Beth wasn't sure if that was a nice way for him to say stupid. "Is that a backhanded compliment or a mild insult?"

Robbie laughed his throaty chuckle. "To tell you the truth, Beth, I'm not sure myself." He nodded at the drink. "Try it."

"I haven't had much experience at drinking."

"Ah, I think I noticed."

She sipped the smooth concoction, tasting chocolate and cream. "Yum. It barely tastes like alcohol at all."

"Makes it all the more dangerous, though. Thus, the food."

"Do I need to worry?" She said, blushing when she realized it sounded like teasing.

"Maybe with some guys. I'm not going to pounce on you, though. So, don't worry. And one of those won't get you loopy."

"You hope not."

He leaned his chin on a hand, eying her with half a smirk. "You would be interesting loopy."

She shook her head in denial. "I don't think so. Besides..." Beth looked down at her drink. "I haven't had a lot of, ah, dating experience." Her face grew warm.

What was she saying? Were they dating? She tried to puzzle it out in her mind. Did they have a "relationship?" She put mental quotation marks around the word, then chided herself for being grammatically correct even in her thoughts. To distract herself, she ate a chip, as they called fries in the U.K.

Robbie sighed and took a sip of his ale, licking his lips to wipe off the foam. "Tell me about your grandfather."

Beth blinked at Robbie's sudden change of subject. "Well, it's funny that you should ask, because I was just thinking of him a little earlier. He wouldn't like that movie we just saw."

"Why?"

"Well, although he likes movies, he prefers ones set in the thirties or forties or fifties. Or movies that tell a good story. This one, though exciting, was a little too predictable."

"You're a movie critic as well as a literature aficionado?"

"I think I told you before that my grandpa and I have a standing date to watch an old movie on the first Friday of every month. The other Friday nights during the school year, I take in art films on either the Shippensburg or Dickinson campus. Dickinson is a college in Carlisle. A private, pricey one. Shippensburg is a State University."

Beth took another sip of her drink. "Grandma always complains about the cost of cable, but Grandpa said he didn't spend money on wine or women, so TV was a lesser vice."

Robbie smiled. "I think I'd like your grandfather. He reminds me a bit of mine. My mother's father. Sort of ornery in a very nice way."

"My grandfather is such a gentleman. Even his jokes are gentlemanly. But Grandma never seems to find Grandpa's jokes funny. She just says, 'Henry Schmidt, I'm taking my migraine medicine and going to bed.'"

In her mind, Beth saw her grandfather's sad eyes follow her grandmother out the door of the television room. "As an adult, I think I realize their marriage is pretty empty. I've often wondered why they married."

She was surprised to hear herself say this out loud to Robbie. She had never mentioned her opinions about her grandparents' marriage to anyone.

Robbie nodded, smoothing his beard, something she was starting to realize he did in thought. "You know, I've had the same thoughts about my parents. My father is away from home so much. But my mother always seems content with their life. She's a primary school teacher and does a lot of volunteer work. My sister says she likes her independence and that their weekend marriage is probably what has kept them together."

Beth shook her head. "But my grandparents have never been away from each other, I don't believe, in all the years they've been married... which are fifty-some, I guess."

"Have you always lived with them?"

Beth nodded. "My mother and father met when my mother was in graduate school in Washington, D.C. during the Vietnam War. They fell in love, and he went off to war and was killed, and then my mother discovered she was pregnant."

Robbie made noises of sympathy.

"Well, it's all just someone else's history, you see," Beth said, shrugging. When she turned twelve, Henry had given her a large scrapbook with photos of Susanna growing up, childish drawings, report cards, newspaper clippings of dance recitals and parades where she marched as a majorette in high school, of college awards, and graduation invitations.

"It hardly seems like my own. I never knew my mother. She left soon after I was born. They didn't tell me that. They told me that she died when I was a few months old. When I was in high school, I found a newspaper clipping in some old stuff in the garage attic with her obituary."

Beth took another sip. "She died in Haight-Asbury. It didn't say of what. Sudden death. But I figured it was a drug overdose. It was only about eight months after I was born. It said she had been living with friends in San Francisco. I figured she couldn't cope with a baby and a dead lover."

Robbie sighed. "That's tough. Your grandparents never told you the whole story?"

"No, I think they're too old-fashioned. It was pretty scandalous back in a small town like Carlisle. I mean my parents weren't married. I'm sure of it. I never saw a wedding picture or even a picture of my father. Maybe it was just a one-night stand."

Beth gulped down the rest of her drink to hide her own astonishment at what she just said. What was it about Robbie that inspired her to tell him things she had thought about, written in her journal, but never shared?

Robbie was quietly attentive, so she went on. "If the question of my parents, say at school, would come up, my grandmother would say, 'They died when you were a baby and left you to us to tend.' She always said it that way. *Tend*. Like I was a cow. She never said it with much sympathy or even sadness. I think my grandmother resented having to raise me." To think people always said she looked more like her grandmother than her grandfather.

"What do they think about you being here?"

"Oh, my grandmother thinks it's a ridiculous waste of money. Those are her exact words. *A ridiculous waste of money*. She used that phrase for a lot of things."

"And your grandfather?"

"He thinks it's a wonderful experience. He was always defending the idea to my grandmother. He gave me that list of things to see, remember?"

Robbie popped the last chip in his mouth. "Speaking of things to see, let's get an early start on our trip to Stirling tomorrow. I could pick you up at nine, and we could stop for some traditional Scottish breakfast on the way. It's only about sixty-five Ks on the M9."

"We're just finishing up one meal, and you're already planning another?" Beth chuckled.

"I can't help it; I'm still a growing boy. Besides, this is just a snack, and we're sharing it."

Beth found herself filled with a warmth that she didn't think came from the alcohol.

"What are you grinning at?" he said, laughing. Beth didn't know how to respond. She could hardly say, "I can't believe you're making plans to spend more time with me." But to her shock, that's exactly what she said and then she burst out laughing at the astonishment on his face.

"You don't know to play coy, indeed," he said after a moment.

She was still giggling. "I told you. I don't have much...experience, and the alcohol has made me fuzzy."

"You only had one drink."

"Two."

"You spilled most of the first one."

Beth looked disconcerted at that memory, but after chugging back the remainder of his ale, Robbie said, "Well, I don't mean to cut the evening short, but I promised to call my sister tonight. It's her birthday."

He stood up and helped her into her jacket, an awkward moment for Beth who was unused to such manners and graces. As he settled her jacket onto her shoulders, he rested his hands lightly on them and said in her ear over the din of the music, "Would you like to come to Tain the next time I go home?"

Beth stood very still. He was asking her to come home with him.

When she didn't reply, he dropped his hands and said, "Oh, it's nothing. Don't worry. I mean, it was just a random thought."

She turned around and looked up at him, trying to make her face passive. It wasn't random at all. He was asking her to meet his family. A burning sensation at the pit of her stomach felt like something near to terror. She swallowed, trying to find the right words, but he was still talking. "Just some time. See a bit of the northern part of Scotland."

To Beth's surprise, he was stumbling over his words, as if her answer mattered, as if he was afraid she'd say no, or embarrassed at his impulsive invitation. Again, she felt astonished at the interest this man had in her.

"Ah, well, I..." She hated her inability to put a sentence together. "I would like to, really." To her surprise, she found it was the truth. "Sometimes."

He laughed offhandedly, shrugging his shoulders, his voice nonchalant. "It's all right. No big deal. Just a thought. That you'd maybe like to get out of Edinburgh for a weekend."

"Yes, sometime... in the future," she interjected. She was making excuses, but in reality, she didn't feel secure enough to meet his family. His sister. Mother. His intimidating father, perhaps. And she wouldn't know how to dress.

"What I mean," she quickly said, "maybe later, after we've seen some of these other places on my grandfather's list. Is that alright with you?" She hoped she hadn't totally blown it with her graceless response. She'd hate to cut short this friendship. She refused to think of it as a "relationship." That sounded too intimate. It was just so astonishing how it was all developing.

She followed him through the smoky, crowded pub to the door, which opened as someone came. As she walked out, she glanced at the guy holding the door.

"Beth!"

Beth stopped short. "Iain!"

"I thought you didn't go to pubs." His voice was accusing.

"I didn't... I don't usually." Her mouth was suddenly dry. She saw Iain look from her to Robbie and then back to her. "I see," he said bluntly.

"There's nothing to see!" Beth grew angry. Why was she defending herself to this guy she hardly knew?

"So, are we still on for Sunday night?" Iain demanded in a voice loud enough for Robbie to hear, who took a step in their direction.

"Yes, yes. Of course. Why not? I'll see you then, like we said."

Iain's stormy face grew calmer, but Beth saw him glare at Robbie.

"Yes, I'll pick you up at your dorm. Sunday night. At seven."

"Okay. Yes." Beth walked quickly in Robbie's direction, disconcerted by the situation. She was grateful Robbie said nothing as he hailed her a cab.

"I can take the bus, Robbie, really."

"No, if you're not going to let me escort you back to your dorm, then I'm going to send you home in a cab."

"*She hath no loyal Knight* is what you're thinking?"

"Seems like you have at least one other."

Beth blushed at his obvious reference to Iain as Robbie opened the taxi door for her.

"Guess I'll have to sharpen my lance." He chuckled. "See you in the morning."

With the lightest of all possible kisses, he said goodnight.

That night she dreamt that Robbie and Iain were in a jousting duel as she sat in the stands waving a lace handkerchief. All the while, a Lancaster bomber circled overhead.

SEVEN

Saturday morning, as Robbie was fixing a cup of coffee, he noticed that Andrew had left his car keys on the table with a note, "Wake me. Something important."

Worried his plans would go awry from car trouble, he knocked on Andrew's bedroom door and went in. Andrew immediately sat up, bleary-eyed from a late night of pubbing.

"What's the problem, Andrew? Is the roadster out of commission, or has the fee gone up?" He was stopped short by the serious look on his friend's face.

"Not so simple, I'm afraid."

Robbie sat down on Andrew's desk chair. "What's not so simple?"

"Ran into Craig last night," Andrew answered, referring to an older professor in their department that both of them liked. He rubbed sleep out of his eyes

"And?"

"Said he saw you outside the Black Bull."

"And?" Robbie was growing impatient with the subterfuge.

"Said he saw the girl you were with."

"What's that got to do with..."

Andrew interrupted. "Said she's in one of his classes."

Robbie frowned. "I don't understand..."

"He suggested I pass along a warning."

"A warning?" Robbie felt his ire rising.

"Yeah. Remember that lecture on student-faculty relationships?"

All too well. "What of it?"

"Well, Craig said it looked like you were crossing the Rubicon."

Robbie growled, "How like Craig to bring Caesar into any discussion."

"He was serious, Robbie. You know it's a breach of conduct to date a student. And you're a new professor. Still under the microscope."

Robbie stared at his flatmate. He hadn't told Andrew anything about Beth. They weren't in the habit of sharing that part of their life, unless it got serious.

"So," Andrew prodded, leaning back against the wall beside his bed. "Who is this girl?"

"An American."

Andrew shook his head. "Of course."

"What's that mean?"

"You've always been a bit soft in the head for American girls."

"So I've taken her to a few historical places. She's interested in history."

"Of course."

"Knock it off, Andrew. I'm helping her with some research on World War II."

"Is that the only kind of research you're doing?"

Robbie began to pace the tiny bedroom. "We went out to dinner. Once. I took her to the movies last night and for a drink. She's different..."

"Naturally."

"I mean it. She's more mature than the other students in her class and rather old-fashioned."

"Ah, I see," Andrew said, smirking. "Didn't give it up on the first date?"

Now Robbie was angry. "It's not like that at all. She's interesting. Easy to be with. Easy to talk to. I... I suggested she might like to visit Tain."

Andrew whistled long and slow. "It's like that, is it? Bugger. Sounds like more than nothing."

"Yes, well, I'm not sure; that's the point." He glared at Andrew.

"But she's a student, Robbie. And you're treading on dangerous ground."

"She's not my student!" Robbie shot back resentfully. "And she's a visiting student."

"You're splitting hairs with that argument. Lay off a while. Retreat back across the Rubicon till the end of the term. When term's over, then you can get on with things."

"When term's over, she'll go back to the States."

"So persuade her to stay for the summer."

Robbie sighed heavily.

"Look, mate," Andrew said, his face cloudy with concern, "Tell her you need to keep things on the up and up until May. If she feels the same way about you, she'll understand."

Robbie shrugged, walking toward the door. "Thanks for the loan of the car... and the advice. I'll give it some thought."

Beth didn't know whether to be relieved or hurt by Robbie's impersonal demeanor as they made their way to Stirling. From the moment she got in the car, he filled the time with a history lesson on William Wallace and the Stirling monument, apparently one of twenty in Scotland honoring the man, though by far the most spectacular one.

Robbie made no mention of his invitation to visit his family or the encounter with Iain. Nothing about his attitude hinted at his brief but tender parting kiss, which had kept her awake for a good part of the night. The last time she kissed, she was the one to give it, and Jason... had been... well, stunned. He had literally jumped back. To be fair, he did tell her afterward that he was gay—a surprise she soon accepted—but still, not a reaction a girl would want again. Last night wasn't that at all... until now. Did Robbie regret the kiss?

After thirty minutes of the nonstop lecture, as they headed west on the motorway, they stopped in a little village for some traditional fare. Beth had a bannock, a type of Scottish pancake, and tea, of course. Robbie ordered a "full Scottish breakfast."

She made a face when she saw his plate of eggs, sausage, haggis, black pudding, a potato scone, toast, tomatoes, and beans, all fried. Except for the beans.

"Beans for breakfast? And all that fried food?" she asked. "I see you Scots don't worry about cholesterol, do you?"

But Robbie said, "Some things are worth it," and concentrated on his breakfast. His unusual reticence made her edgy. She tried to keep her thoughts off his brief kiss and the ridiculous dream as she sipped her tea, trying to puzzle out his change in demeanor. At least he couldn't read her thoughts.

Maybe he was really insulted when I didn't jump at the chance to go to Tain, she mused as she watched him surreptitiously. *Maybe he's sorry he invited me. Maybe it was just an impulse gesture, and he's relieved I said no. Guys don't usually invite you home to meet their mothers, so maybe it was really just an invite to see a different part of Scotland. Or maybe he thought Iain was my boyfriend. Iain certainly put on the jealous lover act. What was with Iain, anyway? I've only just met him. He had no business acting like that.*

Beth poured more of the steeping-hot tea into her white china cup. She loved the way tea was served in Scottish restaurants—a small, individual china teapot, a cup and saucer, a tiny pitcher of milk, and a miniature bowl with several cubes of raw sugar, all presented on an oval china serving platter. She couldn't get in the habit of putting milk in her tea, though.

"You like builder's tea," Robbie had said the first time he noticed at Haddington after they had left Drem. When she asked what that was, he'd said, "Good, strong, black tea with no distractions." She did like her tea sweetened, though, and as she dropped two cubes of sugar in her cup, she continued to think about Robbie's lack of sweetness this morning. He was being polite and friendly, but more like a tour guide than a knight getting ready to do battle for her, which he had hinted at last night.

Maybe he figures I'm only interested in him as a guide. Maybe his history spiel was his way of saying, "Let's keep this impersonal." But why would he have kissed me?

To stop the endless round of thoughts, she asked him why the English drank tea rather than coffee, and he perked up, giving her an amusing history of the English tea trade. Back in the car, Beth said, "I saw that movie, the one about William Wallace. With Mel Gibson."

Robbie snorted. "Yes, there was quite a bit of press about it when they filmed near Glen Nevis, up by Fort William, though most of it was filmed in Ireland. Imagine a movie about Scotland being filmed in Ireland! They premiered it in Stirling. I have several friends who do reenactments, and they were extras on the set...everyone was trying to be an extra. Everyone wanted to be on the big screen."

"Not you?" Beth asked.

"Nah."

Beth thought Robbie sounded thoroughly American at times. "So you'd rather read about history than experience it?" She felt rather than saw his frowning glance

"I'm not into reenactment. Are you?"

"I have a couple of classmates who get into the July Fourth Gettysburg battle thing. Might be fun to experience history more physically."

"But you're always in that bomber jacket. Isn't that what you're doing in a way?"

Beth thought there was an edge of sarcasm in his voice and said gruffly, "No, I mean, well, what if you could... in your imagination... experience what people felt in a different time."

"Like a time traveler," he replied.

"Well, an emotional time traveler." Beth's statement was greeted by silence that grew a little strained. Finally, she said, "Is that so weird?"

"Well, a wee bit weird."

She shrugged, but didn't reply. She pondered their conversation as they returned to the car and continued toward Stirling.

Now would be a perfect time to tell Robbie about her more recent dreams, how real they seemed, how often she woke with the smell of engine oil in her nostrils and the taste of fear in her mouth. Though the dreams in the last two weeks had been fewer, they had lingered longer after she woke, along with the emotions Colin was experiencing in them.

But telling Robbie wouldn't be a good idea, she was sure, remembering how he had reacted at Holyrood—with skepticism, even alarm, accusing her of taking drugs or being carried away with romantic notions. *No*, she concluded. *I didn't tell him about sensing Colin's presence at Traprain Law and Drem, and I lied when he asked me if I was still having the dreams. If I told Robbie that sometimes I feel like I am Colin in the dreams... no, no... I can't risk it. Robbie would think I am a mental case. Or infatuated with someone who's been dead...*

Her brain suddenly froze. Who said he was dead? Her grandfather had lived through the war. Surely Colin had. Yet all her recent research on the bombing campaigns over Germany was full of staggering casualty rates among the pilots and crew. The thought of him dead suddenly filled her with heart-wrenching grief.

Beth stared out the window trying to rein in the urge to weep. Robbie didn't say anything for awhile, and Beth was glad. He probably thought she was angry; she hadn't replied to his last question. She could feel the tears in her throat and didn't dare comment. To her relief, after some time of silence, he went back to talking about the way Hollywood distorted history. It distracted her and gradually calmed her enough so she could start conversing again.

After another half hour, they pulled into the parking lot of the National Wallace Monument, which was situated on a volcanic outcrop known as Abbey Craig, where once stood a Pictish hill fort, Robbie said. Through the leafless trees, she could glimpse a tall, square stone tower topped by what looked like a crown. Though it looked very old, Beth had learned that it was completed in 1869, after eight years of construction. It had a Victorian flair with its fancy stonework, elaborate stone spirals on the crown, and gemlike stained-glass windows.

She got out of the car, glad to be in the brisk air. The day was bright, with wisps of clouds stretched like gauze across the sky. Though it was late February, there was a hint of spring in the air. They took the path from the parking lot, a combination of steps and a curving pathway, which led them to a concrete patio at the foot of the towering monument.

"We have to walk around to the entrance at the front," Robbie said, and he started in that direction, but Beth was too absorbed in the sensation of staring up, trying to glimpse the crown another 220 feet over her head. It was a dizzying effort, causing her to blink and step back, right into Robbie's arms, which closed in a protective embrace. One that was too comfortable.

"I wondered where you were and found you back here gaping like a tourist."

"I am a tourist," Beth retorted, stepping out of his arms quickly. He gave her a questioning look but then said. "Here, this way. The entrance is right next to the two-story Keeper's Lodge, which is actually built into the side of the monument."

Beth followed Robbie to a heavy glass door set into a stone archway topped with a carved stone coat of arms. Beth could see a sword-wielding statue of the hero of Scotland further up. Upon entering, they were greeted by a young female attendant standing behind a large wooden reception desk, who said a cheery, "Good day to ye," in a lilting accent more pronounced than Edinburgh speakers. "Care to climb and take in the view?"

"Oh, yes," Beth said, smiling at the girl's enthusiasm.

"That'll be four pounds fifty for ye each."

Robbie pulled out his Historic Scotland membership card, telling Beth, "Remember, I said it was on me."

"Ye may want to look round here or haid right up. There's three layvels with displays on th' way and then the crown wi' the view. Ye may have a booklet if ye wish."

Beth looked inquiringly at Robbie, who suggested, "I can explain the exhibits and the view. Let's head to the top then stop at the exhibits on the way down... unless 246 steps are too much at once." He said it jokingly, but there was a challenge in his voice.

"Well, I did okay climbing up from the car park," she said mildly, "But you go first. I'll follow at my own pace."

She expected him to say, "No, I'll walk up with you," but he replied, "Sure, I can get in a stepping jog. Over here is the entrance to the stairway.

It's a spiral, tucked into the corner of the monument and opens up onto each floor. Take your time, the stairway is a bit steep."

"Okay," she said, as they reached the first of the stone steps.

"Meet you at the top." He briskly vanished up around the first curve.

Beth followed more slowly. The outer wall of the staircase was punctuated by narrow slits that let in chill February air and filtered sunlight. The stone handrail carved into the stairwell ran along the inner spiral where the triangular-shaped stairs came to a narrow edge. She felt more secure hugging the outer wall. As she carefully mounted the steps, she felt the dampness of the stone and the winter cold seep into her body. Almost as chill as Robbie's mood today.

The narrow stairway gave her a sense of claustrophobia, so she began to mentally count the stairs to distract herself. After some time, the spiraling ascent began to make her lightheaded. At step seventy-one she reached the first level and walked out into an open room filled with display cases and hanging tapestries.

Robbie was nowhere in sight. She wandered to the huge sword in the tall, narrow glass case and stood there, pondering what it would mean to charge into battle wielding such a weapon. Was that courage? Or madness? What would it take for her to be so committed to a cause that she'd take up a sword and go to war?

It was then that she began to sense a presence and glanced around, thinking it was Robbie looking for her. The area was empty. Shivering even in her warm coat, she returned to the staircase and hurried up the next sixty-four steps, continuing her mental count: *eighty-seven, eighty-eight, eighty-nine...*

She didn't bother to look at any of the displays on level two but climbed the next set of stairs more quickly with a driving sense of urgency. The echo of a masculine voice with a Scottish accent seemed to float down the stairs from above.

Her breath was growing shallower.

As she climbed, she felt a sensation of increasing height, accompanied by an impression of being lifted by each step, almost as if each were floating, disconnected from the one below and above it. It was exhilarating and frightening at the same time. By the third level, another sixty-two steps, she was almost running, driven by a need to get to the top, pulled by the echo of a masculine voice just around the next curve of the stairs.

Beth scrambled up the last of the stone steps and walked out into a narrow outer corridor open to the sky, a sudden, brilliant blinding surprise after the dimness of the winding stairway. Four more steps and she was on the walled walkway that ran around the outside of the square tower, just below the crown, passing through arched passageways at each of the four corners.

The walls rose several feet above her and were pierced by small openings on each of the four sides through which she could see the surrounding countryside and, if she wished, could look down the dizzying drop to the bottom of the tower.

She circumnavigated the tower, taking the last few steps that led to the top of the monument. A flat, open area spread out before her with eight narrow, soaring stone arches sweeping up to the crown. A low wall ran between the arches. A wood-plank bench lining the wall gave seating space to contemplate the stunning vista. Light and wind poured in on all sides.

There he stood, facing her, a dark silhouette against a light-filled archway. He was in dress uniform; the one he'd been wearing in that crowded room filled with Tommy Dorsey music. His face was lost in the shadow beneath his officer's cap. Was he looking at her, or was she looking at herself, or was there someone else there, looking at both of them?

Her head spun as if she were on a very slow merry-go-round. She felt weightless, disconnected from the earth, soaring in a space of intensely white light. There was no tower of stone, securely anchored in the earth. There was no car park, many feet below. There was no display of ancient weapons or long-forgotten history. There was only this moment.

She leaned over, her breath constricted, pressing her palms against her thighs just above her knees to fight the oddly delicious sensations, yet wanting desperately to give into them and let them take her where they would.

"Here, come sit down on the bench. You took the steps too quickly," she heard him say in his warm, soft Scots burr, yet from a distance, as if across miles, or years.

He noticed that she was perspiring, hot from the rush up the stairs. With his arm around her, he led her to one of the slatted wooden benches that anchored each of the eight arched openings of the domed space. The moisture on her face gave a lovely sheen to her glowing skin.

He helped her sit down, and she leaned sideways against the cold stone tower arch, closing her eyes, but placed her hand over his, which rested on the bench between them. Her touch was reassuring and electric at the same time. To cover his reaction, he said calmly, "Tis the vertigo, merely. You took the steps too fast. That American blood of yours is a wee bit too thin for these altitudes."

But the continued touch of her soft hand, her nearness, the light, flowery scent of her perfume penetrated his mind and made him dizzy.

The stone solidity of the tower slowly seeped into Beth's awareness making her feel cooler, calmer, grounded. She could feel him perched on the bench, to her left. In a moment she sensed him turning toward her and she sat up, opening her eyes. In the sparkling light of midmorning, she barely made out his brown eyes, dark as a Scottish loch. A gust of wind blew a stand of hair across her face and she closed her eyes, startled. When she opened them, there was no one there. She was suddenly chilled to the bone.

Just then Robbie appeared in front of her. "Oh, there you are," he said. "How odd, I didn't even hear you come up the steps. I was over there looking at the view to the south and..." He stopped in mid-sentence, and squatted in front of her, putting his hands on her knees which trembled slightly with the chills that shook her.

"Have you gone lightheaded from the climb? You're as white as a sheet. I'm sorry, it was stupid of me not to stay with you." His voice was apologetic, his eyes filled with worry. When she didn't reply, he added, with what seemed to be an apparent attempt at levity, "You look like you've seen a ghost. Was Wallace haunting you?"

Beth let out a deep breath in a shaky rattle. "It wasn't Wallace that I saw."

Robbie frowned, looking even more concerned. "That you saw? I was only joking, Beth."

She shook her head. It hurt to do so, so she pressed the tips of her fingers against her temples. For the length of another breath, she resented Robbie's presence. Would Colin have lingered if Robbie hadn't appeared? Would this American girl that confused and disoriented Colin have become visible too?

Then she remembered that just before Colin vanished, he had turned in her direction. She could still clearly see his brown eyes with flecks of green. As if he knew she was sitting next to him.

Beth gasped. "He saw me! He could see me!" She was lost in a memory of a minute ago, that was decades ago. How many decades? Four? Five? Was she there or was he here?

"Who saw you?" Robbie looked around at the deserted floor, his voice laced with concern. "There's no one here. Did someone come up behind you?"

How could she explain? She was pulled between a desire to have Robbie understand and a need to hold this newest revelation close to her heart. When she said nothing, Robbie stood up, his mouth pursed in a frown.

"Come see the sights. I can explain the view," he said in a voice one would use with a recalcitrant child or a fussy old woman. When she didn't respond, he took Beth's hand and pulled her to her feet.

She reluctantly let him turn her around to see the view behind her. He kept hold of her hand, and she found the sensation of flesh on flesh pulling her back to the present, away from the feeling of being a disembodied visitor. It was both comforting and unwelcome, yet without intending to, she interlaced her fingers in his, and he glanced at her with a speculative look.

Pointing with his free hand, he said, "Here... this is the north view. The Ochil Hills. That hill to the north is Dumyat."

Beth thought the hill, rising above a valley that swooped down from the Wallace Monument, looked like a moonscape. It was barren of any vegetation. Snow clung to the crevices and rocky pockmarked surfaces.

It was gray, with twinges of pink and purple veins, and dark spots where gorse, the native mountain shrub, clustered.

The mountain, the monument, the moment felt familiar, yet apart from her, as if she were there, yet not physically, as if she had been there before, and a part of her remained as a shadow. As if once she were at a place and noticed and remarked and commented on that place, she left a part of herself like invisible graffiti on a wall or an invisible thought on the air. Yet she had never been here. Had never seen this place.

Robbie didn't seem to mind her silence as he led her around to face each direction, explaining the view: the Forth Valley to the east with the silver snake of the Forth River twisting away in the distance; the village of Stirling to the south, dominated by the Castle perched on a volcanic rocky promontory above the quaint town and the loop of the Stirling River in front of it; to the west, the Trossachs with their blue-green hillsides and the shimmering glimpse of Loch Lomond in the barely-perceptible distance.

Between Robbie's words, Beth heard snatches of a deep voice with a Scots accent singing *by the bonny, bonny banks of Loch Lomond*, but she didn't know if it was in her head or hanging in the air, lingering for years, or decades.

Colin's voice.

Was she awake? Was it an illusion, a wish, an overwrought imagination? It was only the warmth of Robbie's hand and his easy-to-listen-to timbre that kept her from following that other voice, falling into the shadow of the past, which was so alluring and ever more insistent.

"Perhaps I should do this on my own." She said it softly to herself, but apparently loud enough for Robbie to hear. His sudden fury shocked her into attention and obliterated the music barely perceptible to her ear. "Well, bloody hell, that is fine with me."

She watched him pace across the soaring chamber and disappear down the steps. The echo of his footsteps quickly grew faint and then vanished. As if he too, were a ghost.

After a headlong rush down the twisting stone stairway, past the astonished tour guide, and down the hill to the carpark, Robbie spent the next fifteen minutes pacing furiously back and forth by the passenger door of Andrew's sleek sports car, his jaw clenched. Jingling his key ring off the end of one finger in a rapid, staccato rhythm, he berated himself for his loss of control and tried to resign himself to calling it quits with this girl.

He thought they were visiting Stirling and the Wallace Monument because it was on her grandfather's list. He didn't think it had anything to do with the bomber pilot, as the site was unrelated to World War II. Now, here of all places, she seemed caught up in some romantic or psychotic illusion about being able to see the guy, like he was a spirit.

What was it she'd said? *He looked at me.* Her words echoing in his head made him go suddenly cold. Pacing more rapidly, he reminded himself that she was, after all, just a girl, in spite of being older than the typical college student, and seemingly more mature. But if he really thought about it, in many ways she was really an innocent abroad, so little exposed to life. And then there was the fact that she was a student, and he was a faculty member.

Robbie contemplated Andrew's words as he watched Beth walk slowly down the hill, her hands tucked in her jacket, her eyes on the ground. He liked her. A lot. But Andrew was right. Dating a student, or even giving the appearance of doing so, could be a fatal blow to his newly-launched academic career. Plus he didn't know how she felt about him. If she felt anything at all.

And then she slaps me upside the head with her comment about 'doing this alone.' Pretty well put me in my place, he brooded.

When she reached the car, his manners overcame his anger, and he opened the door for her, ignoring her confused look. He suddenly recalled the young guy they encountered on the way out of the bar last night, the kid who looked mightily upset that Beth was with Robbie. *Same kid she was talking to in the hall earlier in the week. Maybe that's what this is all about*, he thought, his ire up again.

Robbie threw himself into his seat, pulling the door closed with a bang and started the car with a jerky motion. He shoved the gearshift into reverse and thrust the car backward out of the parking space. With a push of his palm, he slammed the gearshift into first and pressed on the gas pedal. As the car leaped forward, he heard Beth gasp but refused to look in her direction. Instead, he focused on maneuvering this vehicle made for curves through the narrow, twisting streets of the old section of Stirling at a ridiculously reckless speed.

The town vanished in a blur as they hit the open road, racing north. Though the roar of the engine filled the car, Robbie wouldn't have been surprised if Beth could also hear his molars grinding and the artery pulsing at the side of his neck.

"Where are we going?" Beth finally asked after the speedometer had clicked off kilometer after kilometer.

"I don't know," he muttered truthfully. He was driving only to feel a sense of motion.

"You don't know." Her statement was filled with resignation. Then she spoke, facing the window so her voice was muffled, and he had to strain to hear her over the whine of the engine.

"You think I'm out of my mind."

He didn't jump in and offer a soothing contradiction.

She tried again. "You think I'm some sort of crazy American college student on a romantic adventure to find some Scottish bomber pilot."

This time he did reply. "Well, some of those statements seem to be accurate."

"Which ones?" she asked.

He began to ease up on the gas pedal, getting his anger under control. A picture of himself in the passenger seat of this father's car roaring down the A9 toward St. Andrews flashed uncomfortably in his mind.

"Well, you are an American college student."

"Yes."

"You are on an adventure, it seems."

"Yes."

"You are trying to find out who this Scots pilot was."

"Yes."

"And obviously the pilot is..." Robbie stopped abruptly, his logic giving out. "Dead" was the word he was going to use. But that wasn't obvious. Many pilots survived the war. Some were still living, though now into their eighties.

"A figment of my imagination." She finished his sentence as a statement, not a question.

"No, that wasn't what I was going to say. Someone wore that bomber jacket, so he was, is, well, a real person."

"But you think I'm crazy for looking."

His words were more carefully chosen. "No... I think you are... maybe... a bit obsessed."

"Obsessed?"

"Aye. I mean, you seem to think you can see him in places, and that's just..." Was she clairvoyant? His logical mind rebelled at that thought, though his Celtic blood was stirred by the idea. "I'm a historian, not a ghost hunter," he insisted.

"You think I'm imagining it?"

Robbie struggled to convey his meaning without belittling or insulting. He thought about the way she talked of poets and writers. The writers were real to her. She didn't just study their words; she was endlessly curious about the times in which they lived and who they loved. They weren't just names on a page in a literature course or in a lecture by some doddering professor. She seemed genuinely affected by their thoughts and words. History, to her, was a collection of passions for which the famous, infamous, and the unknown had lived and died.

She, this young chit of a girl from a country with barely two centuries of existence, seemed to think she could somehow touch the past, a past that happened in his own ancient country, although a mere sixty years ago. And he, the history professor, looked at history as though it were a collection of facts and figures, not flesh and bones.

With a growing realization, Robbie began to acknowledge that he lacked her passion. Her ability to transcend time and be there in spirit made ashes of his pretense of being enmeshed in the past. Only twice in his life had he experienced that transcendence, that sense of being in the presence of those who had made the history he studied in books: once at the chilly, foggy fields of Culloden and the other time in the shimmering July countryside of Gettysburg.

With an irrefutable logic that would have made his father proud, he realized he had been proclaiming that history was his passion, but he had been approaching it just as coldly and logically as his father approached engineering. It was a problem to be solved, a theory to be proven, a story to be told.

The revelation was so unexpected and so blindingly true that he nearly ran off the road. Only Beth's gasped, "Robbie," alerted him to the stone wall precariously near the left front bumper. With years of experience driving over the twisting, winding, single-track back roads of the Highlands, Robbie effortlessly steered the car back onto the roadway and around the next few bends and curves.

Spotting a sign, he said, "Let's stop for coffee. There's a café up ahead."

He saw Beth's nod and blanched face from the corner of his eye. He had given her a fright. *Well,* he thought, *now we're even.*

EIGHT

ROBBIE SAID LITTLE DURING their lunch and even less on the drive home. When he did talk, it was to tell her more about the history of Scotland in the late twelfth century and the impact of William Wallace on the Scottish psyche. He avoided any mention of Colin.

They were back in Edinburgh by midafternoon. When Robbie pulled up in front of her dorm, he put the car in park and sat, looking at her impassively. She was at a loss for words, not knowing what he expected, so she said, "Thanks for the day, the tour... for everything."

It sounded like a goodbye and she flinched, adding in a rush, "It's meant a lot... your help, and... everything." Unwilling to cry in front of him, Beth scurried from the car without looking back. She heard him roar out of the car park but didn't watch his departure. Nor did she return to her dorm. She simply started walking.

She wandered aimlessly through the campus, into town, down streets, looking at nothing, seeing nothing. Simply walking. Finally, hours later, exhausted and too disoriented to find her way back by bus, she hailed a taxi and spent the last cash she had in her wallet to get to her empty dorm room. As usual, Anja was with her boyfriend

Despite being drop-dead tired, she sat up well past one, wrapped in Anja's comforter, detailing the day in her journal as she mulled it over. *He saw me. I swear he saw me. He knew I was sitting there.* The statement seemed unreal, freakish. Beth poised her pen over the page and waited for the courage to write her next words. With a deep breath, she penned the thought that had been haunting her since that moment.

He wants something.

She stared at the sentence for a long time, her hand trembling slightly, her breath quick and shallow, her head woozy, as if she had just finished climbing those two hundred and forty-six steps. Then she finished the thought.

He needs something.

———————⋈———————

Sunday came and went in a blur. At lunchtime she nibbled on an apple and crackers in her room, unwilling to be distracted from her thoughts and not wanting to run into Iain in the dining hall. The thought of idle evening chatter with a college boy at a bar was almost revolting.

She had intended to write her grandfather in the afternoon but couldn't concentrate. Instead she took a nap which smelled richly of a dew-drenched grass airstrip at dawn.

To her complete surprise, her date with Iain was delightful.

His lighthearted and slightly sarcastic banter was distracting and amusing. He took her to a sports bar where he introduced her to a small group of friends watching an American pro hockey game. The guys, another Canadian, two Scots, and a Dane, were all fellow members of the university ice hockey club. The girls were Scottish.

They asked her friendly questions about life in the States and what she thought of their country. She answered simply and politely and cheered for whichever team was winning, which Iain thought was hilarious. He bought her a beer, which she sipped all evening. By midnight, far later than she usually stayed up on a Sunday, he had her back at the dorm and said, "Well, cheerio. Do you want to come see me play Tuesday night?"

It didn't occur to her to say no.

And so, her life fell into a pattern: lunch several days a week with Iain at the Student Union center, attending his scrimmages on Tuesday and Thursday evenings, out with his friends on Friday and Saturday evenings to a pub or the movies or some sports event.

He began helping her with her "research project" on World War II, walking her to the library after their history class. Most of his help consisted of watching documentaries with her in the media center or looking at magazines and newspapers from the era and pointing out facts he thought relevant or interesting, while she took notes or organized her research.

At first, he held her hand when they walked and sat with his arm around her at the movies. Then one evening he kissed her goodbye—a simple, straightforward kiss. It startled her, but she liked it. Slowly the kisses at her dorm room door were growing more intense, with more pressing of bodies and entwining of arms, and she sensed that if she invited him in, he'd be more than happy to see what happened next.

She supposed they were "a thing." This was the pleasant, fun romance she wanted two years ago, it seemed.

Knowing she was to meet him at class or lunch got her out of bed on the many days she longed to linger and recapture her latest dream. She now knew some of Colin's crew members by their nicknames: Fitz, the bomb aimer; Tack, the navigator; and Ox, the rear gunner. But she still hadn't learned Colin's last name. Robbie's list of twenty-seven names seemed too overwhelming to research without his help. She counted on the dreams to reveal more about who Colin was.

She didn't tell Iain she was worried about her grandfather, who assured her in their twice-monthly phone calls that he was fit as a fiddle, but whose health her grandmother harped on in her weekly postscripts to Henry's letters.

P.S. I should take your grandfather to the doctor. He's so short of breath.

P.S. He stumbled today walking out front. Thought he was going to hit the sidewalk.

P.S. I wonder if he should be driving. He seems so distracted.

And at the tail end of each postscript, Naomi always added something like, *Don't tell your grandfather I said this. He'd have my neck. He doesn't want to worry you. After all, how you could do anything being so far away is beyond me.*

She caught occasional glimpses of Robbie on campus, not sure if he saw her. She was surprised by how much she missed his company, his laughter, his warmth. She wondered if she had begun to fall in love with him. It was useless to speculate; their relationship was clearly over.

Since the trip to Stirling, there had been no more "sightings" of Colin. Iain kept her free time occupied, and she never suggested visiting other places on her grandfather's list, another thing she didn't share with Iain.

Colin needs something.

Those words frequently surfaced in her mind and on her journal pages, commanding her attention and pulling her back to that sunlit tower in Stirling. But just as quickly, the image and sensations would fade.

There were moments when Beth wondered if she should give up this search. It was so exhausting and slightly terrifying to be so pulled by... what? What was Colin? A spirit? A ghost? No, he wasn't dead! It must be her, with this disorienting ability to see into the past. Yes, Colin needed something. But still, she owed him nothing. And this obsession, as Robbie called it, had already alienated him. Anyone else would walk away, thinking she was mad. What was this worth?

But no matter how she argued with herself, she couldn't stop now.

After some weeks, Beth decided she needed to revisit Drem. A history department field trip in mid-March provided the perfect opportunity. Iain's commitment to a weekend ice hockey tournament at Aberdeen University offered her an excuse to go to Drem alone. Though he asked her to go to Aberdeen, like some of the other girlfriends, she pleaded a backlog of school work.

"Iain, you've kept me busy every weekend since we started dating," she protested. "I'm way behind in all my reading."

"Yeah, cool, right?" he had responded triumphantly.

She frowned. "Which part is cool?"

"The fact that you've been too busy to read, because of me!" He laughed, adding, "Well, you are a scholar, so I guess I can let you be scholarly this one weekend."

She formulated a plan to remain at the airfield when the other students left. In her research, she had discovered that the nearby village of Gullane was practically taken over by the RAF during the war and that the

Greywalls Hotel had been requisitioned for pilots on rotation from the airfields of southern England for R&R—rest and relaxation.

With the help of a friendly staff member at the Edinburgh tourist center, Beth made a reservation at Greywalls and learned which bus would get her back to Edinburgh on Sunday afternoon. She cringed at the stunning cost of one night's stay, even off-season, at a well-appointed country hotel.

Six weeks after her Stirling trip with Robbie, Beth was on her way to Drem with a van of students, her backpack doubling as an overnight case. She brought her nice outfit should she opt for dinner in the hotel. The graduate assistant leading the day's tour just shrugged when she said she was skipping the bus trip back to meet a friend.

The field trip stopped first at the Museum of Flight. While the other students toured the museum, she lingered in the gift shop, purchasing three books on World War II. On the ride to Drem, she listened while the other students chatted about impossible professors, last night's pub crawl, tonight's party choices, or which Mediterranean beach they were going to on spring break.

Surrounded by such babble, similar to Iain and his friends, Beth longed for Robbie's intelligent and witty repartee. That was a bit unfair, she told herself gruffly. Iain has his own charms, actually quite similar to Jason, who was polite, funny, and talkative. He had been a big hit with Henry and even managed to charm Naomi with his flattering comments about the desserts she always had ready for them when they returned from their dates. Her grandparents would like Iain too, she was certain. Like they would ever meet.

To distract her thoughts, she opened her recently purchased history of the aerodrome. She learned that at the beginning of the war in September of 1939, Drem was ideally situated on the east coast to defend the Scottish Lowlands and that in October 1939 three squadrons of fighter pilots with their Spitfires were stationed there. One of the Squadrons, the 602 from Edinburgh, was posted further south in 1940 to help defend southern Britain.

Beth frowned. Robbie had said Drem wasn't a bomber station. It was always a fighter station or coastal defense site. Why was a bomber pilot there? Yet, she had sensed his presence.

The van drove to a cluster of buildings at the edge of the field she had seen on her brief visit with Robbie. Everyone assembled around the graduate assistant, who explained what she already knew, that most of the buildings had been barracks and airplane hangars during the war, but now housed retail shops, a café, and other commercial enterprises, along with some modern housing.

Beth stood slightly apart, shivering in spite of her bomber jacket, boots, and scarf, not because of the March chill, but in anticipation of being alone on the flat, deserted aerodrome. She tried to picture what it would have been like in the war, with planes coming and going next to a small farming community. Closing her eyes, she tuned out the drone of the tour guide, listening for the hum of incoming planes. But the only hint of air traffic was a twentieth-century jet far overhead, barely perceptible over the voices of shoppers entering the buildings. No sense of Colin, not like the time she and Robbie were here.

There were too many distractions.

When everyone headed for the café, Beth studied a 1939 map of the aerodrome. Picking up her backpack, she headed out onto the grassy field. Several hundred feet away from the converted barracks and hangars, filled with shops making and selling jellies and jams, woolen goods, furniture, and other tourist goods, she stopped in the midst of the former grass airstrip, now a farm field, lying fallow in the late winter sun.

She stood, with her eyes closed, and waited.

And waited.

Skirting the clouds, the sun caressed her face with warmth when it peeked out. She could hear her breath, feel the rise and fall of her chest. After a while, she used her backpack as a seat, stretching her legs out in front of her, her arms crossed.

And waited again. But there was no hint, no sense of Colin's presence.

At last, opening her eyes, she noticed the sun had moved westward on its journey toward the horizon. That's when it occurred to her. She'd need to be here at sunrise, not a late afternoon. The dreams always ended at sunrise on a grassy runway. Yet, Colin couldn't have been landing his Lancaster here; the bombers were stationed at airbases in southern England.

Yet it wasn't sunrise when she and Robbie had been here in February. It was about this time of day, though they had been parked along the road on the opposite side of the field. She had sensed Colin then in those few moments, had felt that dizzy sensation like vertigo, even stronger than she'd felt at Traprain Law, which signaled some gap in the barrier between their decades.

Why had she sensed him here? The book said there had been a flight school at Drem. Could that be it? Was he here in training? But in her dreams, he was piloting the huge Lancaster bomber, returning from a nighttime raid. Floating above the moonlit channel, heading for home. From her research, she knew the Lancaster didn't go into action until 1942, yet if Colin was stationed at Drem, he must have been flying on coastal patrol.

Beth sighed in frustration. Standing up, she headed back toward the café. A snack might help. Forty-five minutes later, after a restoring cup of tea, a scone, and a reread of the small book on Drem Airfield, she decided to wander around the few buildings that hadn't been converted into a strip mall.

The campus van had disappeared. The afternoon had grown cloudy, more like the day she and Robbie had been here. *Stop it,* she mentally chided herself. *Stop thinking about Robbie. Think about Iain instead. Going out with Iain is so much less complicated.*

A metal hangar at the edge of the older buildings looked the most deserted. Weather-worn, the huge sliding doors hung slightly askew. A "for let" sign was posted on the small door at the right of the building. The door wasn't locked and opened with a protest of rusty hinges. Beth stepped inside the vacant, soaring space. But it wasn't the echo of creaking metal she heard.

It was Tommy Dorsey.

The enthralling beat of swing music filled Colin's ears as he walked out of the rainy night into the chilly hangar, packed with people celebrating the last night of 1940. Through the magic possessed by the local civilian auxiliary, a corner of the large, cavernous space had been turned into a dance hall befitting tonight's New Year's Eve celebration. Spitfires and Hurricanes had been rolled out onto the tarmac and replaced by a long, low stage, currently occupied by a band possessing the musical verve, if not the expertise, of a Glenn Miller or Gene Krupa ensemble.

A huge Union Jack hung on the wall behind the stage, and a large net of colorful balloons was suspended over it, along with a sign that read, "Welcome, 1941." The flag displaying the blue and white cross of St. Andrew stood gallantly to the right of the orchestra, reminding any doubters that this RAF station was located in a Scottish town. On the left were the unit flags indicating which squadrons were currently based at Drem.

In front of the stage, a temporary wooden dance floor had been laid over part of the cement, covering the oil stains, grease puddles, and wheel tracks. Very little of the dance floor could be seen beneath the crowd of uniformed RAF men and women and local girls in their party finest. The dancers, whose inhibitions had been loosened by the wares peddled at the temporary bar set up near the stage, danced with abandon to the rhythmic American music.

Rectangular folding tables brought in from the mess hall and briefing rooms were arranged randomly on two sides of the dance floor. Each table was surrounded by wooden folding chairs. Fresh-cut pine boughs that lay on the tables and hung from the metal roof supports filled the air with the scent of Christmas. A fog of cigarette smoke hung over the room like the mist on a fall morning.

Colin headed to the bar, a set of long tables littered with bottles of every possible shape, size, and inebriating content. Several airmen were serving as barkeeps with the willing help of some local girls. Just as he stopped for a dram of whiskey, the band took a break. Spying several of his mates with girls in tow heading toward a table, he threaded his way through the crowd to join them. By the time he got there, the table was packed with men and their female companions, WAAFs, girlfriends, a wife or two, and local girls were there to help mark the turn of the year.

That's when he saw her. It brought him up short.

Rich, thick, chestnut hair tumbled to her shoulders in waves, reflecting the glowing light from votive candles on the middle of the table. Her china-smooth cheeks were pink with enthusiasm, her lips were painted a sultry red. She wore a fitted, low-cut evening dress in a silky pine green set off by a luminescent pearl necklace from which dangled a ruby-red stone that caught the light and seemed to twinkle like the warning beacon atop the nearby hill of Traprain Law.

"Ma'am? Ma'am?"

Beth blinked, shaking her head slightly.

"I'm sorry, ma'am, but this hangar is off-limits."

The voice came from the doorway behind her. She turned slowly, for the dizziness of an unexpected return to the present made her lightheaded. A man in the dark blue uniform of a security officer stood eyeing her with a frown. When she looked back into the hangar, it was empty. Dark. She took a deep breath and inhaled cold dampness. She felt bereft.

The security guard walked up to her.

"This building is off-limits. Didn't you see the no-trespassing sign?" His voice was crisp and clipped, but with that defining Scots burr.

She cleared her throat, suddenly longing for a warm, strong drink. "The door was open," she said by way of explanation. She took one last look into the unlit, cavernous space and walked past the guard into the bleak, late winter afternoon of 1997, her head still filled with the sounds of the last night of 1940.

Beth caught a bus to the Greywalls Hotel, two miles away at the eastern edge of the village of Gullane. Its sweeping driveway, curved frontage of tan stone, brown tiled roof, imposing chimneys, and pleasing symmetry made the hotel every bit as impressive as the price.

The perky young female receptionist asked, "Are ye here from Americay for the golf?" to which Beth smiled and shook her head.

She had barely spoken, yet her nationality was pinpointed. "Golf in March?" she replied.

The girl laughed. "Ye're clearly not here for the golf, for it's golf in the rain, sleet and drivin' wind if they could."

"All I want is a shower and a lie-down," she said, still distracted by the sound of Big Band music playing in her head.

"Wael, don't forget to get up for dinner. We start servin' at six and quit at nine thairty, though the dining room stays open tael elaeven. That's our winter hours."

Beth nodded, wondering if she could even afford a cup of soup. On the way to her room, she had glimpses of a gorgeous library and a cozy bar off the main hallway, giving the air of a well-heeled baron's private home.

After a luxuriously-long, hot bath and a thankfully-dreamless nap wrapped in a delicious duvet, she dressed in the outfit she had worn to dinner with Robbie in February. She had shamelessly absconded Anja's sweater and jewelry since her roommate wasn't there to give her permission. She fussed with her hair. Maybe Anja was right; she should consider a short style.

By the time she nervously made her way to the dining room, it was nearly eight, and she was almost trembling from hunger. Though uncomfortable to eat alone in an upscale restaurant, the impeccable manners of the waitstaff set her at ease, as did the quiet, relaxed surroundings. The dining room was crowded, but they seated her by a quiet spot overlooking the garden, though at this hour it was shrouded in nightfall.

She decided to treat herself to Scottish salmon and garlic smashed potatoes, trying not to blanch at the price. *That's what a credit card is for*, she reminded herself. When the waiter suggested a glass of wine, she asked for his recommendation, and savored a crisp, chilled glass of chardonnay, mentally smiling at her sophistication.

And then, quite suddenly, she longed for Robbie to be sitting across the table from her.

But he wasn't.

Instead, she kept herself company with one of her new books.

The helpful waiter, whose name was Alistair, recommended sticky toffee pudding for dessairt, as he said it. "It's my favorite," he added encouragingly. He was so nice that she said yes and ordered a cup of Earl Grey tea to accompany it.

Though it was nearly nine-thirty when she finished dinner, she wasn't ready for bed. The receptionist had said to avail herself of the sitting areas, so Beth decided to explore the library. For an hour she wandered around the softly-lit room, browsing among the hundreds of books, sitting in a leather easy chair by the fireplace, staring into its mesmerizing dancing flames, losing herself in the vision of a hangar converted to a New Year's Eve venue for 1940. Hearing once again the driving beat of a Benny Goodman tune.

"Let's get a drink in the bar."

Beth started, pulled back instantly to the present.

She gazed at the young couple who had also been meandering around the library.

A drink is a great idea, she mentally agreed, though she had never gone into a drinking establishment by herself. But the hotel's bar felt more like a large living room with a few comfortable chairs and sofas and several small tables in one corner. It certainly was a far cry from the popular watering hole she had gone to with Robbie.

Beth sighed. Between thinking about Robbie and Colin, her mind was once again exhausted. Remembering that there was no table service in English pubs, Beth worked up her nerve to approach the six-seat, polished wooden bar, tucked in one corner of the room.

"Can you make me something creamy and rich?" she asked at the bar, trying to sound self-assured.

The young, quite dashing barkeep dressed in a crisp white shirt, a plaid vest, and a bowtie, smiled warmly. "Oh, aye. I have just the thing for you. A favorite with the lassies." He winked flirtatiously at her, which made Beth giggle. He didn't look much older than Iain.

She enjoyed the drink so much, relaxing with it at one of the tables, that she went back and ordered a second one, to which the young Scot replied, "Let me make you something a little different. You'll like it, I promise."

Back at her seat, she nursed the second soothing drink, which probably had twice the alcohol, the way its sweet warmth spread throughout her body.

That's when she saw him, standing by the bar.

He was in his dress blues, his officer's cap tucked under his left arm, his right foot resting on the brass railing, leaning slightly forward, staring into a tall glass of amber liquid.

Just as she noticed him, he turned and looked in her direction.

Beth's heart nearly stopped as he stood away from the bar and, picking up his ale, headed toward her. She felt a slow, spinning sensation and wondered if she was drunk. But he walked past her to a table beyond her, as if he didn't see her. As if she weren't there.

Turning to watch him, Beth could make out vague, wavery outlines of several people seated at the table where Colin stood. She heard a female voice, a Scottish one. "*Colin, what a delight! Join us.*"

"*Yes, do.*" Beth recognized the voice of the American girl who added, "*But first, how about a dance?*" Someone was playing a slow song on the gramophone.

Colin didn't want to dance with her. It had been hard enough at New Year's Eve. The memory of that experience came rushing back so fast it made his head spin. As if he'd had too much to drink.

At the New Year's Eve dance, he had taken her right hand in his left and placed his other hand on her waist, formally, stiffly, holding her at a distance. But before he could stop her, she crossed the inches of empty space, filling it with her body. Reaching out slowly, she had brought her left hand up and placed it on his shoulder, splaying her lacquered fingertips just a hair's breadth from his neck. They rested there so softly, so gently, that he could not have possibly felt them underneath the thickness of his uniform coat, but he had, and he had winced, but quickly flattened his expression to neutral alertness.

Even now, he could feel his pulse beating in his neck, as it had that night.

Though he was a good four inches taller, she'd stood just below his eye level in her strappy, three-inch heels. She'd looked slightly up at him, smiling warmly. He had not looked away but stared back. She leaned against him, putting her lips to his ear, and whispered, "All I want is a dance."

He'd blinked, once, then with an excruciatingly slow movement, pulled her solidly against his lean, muscular body. "I'm not verra good at these modern dances," he had muttered, then made a lie of his words by suddenly and smoothly sweeping her into an accomplished, disciplined three-corner waltz step that meshed perfectly with the throbbing notes of the slow music. He'd heard her sigh, and then she had ever so lightly leaned her head against his and meshed the rhythm of her body with the fluid movement of his.

"Miss. Miss?"

Beth looked up at the bartender, who stood in front of her table.

"I was a wee bit consairned for you. You look a bit done in. Like you were miles away."

Beth laughed shakily, nodding in agreement. "Or decades," she muttered.

"Are you here on your own, then?"

Beth looked around. There was no one else in the lounge.

"If you want some company, you can sit over by the bar and we can chat. Would you like another drink?"

"What time is it?" she asked, feeling woozy and disoriented. How long had she sat, lost in 1940 or 1941, or whatever year it was. Before the bartender could reply to her first question, she asked, "Do you know anything about this hotel? Its history... during the war. The 1940s?"

"It's nearly one. Last call is at two." He paused, answering her first question, then added, "But look, here's the owner. He's just come in. He always likes a nightcap about this time. He could tell you. His father ran it and he was a wee boy during the war."

She followed him across the room, and the young bartender, who introduced himself as Michael, hovered nearby, keeping her glass of soda constantly full, for Beth refused to muddle her brain with more alcohol.

Thus Beth found herself at a bar in an upscale Scottish country hotel being regaled until two o'clock in the morning by its distinguished, white-haired owner with stories about East Lothian during the war. He told it from the perspective of an eight-year-old when the war began in 1939. He talked about the villages of Gullane and Dirleton, the pilots who came and went from Drem, catching a week or two of respite at the hotel from their sorties in the south, and his deep disappointment that the war ended before he was old enough to fly a Lancaster bomber.

Every now and then, from the corner of her eye, Beth caught a glimpse of one who did.

NINE

THE NIGHT AFTER THEIR disastrous trip to Stirling, Robbie had a dream that was so detailed he could've painted it.

The classroom in his American junior high school was under construction, with a concrete floor and walls framed out in two-by-fours with openings for the windows and door. A blackboard at the front of the room was suspended in the air.

The classroom was filled with students, not the thirteen-year-old American students he had been in school with, but rather, famous Scots—William Wallace, Robbie Burns, Mary Queen of Scots, still with her head, Sir Walter Scott, Bonnie Prince Charlie, Robert Lewis Stevenson, Saint Columba. There were statesmen, heroes, soldiers, monks, scientists, explorers, kings, and queens, all dressed as they would be for their time period, and all looking a little waxy as if they had just stepped out of Madame Tussauds.

Standing in the front of the room, Robert the Bruce was teaching a history lesson. William Wallace kept raising his hand and saying in Mel Gibson's voice, "But Sir Robert, it happened this way. I remember. I was there."

All the while a spider, the one from Bruce's famous experience in the cave, which gave him the object lesson to persist and persist, was weaving the names and dates and places on the chalkboard with spider threads so the students could take notes, which they did on various writing apparatus befitting their period in time.

That's when Robbie noticed his father in the framed-out doorway, wearing a yellow hardhat and carrying a clipboard. He was taking notes as Robert the Bruce talked. Just after Robbie noticed him, his father stepped into the room, interrupting The Bruce's lecture. Everyone gasped at his audacity. Robbie hid his head in shame.

But The Bruce said, "Ah, Sir McLeod, you've come today to lecture us on what, sir?"

Robbie's father replied, "The history of engineering."

Everyone in the room clapped with delight, eager to hear about this subject. Astonished, Robbie stood up to protest. Why would they want to hear about such a dull subject? "Scots, what hae ye?" Robbie shouted the famous opening line of Sir Walter Scott's poem.

"Ye cad," the Bruce shouted back. "Hae ye no respect fer your own da? Off with his head." Everyone stood and began to shout at Robbie. "Off with his head."

"No, no," Robbie shouted back. "You don't understand. Da, make them understand."

But his father simply stood, as unblinking as a wax figure, while William Wallace picked up his broadsword and swung it in the direction of Robbie's neck.

He woke up screaming with Andrew pounding on his door, "McLeod, are you being murdered in there or what?"

Memories of that night's bizarre scene lingered for days. His thoughts of Beth increased, for when he thought of dreams, he thought of her and wished he'd asked about the ones she had been having of the bomber pilot.

Six weeks later, as cold Sunday rain pinged against the windows of his sitting room, Robbie found himself pacing his apartment at the end of a long dreary weekend. He threw himself in exhaustion on the ugly plaid armchair in one corner and stared into the blackness of the uninviting March night.

The room was cast in shadows above and around the small reading light by his chair. It was also distractingly quiet. Andrew was out, and Robbie hadn't bothered to turn on the tube or the radio to fill the emptiness. The lingering odor of the bangers he'd fried for his supper filled the apartment, and the taste of onions and mashed potatoes remained on his tongue. Thoughts of seeing Beth at Holyrood bounced around in his head like echoes in an empty room.

To her quote, *"But the shadows of the past still loom large in this place,"* he'd replied, "Yes, and also the shadows of the world," and pointed out the sound of the jet overhead. Then she'd quoted Tennyson's poem, *"...and moving through a mirror clear, that hangs before her all the year, shadows of the world appear."*

Could she see into some ghostly mirror and glimpse the past? It didn't bear thinking about—right? Either way, he... missed her.

He got up, restless. Once again he paced the short distance between the sitting room, kitchen, and hallway. The miserable day had kept him from his morning jog. He felt confined, physically and mentally. He couldn't work up the motivation to walk to the gym. Strutting to the window, he yanked the blind down to shut out the night.

He picked up the evening paper, glanced at the headlines, and tossed it aside. He headed for the kitchen, opened the refrigerator door, and stared into the brightly lit space, which stood out like a box of white in the dark kitchen. After untold minutes, he took out an American beer, popped the cap, and flung the bottle opener onto the kitchen counter. Not bothering with a glass, he carried the bottle back to the living room. The phone on the end table taunted him with silence.

He downed half the bottle in one go. Then with his free hand, he grabbed the phone and placed it on his lap. With another swig for courage, he punched in Beth's phone number. Like an important date in history, it had become embedded in his memory.

The phone rang repeatedly. He was about to hang up when he heard a sleepy, "Hello?"

"Beth? Were you sleeping?" He glanced at his watch. It was only eight o'clock.

"Oh, hello, Robbie." Her voice was soft and dreamy as if she had just awoken from a lovely nap. He could picture her lying on her side, knees slightly bent, hair falling over her face, holding the phone to her ear. It stirred an aching tenderness in his heart.

When she said nothing more, he asked again, unable to think of what to say now that he had her on the phone, "Did I wake you?"

Her soft, even breathing made him think she had fallen back to sleep, but after a moment she said with a sigh, "I don't know. I guess so. I was away over the weekend and then at the library writing a letter to my grandfather, and came back and, and... what time is it?"

Robbie felt a punch of jealousy in his gut. *Away? With that Canadian kid?* But he responded in an even voice, "It's eight."

"A.M. or P.M?"

Robbie thought she was joking and then realized with a frown that she wasn't. "Evening. You can't have been asleep long."

"Oh, it's early then. I thought it was much later. Guess I only dozed off for a bit."

"Did you go to the library in this rain?"

She laughed softly. "I don't melt, Robbie."

"No, you're made of heartier stuff than that." There was a pause in the conversation, and Robbie scrambled around for something safe to say. There was a pause in conversation and Robbie scrambled around for something safe to say. He settled on, "Did you eat?"

"No, I didn't. I meant to. I mean, I missed dinner, and then I was at the library and was going to stop for a slice of pizza, but it was so miserable out..."

Impulsively, he said, "How about if I bring a pizza over?"

There was stillness on the other end of the phone that Robbie couldn't interpret. At least she hadn't said *go to hell* or hung up on him.

"Well, that's awfully nice of you, but it's too miserable a night out for man or beastie."

"Even a Scottish beastie?" He kept his voice deliberately light.

"Are you a beastie?" was the prompt reply. Clearly, she was waking up.

"I... well, I guess that's for you to decide."

She didn't reply. After a pause, he said, "Sorry about that trip to Stirling. I was a nyaff."

"A what?"

"Oh, a worthless git."

"I wouldn't say that."

"Well, what would you say?" He waited on edge for her reply. It was slow and halting.

"I'm not sure... I understand why, well, why you were so angry. No, that's not true. I mean, I think I know. Well, I guess I sounded ungrateful for your help."

He assumed she was referring to her remark that she'd be better off doing her research alone. Robbie took another sip of his cold beer, pondering her statement. He wasn't sure he wanted to expound on it. Instead of explaining his revelation on the journey out of Stirling, or telling her about his ironic dream, he said, "I can't figure you out."

"And that makes you angry? I never thought I was difficult to understand."

"I think, really..." He tried to find the words. "I think I was angry at myself."

"Really? Why?"

"You make me question why I'm a history professor."

"Oh, Robbie, why would you say that?" Her voice was astonished. "You are so good at what you do. All the students rave about Professor McLeod."

He felt a sense of relief.

She went on. "No, tell me; I need to know. Why would I... me... stupid, silly girl from America, have that kind of impact on you?" She was earnest, intense.

He sighed, recapturing the confused emotions of their last encounter. "I may be good at what I do with facts and figures and biographical data..."

"Robbie, the students say you make history come alive for them. That you're the best history professor on campus."

"That's just because I'm closer to their age than some of the old geezers."

Beth wasn't being put off. "Robbie, honestly."

"But Beth, you seem able or at least willing somehow to live history in a way that..." He hated to say it. It sounded like a confession.

"Yes?" she encouraged him, softly.

"Well, in a way I can't comprehend. That I..."

"That you what, Robbie?"

He said it at last. "Envy."

"Oh." She was silent for a long time, but he could sense her presence on the other end of the phone. When she finally spoke, he could barely hear her. "I'm not sure it's something to envy. It's very... exhausting."

Her reply stirred up a wave of tenderness.

"Well," he replied, softly, "you need a change of pace. Edinburgh in early spring can still be depressing. How about a trip to Skye?"

Robbie was stunned by his own impulsive invitation. He wasn't sure what he'd expected of this phone conversation. He hadn't intended to do anything more than try to apologize for his regrettable behavior six weeks ago. If Andrew could hear him, he'd whack Robbie upside the head. Robbie leaped up and began pacing, stretching the phone cord as he did.

After a moment of silence, she said, "I'm really busy with schoolwork." Was she looking for an excuse? At least she hadn't brought up that Canadian boy. He really shouldn't be interfering in their relationship. He had seen them walking hand in hand, a sight that had left him flummoxed and then filled with surprising sadness. But if she didn't mention the kid, he wasn't going to either.

He tried again. "Or some other place on your grandfather's list. Midterm break is coming up at the end of next week." He hated the eagerness in his voice as if he were a schoolboy. Like that Frasier kid. Oh, he knew all about him. Had checked him out. Hockey jock.

"Aren't you going home?"

"Two weeks of a break leaves plenty of time for a home visit. We could take a couple days and see Skye. Early April can be pleasant in the west of Scotland."

When she didn't say anything, he added, "If you get bored with me, you can spend the days on your own. I'll just be a chauffeur. But then, maybe you've got traveling plans to the Riviera with some of the other students." *Robbie just shut up*, he thought to himself.

"I can't ever imagine getting bored with you." She said it so quietly he barely heard her. But when he realized what she had said, he felt an odd twist in his stomach. After a moment of quiet, she added in a hesitant voice, "Oh, well, I guess so."

Surprised, Robbie nearly danced a jig, he felt so suddenly lighthearted. "Okay then. I'll pick you up on the fourth... about..."

Beth interrupted. "Robbie, ah, wait. First of all, I can only get away for a couple days, a long weekend at the most. I've got some things I have to do later during break."

Robbie felt the green-eyed monster creeping into his brain, sure the other things must have something to do with that boy. He nearly missed the rest of her parameters.

"Don't misunderstand, but I want this to be *history* expedition, not any other type."

He found himself stumbling over his explanation of good intentions. "Of course. I wouldn't... I didn't mean it to be anything else. I'll make reservations for two rooms, and you can pay for your own room and meals and such. Can you do six days? If we leave on Friday, the fourth, and come back on Wednesday, the ninth? That's five nights. That'll give us a couple of days on Skye and then stop at Loch Lomond and the Trossachs National Park on the way back."

He knew she was on a very strict budget and wanted to offer to pay part of her room but knew that would be misconstrued.

"Well... I guess. Five nights. Not too pricey of a place?"

"No, I'll get inexpensive places. Besides, it's off-season, so the rates will be very low. Consider me a paid guide... ah, but one you don't have to pay. Remember, I'm a pro at this." He whacked himself on the side of the head to make himself shut up.

"Good. Great." She didn't seem bothered by his blather. Her voice was stronger, more alert.

He sensed a smile in her voice as she said, "I'm excited. I'd like to see Skye. Every time I go to a place on my grandfather's list..." She stopped abruptly.

He filled in jokingly, "...we have an argument?"

Her laughter made him smile. "Sure, Robbie, that's it. But no argument this time, okay?"

"Of course. I mean, of course not. I'll see you Friday," he said, "unless, I mean, we could get together and do a little planning…"

The sudden coolness in her lack of response told him he had pushed too far.

Finally, Beth said, "Thanks, Robbie, but I'm overwhelmed with work, and I'd better concentrate on things till then."

"Fine. Sure. No problem. Can you get away by two o'clock?"

"I think so," she replied.

"Okay. I'll pick you up next Friday about two-ish. The weather on the islands at this time of year is always chancy, so bring warm things and rain gear. Just casual stuff. Jeans. Walking shoes or hiking boots if you have them. We can do some hill walking if you'd like."

"I would. Okay. The fourth at two-ish."

"Yeah, I'll call you the night before to confirm it all."

"Okay. Great."

"Yeah. Great. See you then. Or maybe around campus."

She didn't respond to that last statement, but simply said, "Night, then."

"Goodnight Beth."

He replaced the phone gently on its cradle, his smile stuck to his face.

He had caught her off guard, waking her up from an exhausted, surprisingly dreamless sleep and then thawing her reserve with his self-deprecating apology and his unexpected invitation. She had thought she wouldn't ever have a chance to spend time with him again. The idea of a weekend away with Robbie was both exciting and alarming.

More distractions. Especially after the events yesterday at Drem and Gullane.

But wasn't Iain also a distraction? While he was fun and entertaining and she was flattered by his attention, she knew that if she had the choice of going to Skye with Robbie or Iain, there'd be no difficulty in deciding. Yet, if she was Iain's girl, then she was two-timing him.

Beth shook her head. No, she couldn't go away for a weekend with one guy when she was dating another one, serious or not. It felt too confusing. It would be so much simpler if she didn't date anyone. Not that she was dating Robbie, she reminded herself, ignoring the fact that he had just invited her to spend a week with him.

If I didn't see either Robbie or Iain, I could concentrate on Colin and try to figure out what he wants. What he needs. She was sure whatever he wanted had something to do with the American girl, the same one who had been at Holyrood, Traprain Law, and most recently at the hangar dance at Drem and in the bar at the Greywalls Hotel.

I'm American. Maybe I need to take a message back to her when I go home. Maybe he was in love with her and never told her, and now he wants to be sure she knows how he felt. *Why couldn't Colin tell the girl himself,* she wondered. Maybe because....

"No! No! No, no, no!" Beth shouted the words to the empty room, refusing to consider the real possibility that he couldn't tell her himself because he was...

Beth sank to the floor, sobbing, mumbling, "Please, Colin, don't be dead. Don't be dead." Her unexpected grief was an overwhelming wave. "I don't believe it. I won't believe it. I'll do whatever it is you need me to do. But please, just don't be dead."

She cried until the tears dried, but her head throbbed and her heart ached, so she crawled back into bed and fell asleep in her clothes, never hearing Anja come in.

Figuring out what to do about Iain was much easier than she'd expected.

On Tuesday, after their History and Culture of Scotland class, Beth and Iain were stopped in the hall outside their classroom by one of Iain's buddies.

"Go on, I'll catch up to you," Iain said, surprising Beth.

"Oh, sure, I've got a question for Dr. Craig about a point he made in today's lecture," she said and ducked back into the classroom. A few minutes later, as she was about to step back into the hallway, she overheard Iain say, "Well, I don't know what I'm going to do about Beth. It's really awkward. I mean, Karen and I planned this before I left Toronto. She bought her ticket in December. I can hardly tell her not to come."

Not wanting to be caught eavesdropping, Beth called out, "Thanks again for clarifying that point, Professor," and then walked through the open doorway.

Iain was leaning against the wall, trying to look nonchalant. He was unusually quiet on their walk to the library. She actually felt sorry for him, so she said, "Iain, I've got something rather awkward to talk to you about. Can we sit over here on the bench before we go into the library?"

Iain looked guilty. "I can explain, really. I know it sounds like I'm a jerk and..."

"I'm sorry, I didn't mean to overhear. Your girlfriend is coming for spring break."

He literally hung his head. She nearly laughed at how he looked like a naughty puppy. How young he was compared to Robbie. Or Colin. Yes, instead very much like blonde, well-built, innocent Jason, down to his sad face as he was rejecting her. The only difference here was their sexualities. And her. *You're a nice girl*, Jason had said, awkwardly trying to comfort her.

Well, she wasn't made of glass anymore.

"Iain, I'm not mad. I'm not hurt. These last weeks have been great. You've helped me deal with a big problem, and you've made my life here at school more of what I hoped for. I've felt like a real college student. Going to sports events. Hanging out in bars. Having a boyfriend."

At that, Iain turned a bright shade of pink. "I do feel like a jerk. I mean, I really like you... I mean Karen and I didn't say we'd be exclusive while we were away, and..."

Beth kissed him gently on the cheek. "Can we still be friends? I mean, after spring break, can I still come to your games and hang out with you and your friends? I'd miss that."

Iain leaped up off the bench with a whoop, pulling her into a huge bear hug.

"Beth, you are the best. Absolutely. Who else would I get to explain all this history and culture jazz to me? Besides, I'm becoming an expert on World War II. When I talk to my dad on the phone, he's totally amazed at what I've learned. In fact, he wants me to look up some distant relatives who were lost in the war. He said to go to the Scottish War Memorial right here in Edinburgh. Maybe you and I could go sometime?"

The taste of bile in her throat almost prevented Beth from answering. *Was Colin's name among those lost?*

"Yeah. Maybe. Sometime."

Ian nodded, looking relieved. "And I'll be watching out for you, make sure you don't take up with some jerk. You got somebody in mind? That professor guy, maybe?" Iain's voice displayed a hint of jealousy.

Beth tried to look indifferent at his accurate guess, but held back the fact she was going on spring break with "that professor guy." Iain had no such scruples and regaled her with details of his upcoming two-week vacation throughout the U.K. with his Canadian girlfriend.

Now that the air was cleared, she began to look forward to her trip to Skye with Robbie. He was right, she did need a break from school, but after this trip, she'd contact the Imperial War Museum and begin in earnest to find Colin's military record.

It was time to know his full name and visit that grassy airfield she kept dreaming about.

TEN

TWELVE DAYS LATER, WHEN Robbie and Beth arrived at Hotel Sligachen after an exhausting six-hour trip by car and ferry, the young hotel clerk said in his heavily Gaelic-accented English, "I'm sorry, we've just got the one reservation for McLeod. A double, and we're full up, ye see." Clearing his throat in an annoying manner, he said, "Ach, no room at the inn."

After deciphering his words, Beth felt her own throat grow thick and had to resist the temptation to imitate the clerk's annoying throat noise. She took a mint from her jacket pocket and filled the silence with the noise of crunching cellophane.

"But I asked for two rooms..." Robbie started to say, but the clerk cut him off.

"Sorry laddie, it's right here in the computer. Nothin' I can do for ye."

Beth could feel Robbie's temper boiling, but continued to concentrate on the floor as he said tersely, "Fine, we'll go up the road and find another place."

"Wall, gud luck to ye," the clerk replied cheerfully, clearing his throat again. "The area is pretty full up, ye see. All these Uni kids come out here on their wee holiday and go hiking..."

"Yes, yes. I can make a couple calls," Robbie replied in a stiff voice.

"Ye can try the country inn up in Portree; the rich American tourists don't usually book that one up till summer. And it's only one twenty a night off-season... per person."

Beth nearly gasped at two hundred dollars a night on a hotel room, though she had spent more than that at Greywalls. But her savings were dwindling faster than she had planned. She finally looked up at Robbie, whose face was flushed.

He said in a strained whisper, "I swear I booked two."

"I'm sure you did. So, since it's already going on nine, let's work it out for tonight and then see about tomorrow in the morning. As long as it's got two beds, we can hang a sheet between us like a curtain and pretend we're Clark Gable and Claudette Colbert in *It Happened One Night*."

Robbie's look of complete bewilderment made her laugh. "I'm sorry," she said, grinning. "It's an old movie."

She must have spoken loud enough for the clerk to hear because he chimed in, "Aye, a classic 'tis," clearing his throat again. Beth handed the young man a mint.

"Thanks," he said. "I've done worn out my throat today," then added, "My gran and I love those old Hollywood movies from the thirties and forties," and launched into a list of his favorites.

Beth felt Robbie tug on her arm. "So, it's okay to stay tonight then?" he asked.

"Sure." She wasn't sure why she was feeling so mellow, but she instinctively trusted him not to take advantage of the mix-up. As old-fashioned as it sounded, she wanted her first taste of love to be just that, love. She wasn't about to fall into bed with any guy just for the sake of losing her virginity. Though Robbie wasn't just any guy.

When they opened their room door and turned on the lights, Beth was relieved to see that a "double" did mean two beds. The room was lovely and even had a fireplace. She walked to the window and marveled at the view of stars beginning to dot the clear, dark sky over the nearby mountains. Robbie interrupted her reverie to plead starvation, reminding her it'd been hours since afternoon tea.

They ate dinner at the pub across the street, a place crowded with young holidaymakers, who were loud and increasingly inebriated, making conversation challenging.

"Let's have a nightcap at the hotel bar," Robbie suggested. "It'll be quieter."

Beth shook her head. "In truth, I'm rather done in, I think I'd like to get ready for... ah, put my paj... ah, turn in."

At Robbie's solemn face, she added, "But you're welcome to have a nightcap in the hotel bar if you'd like. Maybe the clerk would be free now and he could join you and discuss classic American movies."

She giggled at Robbie's glare, and then they laughed together, easing Beth's tension.

As they entered the lobby, Robbie said, "I think I'll skip that drink but check on ordering a hiker's lunch and see about tomorrow's weather."

He entered their room twenty minutes later and gave her a quick glance. By then, she had washed her face, brushed her teeth, and was sitting with the covers tucked under her arms, a book in her hands, appreciating the fresh linens and downy comforter.

"How was the clerk?" Beth asked in an innocent air.

"As annoying as ever." Robbie huffed. "He couldn't give me the weather without blathering on about another old Hollywood movie. As though I've never seen an American film."

Beth grinned.

"Are you warm enough?" Robbie was digging in his suitcase.

"The air's a bit chilly."

"Scottish heating systems have their flaws," Robbie explained. "Shall I look out an extra blanket? Or light the fireplace?"

"No, I'm fine. I'm too tired to stay up and enjoy a fire." She didn't want to suggest anything that would add even a hint of romance to the awkward situation. Though she couldn't imagine how romantic he'd think she was in her long-sleeved, full-length, flannel nightgown.

Robbie took his nightclothes into the bathroom and emerged a few minutes later in sweats and a t-shirt, then settled himself in the other bed. They read in companionable silence for more than an hour.

When she curled up under the covers, Robbie said. "I'm going to set the alarm. We'll do an easy hike tomorrow along Loch Sligachan."

At her mumbled, "um huh," he put down his book and turned out the lamp that sat on the table between their beds. "Have a good night, Beth."

"You too, Robbie," she whispered, wondering what was on his mind as he lay just a few feet from her, facing in the other direction. It really did feel like a scene from some romantic comedy, but she was so tired, and the bed was so enveloping, that she was soon asleep.

Beth woke as the alarm rang and sprang from her bed towards the bathroom, taking the clothes she had laid out on a nearby chair.

"Robbie, is it okay if I take a quick shower?" she asked, peering back out the bathroom door.

"Sure," he grunted. "Just wake me when you're done."

Then while Robbie showered, Beth made her bed, put away her night things, and sat down at the small desk to write in her journal. There'd been no dream last night. She frowned, for the dreams had become regular companions, though not always comfortable ones.

Some nights he'd wake up shaking in the grip of a cold, black fear, shouts filling her ears, the bouncing plane concussed by anti-aircraft fire churning her stomach, and the sight of fiery explosions below filling her eyes. She'd lay awake, calming her breath, matching Anja's soft breathing. Yet other nights were filled with a quiet, calm journey through the sky, where the stars glistened, and the steady drone of the engine was like a lullaby.

She had started dozing in class, staring off into the distance, her ears filled with echoes of conversation or the throb of an engine, her mind reveling in the atmosphere of a Christmas-scented hangar at Drem or the sight of Colin at the Greywalls bar.

Iain had jostled her awake more than once.

Beth longed to tell Robbie about these inexplicable experiences. She so much wanted his calm, logical advice, his help in working out what they might mean. *And what Colin needs me to do. But if I told Robbie my bomber pilot wanted something from me, he'd be signing me into a mental hospital.*

After breakfast they headed to the nearby trailhead. It was a bright, sunny day with no wind, and she was comfortable in her jeans, turtleneck, vest, new lined waterproof jacket, comfy socks, and sturdy walking shoes. They ambled in companionable silence along some salt flats and across several small streams. In the far distance were tall, snow-capped mountains. The trail was fairly popular, and several faster hikers passed them with "a good mornin' to ye."

"This is an easy walk, so you won't get to bag a Munro, I'm sorry to say," Robbie said after an hour.

"What? Bag a what?

Robbie explained that Munro-bagging meant climbing a hill of three thousand feet and that it was a national pastime in Scotland.

"Are there many hills that tall?"

"Two hundred eighty-four of them," he replied. "If you do them all, you're a Munroist."

"Sounds like a religion," she said, laughing. "Was Munro a priest?"

"No, Sir Hugh Munro apparently just liked mountains, especially those over a certain height. He listed 283 of them in the Journal of the Scottish Mountaineering Club in 1891. The club took over the task of keeping the list up to date. An attempt to climb all of them became known as Munro-bagging."

She smiled at him. "Robbie, you know some of the most obscure facts of history."

"Well, they're not obscure to a Scot. Here's another Munro fact. Sir Hugh never climbed all the hills on his own list. It was the Reverend A. E. Robertson who was first to complete the summits in 1901. Story goes, when he finished his final climb, he kissed the cairn—the pile of rocks at the top—and then kissed his wife."

"So, the Reverend loved the mountains more than his wife?"

Robbie shrugged. "Scots love their Munros. If you finish them all, you are a completer."

"And I'm not even a starter," Beth declared.

"Oh, you've plenty of time before you go home to bag at least one Munro."

They walked an upward ascent to the crest of a treeless hill covered with short, brittle grasses and bracken. From there Loch Sligachan lay about fifty feet below. A bit out of breath, she was grateful for the extra pair of walking poles Robbie had brought along for her.

"Let's have something to snack on," he said, sitting on a dry, rocky outcrop and pulling out water bottles, apples, cheese, and trail mix from his backpack. As she looked around at the stark beauty of the water, sky, and mountains, Beth could understand how hiking could become addicting.

When she said it'd be nice to head up into the hills, Robbie replied that they were not equipped for serious hill walking, only a "little stroll."

"You call seven miles a little stroll?"

"Oh, aye. To a Scot."

"What are we lacking for some *serious* hill walking?"

"Well, an ordinance map. A compass. A whistle."

"Really?"

"Novice walkers keep the mountain rescue people rather busy, I'm afraid. Every year some idget gets stranded in unexpected weather or in fog or falls down a cliff. People do die."

"That's comforting."

"No worries. The walk we're on is simple. You can't get lost... you just walk from the lake through the glen and back to our hotel and a glass of whiskey."

"Hmm, I might be interested in one myself tonight."

"Aye, we'll make a Scot of ye yet, me lassie," Robbie said in an exaggerated brogue.

Beth stared at the hills dominating the horizon that offered an odd sense of openness, of invitation to possibilities.

"What is it you want from your life, Robbie?" she said almost to herself, staring past him to the grey granite peaks.

Robbie smiled. "Makes you thoughtful, this walking business. But you first, Beth. What is it you want from your life?"

"It's a good question. I've thought about it a lot, especially in the years I've been going to college. A slow process, working and taking classes on a part-time basis." She took a bite out of the crisp, sweet apple.

"I admire your persistence. A lot of students wouldn't stick to it. They'd be lured away by the income of a steady job."

Beth took a deep breath and then said hesitantly, "I think what I really want, and it's ever clearer after spending this time in Scotland, is to find a place where I truly belong."

Robbie looked at her with thoughtful eyes, "Carlisle isn't where you belong?"

"Well, it's all I've known, really. And I know you're going to find this strange…"

"Maybe not."

"But in a lot of ways, I've felt more at home in Scotland than in my hometown."

"Hmmm," was Robbie's only reply.

"I'd like to, I don't know, have a sense of roots."

"Well, that's understandable. You've never known your father. Or your mother. It's a natural enough desire."

"Yeah, I know. It's odd. I've never really thought about my father much. I don't feel connected to him. How could I? I don't even know his name. I'm just an accident. But then, maybe his family is Scottish, and that's why I feel so at home here. Wouldn't that be funny?"

"Well, if you're an accident, you're a very pleasant one, I say."

Beth smiled at his sincerity.

He added, "And you know, there are an awful lot of people walking around this world that are what you call accidents. A planned child is still a new thing."

"Yes, true. It just so happened my father and mother didn't have the opportunity to get married before he went off to war."

Robbie nodded. "As to his possible Scottish roots, there are lots of Americans descended from Scots. So you could easily have Scottish roots on your father's side. But you've got your grandparents. That's more family than some people have."

"I do miss my grandfather a lot," Beth sighed, thinking of him sharing that big house with her uncommunicative grandmother. "But I always wished I had a brother or sister. Or some cousins. I envy people with big families and think they haven't a clue when they say I'm lucky because I'm an only child."

"No aunts, uncles, cousins?"

Beth popped a handful of granola into her mouth and chewed thoughtfully.

"Well, my mother was an only child. As I said before, my grandmother's sister and brother—Gretchen and William—died in the war. Never had children. It'd be nice to know something about them, even if they are no longer living. After all, they are a part of my history. My grandfather has some siblings, but we rarely see them. Only one of them has children, but none of those started families."

"You also have your grandmother, though you've said you've had your differences."

She thought about Naomi's iciness, the way she told Beth about her parents leaving her to them. "This might sound awful, but I've never had the sense that my grandmother was happy to have me around." The brisk air nipped her face.

"That's rough."

"Yes, well. Everyone has some pain or emptiness in their life." The stark, wild beauty all around would be a sweet balm to aching hearts, she couldn't help but think.

"Very philosophical."

"No sense in wishing someone was different from what they are. I long since accepted my grandmother as a rather unhappy, crotchety old woman. I sometimes wonder how she and my granddad ever got together... he seems so much happier and more positive than she is."

"So, roots, it is," Robbie brought the conversation back to the original question. "And someone who's happy to have you around."

"Oh, and then all the usual stuff," she added.

"Like what?" Robbie asked, beginning to pack up the remains of their break.

"Just to, well, have a little adventure, excitement, travel, discovery, romance. Some day to find someone who finds me attractive, desirable, and stirs my soul."

She felt the heat of embarrassment rise across her cheeks at her words. To cover up, she blurted, "And to find out who this Scottish bomber pilot is." She could've bitten her undisciplined tongue as Robbie's face shifted from interest to wariness.

She jumped up and started on the trail and in a moment heard his footsteps behind her.

"Beth."

She refused to turn around. Inside throbbed this genuine sense of loss that she could not share this most important of all things with him.

He tried again. "Beth, I'm sorry. It's just that..."

She did stop this time and turned around. She tried to hide the moisture in her eyes, but it was all too apparent.

He said softly, "You just worry me about this..."

"Obsession?"

"You used the word, not I."

"But it's what you think."

There was a pause before he responded, almost resentfully, "I don't understand how you can be so absorbed by this. Here you are in another country, having that adventure you've always wished for, having an opportunity to learn new things."

"I can't explain," she said. "Let's just skip it. Get on with our walk."

Beside her, Robbie nodded, a slight frown on his face. "Sure. Lead on."

The rest of the walk, with its uphill and downhill path along the shore, beneath a waterfall, and through a wooded ravine, was vigorous but not exhausting. At the end, in a tranquil farming area, they ate the lunch Robbie had obtained from the hotel kitchen. Their conversation was limited to Robbie's occasional commentary on the surroundings and Beth's responses, but the earlier tension had dissipated.

She found herself once more comparing Robbie's easy-going companionship versus Iain's often frenetic company.

Sunday dawned grey and overcast. The mountains were lost in mist, and a chill rain had settled in. Robbie suggested a trip to Dunvegan, the ancestral home of Clan McLeod. In comfortable quiet, they drove twenty-five miles up the island's west coast, taking in the contrast of green-gray sea, gray sky, and blue-gray mountain.

"It's a real Isle of Skye day," Robbie said finally, breaking the elongated silence.

"Yes," Beth said, ready for some conversation. "Tell me about the McLeods."

Robbie cheerfully set off on a long-winded talk about his clan, with stories both silly and sad. "Good thing your name isn't McDonald," he said partway through his ramblings.

"Why's that?" Beth asked.

"Why, then you'd be my sworn enemy. Let me tell you..." and off into another century, he went. By the time they reached the castle, the sky turned suddenly blue, and the misty rain blew out to sea. Though it was chilly, the air was bracing, and Beth felt her spirits lift.

As they took the guided tour of the castle, Robbie's whispered hysterical and historical side comments had Beth restraining her giggles. As there were only two others on the tour, the guide was none too pleased. When they entered the drawing room to view the famous McLeod Fairy Flag, the guide turned to respond to Robbie's muttered comment about it being a true fairy story, then noticed Robbie's lapel pin.

"What? Ye're a McLeod then?"

"True enough."

"And ye would scoff at your own family history?"

"History, hogwash. It's mythology. A flag is given to the family by fairies blessed with the power to protect the clan in times of danger. It didn't help the McLeods when the Campbells of Uist set fire to the church at Trumpan."

And off they proceeded on a drawn-out argument about the role of myth in history, with Robbie insisting it shouldn't play a role in the late twentieth century. That myth is what gets wars started.

Their argument got so heated that Beth wondered if they would pull down two of hundreds of swords and rapiers that hung on the wall. She lost track of the argument as they talked about whose father was whose, clans and half-clans, and this town or that island, when suddenly the guide clapped Robbie on the back and grinned widely.

"Come on, then. We'll have a wee toast to our great, great, great grandda."

Turns out they were fourth or fifth cousins.

The next thing Beth knew, she and Robbie and the other couple were escorted into the family rooms of the castle, drams of whiskey were poured all around, and with toasts of *Slainte* and *Bottoms Up*, they all became fast friends.

Beth had eaten very little for breakfast, unable to do the "full Scottish breakfast" offering of fried eggs, fried toast, fried sausage, fried tomatoes, and beans. She opted for tea and toast, so the whiskey, even though she took it in small sips, made her feel fuzzy and giggly.

They left the castle arm in arm, Robbie teaching her the clan motto "Hold Fast" in Gaelic.

"You'd better hold me fast, me boy," Beth said, giggling.

Robbie replied in an exaggerated accent, "Is that an invitation, me wee lassie?"

"I'll think on it," she laughed in return.

They stopped in Carbost on the way back to Sligachan to visit the island's only distillery. There Beth got a complete education in distilling, the impact of peat on the Talisker brand, and learned Scotch whisky is spelled without an "e", while Irish whiskey has the extra letter.

At the end of the tour, Beth said, "You'd better feed me, otherwise, my laddie, I'll be a layin' here in the road, napping."

They ate in a nearby pub, sitting by a fragrant peat fire that made her eyes water. By the time they got back to their hotel, the skies had grown leaden, and the rain let loose. They ran through a cloudburst from their car to the hotel, arriving nearly drenched.

Robbie lit the waiting logs in their room's fireplace while Beth changed into dry clothes in the bathroom. By the time she emerged, toweling her hair, Robbie had done the same. They sat by the blazing fire to warm up.

Robbie poured a dram of golden liquid from the bottle he had purchased at the distillery. Over Beth's protest at the expense, he had insisted on purchasing the small authentic glass snifters so she could have the "complete tasting experience."

"You can take them home as a souvenir. A gift for your grandfather."

"I've never seen Grandpa drink any hard liquor," she countered.

"Well, then, be sure to take home a bottle of Scotland's finest. I'll help you pick one."

Afternoon tea fixings—a staple of every good Scottish hotel or B&B—had been left in their room. Beth had at first declined Robbie's offer of more whiskey, opting for strong, hot tea, hoping it would put a bit of sense into her head. But now she was well into her next glass.

Robbie was leaning on the mantelpiece sipping his dram and nibbling on a chocolate cookie, or biscuit, as they were called in the U.K. Beth admired his lean profile, the way his hair curled around his neck, the firmness of his arm against the mantelpiece, the reflection of the firelight in his eyes and how soft his lips looked. She felt a sudden urge to put her hand among those curls. *You're a nice girl,* Jason had whispered once.

Sorry, Jason. I'm not. She took another sip of the fiery liquor, set the snifter down as she rose to her feet, and crossed the short distance between them.

The smile disappeared from his face, flushed red from the warmth of the fire and the whiskey. She reached up, took the glass from his hand, and set it firmly on the mantle. His eyes grew wide, then narrowed slowly.

She leaned toward him and touched her lips to his. Barely.

He stood very still.

She backed away slightly. He didn't seem to be breathing. She reached up and tangled the fingers of her right hand in the curls by his neck, enjoying the thick, wiry texture, gently pulling at the curls and letting them spring back.

Distracted momentarily by this sensation, she was unprepared. The touch of his lips to hers startled her, so she took a breath, tasting peat and chocolate, and felt dizzy all over again. The room seemed to spin in a slow, gentle movement, and she pressed up against him to keep her balance.

He pulled her into a deliciously tight embrace. His kisses were slow and luxurious, promising something more. Without thinking, she reached her hands under the back of his shirt and felt the heated warmth of his bare skin against her fingers.

He stopped, suddenly, and putting his hands on her shoulders, leaned her away gently.

"Beth, this isn't a good idea. I can't..."

"You can't?" She couldn't help giggling, for she knew he "could." She had been pressed tightly against him and knew very well what he was able to do.

"Oh, hell, of course I *can*, but what I'm trying to say, is... are you sure?"

Beth already missed the heat of his body against hers, the wet moistness of his lips, the caressing pressure of his hands on her back and bottom.

"Robbie, I'm a grownup."

She leaned against him and started to touch her lips against his but he gently eased her away again, "I didn't... it wasn't my intention to make you drunk... to take advantage of..."

She stopped his words with her mouth and said, after a long, deep, increasingly passionate kiss, "Maybe I'm the one who's taking advantage of you."

After that, he made no more protests.

It was like learning a new dance, and he was a patient and passionate teacher. With each new step, another piece of clothing was removed, and the sensations intensified. She had long wondered what it would be like, to be touched like this, to be tasted, to be loved.

They lay on the bed, afterward, their skin glimmering golden in the firelight, the sheets scented by fresh air, sky, and wind. Night had darkened the room, lit only by the flickering fireplace. But she had her own glowing fire inside her, spreading from deep within, through her stomach, chest, head, groin, and every other part of her body, drawn out by his touch and his thousand delicious kisses. A million sensations of touch and taste and smell and sound.

Yet her first taste of love had been a confusing paradox of sensations. There had been breathlessness, waiting for something spectacular to happen, but in the end, she felt oddly let down. Confused. Still waiting. Wanting.

Did she do something wrong? Even the bit of discomfort when they were completely joined took her by surprise. But it was so wonderful to lay there now, molded against him, skin against skin, cooling in the air, the chill raising slight goose bumps on her flesh. She felt alive. Cared for. And at the same time open, exposed, and vulnerable. And to her great amazement, not afraid or embarrassed.

Robbie was quiet for so long she began to get worried. He had been so full of life, amusing and energized, tender and passionate. She didn't want him to feel guilt or obligation.

At last, he said in a scratchy whisper, "I... I've never been, well, the first for someone."

It made her smile, the puzzle in his voice.

"Someone has to be first."

"Yes, I mean, well, did it... hurt? I mean, I figured you weren't real experienced, but I didn't realize..."

"No, it didn't hurt, really. Just a little... surprise."

"Oh. I'm sorry. But, was it... good... I mean."

Beth chuckled deep in her throat. "This sounds like dialogue from some B-grade movie."

He laughed, letting out a sigh of tension. "It does. But, the first time isn't always... well... the best for the woman. Takes a little practice to make the moves work just right."

"Really?" Beth was fascinated. "How much practice?"

Robbie nibbled on her neck. "Oh, a wee bit. Tis early, we could practice a bit more."

And Robbie was right. She felt like a musical instrument that had never been played, coming alive under the touch of a master musician. No romance novel, no movie, no imagination could ever have prepared her for the reality.

After a while, they sat by the fireside wrapped in sheets, sipping the wine Robbie had retrieved earlier from the pub, nibbling the last hiking snacks. Then they made love again next to the crackling logs and eventually fell asleep tangled in the sheets and blankets and each other.

In the morning they took a shower together, an amusing challenge in the tiny bathroom, made love again, and fell asleep until nearly noon. Monday afternoon they went out for lunch, nosed around the shops for a couple hours, came back, had tea, and made love again. Later they went to dinner, shared a bottle of wine, then went back upstairs, laughing and delighting in each other.

Tuesday they went further afield, but by noon it had turned ugly and raining, so they came back, lit a fire, and lay on the bed, kissing, touching, and whiling away the afternoon and evening. Somewhere in between, Robbie went downstairs and ordered dinner to bring up to the room, as they didn't have room service.

This is what a honeymoon must be like, Beth thought at some point.

You're supposed to get married before you have a honeymoon, her conscience replied.

Well then, not a honeymoon, a love affair, she told her conscience. Her conscience had no reply to that statement.

Wednesday morning, after breakfast, Beth packed her bag, smiling to herself. Robbie had stayed downstairs to settle the bill. He said "no way" was he going to let her pay for any portion of their weekend; it was his gift, and besides, she "earned it."

She had slapped him playfully on the arm when he said it, and he had given her a quick kiss on the cheek.

The day's weather was a continuation of Tuesday's—cold, damp, and miserable. Robbie came upstairs to help carry the bags to the car he had rented for the trip, as Andrew was off on his own midterm adventure and couldn't spare his lovely Austin.

Robbie offered to pop over to the newsagent for a stamp so she could mail her postcard to Pennsylvania, despite the now pouring rain.

"I'll stay out here for some air," she said, standing on the porch of the hotel while he dashed across the street.

A sudden sense of vertigo struck her, and she had to lean against the wall to steady herself. A sound to her left drew her attention. Beth turned slowly, afraid to breathe. Narrowing her eyes, she saw an outline in the shadows. *Him.*

A voice called to him from inside. The American woman. *"Donald Colin McCauley, I know you're here somewhere."*

Colin looked right in Beth's direction. He was no longer an outline, but clearly visible, even in the shadows. Clearly present. If Beth walked the few feet toward him, reached out, and touched him, she would encounter flesh and blood.

A living, breathing man.

"What do you want?" Beth whispered out loud. "What do you need?"

His deep brown eyes seemed to shimmer. *"I want you to know the truth."*

Robbie was yelling from across the street, "How many postcard stamps do you need, Beth?" and Colin began to fade.

"No, no, don't go," she whispered, anguished. "What truth do you want me to know?"

"I want you to find out the truth. You need to find the truth." His voice was urgent.

Robbie shouted again, his voice drifting across the street over the rain drumming on the porch roof. "Beth? How many do you need?"

Colin faded into the shadows, becoming only an outline, and then indistinguishable from the gloomy recesses of the porch. Her mind whirled with the realization that Colin had been completely present with her, and talked directly to her.

What did he mean? What truth? With a shock, the choice before her came into laser focus.

Past or present. Colin or Robbie.

She could not go on like this, torn between the compelling, demanding past and the delicious, alluring present. She had to find out what Colin needed, what truth he wanted her to know, and what she was expected to do with that truth. That search demanded all of her attention.

And she now knew his full name. Donald Colin McCauley.

A feeling of seasickness came over her. Holding onto the porch railing, she struggled to gain control of the nausea. Swallowing her tears, she took a deep breath and shouted to Robbie, "One." Under her breath, she whispered, "It can only be one of you."

She knew in her devastated heart which one she would have to let go.

ELEVEN

BETH WAS UNNERVINGLY QUIET on the drive back to Edinburgh in the steady rain. Robbie tried to engage her in conversation, but she finally said in a flat voice, "Robbie, would you mind if I took a nap? You just plum wore me out."

Robbie relaxed. He was a bit tuckered himself, yet at the same time deeply content yet excited and energized. As she slept, he formulated plans to take her to Tain for the rest of the break. He had promised his mother and sister that he would come up for one of the two weeks, and this would be the perfect time to introduce them to Beth.

Beth and his sister Caitlain would get along great, and though his mother was always graciously welcoming to everyone, there was something special about Beth that she would really like. Her freshness, innocence... well, he chuckled to himself, maybe not quite as innocent as she used to be.

A twinge of conscience caught him off guard.

It wasn't as if I took advantage of her... he argued with himself. *She was very much receptive. More than receptive. She's the one who made it clear what she wanted, even if I didn't realize she was... inexperienced. And damn it, I did make reservations for two rooms; wasn't my fault that the inept clerk couldn't get it right.*

"Then there is the issue of ethics," the strident voice of that presenter from the orientation lecture blared in his mind. "Having a sexual relationship with a student can be cause for dismissal. Even if the student is not in your class, there is the issue of implied power. It can go both ways. It isn't unheard of for students to lure professors into bed and then demand grade concessions."

"Well, I've certainly crossed the no-fly zone," he muttered, then stopped when Beth stirred, though her deep, gentle breathing soon came back.

In his first year as a professor at a prestigious university, he'd already broken the cardinal rule: don't sleep with your students. Student, he corrected himself. It was as simple as that. Ethics, morals, and professionalism aside, it's just a stupid thing to do. And he knew it.

But Beth isn't my student, he silently yelled back at his conscience. *This is different.*

"Oh yeah, McLeod." He could hear Andrew's scornful voice. "Because she's an American? You're a dolt, and you're going to get yourself called up before the University Board. Maybe even get dismissed."

Robbie contemplated the shaky ground ahead: another ten days of spring vacation, then revision week, and finally four weeks of exams. He'd have to find a way to ratchet back their relationship, just till the semester was over. *We could go away on the weekends; that way no one on campus would know*. He smiled at the delights of the weekend just ending.

That's not ratcheting back, you bloody idiot. Again, the warning tones of his flatmate echoed.

Fine, Andrew, fine. Maybe we'll just do day trips. It's only a little more than six weeks. Then it'll be summer.

He would convince her to stay for the summer, and they could go biking or backpacking through Europe. She'd like that. He pictured days and nights in Paris, Tuscany, Greece.

Focused on planning all the places he'd take her, Robbie drove through the steady rain toward Edinburgh, Beth's gentle breathing keeping him and his thoughts company. Halfway into their return trip, he pulled off the main road and entered a small town. Beth woke up at the change in momentum, and he told her it was teatime.

"What are your plans for the summer?" he said over a bowl of piping hot Scotch Broth. She was having her favorite "cream tea"—tea with scones, clotted cream, and jam.

She shrugged. He thought she looked genuinely tired. "Are you still worn out?" he asked with a devilish undertone.

He was disconcerted when she simply stared at him for a moment, then nodded, "I am. Really. All the hiking and stuff..."

"... and stuff?"

Her smile set him at ease. "Nice stuff." He laughed and went back to eating. She asked him questions about the town they were in and continued with similar questions about the areas they drove through on the rest of their trip back to Edinburgh. It helped the remaining three hours go much faster, he thought, but realized later she never answered his question about her summer plans.

It was late afternoon when they reached her dormitory.

"Beth," he said pointedly. "Why don't you come with me to Tain on Friday? There's still a week and a half of vacation left. Isn't Anja traveling? Won't you be lonely? Give you a chance to see a bit of the northern highlands."

The alarm on her face startled him. She stammered, "I would really... I mean... I can't. I'm sorry, I can't."

"You can't?" He felt a sudden alarming uneasiness about her tone.

"I can't. You see, I've...I made..." she said, then sped through the rest of her sentence, "some plans for the rest of the break."

An image of the blonde Canadian boy instantly filled his mind.

"With whom?" He heard the jealousy in his voice.

Beth looked away and put her hand on the door handle. Probably to hide her guilt, he thought, beginning to grow angry. He had been so sure that she was going to say yes. He changed his approach, making his voice neutral.

"Well, I don't have to go. I can stick around, and we can do some day trips. There's still..."

"Robbie," she interrupted, "Robbie, really. Please. That isn't fair. Your family is expecting you, I'm sure. I don't want to keep you from your family." But she didn't look at him.

"Beth," he said softly. "Beth."

She turned back and he was stunned by the ravaged look on her face. He took her hands hurriedly. "What is it? What's wrong?"

She startled him by yanking back her hands. "Don't. Please. Don't."

"What? Don't what? Beth, what the hell is going on?"

Her words were so soft he could barely hear them. "Robbie, this was an... an amazing... an... I can't even find the words for it. You are... so... so ... such a gentleman."

"A gentleman?" Robbie scoffed. He was hoping for something a little more flattering. His awareness of their unequal status tweaked his conscience again. *Maybe that's what's bothering her, now that we're back on campus.* Or perhaps she's worried about getting... No. They—he—made sure to be as safe, as careful as possible.

He softened his tone. "I know, I've broken all the rules about how a professor is supposed to be with a student. I'm sorry, but not really. I'm not your professor anyway." He sounded defensive, he realized.

She suddenly took his face in her hands and kissed him with soul-aching tenderness. She tasted like strawberry jam. "I'm not sorry, either, but..."

"But what?" His mind was whirling, his heart a stone, pulled down by that hope-smashing three-letter word.

"But it's just that... I... well, it just isn't going to work between us."

Robbie blinked. She said it. She couldn't have. She couldn't mean it.

"What did you say?" He enunciated the words carefully to give himself time to adjust to this alternate reality.

She was trembling. "I can't explain. You wouldn't understand. It's too complicated."

"Complicated," he echoed in a flat voice.

"You've been so... kind...."

"God dammit Beth, stop saying that. You're right, I don't understand. What did I do wrong? Tell me. This isn't making any sense. I thought we..."

"No!" She was nearly shouting, shaking her head vigorously. "I'm so sorry, I'm sorry. I..." She stumbled out of the car and pulled her suitcase from the back seat as Robbie sprung out of the driver's side and sped around the car, grabbing her by the arm.

The tears on her face did not console his shock, his fury. He almost shouted, "Don't say something stupid like *This is hurting me more than it's hurting you.*"

She stood silently before him, tears dampening her cheeks, clutching her backpack and suitcase. But she said nothing.

He withdrew his hand, and she turned away.

"That's it? That's it!" he said, more to himself, but loud enough for her to hear.

Her only response was to pick up her speed as she headed up the sidewalk to her dorm.

<hr />

He didn't go to Tain. He made some excuse to his mother and spent the rest of the break rattling around his empty flat, drinking too much in bars, and going for long, torturous runs. Endlessly he ran through the details of the days in Skye. What had he done to make their amazing time together end with such stunning abruptness?

Repeated calls to her dorm room remained unanswered. Once, he went to her room and knocked on the door, but no one answered. He figured she wasn't even on campus. He couldn't think. Couldn't concentrate.

On the last weekend of the semester break, in a desperate attempt to put her out of his mind, he had an encounter with a sleek and slender blonde law clerk, which ended in a grope and a feel in a dark alley and her invitation to "come up to my place." But when he did and she started peeling off her clothes as soon as he closed the door of her apartment, he found himself suddenly and unaccountably repulsed.

He didn't want a quick screw with a girl he didn't even know. He wanted something more with a girl who meant more, he thought, walking home through the dark streets of Edinburgh.

Could that be Beth?

He mentally ticked off her characteristics. She was odd, intense, and sometimes aggravating. Yet she was intelligent, witty, hardworking, and refreshingly devoid of game-playing. But wasn't this sudden rejection a game she was playing?

No, it seemed too sincere. Like she suddenly regretted the sexual entanglement. Given her lack of experience, that made sense. Yet she seemed to thoroughly enjoy their lovemaking, to be genuinely delighted with his company.

On the other hand, she was mature in ways other girls her age—women, he corrected himself—weren't. Maybe being raised by her grandparents gave her this air of belonging to a different generation. Even her tastes in music, clothes, books, and movies were surprisingly old-fashioned, yet appealing to the historian in him.

However, compared to the sophisticated women of Edinburgh, she was naïve, though charmingly so. After all, she was twenty-two and still a virgin. *Was a virgin*, a voice taunted him.

The thought of their sensuous, intimate, delightful time together was a punch in the gut. Apparently, she wasn't old-fashioned enough to think that her "first time" meant the beginning of a relationship.

The days came and went, and every day he had to stop himself from looking for her on campus, picking up the phone to dial her number, or heading in the direction of her dorm. He constantly analyzed how he must have sabotaged the beginning of something special. Something he hadn't ever felt in any other relationship.

He tried to be honest with himself. Maybe he was just ticked because he was the one that always ended relationships with girls he found too clingy, too dependent, too insistent on commitments he wasn't willing to make? Were his feelings for Beth intensified because she wasn't falling all over him? Day after day, he still had no idea.

One evening during the first week of exams, he and Andrew were watching some mindless comedy on television. After the fifth time that Robbie got up, opened the fridge, and stared into it for a minute, before coming back to the living room empty-handed, Andrew finally said, "Robbie, what the hell's the matter with you?"

Robbie just grunted.

"You've been as jumpy as a popcorn kernel on a fireplace ever since you came back from semester break. Something happened you didn't tell me about?"

"Jumpy as a popcorn kernel? Pretty stupid analogy for a guy who's been educated at Cambridge and Oxford," Robbie shot back. He'd told Andrew that he went hiking in Skye during the first part of his break and spent the in Edinburgh because his father was in Tain and he didn't feel like dealing with him. He hadn't mentioned Beth's part in it.

"Ah," Andrew said with a knowing tone. "It's a woman. That American girl."

"What?" Robbie shot him a disgusted look. "What would make you say that?"

"I've known you for... what is it...two years at Cambridge and four at Oxford? You can't share a flat with a guy all that time and not get to know him. I've seen the look before. I recognize the anguished pacing."

Robbie just groaned. He could rarely keep anything from Andrew.

Andrew said in a coaxing tone, "Female troubles, the deadliest kind. Tell Uncle Andrew."

"Andrew, could you just..."

"Not a chance. Show's boring anyway. You're never quite like this unless you've got romance problems. Did she jilt you?"

At Robbie's glare, Andrew sat up. "Hey, mate, I was just joking. Really. Is it serious?"

"I... well, I took her to Skye."

"Oh, you idiot! Didn't I tell you to lay off until the end of the semester? What, you gave her the full romantic treatment, and now she's threatening sexual harassment?"

"No, it's nothing like that."

"Right-oh."

"Really. It was just... I made two room reservations, and when we got to the hotel, there had been a mix-up."

Andrew snorted. "Well, you did learn something from your years at Britannia's finest institutions of higher learning."

"No, I mean it." Robbie was getting angry. "I didn't intend for it to happen."

Andrew held up his hands placatingly. "Look, mate, I think that whole student-professor relationship shit is for the birds... I mean the sexual harassment thing from the professor's point of view." He grinned. "I'd be perfectly happy to be sexually harassed by some of my students."

Robbie glared at his flatmate, "Well, have you ever been tempted?"

Andrew turned suddenly serious. "Well, sure. But I can't get that woman's voice out of my head from last August. The one who kept talking about quagmires or was it..."

"Land mines. She said the student-teacher relationship is filled with land mines."

"And it seems like you've stepped on one, mate. So, is she putting on the pressure? Threatening to take you to the dean?"

"No, actually," Robbie sighed. "Just the opposite."

"So, you're threatening to take *her* to the dean?" Robbie glowered and Andrew said, more sympathetically, "So, you like this girl."

Robbie simply stared back.

"You more than like this girl."

Robbie still didn't reply. "What is this, a guessing game? Hot and cold? Give me something, here."

"I don't know how I feel, but I can't get her out of my mind. I just want to be with her, but she's... different."

His roommate seemed to roll his words around. "You want to be with her because she's... different?"

"She's young, only twenty-two, but she's very mature." At Andrew's raised eyebrows, Robbie said with disgust, "Not that way, you prick."

"Oh, prick? Who's been doing the pricking here, mate?"

"Let's just say the more time I spend with her, the more I like her. It's just that she's on a weird sort of quest."

"A 'knight in shining armor' quest? Don Quixote? The Knights Templar? Indiana Jones?"

Robbie threw himself down on the couch. "No, I mean...it's hard to explain without making her sound mental."

"Uh-oh. Like that girl at St. Andrews. The one that tried to commit..."

"No, it's nothing like that. Not at all. Beth... that's her name. She's trying to find out about a pilot from the war."

Andrew leaned forward. "History. Right up your alley. So, what makes that weird?"

"It's, well, she bought this bomber jacket in the States. In a vintage clothing store. And started to have dreams..." When Robbie said it out loud, he realized how weird it did sound.

Andrew's waiting silence carried growing dread. It was going to sound as if Beth were... over the edge. "She began to have dreams about the bomber pilot, and when she went to a few places thought she..."

"Yes?"

"Well, thought she could... ah... sense him." He had been about to say "see him," but that would have been too much for Andrew.

"Hmm. A psychic."

"Knock it off, Andrew." But something about that idea seemed attractive.

"Look, I'm on your side. So, that didn't bother you, her... obsession..." Robbie's scowl had him amending. "...her unique abilities to contact the other world?"

Robbie shook his head in frustration. "Yes, it did, some, but not enough... it didn't seem... well, she only talked about it when we first met."

"I see. So, a cute, psychic American girl you like a lot. So then, what's the problem? Other than you'd get fired if the University found out about the trip to Skye."

"She said it couldn't work out between us."

Andrew let out a low whistle. "So you were a one-night... well, one-weekend stand. No wonder you're bummed out. But it's modern times, mate. Chicks do it to guys, these days."

"Sure, rub it in," Robbie growled.

"Look, sorry, Robbie, but what are you going to do? Have you tried calling her, or dropping her a note? Like you really care and aren't just relieved that it *was* a one-night stand?"

"I tried calling and going by her dorm room the week after we got back, but she never answered. I think she was away."

"And since then?"

"No... I got... discouraged."

"True love never gets discouraged. Try again."

Robbie shrugged. "I'll think about it."

After a day or two, he took Andrew's advice. He started calling Beth every evening around nine o'clock. After five days of no answers and no responses to his answering machine messages, he started calling her at random times. Still no response.

On Monday, he was contemplating what he would say in a note to her when unexpectedly, he saw her. He had gone to the café in the student center for coffee, and as he walked away with his to-go cup, he saw her sitting by a window, huddled over some books and a cup of tea. He almost didn't recognize her because she had gotten a haircut, and she wasn't wearing the bomber jacket. She had on the lined windbreaker she had worn to Skye.

Maybe I should just go, he debated with himself, now that she was within reach. *She hasn't returned my calls. Obviously, she doesn't want to see me.*

Ignoring his own advice, he walked over and stood a full minute at the edge of the small, round two-seater table until he worked up the nerve to say, "Beth."

She looked up, startled. The haircut, an extremely attractive short bob, framed her pale face. He was shocked at how exhausted she looked. As if she hadn't been sleeping at all. There were dark circles under her eyes, which looked unfocused and gritty.

She stared at him as though she didn't recognize him. Unwilling to sit down unless invited, he said again, "Beth."

"Robbie? Oh." She blinked, seeming to wake up. "Oh?" Her drawn face flushed a slow, attractive pink, which made her look young and lost.

He sat down because he had to. Seeing her so frail was a punch in the stomach.

"I've been worried." He had wanted to be aloof, cool, indifferent. Instead, he was intense, emotional, and confused. "Why haven't you answered my phone calls?"

"I've been... busy."

It was lame, and he would have been angry if she hadn't looked ill. It frightened him. "Are you all right?"

She shook her head no but said, "Yes, fine. Just busy. You know. All the reading, exam prep. Study. Research and all." Her words were strained, as if she had to concentrate to say them.

"Research? Can I help? This is my field you know, research. History." He hated the pleading in his voice. Mentally kicked himself for sounding so needy.

Get over it, McLeod. She doesn't want you.

"No, thanks. I appreciate the offer, but I've got to do it alone." She had started to sound a bit more coherent. He took it as a signal and stood up.

"I see. Aye. Well." He worked to control the emotion in his voice, the spiteful words waiting on his tongue. "Yes, well, then, good luck."

He turned to go and heard a soft, "Robbie?" He halted, then slowly turned back. "Yes?"

But she was looking down at her papers and mumbled, "Nothing. Really. Nothing."

"Yes," he replied with a bitterness he couldn't keep out of his voice. "It is nothing."

TWELVE

ROBBIE WANDERED THROUGH THE next week vacillating between fierce resentment and debilitating lethargy to the point he could barely concentrate. His morning runs usually cleared his mind, but his feet insisted on taking him by her dorm, past the student center, and through campus areas she frequented. Every day, he would return to his flat, dreading Andrew's questions and interventions. Which were even before the dean asked Andrew, "What was up with McLeod?"

Nothing helped. He was mired in memories. Then the present yanked him rudely back. Iain Frasier, of all people, burst into his office one morning, looking all angry and righteous. "I know it's your fault."

Robbie nearly dropped the coffee he was about to sip. Glaring at the boy, he set his cup down with exaggerated care. How he'd love to throttle this whiny interloper.

But the kid snarled on, waving a note, "You've screwed up Beth's life; I'm sure of it. I knew something was up, ever since the time I saw you with her at that pub. I should report you to the dean, and I will if she doesn't come back soon."

Alarm swept Robbie to his feet. His wheeled office chair slammed into the wall. "What do you mean, if she doesn't come back soon? Come back from where?"

Iain stared at him across the width of the desk. "Figures you don't even know she left."

"Left?" The word stuck in his throat, and he had to swallow hard. Beth's face reappeared, gaunt, exhausted. She had flushed so vulnerably pink when she saw him. His heart wrenched anew. "What are you talking about?"

It took a couple deep breaths to calm himself and convince the kid to show him the note.

Iain, I have to take an unexpected trip out of town. I don't know when I'll be back. Don't worry, it's just something I need to take care of. If the semester ends before I get back to campus, please know I wish you well and thank you for being such a good friend. You made my time in Scotland so much fun. Sincerely, Beth.

He reread the note. *It's just something I have to take care of...* He asked Iain if Beth had mentioned anything about the pilot she was researching. The one whose bomber jacket she wore.

"Pilot? What the fu... what are you talking about? She was researching the war. The bomber war, yes, but she never said anything about one particular guy."

Somehow, this made Robbie unreasonably happy. "Did she ever say anything about doing research in London? At the Imperial War Museum?"

The boy stuck his hands in his jeans and scrunched up his face in concentration, "Well, yes... she did say something about some war museum and London. A couple days before she left. We were watching a soccer game at the pub. I didn't hear everything she said."

It was enough for Robbie. His mind still swam with questions, with memories, but he focused and walked around his desk, sticking out his hand. "Iain, thank you for coming to see me." He was surprised at his sincere gratitude. "I promise I'll find her. I've a pretty good idea where she went. And I'll let you know what I find out. I know you care about her. You've been important to her. I appreciate that you've looked after her."

All the stuffing went out of the kid. He shuffled his feet, "I'm just worried, you see. We'll be leaving school soon. I wouldn't want to go without a goodbye, or at least knowing she's okay."

He wrote his campus address, phone number, and Canadian home number on a notepad, tearing out the page. "Here, in case I'm gone till you find out. And you'd better let Anja know too. Beth left the same note for her. You promise, you hear?"

Robbie placed the note in his dress shirt pocket. "Aye. I promise."

———⋈———

Robbie mulled over his next step, then reread the note. Stared out the window. Finally, he overstepped his faculty privilege again to obtain Beth's emergency contact information and trod anxiously through the day as the clock ticked toward four p.m.—eleven in the morning on the eastern coast of the United States. His students must have thought he had lost it as he stopped a half-dozen times while giving them exam instructions, forgetting what he was saying.

At the end of the day, he hurried back to his flat where he dialed her home number with a shaky hand.

"Hello." The man answering the phone sounded short of breath.

Robbie suddenly didn't know how to start and seconds passed I silence. Some static snapped his hesitation. "Mr. Schmidt. Hello, is this Mr. Henry Schmidt?"

"Yes, this is Henry Schmidt."

"Aye, Mr. Schmidt, this is Robbie McLeod and..."

"Is there something wrong with Beth?" Henry's panic was a punch to the stomach. He was back in the café, looking down at her tired, dark-circled eyes.

Don't worry, it's just something I need to take care of.

"Hello? Hello?" Henry raised his voice. "Are you still there?"

"Aye, Mr. Schmidt, I... I'm sorry, you caught me off guard. Please..."

"What is it? There's something wrong; I can tell."

There was a chair scraping on the floor and the huff of someone sitting down heavily. "As I said, I'm Robbie McLeod and..."

"Yes, yes, Professor McLeod."

"Ah, yes, how..."

"Beth mentioned in her letters that she had met a nice, young professor on the train."

"Oh, yes, of course she would have mentioned me." Relief flooded his mind that he was spared a long explanation of who he was... and a little satisfaction. He put away his initial surprise and continued. "I'm really sorry to be calling you, but actually, I was... please don't be alarmed, but... this is very confusing... but, I was wondering if you've heard from Beth recently?"

Henry took a deep breath, and Robbie mentally kicked himself. He was making a terrible impression on someone so important to Beth. Someone he had hoped to meet someday. "Mr. Schmidt? I'm sorry, I didn't mean to alarm you."

"Ah, yes, I... Professor..."

"Please, my name is Robbie, sir. Have you heard from her?"

"She writes every week," Henry said. "And sends postcards when she travels. It's been longer than usual since she's written, but she did say she had exams and might not be able to write. And we talked just on the first of May. We always talk around the first and the fifteenth."

So no one knew where she was. Fresh alarm seized Robbie. She hadn't... hadn't gone and... no. She had looked almost despairing that day. No, she couldn't have. He forced calm assurance in his voice. "You're right. We're in the midst of exams right now. And I've seen her buy postcards wherever we've gone, and she always says, 'Have to send my Grandpa a postcard. He'll think it's cool that I've been here.' "

Wherever we've gone. Slick, McLeod, slick. Henry seemed the protective sort. Best not to test how he would react to his granddaughter going places with some bloke she only "mentioned" in her letters. Places on Henry's list now engraved in Robbie's memory, like Traprain Law, Drem, the Wallace monument, and... he could barely *think* the name... Skye.

"Ah, I see. So, please tell me, Pro... Robbie, what's going on. Why are you calling? Is Beth okay?"

Robbie cleared his throat of the strangling anxiety. "Well, you see, that's why I'm calling. I...she...we had a bit of a falling out, and I...well...I'm worried about her." A falling out? No, a falling off a cliff.

Henry's response sounded cautious. "She didn't say anything about a falling out."

Robbie pushed past that, putting all of his efforts into quenching panic. "The reason I was calling... this young friend of hers, Frasier, came to my office and told me that she had left him a note that she went on a trip. He wondered if I knew where she went. I didn't and hoped she had told you."

"Frasier... you mean Iain. Yes, she mentioned him. She did say she was going to do some traveling at the end of the semester but hadn't decided on the details. She talked about seeing other parts of Scotland. London. France. Germany. But the semester's not over yet, is it?"

"No," Robbie replied. "It ends on the twenty-fourth. Not for almost two more weeks. That's what surprised me."

"Maybe she finished her exams early." Henry's musing sounded hopeful.

Robbie asked the question he most dreaded. "Mr. Schmidt, did she tell you she's been doing some research here?"

Henry's voice took on an odd edge. "Well, she said she was reading up on the War. She always was interested. My fault. I gave her a list of places I thought she might want to visit. You see, I was stationed there, in the War, in the UK."

"Yes, she said. But all the items on your list are in Scotland." He coughed nervously. "She showed me that list when we met on the train."

"Yes, yes. Well, you see I spent a lot of time in Scotland... on leave and such. Lovely place. Nice to get away."

Robbie frowned. Was that wariness, or just him? "Did she tell you she was doing research on a particular person?" Robbie held his breath. Hopefully, Henry could explain this one.

Henry's response was a croak. "A particular person? Who?"

This was it. Robbie barely heard himself saying, "A bomber pilot."

"Why would she be doing that?" Henry's words were shaky.

Robbie proceeded cautiously. "It's kind of, well, weird. And well, I don't know how to explain it without making it sound very... odd. She had me concerned. She got rather obsessed with it, and that's one of the things we argued about."

"Please, Robbie, who was she researching? And why?"

Robbie pictured Beth's pale, pinched face as he'd last seen her. "A Scottish bomber pilot. She was convinced the RAF bomber jacket she had belonged to someone she needed to trace."

"Oh, God!"

He might well have shot Henry. "Mr. Schmidt, Mr. Schmidt? Are you there? Hello? Hello?"

"Yes, yes." Henry sounded to be struggling with his breath. "It's a bit of a shock, you see."

Robbie remembered this man was in his eighties and tried to speak with assurance. "I'm so sorry, I'm sure she's fine. She's a very resourceful young woman, very capable of taking care of herself. I didn't mean to upset you. I just... I wanted to see if I could help her."

"Let me go get her last letter. I'll be right back."

In the few moments it took for Henry to return, Robbie was puzzled over Henry's intense upset at Beth's bomber pilot search. Why did he seem almost frightened? Henry's wartime station, Beth's vivid dreams, her occasional iciness, the bomber jacket... it was all so knotted together...

Henry's words cut in. "Hello, are you still there? It's dated May third."

"That's the last letter? Did she say anything about a trip?" Henry didn't respond. That's a no. "It's very, very odd, you see. She... please don't take this wrong, it sounds very weird, I thought it was weird too, and I think she got really angry with me because I didn't take her seriously, but she said... she said she was... dreaming about him. You know, having dreams, and felt she needed to find out about him. Learn his story." A painful new truth pressed into him. He was so enmeshed in his logical philosophy and distaste for spiritual mumbo-jumbo and dream messages that he dismissed her pilot, not realizing he was also dismissing her. *I wasn't much of a friend or a help to her.*

"Learn... his... story?" Henry's words were halting.

"Well, find out about him, I guess. I'm sorry, I don't mean to worry you..."

"Where are you now, Robbie?" The old man suddenly sounded stronger. Business-like. Robbie collected himself. "I'm at my flat, in Edinburgh."

"Give me your phone number and address. I'm getting the next plane I can and coming there to help you find her. I think I know of some places she might be."

This he definitely didn't see coming. "Oh, no, I think she'd be really upset if you'd do that. I can look for her. Why don't you tell me where you think..."

Henry interrupted forcefully. "No, no. I... it's very important that I come. It's a very long story, and I'll explain it all when I get there.. As soon as I arrange my flight, I'll call you back."

"Are you sure, sir?" Robbie probed cautiously. Perhaps Henry needed to reconsider once the shock wore off. "It's a long way. I feel responsible, and if you tell me where..."

"No, I mean, I appreciate your concern. I have a feeling you care more than you're saying. That maybe there's more than you're saying."

Robbie cleared his throat. "I do care. A great deal." *More than I can put into words.*

They crept back now, moments so small yet so tender they astonished him. Her carefully organizing the papers he so clumsily dumped on her head on the train. Her quirky imitation of a Scottish accent. "Aye, I might be a wee American lassie, but I'm a quick learner."

Her quiet, absorbed face listening to his stories about Da in the glow of soft restaurant lights. The comforting ease of walking arm-in-arm around downtown Edinburgh.

"The students say you make history come alive for them. You're the best history professor on campus," she had told him fervidly, almost surprised this was lost on him.

The giggles she burst into at his expense over the idget clerk on Skye. Her solemn dream—who would've thought he remembered—"to have a little adventure, excitement, travel, discovery, romance. Some day to find someone who finds me attractive, desirable, and stirs my soul."

The warmth of her skin as she leaned in, her face lit on one side by the glow of fire. The deep brown of her eyes. The velvet press of her lips.

"I'm glad that she has had someone there to look after her."

Robbie started, yanked back to the present. "I don't know as I've done such a good job of that, though."

"We'll have a lot to talk about when I get there, Robbie."

"Aye, we will." Robbie suddenly felt so much better. Focused. Here was something to handle and take care of. "By the way, sir, flying into London would be less expensive than coming directly to Edinburgh or Glasgow. I can pick you up there. And..." He paused, remembering. "That Frasier kid did say she'd talked about visiting the Imperial War Museum, which is in London, and some old RAF bases in England."

"Yes, that would make sense, if she... well, I'll see what flight I can get."

Robbie gave Henry his address and telephone numbers at his apartment and the university. Just then, an older woman's voice crackled in the background. "Who are you talking to? What's this address?"

"Not now, Naomi," Henry said in a muffled tone then to Robbie, "I'm sorry, can you repeat that?" He did, and after a moment, Henry continued. "Okay, I have it." He repeated the information slowly. "Yes, yes, okay. I will call you today. Later. Within the next couple hours. What time is it there?"

Robbie checked, "It's nearly half past the hour, four in the afternoon. Call me as soon as you know. I'll stay here in my apartment. I won't go anywhere."

"Call no matter how late it is?"

"No matter how late. And I'm sorry we'll be meeting under these circumstances, but I'm looking forward to making your acquaintance, sir. And I'm sure Beth is fine." Hope was seeping back in. Beth couldn't have gone off to hurt herself, he knew now. Not with someone like Henry in her life. And that phantom of a bomber pilot to hunt down.

Henry's voice was calmer and warm. "Yes, Robbie, it will be good to meet you. Thank you for calling. Talk to you soon."

"You're welcome, sir. Good day till then."

Henry put the phone back on its wall mount. Then he turned to face Naomi, who had taken off her garden gloves and picked up the paper, frowning. "What's this about Beth being fine?"

"It was that Professor Beth met, Dr. McLeod. He said that Beth... that Beth..." Henry again felt anxiety taking over.

"That Beth what? Oh, I know. Let me guess. She's pregnant. Just like her mother."

Rage like he hadn't felt in years seared through Henry's body.

"You horrid, thoughtless woman. How the hell can you say that?"

Naomi's face flushed a mottled red. "Don't you swear at me! You know damn well that going over there was going to come to no good. I told you."

"She isn't pregnant, you stupid woman! She's left school. And he was worried. Wondered if we knew where she is."

"Missing?" Naomi's face lost its flush. "Oh... I... what?"

"He said she went on a trip and..."

"So she went on a trip? That's what she's there for. What does he mean, she's missing?"

"Well, she didn't tell him, and she's not at school, and he's worried."

"Well, if he's worried, let him go look for her!" Naomi was angry now. "And don't you call me stupid, Henry Schmidt. You've deceived me in the past, but I'm not stupid."

Henry walked out of the kitchen toward the stairs.

"Where are you going?" Naomi followed him, shouting. "Come back here!"

"I'm going to see Jim's daughter. The travel agent. And get a ticket to Scotland."

"You are doing what? You will do no such thing. Besides, you have to have a passport, and that takes weeks."

Henry turned and looked at Naomi. "I already have one."

"You what?"

"I've had a passport for years. Always kept it current. Just in case."

"Just in case?"

"Yes, just in case I'd ever need it in a hurry. Like now."

Henry thought Naomi was going to explode but didn't care.

"I'm going to Scotland. I'm going to help Robbie find Beth and I'm going to do what I should have done all those years ago."

Naomi grabbed Henry's arm, squeezing it furiously. "It's always been about her. Always. Always. Well, I can tell you, Henry Schmidt, if you get on that plane to Scotland, you can rest assured that you won't come back here. You're done! I'm done! We're done!"

Henry pried his wife's pinching fingers off his arm. He felt only exhaustion. And regret.

"That's fine, Naomi. If that's the way you want it, that's fine with me."

The British Airways 747 Jumbo Jet coasted its way across the night sky above the Atlantic Ocean. Henry could see nothing from the window seat, just inky black and the steady blinking lights on the wing, reflected against the clouds.

Everything inside the economy class cabin was dimmed and muffled, as though someone had stuffed cotton in his ears and wrapped gauze around his eyes. Most of the passengers were sleeping. It was, after all, midnight. The businessman to his right was snoring lightly, his mouth agape, his seat tilted back. From the front, he heard a fussy child.

The taste of dinner that had been served not long after takeoff still lingered on his tongue... the rich roast beef and the flaky texture of instant mashed potatoes. Overcooked vegetables. A tiny salad. All served in miniature, as though he was to fit his appetite to the shrunken size of the tray and utensils. Naomi would have been horrified and full of complaints.

Not for the first time, he realized how grateful he was to be on this journey alone.

He was hungry. Or maybe it was just fear. There was something in his stomach. Something that defied naming. It agitated back and forth like a washing machine. He shouldn't be excited. He shouldn't be elated. And he shouldn't be awake. But though exhaustion awaited him in London after a sleepless overnight flight, he could not settle his stomach or his mind.

To England. And then to Scotland.

He wondered for the hundredth time since he had talked to that Scottish professor why he had given Beth that list. Why he had left off the most important place. And why he hadn't done as Naomi had said and just burned that stuff in the garage attic.

Instead, he had put the letters and mementos in a safety deposit box so Naomi wouldn't find them again and given away the military clothes fifteen years ago. Who would have imagined...

The cabin was chilly; the Atlantic air seemed to creep through the window glass. Henry looked out into the night again, and in the distance, he thought he could see stars. He pulled the small blanket up to his chin. It seemed very British, like the blanket he'd had on his bed at Drem.

Though the blanket sheltering him against the cold of the cabin was lightweight, it felt heavy, like the weight of promises he had made and broken. Like the lies he had told. And the heartbreak that had followed.

He thought he had left it all behind, escaped his past, but it was all coming back as he sped toward London, where this young Scottish professor would meet him.

They would find Beth. They had to. Soon, so he could tell her the truth before she found out for herself, before he lost her like he had lost everyone else in his life whom he had loved.

He looked out into the dark night, leaning against the window, his breath spreading like a fog across the cold glass. Blurring his reflection.

Like that summer night in 1939. That night he was going to propose.

To Gretchen.

Naomi's sister.

Thirteen

PART 2: 1939-1944

May 1939

HENRY PEERED INTO THE small, white-framed bathroom mirror that hung over the rust-stained pedestal sink. He had opened the tiny window over the tub, dislodging some loose chips of peeling paint, to let out the steam from his bath, but his image was still a foggy reflection of a frowning young man with clear blue eyes straightening a red tie, newly bought for the occasion.

He had been planning this night for months. Agonizing over where to take her. What to say to her. How to put his feelings into words.

He had rehearsed it over and over in his head.

A ray of afternoon sun broke through the clouds into the boarding house's third-floor bathroom. He squinted as its unexpected brilliance bounced off the steamed-up mirror.

What if she doesn't know I'm planning to propose?

His slightly rounded face with its ruddy complexion seemed to waver as if the mirror could see the doubts he refused to consider.

Could I be wrong?

He'd never spoken of love. It had been agonizing to hold his tongue while he waited for her to finish secretarial school this past year, making two trips a month across the Susquehanna River from New

Cumberland to meet her and her friends at some smoke-filled nightclub in Harrisburg.

Gretchen was always chic, classy. You'd never guess that until September she had lived on a farm in southern York County, fifty miles south of Pennsylvania's capital city, where she was enrolled in a one-year program.

Nightclubs weren't his favorite form of entertainment. He would have preferred the cinema or a walk around the city, but the advantage of a nightclub was the chance to hold her close on the rare occasions he could snag her for a slow dance. Respectfully close, of course. The opportunity to feel her slender fingers in his thicker, rougher ones; to savor the sensation of his hand beneath her dimpled elbow, as he escorted her off and onto the floor; to inhale the scent of her lightly floral perfume, like her mother's flower garden on a warm spring day.

At five feet, eight inches, he wasn't much taller than Gretchen, especially when she wore those high heels, but he didn't need to tower over her to lead her smoothly around the dance floor, doing that slow waltz she had taught him when she was sixteen, using him to perfect her steps. Henry knew he was more solid than suave, more ponderous than polished, but he was comfortable with himself. Knew where he belonged.

With Gretchen.

As he put his razor and shaving cream into his shower bag, he pictured her as he'd see her tonight, with her rich, thick chestnut hair that fell in natural waves around her shoulders and her brown eyes flaked with green, which changed color with her moods. Greener when she was angry, browner when she was happy. Her lanky, leggy body, moved with an easy grace.

Tonight was the first time in a year he'd managed to get some time alone with her, away from that rather fast crowd she ran with. Some of the gals got awfully sloshed. Henry was embarrassed for them, but no one else seemed to mind. He was surprised at how well Gretchen could hold her liquor. He had never seen her drink before this year, and it was a shock at first. She even lit up a cigarette occasionally, but nothing like some of those other nicotine fiends.

Henry figured his being there would protect her. Make sure none of the guys got fresh. Not that she couldn't handle them. But once they were married, she'd make new friends. Settled people. Other married couples. At church and all.

At Thanksgiving, Christmas, and Easter breaks, he had driven her home, anticipating the quiet, intimate space of his car as the right place to hint at his feelings. But to his dismay, at each holiday, Gretchen brought her new friend, Fiona Callendar, the girl from Scotland who had come to visit relatives and stayed to attend school. Not that he minded her; of all Gretchen's gang, he liked Fiona the best. She was friendly in a quietly reserved way and never drank to excess.

Of course, Gretchen knows how I feel. Why else would I have spent all those Saturday nights with her and her friends?

As he folded his work clothes and straightened the bathroom, he recalled the first time he met her. She was seven, and he was ten the first year his folks had sent him to help on his uncle's farm near East Berlin, thirty miles west of his home in Lancaster. It was one less mouth for his parents to feed and an extra hand for his uncle, who had only daughters.

His uncle loved having a boy around who liked tinkering with tractor engines and appreciated grease and oil. Gretchen's family lived on the next farm over.

Now she was all grown up.

He had made dinner reservations at The Uptown Room, Harrisburg's swankiest restaurant. Told her to dress up, that he was taking her someplace special to celebrate her upcoming graduation.

"A year of hard work should be rewarded," he'd said.

She had laughed. *"Not that I worked so hard."*

"You didn't need to work hard. You're smart that way."

She gave him one of her dazzling smiles that always made his heart compress, *"Oh, Henry, you're such a flatterer."*

She told him *she* had a big surprise for him. Maybe she had graduated at the top of her class. She *was* smart. Sharp. He wasn't flattering her. Just telling the truth. She could have gone to regular college, but she always joked, *"I don't want to tax my head."*

He was glad she didn't go off to a university. She might have been out of his league then.

That first glance each time he saw her, when he'd been away from her for a while, always startled him and made his breath catch. She was so pretty. *And she's with me,* he'd think, as she would take his arm, toss her hair back with her hand, and give him a peck on the cheek.

Henry, how delicious to see you.

She was so fresh, so unconscious of her beauty or the easy way she walked. Confident. Everyone looked. The men, desiring; the women, envious. She had a zest for living, a glow like she was lit from within. It was an energy she gave off. It did worry him some. Like she was a battery that might wear out after a while.

She needed to be settled. That would be good for her, he was sure. This year in the city after eighteen years on the farm had gone to her head a bit. No surprise. She was still pretty young. Impressionable. Lots of girls got married at nineteen, though.

But he'd give her a year. That's a decent engagement. A year when she could work and not feel like she'd wasted her time at secretarial college. And that'd give him more time to pay on the house he'd picked out. Fix it up some. Make it ready for her. It was a doozy. A cozy little two-story frame house on the east end of New Cumberland, near his job as an airplane mechanic at the Harrisburg-York State Airport. Two bedrooms and a small yard. A home to bring up kids.

Just across the river from the city life she relished.

Henry took one last look in the mirror, now clearing as the cooler outside air filled the bathroom, dissipating the steam. He frowned at his reflection and ran his fingers over his freshly shaven face. But it was Gretchen he saw in the mirror, laughing when he suggested she'd be a great mother.

"Henry, don't be silly. Can you imagine me with babies? What kind of mother would I be?"

He always took her to be joking. After all, she was good around kids, and they loved her. At church picnics and such, they'd trail after her, pleading, "Gretchen, play with us." And she always did, giving herself wholeheartedly to some game, like she was a kid herself.

Next Saturday was her graduation, May 28. She would be getting some awards, he was sure. They'd look nice framed in their little house.

"See, kids," he'd say—he was planning on a bunch of them—*"Your mom's a right smart lady. See these awards. She earned them in college. Yep. Secretarial college. Your mom's real bright. You've got to live up to her example."*

A pounding on the bathroom door startled him from his reverie.

"Schmidt, you gonna spend all night in there? Some of us got plans too, ya know," a husky male voice shouted.

"Right, right," he replied loudly. "Be out in a jiffy."

On his drive to Harrisburg, he rehearsed the words he planned to say to her. *Gretchen, we've known each other for a long time. Twelve years to be exact. Seems like we grew up together.* Now when he said the words in his head, they seemed hollow, stupid. His stomach began to knot. Panic crept into his lungs. The words always seemed so right before.

You're nineteen now. I'm twenty-two. I'm a man, Gretchen. I've got a good job, and you're done with school. You're a woman. A beautiful woman.

As he walked her to the table, she oohed and aahed at the luxury, the upscale refinement, the fabulous orchestra. "Oh, they're playing *Smoke Gets in Your Eyes.* Don't you just love it?"

But Henry was still rehearsing the words, rewriting the script in his head. He barely heard her comments, her laughter. The jeweler he had chosen had special Saturday night hours in May and June. He had planned how he'd tell her that, too. *We can go just down the street. I want it to be your choice. The ring. I've picked out three I think you'll like, but you choose the one that suits you best.*

It was all wrong.

Now that the moment had come, he realized she would want him to get on his knee. Be romantic. Have the ring there. He began to feel lightheaded.

"Henry, what in heaven's name is wrong with you? You look terrible. I don't think you heard a word I said. Take a drink."

He had ordered champagne, an outrageous extravagance, to celebrate her graduation. And his proposal. But nothing was going the way he planned. The champagne was making her giggly and him nauseous. She was chattering on and on about her friend Fiona.

"Well, this is just too fantabulous. I couldn't say before, because it wasn't a done deal. But she said she is sure, rock bottom certain, that it's in the bag. That I've got it."

Henry looked across the starched white tablecloth and glistening silverware. Everything seemed foggy as if he had brought the steamed-up mirror with him, seeing everything in its distorted, hazy reflection.

Gretchen's face was flushed with excitement and wine. Her lips were cherry red, and her eyes were wide and shining. Her red dress was low-cut and clingy and showed off her breathtaking figure. A string of pearls lay in the hollow of her throat.

Through his haze, he could see her beauty but not stop her words.

"Henry, you are so dense sometimes. You never seem to hear a word I say. Where is your mind? Fiona's uncle in Scotland. Scotland! Can you imagine?"

"Her uncle? In Scotland?" he managed to say.

"Oh, Henry where is your head tonight? I just told you! He's got a job. For me! For both of us, actually. I'll stay with them till Fiona and I can get a place of our own. In a flat, she calls it. She said a bunch of us girls there can get a place. I love her accent. I've already booked my passage. We're going to share a cabin. An ocean liner. Ohmigod, isn't it just too much?!"

None of it made sense. His mind was filled with the same haze that was blurring his vision. The same fog from the overheated, dilapidated bathroom where he had been just an hour before.

"But what about our house?" he finally said, struggling to put a sentence together, to see, to hear, to breathe, after her astounding announcement.

Her brow wrinkled in confusion. "What house?"

"The one, the one... in New Cumberland," he said, longing to reach across the table and smooth out those creases on her forehead.

"You're not making any sense. What are you talking about?"

"The house I'm buying for us." He answered too loudly, he realized, by the surprise on her face and the turned heads of the people at the next table.

"For us?" Her brown eyes with their flecks of green grew more intense. The smile left her face. She leaned across the table. "What do you mean, Henry?"

"When we're married, of course," he blurted out.

The look of profound shock on her face told Henry everything he needed to know but hadn't allowed himself to admit. That she had never suspected.

She sat back in her chair, thin, delicate fingers covering her perfect mouth. That mouth he had wanted to kiss for years but never dared. He knew he would see her like this in his mind forever. Staring stunned at him across the table.

"I had no idea... I... it never..." Her eyes filled with tears. And then slowly with anger. She sat silent for a minute, but he knew what was coming. Once she had that look, it wouldn't be long before her ire found words.

"What were you thinking, Henry? That I was going to settle down in a dumpy little town and be a housewife? Now that I have a secretarial degree?" She was working herself into a fine temper, her face flushed. "Throw it all away? Just like that? You know I've always wanted to do something! To see something. To be something. Now I have the chance!"

Some part of his mind remarked that anger did not become her.

"Say something, damn it," she said fiercely.

But Henry could make no reply. His mind had forgotten its script. His tongue had forgotten its purpose.

"Why did you have to ruin this? All these years, and I thought we were pals. That I could trust you. You were never like the other guys. Never grabbing or touching or trying to kiss me." Her words were sharp points, making precise incisions in his heart.

Henry's hands trembled as he drank his champagne in one gulp. He whispered, the bubbles stimulating his tongue, "I respect you."

More people were beginning to glance at them. She didn't notice. Her anger was intensifying. "You were different, Henry. From the time we were kids. Someone I could rely on. A guy friend. And you thought what? That I'd want to marry you?"

The words were punches. He put up his right hand to ward them off, then realizing what he was doing, filled his glass with more champagne and gulped it again.

She picked up her glittering, gold-mesh purse and stood. "I'll call a taxi, Henry."

Others were staring now. The waiter in his formal white jacket and black bowtie was hurrying their way. Henry didn't move. His mind was in the bathroom, where he was straightening his tie. Where there was still time to find the right words. Make it all turn out the way he wanted it.

His anguish must have been apparent, for Gretchen's face suddenly crumpled, the stiffening of anger leaching out.

"Oh, dear Henry, I had no idea," she said, dismay in her voice. She brushed his cheek tenderly with her red-lacquered fingertips as she walked by, the heat of her skin like a scorching iron on his freshly-shaven face.

Later that night, when he looked into the bathroom mirror, he expected to see long, thin, red blisters running the length of his cheek where she had caressed him. But there was only the reflection of his haggard face and stunned eyes.

Henry, he told his image in the mirror, *you are a damn fool.*

Leaning his forehead against the mirror, he began to cry silently, steaming up his reflection with his breath.

Gretchen sat down on the porch swing, grateful for a respite from packing. Her bedroom was sweltering, even with all the windows open. She savored the ice-cold tea, holding the cut-glass tumbler against her cheek, longing for a breeze. It was an unusually steamy June afternoon.

She gazed at the familiar vista, one she had observed from this very spot so many other Sunday afternoons. The long, rutted dirt lane ran between the eighteenth-century brick farmhouse and the faded red bank barn down to the macadam country road. The rolling farmland, undulating south and east, green with promise, which had been in the family for generations. The distant Tuscarora Mountains to the west, foothills of the Appalachians.

Never had she imagined that she would get her opportunity to leave the confining limits of the farm. Tomorrow her father would load her steamer trunk on his flatbed truck and drive her to York, where she would catch the Harrisburg Express. There Fiona would join her for the train ride to New York City and a taxi ride to the dock, where they would catch the RMS *Queen Mary,* the flagship of the Cunard line.

It was stunning to think about, a voyage across the Atlantic to Southampton. They weren't first-class tickets, but tourist class was better than third, according to Fiona. Then a train to London, a short stay with friends of Fiona, and another train to Edinburgh. They'd stay with Fiona's aunt and uncle till they found a flat.

Thank heavens for Fiona! Gretchen never stopped counting her lucky stars that she had befriended the reserved, well-dressed young woman with a funny accent. *Fiona, my ticket to the world. You and Grandpa Dunst.*

Gretchen pictured herself on the ocean liner staring at the Atlantic. She enunciated the words in rhythm with the swing's gentle movement, propelled by her bare toes, their enameled nails matching the newly applied red polish on her fingertips.

The... At... lan... tic. The... At... lan... tic.

She barely heard Naomi come onto the porch. The slap of the screen door hardly registered. Gretchen was leaning against the railing, waving her brightly colored scarf at the hordes of people screaming farewell from the docks. A momentary sadness filled her when she realized no one was waving to her. Only Henry would have come.

The swing creaked as Naomi settled at the other end. "Are you all packed then?"

Gretchen chose to ignore the underlying bitterness. "Almost. Just a few things, yet. It's all so exciting. Hard to leave anything behind, but there's only so much room."

"Yes, of course." The bitterness in Naomi's tone was more distinct.

Gretchen searched for words to express her sympathy that it was she, the younger sister, who got to go to secretarial school. And now to Scotland.

Not that Naomi was the adventuresome type. Gretchen couldn't imagine her older sister wanting to go to secretarial school, let alone taking a job across the Atlantic. She was such a homebody and at twenty-four, practically an old maid. She certainly looked like one, in her frumpy house dresses. She could be a looker though, with her thick hair, similar to Gretchen's but a shade darker. She had a nice, petite figure, and they both had shapely legs, but Naomi never showed off hers. And both their eyes were a lovely woody brown with splashes of green. If Naomi would just smile a bit more, she could be at least... intriguing.

She may as well stay home and help out on the farm. After all, it was Gretchen who had won the scholarship. Between her savings and her part-time job as a waitress, she paid for her room and board. As for the trip abroad, she was using Grandpa Dunst's small legacy, a bit of cash left to her, Naomi, and William, available to them when they graduated from high school. It wasn't her fault that Naomi was too stingy to do anything but save it for a rainy day. Bad times were over. And it was about to be a new decade. Time for new things. Even sixteen-year-old William talked college.

But feeling guilty at her good fortune, said, "Naomi, I'm... sorry."

"Sorry for what? What did you do?" Naomi's tone was accusatory.

"Nothing at all."

"I can't believe Mother and Daddy are letting you go. There's going to be a war. Why would you go where there's going to be a war? If I were Mother and Daddy, I'd..."

"But you aren't, are you? And, anyway, there won't be a war. At least none that will involve us." Gretchen took another sip of her iced tea.

"Maybe not us, but Britain's sure to be drawn in, and you'll be in England."

"I'll be in Scotland. Fiona said Scotland is at the top of England and not to worry. She says England won't go to war. Besides, they're an island."

"Then she's as much of a stupid girl as you are. They just called up their reserves for special training. They're getting ready for a war."

Gretchen took in Naomi's crossed arms and sour frown.

"How do you know, Naomi?"

"I read the papers. I listen to the wireless. I hear Daddy talking to the hired hand."

"Since when do you care about world affairs? You're always up to your elbows in flour."

Naomi made a gravelly sound in her throat but said nothing more.

They sat, an uneasy silence settling. Gretchen was mentally finishing her packing when Naomi said in a more civil tone, "I thought maybe Henry might come. Say goodbye and all. He wasn't at your graduation last week. I was surprised."

Gretchen felt her face grow warm but didn't look at her sister.

"He won't be coming," She tried to sound nonchalant.

"And why not?"

She had worked very hard to forget that night, to erase the anguish in Henry's clear blue eyes, so transparent she thought she knew him to the core. But she was completely mistaken.

"We had words." Gretchen tried to make her voice light, indifferent.

"Words?" There was her sister's censure.

"At dinner the Saturday before my graduation."

"Yes, you had mentioned in a letter that he invited you to some very... what did you call it... *swanky* place."

"It was *very swanky.*" Gretchen tossed her head. "*You* wouldn't have liked it. He ordered *champagne.*"

"Champagne?" Naomi echoed with a tinge of longing.

Some devil in Gretchen made her sneer, "Ever have champagne, NayNay?" using the long-discarded, babyish endearment.

"Of course not. Don't be ridiculous. When would I ever have champagne? I don't get to go out to nightclubs and such. Someone has to *stay* and do the *work.*"

Gretchen refused to rise to Naomi's needling. She was always scolding, always putting a damper on any innocent fun she and Henry had: swinging into the pond on a rope, jumping in the hayloft, hitting the tennis ball against the barn, dancing to 33s on the gramophone. There was always some critical remark, some comment to their mother about how spoiled Gretchen was.

"Did you tell Henry you're sorry?"

Gretchen started, flushing. Had Naomi guessed about that awful night? *Henry wouldn't have told Naomi, would he? No, he hadn't seen her, and besides, I know Henry. He would never tell anyone what happened.*

"Sorry for what?" Gretchen shot back, trying not to sound defensive.

"Well, knowing you, Gretchen, I'm sure it was your fault that you had words."

Losing her battle to rein in her fury at Naomi's know-it-all tone, her voice began trembling. "It was not my fault. He's the one who made a fool of himself. Whatever put it in his mind? I just wanted to cry. He ruined it. Ruined the evening."

Gretchen's eyes filled with tears, remembering the excruciating shock of Henry's proposal and the pain on his face when she turned on him in anger. How callous she had been, how heartless. Uncalled for behavior. But he had taken her completely by surprise. *Marry him? What could he have been thinking?* All these years, he had been like a brother. She never imagined even wanting to kiss him. What had put it in his mind?

Yet as she spoke, Gretchen realized there had been plenty of signs indicating how Henry felt. If she had wanted to see them. She looked up into Naomi's intense stare.

"I can't imagine Henry ever making a fool of himself. He's a very mature young man. Hard working. If he *was* foolish, it was to order champagne and take you out to the nicest restaurant in Harrisburg..." A pause stretched. "How did he make a fool of himself?"

Gretchen looked away, assuming an innocent air.

There was growing venom in Naomi's voice. "He didn't... he couldn't have..."

"Yes, he did," Gretchen spat. "There I was, all excited to tell him about my trip to Scotland, and all he can say is, 'What about our house in New Cumberland?'"

"He asked you to marry him?" Naomi's voice shook.

"Hardly. It wasn't even a proper proposal. I don't even think he had a ring. It was all so queer. So odd. I can't imagine whatever got into him."

"He asked you to marry him?" Naomi seemed unable to comprehend. "He asked you to marry him?"

"Well, he didn't ask, really. He sort of told me. Or assumed. I don't know what it was. I didn't stay to find out."

"What do you mean you didn't stay?" Naomi's shrillness made Gretchen cringe.

"I was shocked. I never expected it. He completely caught me by surprise. I couldn't think of what to do. I got up and left."

Gretchen winced at the words. *Is that what I did? Just left him there in the restaurant? Gretchen, you are heartless.*

Naomi had gone ashen, but her brown eyes were wide and threatening. Gretchen was astonished. She had never seen such a look on her sister's face.

"You... left... him... sitting... there," Naomi said each word like a slap.

Gretchen instinctively pulled back, curling up in the corner of the swing, clutching the glass of iced tea in front of her.

Then she knew. Then she understood why all those times when Henry came from Carlisle for Sunday dinner while Gretchen was still in high school, Naomi would tell their mother that *she* would cook, and do the whole meal, not just the desserts she usually made.

"I'll give you a day off," she'd explain to their grateful mother, and each Sunday that Henry was expected, Naomi made a wonderful dinner and baked fabulous pies and cakes, set the table with Grandma Dunst's willow ware china and cut glass, and put out starched napkins. She was showing off her domestic skills. Trying to impress Henry.

How did she miss it? Naomi was in love with him. *And Henry is in love with me.*

Gretchen didn't realize she had said the words aloud until she felt the sting of an open hand across her cheek.

"You led him on. You must have. Flirted. Played with him. Why else would he have proposed to a chit of a girl like you? You're not even a woman. Just a girl who looks like one."

The shock of Naomi's slap wore off suddenly. Gretchen stood up, glaring at her sister. "I don't want him. He's not my type. You can have him. If you can get him!"

Naomi leaped to her feet. Several inches shorter, she scowled up at Gretchen, then tore the glass of iced tea out of Gretchen's hands, tossing the contents in her face.

Ignoring her sister's gasp of shock, Naomi snarled, "I hope you die of love someday. Die of it! Love somebody who thinks you're worthless. It would serve you right!"

Slamming the tumbler on the floor, shattering glass and scattering ice, Naomi flung the screen door against the wall as she ran into the house. Gretchen could hear her feet pounding up the stairs and the slam of a distant bedroom door.

"Girls, girls, what's going on?" her mother's alarmed voice drifted out to the porch.

Gretchen stood unmoving, her face and dress drenched with sticky wetness as she watched the late afternoon sunlight turn the broken glass shards into prisms that projected tiny rainbows on the wall behind the swing.

Fourteen

September 1939

Shouts from the lower regions of the boarding house woke Henry from a fitful sleep. Lying on the lumpy mattress, he stared at the cracked, plaster ceiling of his small, third-floor bedroom. The smell of Sunday supper drifted up the stairs and crept under the door. Must be near five-thirty.

He came home from work Thursday achy and feverish and went right to bed. His landlady sent up toast, tea, and soup, which he had nibbled between restless bouts of sleep and nightmarish dreams. He declined her offer to fetch the doctor.

Though finally well enough to get up, what was there to fill the long and empty evening ahead?

Henry had kept to himself in the three months since Gretchen cruelly thrust his proposal aside as if insulted by it. Now he was grateful he had moved into a more expensive single room; he couldn't have handled the prodding questions from a nosy roommate.

Not that he ever told the other fellows about Gretchen, let alone his plans to propose. All those Saturday nights when he went out the door, dressed up, they'd razz him, "Where ya goin' Schmidt? Got a girl? Hey, take me along. I'll spot you a brew."

He would just smile and say, "Just going out."

"Betcha got secrets, Henry," Marcus Shute always said, but Henry ignored him. To prevent more prodding, he had continued his habit of leaving the boarding house dressed up two Saturday nights a month. But not for a trip to Harrisburg. Or to see Gretchen.

She was gone. Very far away.

Scotland.

Sometimes he'd just go for a drive, park the car on some back road, and sit, staring at the fields, thinking about those years on his uncle's farm. Or go to a bar where he wasn't known. One weekend a month, he continued to visit his parents in Lancaster, just as he had always done since moving away at eighteen.

More shouts from downstairs caught his attention.

Might as well get up and investigate the kerfuffle. Certainly would beat another long night reading a *Tarzan* novel, going to the cinema alone, or sitting in a smoky, noisy, bar nursing the one beer he never finished, trying to forget her last touch.

Involuntarily, he put his fingertips to his right cheek, feeling the fiery trace of her nails beneath the stubble of his unshaven face and hearing once more her pitying goodbye, "Oh, dear Henry. I had no idea."

Even now, the tone of her voice made him cringe.

With a half-moan that harmonized with the creaking metal springs, he rolled off the narrow bed. First order of business, a bath and a shave, followed by a splash of Old Spice, Gretchen's gift last year at Christmas. He could never shave without thinking about her and had considered pouring it down the drain but never could bring himself to do it.

Thirty minutes later, dressed in tan serge pants and a short-sleeved blue cotton shirt with a button-down collar, he locked his door and ambled down the once-grand mahogany staircase carpeted in a threadbare, faded floral print. In the sitting room, a dozen men of various ages were talking in excited voices.

A thin, wiry young man rushed over to Henry, "It's war. The Brits have gone to war! I knew it. I knew it!"

The words were a punch in his gut. "Are you sure, Marcus?"

"Yeah, yeah," the young man insisted.

"You didn't know it, you damn idiot," Frank, a newer boarder shot back at Marcus. "You said they'd never go to war."

"I'll have none of that cursing in my boarding house, Mr. O'Reilly!" Mrs. Landis, the landlady protested, her round face turning redder than usual. "Surely you can express yourself in ways that don't require taking the Lord's name in vain. And no unruly behavior from you, either, Mr. Shute."

"But I didn't even mention the Lord's name, ma'am," Frank replied in a chastised voice, while Marcus just shrugged.

"Nevertheless, it was implied," Mrs. Landis insisted, sitting up taller in the cracked, leather wingback chair beside the tile-lined fireplace. This was the throne from which she reigned during the evening gatherings, seated next to the waist-high, elegant, dark wood Zenith radio that was her consort. Nearly all of the other boarders were gathered nearby, seated on worn couches and ottomans or leaning against the faded pink Victorian wallpaper.

When Henry had arrived in September, the rotund landlady informed him, "We have conversations in the evenings in the drawing room. We discuss the day's events and what everyone has done to contribute to the good of the country. Of course, we listen to the wireless. Won't have dinnertime disturbed, however. This is a civilized boarding home."

She turned toward Henry, concern on her face. "Mr. Schmidt, are you feeling better?"

"Yes, thank you, ma'am, much better," Henry replied, his mind on a distant land. *But she'd be safe in Scotland, surely. A long way from Germany.* "And thank you for the soup and tea and such you sent up," he said as an afterthought.

"But you've missed supper. Don't think Mable's cleaned up yet. We all rushed in here to catch the six o'clock news."

"I'm fine, ma'am. I'm not a bit hungry. But thank you."

Henry knew things had been looking grim in Europe, though since June, he had tried to ignore the newspapers and avoid the drawing room conversations. When he wasn't working all the overtime he was allowed, he took endless, rambling walks through town, inhabiting his memories rather than his current life.

Though a private person, he was not a naturally solitary man, and his sudden withdrawal was noticed and commented on by coworkers and fellow boarders.

"Whatsamatter, Schmidt? Planning a bank robbery?"

"Nah, betchya it's girl trouble. Always makes a man moody. Women."

"He'll snap out of it. Leave him alone."

"Hey, Henry, my girl's got a friend... ya wanna do the town this weekend with us? She's a looker, believe me."

"Oh yeah, if she's such a looker, what'd she want with Schmidty, here?"

He had shrugged off the comments, entered into the banter long enough to stop the teasing, and returned to his thoughts of Gretchen, constantly replaying that night in his head. What he could have done differently. What other words he might have said. How it might have turned out another way.

He had heard the mechanics and pilots at the airfield discussing Hitler's latest threats, but they all agreed it was Europe's war, not America's. Everyone was more interested in Joe Lewis' latest fight or Lou Gehrig's shocking diagnosis of chronic infantile paralysis.

Henry looked back at Marcus. "But what's this about war?"

"Guess you don't know. You've been locked up in your room. Hope you aren't contagious." Marcus, a bakery helper perpetually chewing gum, tried to fill Henry in on the excitement. "They're going to rebroadcast that Chamberlain guy's announcement at six-thirty."

"That Chamberlain guy is the prime minister of England, you ninny," Frank muttered. A college dropout who worked at the local brewery, Frank prided himself on his knowledge of world news. "He's been an appeaser, you see. He gave away Austria. Then Czechoslovakia. Said it's peace in our time September of '38. Remember?"

"So why declare war now?" Marcus asked.

"Poland," Frank shot back, clearly disgusted with Marcus's ignorance. "They all said they'd come to the defense of Poland. Hitler invaded Friday, the first of September, and they gave the Germans until today to cease and desist, or England would declare war on Germany. And so they did at noon, London time. That was seven o'clock this morning, our time."

"Hitler invaded Poland?" Henry couldn't believe what he missed in one weekend.

"Who said they'd defend Poland?" Marcus asked, ignoring Henry's question.

"Well, Marcus, you clearly know nothing of the world," Frank replied sarcastically. "England and France said, that's who. And now they've got to pay up because Hitler's gone and invaded Poland. With Russia waiting in the wings, no less. They'll be dividing the country up like a loaf of bread. But first, the Krauts are blasting the hell out of Poland with the Wehrmacht."

"Bread? What kind of bread? Is wearmack a kind of bread?" Marcus said at the same time Mrs. Landis growled, "Mr. O'Reilly, your language. I've warned you about your language. This is a Christian boarding house."

Henry's anxiety grew as he listened to this exchange, while Frank continued on his self-appointed task of educating the masses.

"The German Air Force, you dolt. The Wehrmacht. It's Blitzkrieg. Lightning war. Boom, boom, boom, and the Polacks are dead."

"Vatch it thar, O'Reilly," an angry, Polish-accented voice was heard above the babble.

Frank continued unphased. "And now it's war. And Chamberlain's likely to resign, 'cause he had all the Brits convinced that they'd be safe, that Hitler was happy with the Sudetenland and then Czechoslovakia."

Henry, whose grandparents had emigrated from southern Germany in the 1890s, had grown up knowing little about the "old country." His own father, who had been a tiny baby when the family arrived in Lancaster County and settled among the Germans on the "Cabbage Hill" section of Lancaster, refused to speak German to his children. "You're American-born." It was his father who began calling him Henry instead of his given name, Hans, in spite of the fact Henry had been named after his grandfather.

"War," Henry muttered to himself, unable to comprehend it. England is at war, and Gretchen is there. What would that mean for her?

The only news he had of her was an occasional letter from Naomi, who'd first written him the week Gretchen left for Europe, expressing her regret for her sister's cruelty. "She didn't, doesn't deserve you, Henry. She's always been a thoughtless, self-centered chit of a girl. I'm sure now you realize what she's like."

He had cringed at the thought of Gretchen telling her sister about his proposal, making light of it, mocking him. He never imagined she could be so heartless.

Naomi invited him to visit the farm. "I'll be glad to cook your favorite dinner." As if any meal, even Naomi's fabulous cooking, could ease the constant pain in his heart.

He'd sent a brief note praising her as the best cook west of the Susquehanna, but declining, making an excuse about work. "Maybe another time," he had left it.

Naomi had written back saying they'd received a cable from Gretchen, that she'd arrived safely in London. "Typically extravagant of her. Anyone else would just write a letter," Naomi complained. That letter was followed by another several weeks later. "We finally got a letter from Gretchen. More of a note. She could have taken the time to say something more."

To Henry, the news that she loved Scotland, that everything was "fab" and the "lassies" who shared her apartment—flat, they called it—were sweet and welcoming was good news. If he couldn't have her happy in his life, at least he wanted her happy in her own life.

Naomi continued to write, informing him twice a month of news from Gretchen and local updates. She elaborated on how "those incomers from upstate" who had bought his uncle's farm were sprucing it up. Three years ago, in the face of foreclosure, Henry's uncle hanged himself in the barn. His aunt and cousins moved to Pittsburgh and rarely wrote. "He's on. Chamberlain. He's on," someone shouted, drawing Henry's attention. A tense silence fell, and the solemn voice of the prime minister filled the room.

"This morning, the British Ambassador in Berlin handed the German government a final note stating that unless we heard from them by eleven o'clock that they were prepared at once to withdraw their troops from

Poland, a state of war would exist between us. I have to tell you now that no such undertaking has been received, and that consequently, this country is at war with Germany."

Henry heard no more of the speech. All he could think of was Gretchen, longing to hear directly from her that she was safe.

Henry became obsessed with news from Europe. He read the *Harrisburg Patriot* with breakfast. He rejoined the lunchtime chatter at work about the developing war. Every night he rushed through dinner to listen to the six o'clock news. Instead of lying on his bed reading Edgar Rice Burroughs or Jules Verne, he devoured the weekly copies of *Time, Look,* and *Life* purchased at the newsstand.

He listened with alarm as the German rout of Poland and Frank's prediction of the Russian invasion of that unfortunate country came true. Read with awe about the deployment of the British Expeditionary Force to France. Contemplated the horrifying torpedoing of the British ship, the *S.S. Athenia*, jammed with 1,450 Canadian and American travelers trying to get home from Europe, sunk two hundred miles west of the Scottish Hebrides, with the loss of 117 lives.

On Saturdays he traveled to the Harrisburg library, reading the history of Europe, absorbing what he could of the convoluted background of the current conflict. He had never been much for history, seemed too boring as a kid, but now he couldn't get enough of it.

He also spent time talking to Thomas Massey, an older mechanic who had brought his wife and children to the United States from England during the early years of the Depression. The other men thought Thomas was standoffish, but as Henry began asking questions about England, he found Thomas friendly and helpful. He often suggested books to read or authors to pursue.

Thomas even started inviting Henry to dinner once a week, adding a bright spot to Henry's life and expanding his understanding of the British. It was only to Thomas and his wife, Marion, that Henry finally opened up about Gretchen.

In early October, Henry finally accepted Naomi's invitation to Sunday dinner. He wanted to get Gretchen's address. Though he could have just asked for it in a letter, he wanted to see Gretchen's family. They had always been so welcoming, inviting him for a monthly Sunday dinner during the years he lived in Carlisle. Just because his relationship with Gretchen hadn't worked out, that didn't mean he wanted to lose touch with her family.

He wasn't sure if Gretchen had told her parents about his proposal. If he had followed the honorable way of asking Mr. Dunst for permission to marry Gretchen, he might have been warned of her plans, so it was with some trepidation that he made the journey south. But when he arrived that October Sunday, Mr. and Mrs. Dunst greeted him with hugs and handshakes.

Mr. Dunst seemed a bit peaked, but maybe it was the colder weather. The conversation centered on William, who spent most of dinner bragging about his high school football team's undefeated record, due to, according to William, his own particular prowess as the quarterback.

William's parents concurred, though Naomi was unimpressed.

"It's just a game, William."

She was even less impressed by William's new roadster. When he took Henry on a spin down the winding rural roads, Henry learned that William's parents had permitted him to spend his inheritance early, buying a car for his sixteenth birthday.

"Naomi was all put out about it," William told Henry as they sped through the autumn countryside, bejeweled with trees in their fall attire of crimson, orange, and yellow. "She thought it was *shocking*. That's the word she used. *Shocking* that I used good money for such a frivolity."

Henry could hear Naomi's tone.

"She said I should have saved the money for college, but Pop agreed that I'll be getting a football scholarship. He said the way the world is going, I better get my fun in while I can."

Henry was surprised to hear that the stern Pennsylvania Dutch farmer would condone such a thing, but then he figured Mr. Dunst had allowed Gretchen to go to Scotland, so maybe he wasn't as tough as he seemed.

"Oh, Daddy's a pussycat," Gretchen always said. "I can get him to do anything."

Looking back, Henry realized Gretchen was encouraged to do a lot of things, such as play on the girl's tennis and basketball teams and go to secretarial college.

"He said I'm not really cut out to be a farm wife," Gretchen had said. That statement had made Henry's heart drop, but he had thought at the time, *I'm not a farmer. I'm a mechanic.*

When he and William returned from their fevered jaunt, they sat for a while with Naomi and her parents in the parlor. Naomi served pumpkin pie, one of her specialties. Henry made sure to give her lots of compliments about dinner and especially about the dessert.

"Yes, my Naomi will make a fine farmwife," Mr. Dunst said, relaxing in his rocking chair and smoking his pipe, which filled the air with an acridly sweet scent.

"Daddy, stop." Naomi tried to shush her father, blushing.

"No, he's right, Naomi. You're a better cook than I am," Mrs. Dunst remarked. "Why, you just get better all the time. And you're a great help to your father with the paperwork."

Looking at Henry, she continued, "All William thinks about is football, but Naomi will be able to run a farm, not just be a housewife."

Henry said nothing at this.

"You know, Naomi," Mr. Dunst addressed his daughter, "I hear Abram Long is thinking of getting married again."

"Daddy, stop!" This time Naomi's voice carried some anger.

"He's a widower, you see," Naomi's mother said to Henry. "Has the farm in the hollow, down the road. Do you remember the Longs?"

Henry nodded. He had a vague recollection of meeting them when he was at his uncle's farm.

"You're not going to be a farmer, are you, Henry?"

Henry looked at Mr. Dunst, surprised by the question. For some reason, the room seemed unnaturally quiet.

William, so far absorbed by his second piece of pumpkin pie, chimed in. "Henry a farmer? Not on your life. He's an airplane mechanic. That's just the bee's knees."

"The what?" Naomi said, her face suddenly devoid of color.

"Bee's knees. Jive talk."

"Talk like a person, not a jive," Naomi responded with a snarl. "You sound like an idiot."

"Naomi, that's not necessary," Mrs. Dunst chided gently.

To Henry's surprise, Mr. Dunst repeated his question, this time making it sound like a fact. "So, Henry, you're not going to be a farmer, are you."

Four pairs of eyes stared at him.

"I always enjoyed summers on my uncle's farm," he said hesitantly.

"And here, too. You were always willing to lend a hand here, too," Mrs. Dunst piped up.

"Yes. Yes, I was. But... well... I really do like working on engines. I think it was that part of farming I liked best. Keeping the tractor running. My uncle's John Deere, his Studebaker."

"Ever think of being a pilot?" William asked, his mouth full with a last bite of pie.

"Why would Henry want to do such a foolish thing?" Naomi shot back. "He's too sensible for that. Being a mechanic, at least he's safe on the ground."

Henry looked across the room at Naomi, who looked away. Why was she so angry?

"I'm going to join the Navy when I graduate," William bragged.

"Thought you were going to be the big man on campus, Billy." Naomi's voice was filled with sarcasm. "Thought that's why you needed your fancy roadster."

"Naomi," Mrs. Dunst frowned. "Enough."

"I'll go to Annapolis, and then I'll be an officer."

"Well, for now, sail these dishes out to the kitchen," Mrs. Dunst said, laughing at her son.

"That's woman's work," he protested, then dodged his mother's playful swat.

When Naomi stood, her mother said, "No, Naomi, you sit. You made a wonderful dinner. I'll clean up, and William will help."

"I'll do what?" the youngster protested as they walked through the doorway.

"I'm going out for a walk," Mr. Dunst said suddenly to no one in particular and left as well. Henry was relieved. Now he could ask Naomi for Gretchen's address.

Before he could, though, he was surprised when Naomi returned to her father's question. "So, you're giving up farming?"

"Naomi, I never started it," he protested, frustrated at the ongoing interrogation. "I liked the work, the physical work. But I like working with engines. Getting them to run, taking things apart, figuring out the problem, and putting them back together."

"Oh." Her voice was small, still.

"Naomi," he said, taking advantage of the silence, "I was wondering if I could have Gretchen's address."

"Why would you want to write her?" Naomi said, in a tone of such bitterness that it took Henry aback but not as much as her words. "She was so heartless, so cruel. And selfish. And she refuses to come home! Mother and Daddy have begged and begged, but she says it's too dangerous. Dangerous! As if being in England isn't dangerous when they're at war!"

"She's pretty far removed from all that in Scotland, Naomi," Henry replied, trying to convince himself. "And there are U-boats in the North Atlantic, so it is dangerous to travel. Look at what happened to the *Athenia*. It's safer for her to stay there."

"Yes, yes. So happens she's conveniently removed from here, too. Leaves it all to us to do." She jumped up and began to pace in front of the fireplace.

For the first time, Henry noticed her dress. It was a pretty shade of baby blue. He wondered if she was expecting a visit from the widower.

"That's a nice dress, Naomi," he said. "You look good in that color."

Naomi froze in mid-pace. "What did you say?"

Henry was embarrassed by her reaction. "I just said it's a nice dress. A nice color. Did I say something wrong?"

To his astonishment, she burst into tears and ran from the room. He stared at the door, stunned.

In the years he had known her, he'd never seen her cry. Yell. Scold. Be sarcastic. But never cry. At least in front of him. Not knowing what to do, he sat for a while staring into the fireplace. A few minutes later, Mrs. Dunst came in carrying a piece of paper. Henry stood.

"Naomi said you wanted Gretchen's address. She asked me to give it to you."

He nodded, waiting for her to explain Naomi's strange behavior, but she only said the oddest thing. "I never did think you were going to be a farmer."

FIFTEEN

NOVEMBER 1939

WHEN GRETCHEN OPENED HER eyes at seven-fifteen, it was still pitch black outside. It'd be another hour till the sun made its appearance on this morning in late November. The nights were still growing longer, and Scotland winters came early. She curled under her covers, tempted to stay in bed on such a rainy, dreary morning, especially since the bedroom wasn't heated.

Their flat was terribly cute, a fourth-floor walk-up in a converted Georgian townhouse in the New Towne section of Edinburgh. A funny name, Gretchen thought, for houses built in the 1780s. She heard her three roommates bustling about the living room and kitchen, their lilting Scottish accents filling the flat with good cheer and occasional bickering.

"Who wore my red sweater?"

"Where's my scarab bracelet?"

"Fiona, did you see my clutch?"

Gretchen enjoyed sharing her living space with girls who, unlike Naomi, enjoyed life. She yawned again. After years of literally getting up with the chickens, she luxuriated in being the last one to stir. She was happy to take the "late shift" in the bathroom.

The stimulating smell of strong coffee wafted through the open bedroom door. Catriona always put the blue spatterware tin percolator on the tiny two-burner gas stove that filled the small kitchen, along with the tiny icebox, sink, and four-seat rectangular table.

They rationed coffee to one cup each, though Gretchen was permitted two. After all, she had provided the percolator and coffee, two of many practical items she brought with her. Fiona had told her what things would make life more pleasant in Scotland: a set of good knives, linen dishtowels, cocoa, chocolate bars, sheets, towels, and warm clothing.

Gretchen had written for more items, including silk stockings, once the rumor of rationing arose. To her flatmates' delight, her mother constantly sent care packages of tinned goods, flour, sugar, and dried herbs from the garden, convinced Gretchen had nothing to eat.

It had been late June when she and Fiona moved into the flat, already occupied by two of Fiona's friends. Gretchen had thought it was more fitting for two or for a family with one child, but Fiona had said everyone in Scotland lived in small spaces unless you had an estate in the highlands.

Which, to Gretchen's complete astonishment, Fiona's family did.

Gretchen continually thanked her lucky stars that Fiona had not only invited her to Edinburgh but also had gotten her a job in her uncle's wool brokerage office.

"Gretch, ye're gonta be lait," Catriona yelled from the kitchen.

"Nah, I'll be ready in a jiff, Cat."

She heard the slam of the door as Catriona, Fiona, and Eileen headed out. Catriona and Eileen had a longer trolley ride than she did. Fiona, as niece of the company's owner, made it a point to be early, even though she, like Gretchen, had started at entry level in the secretarial pool.

It never took her long to get ready because no matter how late she was out the evening before--even staid Edinburgh had its share of nightspots and handsome men willing to buy a girl a drink or dinner--she made sure that her outfit for the next day was clean and ironed, her hose were runner free, and her shoes were neatly polished.

Gretchen shivered as she eased out of bed and quickly wrapped her long, cotton bathrobe around her, basking in the few minutes of quiet she got each day. She had fifteen minutes to savor the strong, black coffee Catriona had poured for her. Then after a quick but thorough sink bath, she brushed her teeth, combed her hair, and applied just a touch of makeup.

She took five minutes to put on her work attire: silk stockings; high-button, white-collared cotton blouse; slim forest green woolen skirt; plaid cardigan sweater; and low-heeled work shoes, which left enough time to nibble the last scone and eat an apple.

—⋈—

By the time Gretchen returned home, just short of five-thirty, it had been dark for nearly an hour. Fiona had stayed late; Eileen and Catriona would be along in another twenty minutes.

She picked up the mail from the downstairs entrance table, and after climbing the three flights of stairs, turned on the gas light at the entrance to their flat and hung up her coat.

Gretchen never looked to see if there was mail for her. All the letters were the same.

From her mother: *Please Gretchen, come home. Now that England declared war on that maniac Hitler, it's not safe there. Why, we heard they sent all the children out of London. We need you at home. Your father hasn't been well and, oh by the way, William is doing well at school this year as a senior...* or *William made first-string quarterback...*or *William had his picture in the paper after the last game. Here's a clipping.*

Or from Naomi: *Have you had enough of an adventure yet? Father is heartbroken. You are his favorite, as you know. By the way, Henry dropped us a line.*

She rarely replied. There was no sense explaining what they didn't understand—in three months since war was declared, nothing had happened, other than some initial panic involving sandbags, taped-up windows, and air raid drills.

Yes, well, there had been a couple German planes shot down in early September near Edinburgh and that awful U-boat attack at Scapa Flow in the far north in the Orkney Islands. The British Expeditionary Force hadn't even encountered any Germans in France. Some people were calling it the phony war.

As she lay the mail on the kitchen table, she caught a glimpse of her name on an envelope in a familiar, but unwelcome handwriting.

Henry. What could he possibly say?

She hadn't seen him or heard from him since that night in Harrisburg, though Naomi's last letter was full of Henry's visit to the farm: what she'd cooked for him, how they'd chatted in the parlor, and how Henry had complimented her on her new dress.

She'd never told anyone, not even Fiona, that Henry had proposed. Only Naomi knew because she'd finagled it out of her. Since her mother never mentioned it, she assumed that Naomi hadn't told her.

There were times, she admitted to herself, when she missed Henry. He'd always kept the other guys from getting too forward. "Let's dance, Henry," she'd say when one of the other gents had gotten a little too tipsy.

"Sure thing," he'd answer with his soft, gentle voice. He'd take her elbow and escort her onto the floor. Because he had learned to dance so well under her tutelage, she knew it would be a smooth spin, and she wouldn't have to worry about wandering hands or being crushed against a solid chest. Henry held her at a respectable distance.

He had always been attentive but never intrusive, and because of that, she had misinterpreted his feelings. She thought he hung out with her for fun like he did when they were youngsters. Pals. Even now, six months later, thinking of that night got her angry and then distressed, first about his presumption and then the look on his face. She had never, ever wanted to hurt him.

Sighing, she picked up the letter. In her bedroom, she kicked off her shoes and flung off her skirt and blouse. Undoing the tabs on her garter belt, she peeled off her silk stockings then wrapped herself in her robe and sat cross-legged on the bed.

I may as well get this over now before the others come home and ask questions. Eileen and Catriona were fascinated by her family and life in the States. They didn't believe how dull it was compared to here. Occasionally, Fiona would ask if she'd had any news of Henry, and Gretchen would convey whatever Naomi or her mother had written.

"It surprises me that he doesn't write," Fiona remarked once, giving Gretchen a curious look, but Gretchen shrugged and said, "I don't think he's much of a correspondent."

"Really?" Fiona had replied.

Begrudgingly, Gretchen opened Henry's letter.

Dear Gretchen,

Sorry, I haven't written before. Hope you are well there in Scotland.

We've had a lot of overtime at the airfield and I've been happy to take it. Met an English chap there, Thomas—he's American now, brought his family over in the early 30s—we've gotten to be friends. He tells me about life in England; never got to Scotland he says. Too far north.

That's funny, isn't it? He came the whole way across the Atlantic Ocean to live but didn't go to the northern part of his own country. I get to his house about once a week for dinner. His wife's a great cook and he's got two cute kids, a boy and a girl, five and six. Alec and Veronica.

Went to see your family in early October. Everyone is well. Your brother, I'm sure he wrote to tell you, (Gretchen scoffed aloud at the idea of William writing a letter) *bought a 1939 Ford Roadster. It has a removable hard top, cream and purple leather interior, power steering, and power brakes. The engine is fantastic and has a GM 700 R-4 Automatic Overdrive Transmission. A tilt steering column, remote door, and trunk latch. Great chrome. And it's purple. Can you believe that? Purple paint with pin-striping.*

Had a great dinner. Naomi cooked. Your folks invited me for Thanksgiving, which did you know, FDR changed to the third Thursday of November instead of the last. So, this year it's on the 23rd, not the 30th. I had to say no to your folks' invite. My mom wouldn't forgive me if I didn't come back to Lancaster for Thanksgiving to be with the family.

Say hello to Fiona and take care,

Henry

Gretchen turned the single sheet of paper over, scanning for more on the other side, but there was nothing. Stunned, she re-read the letter.

One page. And no mention that he missed her. That he was worried about her. There was a war on, after all. Not a thing about their last dinner. Nothing about his proposal. No declaration of love. Or anything about being sorry for acting like a fool. No, instead he writes about her brother's roadster and some stupid fellow named Thomas. Who would care? She had heard all about the automobile from her mother and Naomi, but not in as much excruciating detail.

Men. Suddenly angry, she crumpled the lightweight sheet of stationery and tossed it across the room, leaning against the wall as she heard the front door slam.

Then she realized the date. Thursday. November 23.

At home, they'd be having Thanksgiving dinner. Or getting it ready, remembering they were five hours behind in the States. Turkey and stuffing. Dried corn. Relish made with whole cranberries and orange peel. Mashed potatoes and gravy. Yams. And, of course, pumpkin, shoofly, and dried apple pies.

For the first time in six months, she was dreadfully homesick. Her eyes teared up.

"Gretchen? Are ye here?" Fiona's voice came from the entryway.

In a moment, the Scottish girl walked into their bedroom. She stopped and picked up Gretchen's carelessly flung clothes and laid them across the foot of the bed. She left the silk stockings lying when she noticed the ball of paper on the floor. Picking it up, she sat on the bed across from Gretchen and smoothed out the letter. Then, looking, up, she saw Gretchen's face.

"Oh, is it bad news, then?" She leaned forward, concern written in her demeanor.

Gretchen shook her head. "It's nothing. Just... I don't know... homesick all of a sudden."

"Who's the letter from that ye tossed it away like that?"

"You can read it. It's nothing."

Fiona frowned but took a moment to read the letter. "Henry? You said he never wrote. Did the letter make you angry? What, your brother got an automobile? Is that it?"

"No. No, nothing like that. It's Thanksgiving at home, today."

"Aye. It's hard to be away from the family at the holidays. We don't have Thanksgiving here. I quite enjoyed it when you took me home last year. But something else is sitting heavy?"

Gretchen rolled her eyes. Fiona was both perceptive and respectfully unobtrusive.

"Is it Henry, then? You know, I dinna believe he's not written before now. And we used to all go out dancin' all those Saturday nights. What fun we had. And what a great dancer. He was quite taken with ye, I think."

When Gretchen didn't reply, Fiona added, "A verra nice fella, that Henry. What did happen that night he took ye out to the fancy nightclub? You came back all in a state, you did. But you never did say."

Fiona looked at the wrinkled paper. "He doesn't even say he misses ye. Does that vex you?"

Gretchen wiped her eyes with the edge of her robe. "Oh, well, if you must know. I've never told anyone. Only my nosy sister wriggled it out of me."

"What? What!"

"That night, oh, I hate to think of it, it was so awful. He, well, he proposed."

"What? And ye never said? Gretchen!" The Scottish girl bounced on the bed.

"Well, he didn't actually propose. He hinted."

"Hinted! How's a fella hint he wants 'ta marry ye?" Fiona's voice brimmed with laughter.

"I was going on about our trip and how excited I was, and he says, out of the clear blue sky, *What about our house in New Cumberland?* So I guess he bought us a house, thinking I was going to marry him."

Gretchen saw Fiona's deep brown eyes widen, but instead of expressing sympathy, Fiona said with a sigh, "How romantic."

"Romantic?" Gretchen protested, flushing. "No. It was humiliating. I mean, I never expected it. It wasn't like that between us. Henry was always, well he was always..."

"There?"

"Yes. Yes. He was always there and he was always..." Fiona waited. "...Safe."

Fiona said nothing, but Gretchen saw the censure in her eyes. "You think I took advantage of him? Used him?"

"He didn't seem to mind, though, did he?" Fiona shrugged.

"I mean, he danced with everyone." Gretchen defended herself. "We weren't a couple."

"Aye, but..."

"But what?"

"All we lassies, we knew Henry was sweet on you. No one even tried to flirt with him."

"No, you're wrong. Everyone was always having a good time."

"I tell ye, Gretchen, a few of those gals had their eyes on your laddie."

"He wasn't mine! He isn't mine!"

"So, I take it ye turned him down?"

Gretchen felt her flush grow brighter. "Yes. And well, I wasn't... very gracious."

Fiona snorted.

"What's so funny?"

"I can just imagine it. Poor Henry." She shook her head.

"Poor Henry? Where's my sympathy?"

"Gretchen, it's hard to have sympathy for a gal who has the fellas fallin' all over her."

Gretchen grunted.

"So, you're miffed because he isn't beggin' ye to come home. To love him and all, eh?"

"Well, it just goes to show he mustn't have really meant it." She knew she was pouting.

Fiona grinned. "So, he's free game, then?"

"What?"

"'Tis it all right if I write to him and take up our acquaintance again?"

Gretchen stared across the bedroom at her flatmate, wondering what she was up to. Maybe Fiona was one of those who was sweet on Henry. "Well... sure... if you want to."

Fiona smiled broadly. "Aye, but havin' such a nice American gent to correspond with, even if he only writes back occasionally, now that's a thing to look forward to. Think how I can brag to all the other lassies at the office and those skinflints at the club."

Gretchen laughed, cheering up immensely. "Speaking of the club, let's go celebrate Thanksgiving Scottish style."

"Aye. But with American gin and tonic, please!" Fiona agreed merrily. "That'll make us thankful!"

Sixteen

April 1940

"'Enry, the phone's for you," Alice said in the Cockney accent Henry found so amusing. Though he had been in London less than a week, Alice and her husband Jonathan made him feel more like a family member than a boarder.

Henry looked up from the Thursday evening paper, filled with the news of the British Navy's expedition to Narvik, Norway, a response to the surprise Nazi invasion of Scandinavia. The petite, middle-aged housewife stood in the doorway of her cozy sitting room, wiping her hands on her striped dishtowel. She had a twinkle in her eyes that made him smile.

"'Ate to get chew up after your log day at the aerodrome, but it's a girl."

Dinner's fried cabbage and sausage suddenly churned in his stomach. There could only be one girl calling him. Well, maybe two.

"Scottish?" he asked, as he got up on wobbly legs, trying to look nonchalant.

Alice tittered. "Oh, blimey, no. It's an American. You got one on both sides of the ocean? Did she follow you here?"

He trailed his landlady to the telephone stand at the bottom of the stairway, where she handed him the receiver, winked, and returned to the kitchen, its swinging door flapping rhythmically behind her. But then, maybe that was the sound of his pounding heart.

He'd been writing to Gretchen weekly since his first letter in early November, one-page missives filled with news of the airport, the characters in the boarding home, his visits to Thomas' family, or trips home to Lancaster.

She had written back only once, a hastily penned note of five truncated sentences: "Thanks for all the notes, Henry. It's sweet of you to write. Sorry, I don't get a chance to reply. Really busy. Working hard."

Her friend Fiona had begun writing in early December—short, cheery letters that eased Henry's mind about Gretchen's welfare. She filled him in on life under the shadow of war, not much different from before the war, except for the rationing and "lots of lads in spiffy uniforms." And from what Fiona said, many of them lined up to squire Gretchen about town.

Henry answered Fiona's letters. It would've been rude not to.

He had written Gretchen in mid-March, telling her about his transfer to Transcontinental's London headquarters but not mentioning the complicated steps it had taken to accomplish that feat. Knowing he might arrive before his letter, he wrote her again once he arrived, including his address in London and, as a hopeful gesture, the phone number.

That was last week.

Once he was settled and could arrange some time off, he could offer to come to Edinburgh to visit her and Fiona. He never imagined that she would contact him. Trying to calm his shaky breath, he put the receiver to his ear, "Hello, this is Henry Schmidt."

"Henry! Oh good glory, it's so lovely to hear your voice!"

Henry put his arm out to brace himself against the wall, closing his eyes and letting her disembodied voice form an image of her in his mind.

"Gretchen. I didn't expect to hear from you," he said in a falsely calm voice.

"You what? You've come the whole way across the Atlantic Ocean, and you didn't think I'd call? What are you doing here? I was so stunned to get your letter!"

"I explained in my first letter. Did you get one or two?"

"Just one. Arrived today. Why does it take a week to get a letter from London?"

"Well, it is 333 miles, as the crow flies."

Gretchen's silky laughter made Henry's head spin. "Only you would know that, Henry. It would probably be faster to send it by fighter pilot. I know a few who'd do me the favor."

Henry didn't doubt that at all. He was momentarily distracted by the thought of Gretchen dancing with some fly boy and missed her next sentence.

"I'm sorry, what did you say?"

"Oh, these English phones. Such bad connections. I said, how long are you staying?"

At first, Henry didn't comprehend Gretchen's question. Did she think he was on vacation? "Oh, it's a permanent transfer. I don't have any plans to go back. Not right away. I told them I'd be here at least a year. Or however long they need me."

"I can't wait to hear all about it. How did you get here?"

"By ship."

"Well, yes, Henry, I guessed that, you ninny. What kind of ship? The Atlantic is so dangerous."

"A British merchant marine. It was a fairly smooth journey," he lied.

"Can't wait to hear about it. How convenient that Fiona and I already planned to come to London next weekend. We're staying with a school chum of hers. The four of us can meet up. Mind escorting three girls around London? We'll go to the most smashing places."

Henry blinked, trying to take it all in.

"We're coming Friday on the *Flying Scotsman*. To King's Cross Station. The 4:10. If it runs on time. Everything's all out of whack these days. Can you meet us there?"

It was hard to put a coherent sentence together once he realized he'd be seeing her in just over a week. "Ah, yes. Sure. Next Friday at the train station."

"Oh, Henry, it'll be so nice to see a face from home. To pal around again. And Fiona's really excited to see you again, too. You'll really like her friend, Lucy, too."

Henry's heart plummeted to his feet. Pal around. But then, what did he expect?

"Ah, yes. Me too."

"Okey dokey! See you next Friday. Bye-bye."

"Bye. Gretchen. I'm really..." But she had already rung off.

Lancaster was the largest town he'd ever lived in, and compared to London, it was a tiny village. London was so disorienting, with the crowded streets and the speeding traffic on the "wrong" side of the road, which required first looking right instead of left before crossing so he didn't step in front of a lorry. Then there was living in a city at war, with huge barrage balloons dangling in the sky, piles of sandbags everywhere, and blackout restrictions.

Meeting Gretchen at the train station meant getting home from work early to shower and change and catching the right bus, then transferring to another through the Friday traffic.

In October Henry had decided he was going to Scotland or England after a German U-boat sank a Royal Navy battleship at Scapa Flow, in the Orkney Islands. Thomas' assurances that Edinburgh was three hundred miles south didn't ease Henry's anxiety. Nor did the idea that Scotland's capital city was three hundred miles north of the English Channel, the twenty-mile-wide barrier between the UK and the German army and air force.

He could never be at peace so far away from her, even if she wouldn't see him.

From the scuttlebutt at the airfield, he'd learned that some American pilots were secretly venturing to England via Canada to volunteer for the Royal Air Force, despite the Neutrality Act which made it illegal for Americans to "aid and abet" a belligerent country. Could result in a possible jail term.

But, he reminded himself, he was a mechanic, not a pilot. So that route wouldn't work.

It was Thomas who suggested a transfer to Transcontinental's London site, where they were short of trained mechanics to maintain the civilian air fleet. Henry's manager gave him a glowing recommendation, though he said, "You're off your rocker. They're at war over there."

Once the transfer was approved, he had to get a passport and permission to work in England from both the U.S. and British embassies. Most Americans had followed instructions to leave England when war was declared on September 3, 1939. There weren't many trying to get into the country. Thomas' cousin in London offered to rent a room with meals.

Thomas also helped Henry figure out how to get there—a job as an engine room mechanic on a British merchant ship from Novia Scotia to Southampton, England. The train trip to Canada was a cakewalk compared with their journey across the churning North Atlantic, infested with U-boats eager to send England-bound merchant ships to the bottom of the sea.

He arrived in mid-April, exhausted from the intense heat of the engine room and the unspoken terror when two ships in their convoy were sunk halfway across the ocean. Everyone lived with the palpable fear of being the next one sent to Davy Jones's locker.

He was glad Fiona was coming with Gretchen. The Scottish girl was witty and charming, her letters fun to read, though she was somewhat reserved in person. He hoped it would seem more like a reunion of friends, rather than a meeting of a rejected suitor with his cherished sweetheart.

By the time the *Flying Scotsman* pulled in, an hour late, his nerves were jittery from all the coffee he drank to fill the time and fight the damp chill of a finicky English spring day.

He spotted her immediately through the clouds of steam rising from the engine. As usual, she was fashionably attired. A heather blue plaid wool suit, with its slim skirt and fitted jacket, showed off her trim figure. A matching beret sat at a perky angle on her dark brown hair. Gretchen was still airy, light, and if possible, even more beautiful.

She greeted him in her old way, "Oh, Henry, dear, how delicious to see you," gave him a light kiss on the cheek, took his arm, and said to Fiona, "Look, it's our Henry." It was as though that night a year ago had never happened.

Fiona tilted her head and smiled, taking his other arm.

After dropping their luggage at Lucy's house, the four of them went out on the town. How his heart survived that weekend, he never knew. He was only able to recall a fog of music, color, and alcohol. All scented with Gretchen's perfume.

A week later, all hell broke loose. The Nazi Blitzkrieg, with its combination of Stuka dive bombers and Panzer tank divisions, rolled across Belgium, Luxembourg, and the Netherlands. When King Leopold III of Belgium surrendered, the British Expeditionary Force and its French allies were cut off and in late May retreated toward the only port remaining open—Dunkirk. There they were trapped.

Henry, along with every citizen of Great Britain, devoured each snippet of information that seeped through the censor's filter into the press and onto the airwaves. When it was over, they learned what happened on that sandy shore of France, barely twenty-nine miles away.

Somehow, in a few days, the British saved 200,000 of their boys and 138,000 more French, Polish, and Belgian troops, ferrying them across the Channel in every kind of floating device they could muster, but leaving more than 50,000 British soldiers and countless allies behind, many dead or wounded from the Luftwaffe's strafing, and the German army took the survivors prisoner.

Fiona's cousin Malcolm, a member of the *1st Royal Scots* disappeared into the haze of war. Wounded, killed, or prisoner, no one knew.

Like others in harm's way, Henry's heart soared as Winston Churchill, named prime minister on May 10, rallied the English to prepare for an impending German invasion.

"We shall defend our island, whatever the cost may be; we shall fight on the beaches, landing grounds, in fields, in streets, and on the hills. We shall never surrender, and even if, which I do not for the moment believe, this island or a large part of it were subjugated and starving, then our empire beyond the seas, armed and guarded by the British Fleet, will carry on the struggle until, in God's good time, the New World, with all its power and might, sets forth to the liberation and rescue of the Old."

As a representative of that New World, Henry set forth on his own liberation and rescue of the Old, taking a job as a civilian ground crew at an RAF airbase east of London. Doing so put him in violation of the Neutrality Act, but he no longer cared. He was going to do his part in the face of the invasion everyone was preparing for.

That didn't come.

Instead, starting in mid-July, there was the dizzying sky dance of British fighter pilots fending off German Messerschmitts intent on destroying the Royal Air Force. Through the bright summer months and into the brilliant days of September, Henry prepped and maintained the Spitfires and Hurricanes that took countless young men, barely out of their teens, into the bullet-riddled skies over the island he now thought of as home.

At night, he drank with them in the pubs as they washed away their gut-wrenching fear with pints of warm ale and youthful bravado, and then the next day, he repaired, refitted, and restored the planes that sent his new friends to their soaring death in the clouds. It was then he began to introduce himself as Henry Smith.

Gretchen and Fiona visited monthly through the summer, bringing a girlfriend or two for a night of dancing and merriment. If Henry could manage a few hours off, they spent the evening with the pilots and ground crew in a nearby tavern. If he managed a rare overnight pass, they went out on the town in London, among the crowds partying as if there were no tomorrow.

The visits helped Henry forget, for a few hours, the mounting toll of lost friends. The burning cities. The droning planes. The dropping bombs. But he could not forget for long. The faces of those young men stayed with him as he worked longer and longer hours to be sure that it wouldn't be the plane's fault if the pilot died.

When the nighttime bombing raids began in London, Henry told the girls to stay in the north where it was safer.

Ironically, the German Air Force's concentration on bombing English cities eased the pressure on the RAF. But that didn't ease the pressure

Henry put on himself. Finally, in late October, he collapsed with exhaustion, which turned into pneumonia and a week in the hospital.

On his release, Gretchen and Fiona took him to Edinburgh, where Fiona's uncle and aunt offered him a place to recuperate. Because he was an American civilian, he was not obligated to return to the English airbase. Thanks to the motherly care of Fiona's aunt, who was silently grieving the unknown fate of her son, Malcolm, Henry was soon on his feet.

With the help of Fiona's uncle, by mid-November, he found work and lodging at Drem Aerodrome, twenty miles east of Edinburgh.

Thus, life settled down into a pattern. Once more he found himself in smoke-filled nightclubs, dancing to the tunes of Tommy Dorsey and Benny Goodman.

With Gretchen. And his heart began to hope.

Again.

SEVENTEEN

DECEMBER 1940

EXCEPT FOR THE INTENSE cold, Henry thought the dim, gray December morning could be mistaken for Eastern Pennsylvania, rather than Eastern Scotland. Even in work slacks and shirt, mechanic's overalls, a fleece-lined jacket, and a cap, Henry wouldn't say he was warm, except for the few minutes each hour when the overhead blowers kicked in and practically melted him if he were directly below them.

His work gloves were too cumbersome for the fine work he was doing on the Hurricane's engine. Blowing on his fingers to warm them, he turned so more natural light fell into the engine compartment. A spotlight would be nice, but Drem rationed its electricity. He tuned out the clang of metal on metal, the roar of another Hurricane in a back corner, and the hiss of welding equipment as someone repaired a Tiger Moth, used for pilot training.

Being the only American on this Scottish airbase, he received resentment at first.

Why the hell aren't you Yanks helping us fight off the Huns? Why did Roosevelt only send some bloody rusty, outdated destroyers?

But once they found out he had been at Biggin Hill during the height of what Churchill called the Battle of Britain, they treated him like a hero.

All the RAF pilots and, by association, the ground crews that kept them flying and fighting during those September days were treated like demi-gods. Lavished with praise by the press, lauded by Churchill with his words, "Never was so much owed by so many to so few," they had, against all odds, fought off the Luftwaffe and turned back Hitler's planned invasion.

Henry felt he was neither an interloper nor a hero. He was a man in a foreign country, caught up in a foreign war, because he couldn't bear to be away from the woman he loved.

The sound of a slamming door and a blast of December wind caught Henry's attention. The air stirred up the smell of oil, gasoline, and stale cigarette smoke permeating the metal Quonset hut, but these were so familiar they rarely registered in Henry's senses.

He retrieved an oily cloth from the back pocket of his grease-stained overalls and wiped his hands on the only clean spot. Stuffing the rag back, he plucked the sweat-stained cap from his head and raked his fingers through his cropped blonde hair.

As he resettled his cap, he noticed an officer crossing the hangar floor towards him. When the new pilot dipped his head in a silent hello, Henry nodded in return. Angular features, pale complexion, and high cheekbones hinted at some Norse ancestry.

After eighteen days at the aerodrome, Henry knew most of the men, a majority of whom were on a three to six-week rotation. The aerodrome was responsible for coastal patrol and was a temporary respite assignment for pilots from RAF bases in England. The latest unit to report was the 258th Squadron, which had arrived on December 4 to join the 607th, both flying Hurricanes.

There was an easy camaraderie between the aircrew and the ground crew, but Henry had learned not to be overtly friendly to new pilots, as class distinctions in British society put him in the lower ranks. Some pilots from titled families let him know it.

"Good day," the man said in a distinct Scottish burr that marked him as hailing from the northern part of the country. Henry was beginning to learn that there was no one Scottish accent. "Getting my plane ready for me?"

"Aye," Henry replied automatically.

"Ye're not from here, are ye?" The Scot looked at Henry intently with dark brown eyes that could be intimidating, despite the pilot's youth.

"You can tell in one word?" Henry chuckled.

"Ach, nay. T'was the way ye nodded your head."A small smile broke the solemnity of the pilot's face, and a gleam in his eye hinted at some drollness.

They both laughed. The pilot took off his dress cap and tucked it under his arm.

"No, that's not it," he contradicted himself. "They said, 'Go check with the Yank and see if your Hurricane is ready.' So I saw there's only two Hurricanes bein' tinkered with, so I figured I'd try the first one. And I figured from your accent, that you must be the Yank."

Henry nodded, warming to the Scot already, almost against his will, and instinctively held out his hand in greeting. He had been wary to make friends with the pilots at Drem, knowing they'd head back south after a couple weeks and possibly die in a fiery crash or drown in the sea. He had kept to himself, spending his spare time reading history, as usual.

"Henry... Smith," he said, using the Anglicized version of his last name, which he had found created less hostility in this land at war with Germany. Unbothered by the grease on Henry's hand, the pilot shook it firmly without hesitation.

"Colin," he introduced himself, then crossed his arms and leaned his broad shoulders against the plane. "MacAuley," he added, "Though if you checked my birth certificate it'd say Domnhall Cailean MacAmhlaigh."

"How on earth do you spell that?" Henry replied, shaking his head in amazement.

Colin complied and added, "As for pronunciation, you fairly well say the beginning and ending of a Gaelic word, but swallow the middle of it."

Henry blurted out, "Well, truth be told, my birth certificate reads Hans Albert Schmidt."

The two men eyed each other. "Been a Yank long?" Colin replied softly.

Henry knew he was referring to family lineage. "My grandfather moved to America in the late 1880s."

Colin nodded. "My clan's been in the western highlands since the thirteenth century. But I'll not hold that against ye."

Henry felt his shoulders relax as he released a chuckle. "I've only been in Scotland a couple weeks, so I've not seen much. What part of the highlands?"

"West highlands. Achiltibuie on the Coigach peninsula. Sure ye've never heard of it."

"No, can't say as I have. Still learning to find my way around East Lothian and Edinburgh." Henry gave the capital it's Scottish "burra" ending.

"Aye, I see ye're larnin' the way to say the names." Colin's formality seemed to be dropping away quickly, which made Henry warm to him even more.

"Aye," Henry replied, and they both laughed. Henry liked Colin's down-to-earth way.

"So why are ye here... at Drem?" Colin asked.

Henry shrugged. "Fixing airplanes."

"Yanks aren't in the war."

"They would be if they'd seen what I've seen," Henry replied with uncharacteristic ferocity. He stared back at the Scot.

Colin nodded. "You've been in the south, I hear."

At Henry's surprised look, Colin smiled wryly. " 'Tis a small place, an aerodrome, and though I've only just arrived, I've already been given all the scuttlebutt. And a Yank 'tis a rare thing, let alone a Yank fixing RAF planes, so you come up fairly soon in the conversation."

Henry shrugged again. "You with the 607th?"

"Temporarily. Until my unit, the 603rd out of Edinburgh, comes north on rotation," Colin replied. "I'm just off extended leave. So we're both outsiders."

"How's that?" Henry asked, confused. "You're the native."

"Most of the Highlanders are in the Royal Guard, or those that grew up on the water in the Royal Navy. Like my brother. Not too many of us took to the air, in spite of livin' in high places. How long have you been here?"

"Nearly three weeks, actually."

"Well then, that makes you an old timer," Colin replied, the smile leaving his face, "especially with what you've seen."

Henry nodded. "Aye," he said, then brightened, "I can show you around, sir."

Colin nodded. "Thanks for the offer, but I've been to Drem before, while I was at university. Belonged to the Flying Club. That's how I learned to fly. Before the war. By the way, ye're not RAF. Don't have to call me sir."

"It's part of the job. Respect and all."

"Well, don't call me sir when we're alone," Colin growled.

"No sir, sir," Henry replied with a straight face.

Colin grinned in return. "Cheeky Yank. Want to grab some lunch?"

"Sure, the Parachute Café does a decent fry-up."

———※———

The first time Colin saw an airplane, he was seven years old.

Colin's father promised a surprise on the last day of their visit to the aunts, uncles, and cousins on the Isle of Lewis, a ferry ride off the west coast of Scotland. He couldn't imagine what could be any more of a surprise than seeing the Bronze Age Callanish stones standing like tall, stiff sentinels on the flat inland plain—Scotland's less famous version of Stonehenge.

The ride on land had been an all-day venture in the back of wagons that jolted and jarred over the rutted dirt road. With the kindling they brought, they lit a fire to roast the basket of clams, fish, and crabs caught first thing in the morning on the shore near their uncle's croft. Colin's brother and sisters were content to play tag and hide-and-seek with their cousins in the shadow of the standing stones. But Colin ignored them and walked slowly between each stone, staring up at its straight, towering edges, touching the strange, pagan carvings.

"They say Merlin put these here, they did," his Uncle Niall teased him.

"Bosh," Colin's father replied. "Don't be filling the boy's head with such nonsense. This is the twentieth century, now. 'Tis a modern age. We need to teach him to be a man of science."

"Science?" His Uncle Niall had laughed. "And what need of science will ye have in the west of Scotland and these islands here?"

"The science that will help us get better crops. The science of agriculture."

"Seems the lad is more into archeology, Bryan, the way he's eyein' up those stanes."

Colin had a taste of a different science on Monday when his parents and siblings visited the new aerodrome in Stornoway.

A distant cousin of his father, Matthew MacGuire, ran a single-plane airfreight service from the islands of Lewis and Harris to the isle of Orkney in the north, and the mainland city of Inverness. Colin's da told them Matthew had been in the Royal Air Corp during the Great War.

Colin's first glimpse of the airplane astounded him. A brilliant red, it stood next to the hangar at the end of the dirt runway. He had seen pictures of airplanes in magazines and newspapers, but it wasn't like seeing one in person. Colin stared, afraid to go closer. He felt a need to touch, to feel, to make sure it wasn't something he was imagining, the same need the stones had inspired. The need to be right next to it, to see the rivets in the wings and the tread in the tires. It was enough to make him jittery.

He imagined, unlike the stones—a substance he was well familiar with living in the rocky coastal uplands—the airplane would crumple under his touch, like the delicate wings of a moth that he once tried to free from its cocoon.

His older brother, at thirteen, seemed to think he needed no one's permission for a closer look and got a sharp reprimand from his father when he tried to climb into the cockpit. "Alasdair, get yourself back here and mind yer manners, lad." Colin hadn't moved a step from his father's side, though he nearly shook from the need to get closer, to touch.

When Matthew MacGuire chuckled, "Come on. I know ye're dyin' to see it up close," Colin looked at his father for permission. At his father's nod, Colin walked to the plane with the pilot, who picked him up and walked him all around it, explaining the purpose of the rudder, how the propeller worked, and how long it took to take off.

"It's a refitted Avro biplane fighter with enough room for a pilot, a passenger in the seat in front of him, and some freight behind. Made for short runs."

Colin listened enraptured, while Alasdair trailed behind, stormy-faced. Then the pilot said something that made Colin's stomach wrench with possibility. "Would ye like ta see inside her now, sit in the pilot's seat, and get the feel of 'er?"

Colin looked around for his da. He probably needed permission for such a profound step, but MacGuire just laughed. "Your da is busy talkin'. Come on now."

Helping him climb up the stepladder to the cockpit, he boosted Colin in, sitting him in the pilot's seat, where all Colin could see were dials and handles. Awash in the smell of engine oil and gasoline, Colin listened carefully as MacGuire pointed out the controls and let him put his hands on the joystick, explaining how it was used to control the airplane.

"I'd take ye up, mind ye, but I'm on a schedule, ye ken, so another time, maybe."

The man laughed as Colin just stared at him. "I know. I see the fever. I know the bug 'ats' bitin' ye. It'll happen, mind ye. Ye've got a bit of growin' up ta do ferst."

Wordless, Colin didn't begrudge being hoisted out and replaced by his brother, who had been clamoring to have his turn. When he watched the plane taxi down the runway and take off toward Inverness, Colin's mind swirled with new sounds as well as new hopes.

On the ferry ride back to Ullapool on the Western coast of Scotland, his stomach heaving and roiling with the choppy Minch Strait, Colin pictured himself flying above the wild seas, over the mountains of Stac Polly, Cul Mor, and Cul Beag. Over the mainland, down into England, and across the Channel to the distant lands of the Continent.

Someday, he vowed to himself, *Someday, I'll be a pilot.*

But it wasn't a wish he said aloud, for his future was laid out before him, as it had been for his father and grandfather, back generation after generation—laird, leader, farmer, fisherman.

Tied to the land, not soaring above it.

———⟆⟆———

On New Year's Eve, the enthralling beat of swing music filled Colin's ears as he walked out of the rainy night into the chilly hangar. Through the magic possessed by the local civilians, a corner of the large, cavernous space had been turned into a dance hall. Spitfires and Hurricanes had been rolled out of the way, some out onto the tarmac, replaced by a recently constructed stage, currently occupied by a band possessing the musical verve, if not the expertise, of a Glenn Miller or Gene Kruppa ensemble.

A huge Union Jack hung on the wall behind the stage, and a large net of colorful balloons was suspended over it, along with a banner that read, "Welcome, 1941." The flag with the blue and white cross of St. Andrew stood gallantly to the right of the orchestra, reminding everyone that this RAF station was located in a Scottish town. On the left were the unit flags of the squadrons currently based at Drem, the 43rd and the 603rd, his unit, flying Spitfires, which had arrived on December 12. The other units had returned south.

In front of the stage, a temporary wooden dance floor had been laid over part of the cement, covering the oil stains, grease puddles, and wheel tracks, though at this moment, very little of the dance floor could be seen beneath the crowd of uniformed airmen and WAFFs and young local women in their party finest. The dancers jived with abandon to the rhythmic American music that seemed oddly jarring to Colin, who usually celebrated New Year's Eve, or Hogmanay in Gaelic, with a traditional Highland cèilidh filled with pipe and fiddle music and energetic Scottish country dances.

Rectangular folding tables brought in from the mess hall and briefing rooms were arranged randomly on two sides of the dance floor, each table surrounded by ten wooden folding chairs. The tables were covered with white starched cloths that fell in flowing folds to the floor, reminding Colin of Father McNichol's robes.

Square linen napkins in rich colors were laid diagonally along the center of each table forming diamonds of color: the purple of Lent, the red of Pentecost, and the green of Ordinary Time, strangely liturgical in theme, Colin thought, for so Protestant a place as East Lothian. Colin imagined that every linen closet in the shire had been emptied in this effort. On each diamond of linen, a votive candle in a small crystal tumbler gave off soft, flickering light.

The transformation confirmed his amazement at the organizational power of a group of civilians, mostly women, who were determined to help their boys forget for one night what lay in wait for them beyond the converted hangar. No one cared that the rain had crystallized into a driving sleet, which pinged in tiny shards on the roof, or paid any attention to the gusts of wind rattling the metal sides of the hangar.

Fresh-cut pine boughs on the tables and hanging from the metal roof supports filled the air with the scent of Christmas and filled Colin's mind with an image of the pine forest on the hills above Achiltibuie. He could almost feel his feet crunching on the long, narrow path that climbed to the lookout point over Badentarbat Bay and hear the tall, straight Scots pines, which grew sparsely on the western hills, rustling in the brisk breeze.

From that lookout, he could see his house, where his ill father writhed in pain, his mother and sisters trying to be brave when he left for Drem to join his former University schoolmates and their RAF squadron as it rotated north on a short respite from southern England.

But the noise in the hangar infiltrated his mind, and the throbbing music of "Lady Be Good," played like Artie Shaw's orchestra, distracted his thoughts. Around the room, the light from the crystal tumblers seemed to jump and jitter to the beat. Cigarette smoke hung like the mist on Mount Suilven on a fall morning.

At the far reaches of the temporary dance hall, the older officers, local dignitaries, and matronly townswomen lingered, providing a pretense of chaperones. Watching most likely, Colin thought, to be sure the local Scottish lassies weren't besmirched by contact with too many drunken airmen, especially the English ones.

Colin headed to the temporary bar, a set of long tables littered with bottles of every possible shape, size, and inebriating content, another amazing collection that probably came from the storerooms of the East Lothian residents. Several airmen were manning the tables with the willing help of some local girls. Just as he stopped for a dram of whiskey, the band took a break. Spying several of his mates with girls in tow heading toward a table, he threaded his way through the crowd to join them.

That's when he saw her.

Rich, thick, chestnut hair tumbled to her shoulders in waves, reflecting the glowing light from votive candles in the middle of the table. Her china-smooth cheeks were pink with enthusiasm, her lips were painted a sultry red. She wore a fitted, low-cut evening dress in a silky pine green set off by a luminescent pearl necklace from which dangled a ruby-red stone that caught the light, twinkling like the warning beacon atop the nearby hill of Traprain Law.

No, she was a light from the Achiltibuie lighthouse or a homing beacon along the Firth of Forth...something beautiful that reminded him to return from his flight among the clouds and the stars, but dangerously distracting if he flew too close to it. She seemed made of ivory and cream, unlike the Scots girls he knew, especially the Highland Scots girls with their ruddy complexions and outdoor ways, their capable hands and reticent looks.

She must have felt his stare, for she turned her hazel eyes toward him. They widened, almost in surprise. Colin felt a wrench in his stomach, an odd sensation of weightlessness, similar to the exhilaration that flight always gave him. Her smile faded, but her look intensified. For a moment he allowed himself to be lost in that look, even though he knew he shouldn't.

A warmth that had nothing to do with his whiskey began creeping along his veins.

She was Henry's girl.

In the three weeks that Colin and Henry had known each other, they had formed a steady friendship, and Henry gradually told Colin the convoluted story of his relationship with Gretchen: his proposal, her move to Scotland, Henry's transfer to London and eventual volunteer work at Biggin Hill, and Gretchen's consistent treks to London with her Scottish friend, Fiona.

"It wasn't me she came to see, though. It was really to enjoy the nightlife," Henry said, but Colin wondered. There was plenty of nightlife in Edinburgh; one didn't have to go to London for it, but then, Edinburgh certainly wasn't London.

Henry explained Fiona's role in his recuperation from pneumonia and arrival at Drem. Colin suspected Henry's real motive was to be closer to Gretchen, though Henry insisted he and Gretchen were just friends, and that he regretted his foolish marriage proposal.

"Whatever you do, don't call her my girlfriend. Because she isn't," Henry insisted earlier in the day when he said Gretchen and her roommates were coming to the dance.

Colin first met Gretchen right after he encountered Henry in the hangar. Colin had a six-hour pass, and Henry arranged for them to have dinner in Edinburgh with Gretchen and Fiona. At the first encounter, he immediately understood Henry's infatuation. Though Henry said he had no claim on Gretchen and often introduced her to other crew members, Colin knew the depths of Henry's feelings.

He had considered making an excuse not to come to the hangar dance but, other than faking illness, could not think of one. So here he was, determined not to be a moth to Gretchen's flame. He couldn't do that to Henry.

———— ✠ ————

Well after midnight, when the band announced the last slow number, Gretchen knew if she was going to dance with Colin, she would have to ask him. He had danced with every other girl at the table but exchanged only a few polite words with her.

He already thinks I'm forward, so why try to change his opinion now, Gretchen thought as she walked up to him and said, in a light, flirtatious manner, "You've danced with everyone but me, Colin. Don't be rude."

"Yes, go on, Colin," Henry urged. "She won't step on your feet."

Gretchen smiled at Henry's joke and waited for Colin to stand. For one moment, she thought he might say no. Or that Henry should dance with her. But he stood and followed her silently to the dance floor. She turned around and waited for him to take her in his arms, something she'd been longing for since the moment she met him.

Since Henry had been at Drem, she and Fiona had met up several times for drinks or dancing with Henry and some pilot or mechanic he knew, no one claiming to be with anyone. She thought there might be something between Henry and Fiona, as they had continued their correspondence once Henry came to London, and Fiona had suggested Henry come to Edinburgh to recuperate. But if there was something, neither Henry nor Fiona was saying.

He was a dear, and she cared about him, but there was no spark, no flame that lit in her when he was near, just pleased contentment that her childhood friend, her champion, was in her world again. She was amused by the men he introduced to her. They were always polite, friendly, and fun, but never forward. She wondered if there was some test they had to pass to meet Henry's standards. She knew he was still trying to protect her. Oh, sweet and comforting Henry. She hoped he had gotten over his infatuation with her.

She loved to flirt but never took any of her admirers seriously. She had yet to meet one she would give up the others for. She enjoyed her freedom, plus she had watched many of her Scottish girlfriends be shattered when their beaus went off to war and didn't come back.

She wasn't even sure what attracted her to Colin. He was nice-looking, but nothing spectacular, though she could imagine him in a kilt and had found herself blushing at the idea. He was lean, trim, muscular, and athletic. She admired his finely shaped fingers and wondered if he played the piano. He had a way of looking at her intensely that she found unnerving yet captivating.

Henry told her Colin had just celebrated his twentieth birthday. Though he was warm and friendly to Fiona and bantered easily with Henry, from the moment she met him, he was cooly distant. It puzzled, confused, and fascinated her. She wasn't used to being treated indifferently. Since that night they met, she had found herself thinking of him at odd moments, anticipating the New Year's Eve dance. Imagining herself dancing with him.

And now the moment was here.

He took her right hand in his left and placed his other hand on her waist, formally, stiffly, holding her at a distance. But before he could stop her, Gretchen crossed the inches of empty space, filling it with her body. Reaching out slowly, she brought her left hand up to his shoulder, splaying her lacquered fingertips just a hair's breadth from his neck.

They rested there so softly, so gently, that he could not have possibly felt them underneath the cotton thickness of his uniform coat, but she saw him wince for a fragment of a second then flatten his expression to neutral alertness. In spite of his utter stillness, she knew he was affected by her nearness, for she could see his pulse beating in his neck and saw a flush begin to creep up his neck, staining his cheeks.

Though he was a good four inches taller, Gretchen stood just below eye level with him in her strappy, three-inch heels, the envy of all her Scottish girlfriends. She smiled warmly up at him while he stared back with his indecipherable brown eyes, as though challenging her to break through his reserve.

She leaned against him, putting her lips to his ear, and whispered, "All I want is a dance."

He blinked once, then with an excruciatingly slow movement pulled her solidly against his lean, muscular body.

Gretchen, her smile shaky now, continued to look at him directly, beginning to lose herself in his eyes, as deep as a northern loch.

"I'm not verra good at these modern dances," he muttered, then made a lie of his words by suddenly and smoothly sweeping her into an accomplished, disciplined three-corner waltz step that meshed perfectly with the throbbing notes of the "Moonlight Serenade."

Gretchen sighed, relaxing, and let him lead her expertly. Closing her eyes, she lightly rested her right temple against his and gave herself up to the fluid movement of his body.

Two days later, Colin eased himself into the pilot's seat of his newly assigned Spitfire, thrilled for the step up from the clunkier Hurricane. He began the preflight sequence of tests and checks that were so much a part of his life that he did it without thinking.

Automatic pilot. The words made him frown. That's what Gretchen said to him at the end of the dance. "Sometimes you act like you're the one that's on automatic pilot, instead of your plane."

As he and Pearson went through the engine check, listening for any sound, hum, or pitch that would give a hint of something wrong, roaring filled his ears.

He tried to think only of this moment. To do anything else was dangerous, even fatal.

Check.

Yet the scent of her perfume lingered in his senses, mingling with the pungent tang of gasoline and engine oil so that the gasoline seemed to hint at flowers and the oil of fruit. He sniffed suddenly to clear it of her smell, clear his head of this distraction.

Check.

Instead of Pearson's Brighton accent through his earphones, he heard her whisper, felt her breath on his ear as she said, "All I want is a dance." But she wanted much more; he had seen it in her green-flecked eyes. Her image hovered before him. She could never be his. It was Henry who loved her.

Henry, who had become the closest friend he had made since boyhood, broke through Colin's natural reserve with his genuine good-heartedness, his quiet, easygoing nature, his willingness to always do what was needed. Henry had come thousands of miles across the treacherous U-boat-filled North Atlantic to be near a girl who didn't even love him.

"No."

"What?" Pearson's voice shouted in his earpiece, startled. "No what, sir?"

"No possibility," Colin replied, still hearing Gretchen's unspoken invitation for something more than a dance.

"Of what, sir? No possibility of what?" Pearson's alarmed voice finally penetrated.

Looking down into his flight director's concerned face, Colin realized it was already too late. Too late to say no, for she had penetrated his mind, his thoughts, his sense of separateness.

With deliberate mental effort, he pictured escorting her to a room and shutting her in, locking the door despite her pleading voice and her tempting eyes. It would be the only way he could survive this duty flight, and all the flights that had yet to come, until this unending war would be over, however and whenever that might be.

And then she would be gone, back to America. Relieving him of the immediate danger of her presence but leaving him lost and his life empty.

EIGHTEEN

FEBRUARY 1941

IN THE MONTH SINCE the New Year's Eve dance, those moments with Colin seeped into Gretchen's consciousness at unexpected times.

She would feel his firm shoulder under her palm, his warm hand enveloping hers, his pulse beating where her temple rested against his. She would hear his polite but distant voice saying, "So I've danced with ye, Gretchen. Is that enough?" And see the look of surprised wariness at her reply, "Not nearly enough, Colin, but it's a beginning."

Lost in memory, her fingers hovered over the typewriter keys until the teasing voice of another secretary punctured the memory, and it seeped away, like a tire with a slow leak.

Henry had twice ventured to Edinburgh with someone other than Colin, as Colin had either volunteered for an extra op or just come off a long gig.

When Gretchen was politely indifferent to the men, Fiona remarked, "Gretchen, what's ailing ye? Have you lost your touch?"

On a Saturday in early February, she and Fiona took a bus to meet Henry for dinner at the Gullane Royal Arms, in a town two miles from Drem where many of the pilot officers were billeted. To Gretchen's delight, Colin was at the bar with Henry.

Colin merely nodded at her but gave Fiona a friendly smile and hello.

To cover her irritation, she stroked Colin's arm, "Why don't you join us for dinner, Colin, otherwise we'll be dive-bombed by these other flyboys. Right, Fiona?" The man practically flinched at her touch but acquiesced. Dinner was full of bantering conversation, yet Gretchen noticed Colin was pointedly reserved toward her.

Before dessert, he said he had an early morning op and left.

Before the band started playing, and he would be forced to dance with me again, Gretchen thought. She wasn't used to men, American, English, or Scottish, being indifferent when she turned on the charm. *I'll just have to work a little harder on this one.*

Her opportunity came several weeks later.

Fiona had organized a sightseeing visit to Stirling, which, like Edinburgh, had a castle dominating its skyline. Through her uncle she also arranged a tour of the nearby William Wallace Monument, closed since the war began.

Henry was excited to see this iconic attraction, built in the Victorian days. "I've invited Colin," Henry told Gretchen. "He finds my enthusiasm for Scottish history amusing but graciously takes time to share his knowledge."

Here's a way to gain Colin's attention, Gretchen perked up. *I could be more interested in local history, like Henry.*

At the last moment, Henry was scheduled for duty. Concerned the Jerries might take advantage of the first extended stretch of cloudless weather in weeks, the Wing Commander put more pilots on coastal patrol. And thus, more ground crew.

Just off a long stint of ops, Colin was allowed to stand down.

"I told Colin you and Fiona would be really disappointed if you didn't get to go," Henry told Gretchen by phone Friday. "Especially since Fiona finagled it through her uncle. Plus, I already arranged to borrow a car. Colin will pick you up at nine like we'd planned."

"I'm sorry you can't come, Henry, but I promise to pay strict attention and tell you everything I see," Gretchen replied in a serious tone.

Henry laughed. "Sure, Gretchen. I know how you *love* history. But this will give you a chance to get to know Colin better. Once you get to know him, you'll like him as much as I do."

Maybe Colin would be friendlier if it was just Fiona and me. It'll be obvious if he isn't.

Saturday morning, Fiona woke with a miserable cold. "It's all been arranged, so just go," she told Gretchen through her sniffles. "I feel bad for Henry, though. He's really into Scottish history. Tis a pity it isn't Colin who's on duty and Henry free, so the two of you could spend a wee bit of time together."

"We do spend lots of time together, Fiona," Gretchen protested mildly, trying to hide her delight at the opportunity for a day alone with Colin.

"Aye, but not just the two of you. We're always a foursome."

Gretchen rolled her eyes. "What's wrong with that, Fiona? Besides, I've told you dozens of times, Henry is just a pal. It's nice to have someone from home around, but I think he spends so much time with us because of you."

Fiona snorted, which sent her into a coughing jag. "Well," she said when she was able to talk again, "enjoy your time with Colin."

"Oh, I'll try. He can be such a prig. I'm sort of dreading it," Gretchen made an effort to sound put out.

"Right-O," Fiona smirked. "You just hate the thought of spendin' a day with a dashing RAF pilot."

"I can think of others I'd rather spend the day with," Gretchen said, shrugging. "I'm doing it as a favor for Henry."

To which Fiona chuckled.

When Colin pulled up in a sporty blue coupe, attired in a dress uniform, the custom of most off-duty officers, she thought he looked particularly dashing.

"Good morning," she said brightly, turning on her full charm.

"Where's Fiona?" He frowned at her.

"She woke up with a bad cold and can't come." She tried to sound sympathetic.

Colin replied abruptly, "We should cancel. She's the one expected. We're just guests."

Struggling to hide her hurt feelings, Gretchen replied sharply, "It's all arranged, Colin. I think Fiona's uncle would be put out if we didn't show up. He's organized a guide to open the museum for us. And I promised Henry that I would tell him all about it."

With a grunt, Colin said, "Well, fine, then. We may as well be on the way."

Colin was sullenly uncommunicative as they headed toward Stirling, a ninety-minute winding journey through the countryside northwest of Edinburgh. Gretchen tried to start a conversation by asking about his ops and his ground crew but got only perfunctory answers. She switched to questions about his family but learned only that he had an older brother, Alasdair, who was in the Navy, two older sisters, Margret and Catriona, and a younger sister, Màiri.

Tired of his vague indifference, she tried chattering about her roommates and her job. When he said nothing more than, "um" or "uh-huh," she gave up and just looked out the window at the small farms and villages they passed. Through the car window, Gretchen saw wisps of clouds stretched out like gauze across the bright, blue sky. Despite the disappointment at her forbidding Scots companion, she smiled at the sight.

Although it was late February, there was a welcome hint of spring in the air. Everyone said the winter of 1940-41 was the coldest one on record. It was certainly the coldest she had ever known, especially with the Scots' strange aversion to central heat. As they rounded a corner in the road, she glimpsed a tall tower on the hill ahead protruding above the leafless trees and strained to see through the windshield.

"Is that the Wallace Monument?" she asked.

"Aye."

"I'm glad I wore my walking shoes and trousers. Are there a lot of stairs?"

"Aye."

Gretchen sighed inwardly.

"You know," Colin said, "most historical sites and museums closed at the start of the war, and a lot of artwork and artifacts have been stashed away in hidden places. Fiona must know people to arrange this. Too bad she can't be here to appreciate it."

"Yes, it is too bad." Gretchen agreed, beginning to think Colin would never warm to her. Though he opened her car door, helped her out, escorted her up the steep approach, and held her elbow as they mounted several flights of stairs that led to the flat patio area fronting the tower's entrance, Gretchen sensed only polite indifference.

A gray-haired man with stooped shoulders greeted them at the door. "'Tis this all of your party, then? I was told there was to be four," he said in a strong highland brogue which Gretchen struggled to understand.

"My roommate Fiona came down with a fever this morning, and our friend Henry was put on the duty roster this morning," she explained.

The guide seemed put out until Colin had a brief conversation with him in Gaelic, which slowly made him smile. Gretchen was intrigued to hear Colin speak his native tongue. Occasionally catching her roommates conversing in Gaelic was pleasant, their tones rising and falling like music, but she never paid that much attention before. Lilting was how she'd heard it described. Listening closely now, she was surprisedly delighted to hear hard, drawn-out k sounds and emphatic g's, like someone coughing. Oddly, it reminded her of the Pennsylvania Dutch dialect of German spoken by older Amish and Mennonites on the farms around her own.

He noticed her smile. "What is it?"

"I've never heard you speak Gaelic before. It's quite a lovely sounding language."

That made the guide smile. He proceeded in a more polite manner to talk at length about William Wallace and his place in Scottish history. Most of it was lost on Gretchen because of the man's heavy accent, but she amused herself by surreptitiously watching Colin.

"There are two hundred and forty-six steps," the guide concluded. "And they go round and round. Might get ye a bit woozy," he added, looking pointedly at Gretchen.

"Is that too much for you?" Colin asked, eyeing her skeptically.

Gretchen laughed. "I played basketball and tennis in high school."

"Aye, but that's been a while, eh?" he replied with a straight face.

Gretchen blinked, not sure if he was teasing. "I'll be fine. What about you? Aren't you used to just sitting in an airplane and letting it do all the work for you?"

The guide looked askance at Gretchen.

"I'm just joshing with him. We Yanks do that a lot." Gretchen smiled brilliantly at the older gentleman, who blinked and then returned a hesitant smile.

"Very well," Colin said and led the way across the entrance foyer to the spiral stone staircase, tucked in one corner of the rectangular monument.

Gretchen walked behind him up the icily cold steps. At step seventy-one, they reached the first level. She trailed Colin around the room, giving cursory glances to the showy array of armor, and paused beside him as he eyed a huge broadsword in a glass case. It was labeled, *The Sword of William Wallace.*

"I'm surprised they've not packed this away in some underground bunker," Colin said.

Noticing Colin's thoughtfulness, she asked, "Was he very brave, you think? "

Colin turned his head to look at her, his eyes piercing and impenetrable, but did not reply.

"And you, do you want to be like William Wallace?" she prodded.

He frowned. "You mean, a hero?"

"Yes."

"I don't know."

"But you're one already? I mean, aren't all pilots heroes? That's what Churchill said."

Colin looked into the display case. "I've only been on coastal patrol and chased away a few Jerries, not gotten into any scraps with them."

She suddenly blurted, "Don't be a hero, Colin. Heroes get themselves killed."

When he frowned at her, she glanced away, her eyes filling with tears.

"I don't want to get myself killed," he said softly. "I have things I want to do in my life."

Gretchen turned back to face him, blinking away the unshed tears.

"But I don't want to be a coward," he added fiercely. Sighing, he said, "Let's go on. We're only at the first level," and walked away.

She followed, but he was already out of sight when she started up the stairs.

After sixty-two more steps, she was at the second level, but Colin, apparently uninterested in those displays, had already disappeared up the third rise of steps. With a quick jaunt around the room, so she could give a report to Henry, she returned to the staircase and continued upward, increasing her pace.

For some reason, Henry's recent comment about another squadron preparing to return south flitted through her mind, and she suddenly realized that Colin's unit had been at Drem for an unusually long six weeks. Did Henry mean Colin's unit?

By the third level, another sixty-two steps, she was almost running, driven by the need to be with him before he was gone from her life. His disembodied voice floated down the spiraling stairway. "Are ye coming? What's taking ye so long?"

She pressed on, filled with an irrational fear that Colin would sprout wings and disappear off the top of the tower, soaring where she couldn't follow. That thought suddenly turned into a horrifying image of Colin's plane tumbling like a fiery comet from the sky. The terror of such a possibility yanked the breath from her lungs, making it impossible for her to do no more than whisper, "Yes, yes. Please wait for me."

At the very top of the stairs, she circumnavigated the balcony to a smaller flight of steps up to the open, domed viewing area at the tower's apex. Brilliant winter light poured in from the wide, soaring archways on all sides, nearly blinding her.

Colin was a dark silhouette facing away from her. *Or is he an illusion? Or just a memory?*

Her head spun as if she were on a very slow merry-go-round. She leaned over, pressing her palms against her thighs, and closed her eyes, gasping for breath.

"Here, come sit down on the bench. You took the steps too quickly."

She heard his voice next to her, soft with unexpected concern, and felt supportive, strong arms leading her to a bench. She sat with closed eyes, leaning against the cold spine of the peaked dome, willing away the dizzying sensation.

Dropping her hand to her side, she encountered his, warmly reassuring and electric at the same time. *He was real! He was still here.* Gently she intertwined her fingers with his, unspeakably grateful for his solid presence.

She felt him tense with her touch, but then begin gently rubbing the place just below her thumb in a caressing, tender rhythm. It was soothing and intimate.

"Tis the vertigo, merely," he said in soft, reassuring tones. "You took the steps too fast." He added, "That American blood of yours is a wee bit too thin for these altitudes."

Colin eyed Gretchen with concern. She was perspiring, probably overheating from the rush up the stairs, even with the damp chill radiating from the stones. The moisture on her face gave a lovely sheen to her already glowing skin. The continued touch of her soft hand, her nearness, and the light, flowery scent of her perfume put every cell in his body on alert.

She sat up slowly and opened her eyes, a puzzled frown on her face as she glanced at him. "Don't look so worried; I'll be fine," she said with a soft laugh, squeezing his fingers.

But I'm not fine, Colin replied in his mind.

Letting go of her hand, he stood up suddenly and walked across the soaring space to gaze out at the stunning snow-covered landscape. He heard her come up and stand next to him.

"What's that water in the far distance?" she asked.

"There, beyond those hills, the Trossachs, is Loch Lomond."

When she didn't respond, he said, "You know, Loch Lomond, as in the song," and sang the chorus that every Scottish child learned in grammar school, but gave it not a childish jauntiness, but a grownup languor:

O, ye'll tak' the high road, and Ah'll tak' the low road

And Ah'll be in Scotlan' afore ye
Fir me an' my true love will ne'er meet again
On the bonnie, bonnie banks o' Loch Lomon'.

As the echoes of his rich, tenor voice fell away into the valley below, he turned to look at her and was stunned to see her face stained with tears, her eyes awash in grief, her arms pressed across her trembling body. His reserve slipping, he struggled to put his feelings back in that hidden room where he had locked them after New Year's Eve.

To counteract his longing to take her in his arms, he reverted to accusation. "You should have dressed in something warmer," he said harshly, nodding at her tan, cashmere sweater.

She stiffened. It was a long minute until she turned angry eyes on him, "You don't have *your* topcoat on!"

"I'm used to Scottish weather." He looked back over the winter countryside, not wanting to see the vulnerability in her eyes. He heard her take several trembling sighs then walk away.

He turned to see her looking out another archway and found his feet carrying him over to her.

"You could be a gentleman and do something to keep me warm." Her voice was a bit more lighthearted, closer to her normal teasing tone.

It seemed her composure was back from that challenging climb and the lyrics of a song so relevant in the midst of this newest war. Then she playfully bumped up against him with her shoulder several times, tempting him to act on her words, but not in a gentlemanly manner.

"Do you have to do that?" he found himself almost shouting. How easy it was to lose his composure in her presence.

"Do what?" She was staring up at him. In her street shoes, she was shorter than the night they had danced. It made her seem more defenseless and increased his irrational fury.

"Tease! Be a tease! Flirt! Do you think you have to conquer every lad who comes along?" He saw surprise and pain on her lovely face. *Get ahold of yourself, Colin.* He heard himself say, "I'm not every lad." in a petulant and spoiled tone.

Her response seared his heart.

"No, Domnhall Cailean MacAmhlaigh," she said, pronouncing his name in surprisingly good, though Yankee-accented, Gaelic. "You are *not* every lad. You're not like *any* of the lads I've met." Her voice was laced with something he was afraid to name.

She paced to another archway. He followed slowly to stand behind her, admiring not the breathtaking view of Stirling's ancient fortress on a hill across the valley, but the way the wind stirred her soft hair that tumbled about her shoulders. He said nothing because he was unable to.

After a moment of quiet, she said in a flat voice, "Tell me what we're looking at. Henry said I was to tell him everything I saw. He's the one who was excited about this visit."

Colin struggled to concentrate on the distant scene, rather than the lovely girl in front of him. He noticed she was shivering slightly. He took off his uniform coat and draped it around her shoulders, pressing the wool sleeves against her arms for the minutest of moments. Reluctantly removing his hands from her body, and his mind from her presence, he gave a thorough description of what lay before them, in a casual, indifferent voice.

As if he were merely a tour guide and she was only a tourist.

When he finished explaining the view in all four directions, he led the way back to the tower stairs, where he paused. "It's verra steep going down, so hold onto the railing. If you tumble, I'll be here to block your fall."

She said nothing but handed him his uniform jacket, which he slipped back into. He felt her on the stairs behind him as they turned round and round the dizzying downward steps.

They thanked the guide on the way out. Gretchen gave the old man a tip, to which he beamed and thanked her for her courtesy.

Colin was impressed with her gesture.

She refused his offer to stop for lunch in Stirling before they drove back. "I'm not really hungry, and I'm sure you have things to do back on base," she replied, not looking at him.

"It's a long ride, and you've not had a bite to eat since breakfast," he protested. Not that he wanted to torment himself with more time in her presence, but he was concerned because the climb had made her so breathless.

"Well, at least have a wee bite of chocolate, then," he urged at her shrug, reaching in his uniform jacket and retrieving a Hershey's bar. "Courtesy of Henry. He says it's made somewhere near where you and he are from."

She smiled wryly at that, unwrapped the candy, and broke it into small squares. As they drove toward Edinburgh, she handed him a square every time she ate one herself. He found the ritual unnervingly intimate.

Gretchen said little, probably mulling over his churlish behavior. Ah, it was easier if she was aloof or indifferent. As if to punish him, the scent of her perfume lingered on his coat for several days, wreaking havoc with his heart.

———⨯———

Henry was both relieved and happy that Colin did not accompany his unit at the end of February when they returned south, though he had the presence of mind not to say so.

"The Wing Commander, the Anglish Wing Commander, by the way, informed me I was needed here," Colin told Henry over a pint in the pub. "When I protested that I wanted to get south and see some action, he said, 'You're local and familiar with the territory. You're an important asset to our job of coastal patrol. You'll be attached to A Squadron of the 43rd that's arriving next week.' I wanted to smack him upside his Sassennach head with a stane."

When Colin got upset, Henry noticed his English became more heavily accented and laced with Scots words.

"I told him every other lad in the squadron was just as local and just as familiar with the *territory*, otherwise known as *Scotland,* but he called me to attention and said I was out of line."

Henry made sympathetic noises in response wondering if Colin, with his usually contained temper, could truly get out of line.

Colin grunted in disgust, "Well, Henry, if I'm stuck here for a while longer, you should come up with me someday. I could take you in one of the Tiger Moths and give you a flying lesson. Besides, you're so curious about Scotland. Ye can't understand the lay of the land unless you've been flying over it. All the maps can't give you a picture of it, the twisting, winding rivers, and the chopped-up coastline."

Henry caught his breath. *Fly? He repaired planes; he didn't pilot them, or even fly in them.* "I'm ground crew. That means I stay on the ground. I'm sure it's against regulations."

Colin scoffed. "You're a Yank volunteer. You don't exactly come under the regulations."

"Yes, I'm a civilian worker, but I'm still bound by regulations."

"The Wing Commander likes you, and he owes me a favor for keeping me here."

"Yeah, he likes me, but sometimes it feels like he's still sizing me up."

"Oh, aye, with your real name being Herr Schmidt and all," Colin chuckled. "I guess they wouldn't want you up in our planes getting a birds-eye view."

"It's not funny. I could get sent off to a detention camp just for having German ancestry."

"Only if you're not a British citizen," Colin protested.

"I'm not a British citizen," Henry reminded him. "And I think there's been some British citizens put in detention camps."

When Colin looked concerned, Henry returned to the subject at hand. "Being stuck here has one advantage. We get to spend time with Gretchen and Fiona."

"Sure," Colin used the Americanism with a decidedly Highland drawl, which made it difficult for Henry to decide if Colin was enthusiastic about the prospect or not. He had hoped that something would flare up between Colin and Fiona, but despite the many times they'd been together and the casual warmth between them, there didn't seem to be more.

Henry's guess was affirmed in mid-March when the four of them were at a nightclub in Edinburgh. Colin had only agreed to come because Fiona said she'd had an important announcement.

Her news was astonishing—she was joining the WAAF's, the Women's Auxiliary Air Force.

"What's your family say?" Henry asked. Though he had gotten used to women in uniform—there were several WAAFs at Drem serving as drivers, secretaries, and other support—women in the armed forces still seemed an oddity to him. He had heard there were even women service pilots ferrying planes between aerodromes. He'd yet to meet one.

"They're a wee bit taken aback, aye, but my brothers are both in the service, my father is off to some hush-hush job in Whitehall, my uncle in Edinburgh is an Air Raid Warden, and my mother up home is in the Red Cross, as is my aunt in Edinburgh."

Then she added, looking at Henry intensely, "I can't just sit here and watch all the young lads I've known go off and..." Her sentence came to a sudden halt.

Henry was touched by the emotion on her usually calm, contained face. Gretchen had told him that two of Fiona's schoolmates had recently been killed in action, one when his Merchant Marine ship sank off the coast of Ireland and another when his bomber was shot down in a daylight raid on the docks of Calais in France.

Colin spoke up, filling the pained silence. "Well done, Fiona. You've got the spirit. We're all in this together, and everyone has got to do their bit."

Henry figured Colin would have been upset by Fiona's decision if he had been romantically interested in her. So much for his matchmaking.

"Very patriotic speech," Gretchen fired at Colin, surprising Henry with her sarcasm.

"Aye, but then it's not your war, is it?" was Colin's equally biting reply. Gretchen glared back at him.

"But it should be," Henry interjected, trying to make peace. The animosity between his friends was still puzzling, and it seemed worse since their trip to Stirling. He wasn't sure how Gretchen felt about her flatmate's enlistment. He was surprised she hadn't mentioned it. When they were alone at the table later, he asked her.

"There'll be just the two of us now in the flat, Eileen and me, since Catriona joined the Women's Land Army, and now Fiona's leaving. And even Eileen is making noises about the WRENS. I'm either going to have to find new flatmates or a smaller place," Gretchen sighed.

He noticed she didn't really answer his question. When he pressed her, she finally confessed, trembling in a way that made Henry want to comfort her. "Oh, Henry, Fiona's been my lifeline since I got here in '39. I just feel so out of place. Everyone is doing something important."

"But you're doing something important, Gretchen," he answered. "You're supporting the civilian work to get wool, make uniforms. That's important."

Gretchen shrugged indifferently, "Not really."

After Fiona left, Colin stopped going with Henry to Edinburgh. "Three's a crowd," he'd say, though Henry was confident Gretchen could easily find a girl happy to make a foursome.

Colin scoffed, "I don't need any giddy lassies pawing my uniform."

Which made Henry wonder if Colin did care for Fiona, yet when he asked if Fiona wrote, Colin said no.

But Fiona continued to write Henry brief, breezy letters full of the ironies and antics of life in the WAAFs, keeping up the correspondence she began in late 1939. Only now, her letters no longer contained details about Gretchen's life, just her own.

More than ever, Henry struggled with his limited time off. His schedule of six twelve-hour days on duty and one day off rarely coincided with Gretchen's weekends off, and 48-hour passes were only doled out once a month. When he got one, he traveled to Edinburgh for an afternoon at the movies, dinner out, or a walk around the city.

It was ironic, he mused, that it took two years, a war, and a trip across the Atlantic to get his wish of spending time alone with Gretchen, and now that time was limited by the very means he used to get near her.

Still, he kept his tone light and easy-going. They talked about their jobs, about Fiona's letters, and about Colin, as she always asked about him. Henry would tell her details about Colin's ops and his frustration with coastal patrol. But he never spoke of his own feelings for her. He wasn't about to scare her off again.

Patience and time were on his side.

Nineteen

May 1941

On a Saturday in early May, Henry's plan to see Gretchen was again canceled from last-minute changes to the duty roster. The base was on high alert. There had been three high-explosive bombs dropped the morning of May 6 near the west end of the aerodrome. Broken windows, but no casualties.

Everyone was still talking about the Luftwaffe's eight-hour firebombing of London on April 28. News from North Africa wasn't good either: in ten days the Germans recaptured ground which had taken the Brits eight weeks to claim. The Suez Canal was again in danger.

Henry ran into Colin having breakfast at the Parachute Café. Even with the base being on alert, Colin was due to stand down after an extended stint of ops.

Henry said, "I wouldn't ask you, knowing how exhausted you are, but I need a favor. I had the day with Gretchen planned. We were going to Holyrood—today's the one day this month it's open. Then we were going to dinner and to a play. It's something you'd like. Shakespeare."

Colin nearly choked on his coffee. "You're taking Gretchen to Shakespeare?"

"Yeah. I mean, I'm not a literature buff like you. Weren't you studying all that when you were going to college?"

"Aye, I was reading British Literature, but I only did two years at University."

"Well, then. You would be the perfect one to accompany her. I'm sure it will be interesting, but I don't know that I would've understood it."

"So why did you get the tickets?" Colin studied his morning beverage.

"Well, I know you might find this odd, but Gretchen said she wanted to go."

Colin looked up at Henry, shaking his head. "Gretchen wants to see Shakespeare? Which play?" The idea of Shakespeare and Gretchen didn't mesh in Colin's mind.

"One of the historical ones. Henry IV. She knows I like English history, that I've been reading a lot of it. She even said, 'Won't Colin be shocked that I went to Shakespeare.' You know, since the two of you went to Stirling, she's been a lot more into learning about history. Fiona even lent her one of her old school books."

"It might be amusing to see Gretchen's reaction to Shakespeare," Colin replied, imagining watching her, but realized he was sounding willing. Which he wasn't.

But Henry had taken his statement as a yes. "Great, you'll go? I was going to meet Gretchen at Holyrood at two. If it's too late to catch the train or bus back, you can stay with Fiona's aunt and uncle. I've done it several times."

Colin wished Henry would stop throwing him and Gretchen together. How could he explain that being around Gretchen was agony?

"I don't think she'd want to spend the day with me," Colin replied at last.

"Oh no, she won't mind. She's been so glum since Fiona left, and now her other roommate is leaving at the end of the month, joining the WRENS."

"So that leaves Gretchen alone in her flat?" Colin said.

"No, actually Fiona's aunt and uncle invited her to come live with them and rent a room, though knowing them, they won't charge her. I'm glad. I don't think it's good for her to be alone. A girl by herself in a city and all."

Colin noted Henry's protective attitude.

Henry continued, "I won't be able to let Gretchen know that it'll be you coming. They had to give up the phone in her flat since they're moving out; I always call her during the week at work. So she'll be surprised to see you."

"I'm sure she will be," Colin said truthfully.

On the bus ride into the city, Colin thought about that March evening he'd last seen Gretchen, the night Fiona announced her plans to join the WAAFs. During a slow dance with Fiona, she made some odd comments about Gretchen and Henry.

"You know, Colin, Gretchen sees Henry as one of her pals. Just the way it was back in America. When she and I were in school together, we all went out with Henry and others."

Colin looked at her warily, uncertain why she was saying this. His feelings for Gretchen weren't really evident. Maybe Fiona had designs on Henry, though she'd break her heart there.

"She's fond of him, aye, but it's nothing romantic," Fiona was saying. "She goes out with other lads. She'd got a whole squadron of admirers."

"Any squadron in particular?" Colin retorted. "The 609th?" he asked, referring to Edinburgh's home-grown unit.

Seeing Fiona's speculative look, he felt the need to clarify. "It's not my squadron anymore. The Wing Commander pulled me out."

Fiona snickered. "Well, 609th or 607th. Pretty much every squadron, I'd say. But then, there's nary a fighter boy that has her eye... or her heart." She looked at Colin intensely.

With an impatient grunt, he asked, "Why are you telling me this?"

She shook her head in disbelief. "There are none so blind as will not see."

"Will not see what, you daft lassie," he shot back, bringing them to a complete halt in the middle of the dance floor.

"It's not for me to say, Colin, if you haven't realized it. Either way, it'll be a mess."

He resumed their three-step waltz, thinking, *It already is.*

And today just proved it because it wasn't really for Henry he was doing this; it was for himself, for he longed to see Gretchen again, bask in her glowing personality, hear her laughter, politely take her elbow and help her across the street, smell her perfume.

She's not available even if she thinks she is. At least not to me. I shouldn't be seeing her alone. And yet here he was, once again, thrown into temptation by his very own friend.

Henry, don't you know what you are doing to me? Or to yourself? But how could he tell him? It'd be the end of their friendship. At least he was protecting Gretchen for Henry. He steeled his nerve. His cool Scottish demeanor would have to get him through this day.

But the moment he saw Gretchen by the ancient iron gates of Holyrood Palace in a short-sleeved peach dress and a wide-brimmed hat, as fresh as the spring day, and so American in her bright colors, he came to an abrupt stop. She hadn't seen him. There was time to go back and make some excuse to Henry.

But he wouldn't. He couldn't.

Damn you, Henry. Why have you done this to me?

Gretchen stood by the large iron gates of the palace and breathed in the spring air. Edinburgh was bursting with flowers and tourists. All the trees were in bloom, and every window box in the city overflowed with color. She had walked up from her flat in New Towne through Princes Street Gardens, which was filled with families and young women hanging on the arms of young men. If not for the presence of uniforms, she could have forgotten about the war.

And she was ready to. It had been nearly two years since her arrival in Edinburgh, and her early excitement had worn off as the war had worn on. Fiona in the WAAFS. Eileen in the Women's Land Army. Now Catriona to join the WRENS. And like some old maid, she was moving in with Fiona's aunt and uncle, again under the eye of a protective older couple.

The job, once stimulating and thrilling, was now tedious and stressful as she'd taken on more responsibilities. And the young men she stepped out with to restaurants, clubs, and cinemas were names and faces that passed through her life like water in a Scottish burn. She'd barely learned their names, and they were off to distant Indochina or northern Africa or out in ships in the Atlantic or in planes over the English Channel.

In harm's way.

She finally told Henry to stop bringing airmen around. She didn't want to dig up girls other than Fiona for party nights. The one young airman she did wish to see pointedly avoided her. Henry's once-monthly visits were calming and comfortable. She was looking forward to their day of culture, something that would have astonished Naomi.

"See," she'd tell her, "I'm learning about history. And the theater."

It was unlike Henry to be late. She glanced at her watch. He had said two o'clock. Of course, buses were often delayed, or he could have been called back to duty. She looked down the long drive leading from the palace entrance to the street and blinked against the brilliant sun. There was an RAF officer leaning against a lamppost smoking a cigarette. When he straightened up with a last drag, crushed his cigarette with his foot, and started her way, she realized it was Colin.

Gretchen immediately attempted to dress herself in indifference. But her heart was racing, and she was nearly breathless by the time Colin walked up the macadam driveway to stand in front of her. She hadn't seen him in two months. She tried to hide the look of surprised pleasure and delight from her face.

Instead, she spontaneously put her hand on his forearm. "Why, Colin! What in heaven's name are you doing here?" A horrid thought struck her, and she took a step back. "Henry... there's something wrong with Henry."

"No, no, he was called back on duty," he reassured her. "Another mechanic got ill, and Henry had to fill in. He's fine. Really."

"Oh." She laughed with a nervous titter. "I'm sorry. It's just, Henry's my..." Gretchen stopped in midsentence when she saw Colin staring at her. His gaze disconcerted her.

"He's your what, Gretchen?" he asked, in a flat, serious voice.

She had a sense that her answer was important in a way she couldn't understand and chose her words carefully. "Henry's my connection to home. My anchor. And like a... well, like the big brother I always wanted."

"Is that right? I thought you had a brother." His voice held a hint of sarcasm.

"A younger brother. William. Just finishing up his first year of college at Dickinson."

Colin made a nondescript noise. She steered the conversation back to her original question. "So... why *are* you here? Are you meeting someone?"

At his "aye," her heart sank. Fiona said he didn't have a steady girl, and Henry once mentioned he never saw Colin with girls unless they were in a crowd.

"Where is this someone?" Gretchen looked around, trying to recover her air of indifference.

"She's right here in front of me."

She blinked and looked back at him. When Colin began to smile, she felt her heart turn over. "You mean me?"

"Of course, you. Henry sent me. To the rescue. Your knight in shining armor."

"You volunteered?"

"Henry didn't want you to be disappointed. So I'm doing him a favor. Besides, I wanted to see *you* at a Shakespeare performance."

Gretchen, entirely pleased, was nevertheless a bit put out. Colin never teased her, so she wasn't sure if he was serious or making fun.

"Henry didn't have to send you in his place. I'm quite capable of finding someone to take me to the play. Catriona's not joining the WRENs for another couple weeks; she could have come. And you don't have to do this. I don't like being someone's favor. Besides," she added, getting angry as she thought more about his words, "I'm not stupid. I've been to plays. I was *in* our high school plays. I had the lead role in *Daisy Pulls it Off*, which, by the way, was set in an English boarding school."

Colin casually picked a bit of lint from his uniform. "Well don't get yourself in a mixter-maxter. I've delivered my missive, as instructed. I can go on my way if ye please."

THE BOMBER JACKET   249

Now Gretchen was speechless. Colin's demeanor got her so befuddled, first acting gallant and then shrugging her off. Always an air about him as if he were judging her, finding her lacking in some way. Gathering her wits, she tilted her head and smiled haughtily.

"No, if you're hoping I'll let you off the hook now, I don't think so! We shall go to the palace and the grounds. I was going to play docent and give Henry the tour. I even studied the guidebook. So you shall have to pretend you are Henry and be polite and interested in everything about Scottish history, which you probably find boring because you learned it all in school. And for my reward, you shall take me to a nice restaurant for dinner and then to the play and not be put out if I ask you a question or two."

She was pleased that Colin looked taken aback, even if it was momentarily. And even more pleased when he smiled wryly and said, "Very well, ma'am. Lead the way."

Colin followed docilely as Gretchen took him through the palace, guidebook in hand. On this May Day holiday, the place was thronged with visitors, many like himself in the ubiquitous uniform. Every room featured a stern-faced armed guard standing watch, probably to keep the rabble from filching the antiquities.

Gretchen surprised him by the thoroughness of her tour. She knew all about Mary Queen of Scots, whom she found a sad and romantic figure, and gave details about the various rooms and their historic significance. However, once she left the building, she became quiet. To fill the silence, he told her how the palace and now ruined abbey came to be named.

"In 1127, while King David the First was hunting in the forests to the east of Edinburgh, he was thrown from his horse when it was startled by a hart, a deer," Colin explained how the king was saved from being gored when it was frightened away by the appearance of a cross descending from the skies. "Thus, the name Holy Rood. Holy Cross."

"Let's look at the garden," was her only reply.

He trailed behind her as she wandered the pristine grounds fragrant with lilacs, watching her graceful movements as she touched overhanging leaves, ran her fingers over the bark of a twining, twisted tree, and stooped to get a closer look at a bed of tulips. Still silent, she walked over to a park bench near the front of the abbey. Taking off her broad-brimmed hat, she held it in her lap and stared off at Arthur's Seat, the distinctly shaped volcanic hill which was a favorite with hillwalkers. It was covered in yellow spring gorse.

He sat down next to her, wondering at her pensive mood.

"You're unusually quiet. Is the tour done?"

She stared ahead again. "Is that a criticism of the fact that I am not usually quiet?"

Colin grunted in frustration. Anything he said seemed to set her off. Of course, he knew he had set up their dynamic with his deliberate attempt to be indifferent. He really had been enjoying this day with her and had begun to relax.

"Now what?" she asked in an accusatory tone.

"What do you mean, *now what*?" He was equally accusatory.

"Well, you just huffed and puffed like you're all beside yourself."

"I'm not beside myself; I'm beside you."

"Oh, so now the oh-so-solemn-and-sober Scot is making jokes and teasing me."

"Gretchen, what is wrong with you?"

"Here's what it is, Colin. The last time we spent a day together you were... you accused me... of being a floozy."

Colin was stunned to hear her voice tremble and turned to her, frowning. "I never said you were a floozy, whatever that is."

Ignoring his answer, Gretchen went on, still staring ahead, but he noticed her face had taken on a pink tinge. "So today, I try to be all intellectual, and I get criticized. Why do I always feel as if you're judging me? What have I ever done to make you so unfriendly? And then today *you're* being the tease and the jokester. Is that a new way of making me feel bad?"

Colin caught his breath. The hurt in her voice made him feel small. Of course, it was obvious to her that he appeared critical and judgmental.

That's the tone he always took around her. What he couldn't say was, *Gretchen, it's the only way I can keep myself from falling for you. You're Henry's, and that's all there is to it.*

Instead, he sighed deeply, "I'm sorry. It's just your..." he tried to think of a reasonable excuse for his ungentlemanly behavior. "...American ways."

Now she did turn, hurt replaced by fury.

Good, he thought to himself, but with regret. The lovely day was going sour quickly, though he could better deal with her anger than her tenderness.

"My American ways? What's that supposed to mean? Henry's an American. You and he get on just swell."

"It's different. You're a lassie."

"No shit," she said, standing. "Tell me something I don't know."

"Your ways are different from the girls I grew up with."

Glaring down at him, she said, "Go on. Explain."

Henry. Think of Henry. Colin cringed inwardly as he stood slowly, speaking the worst dismissive insult in mind. "You came here to have a good time. Right as our country was about to go to war. And your family back in the States—you don't seem too worried that they might be consairned about you. And, on top of all that, I don't see you doing anything for the war effort."

Gretchen's face grew pale. Her eyes widened and then filled with tears. She staggered an alarming step backward. Colin instinctively reached out to grab her arms.

"Take your hands off me," she shouted, drawing the attention of a nearby tourist.

Colin stepped away, wanting to avoid a scene. "Sit down, then. You look ill."

"Wouldn't you look ill if someone just insulted you? So now I know. Now I understand. I'm a good-time girl. That's all you think of me. And Henry? What does he think?"

"You're his friend," Colin replied with a shrug.

"Clearly you are not *my* friend."

"We can never be friends, Gretchen," he answered, lowering the final blow to any hope he might have with this beautiful, vivacious, alluring American girl.

"I say amen to that, Domnhall Cailean MacAmhlaigh," her American-accented Gaelic twisted his heart with every syllable. "And goodbye."

She spun away from him, marching toward the exit.

Colin followed. "No, let me escort you home."

She waved a hand dismissively at him and maintained her pace.

"Henry would skin me alive if some drunken lout accosted you on the street."

That did get her attention. She stopped in her tracks and turned slowly, her face a play of anguish and agony. Colin felt sick to his stomach, knowing he was the cause.

"As opposed to a vile Scot who insults me in a garden? He would skin you alive *if* he knew the horrible things *you said*, but I'll never tell him. I know how much your friendship means to him, though in God's name, I don't know why. "

"I don't know why either," he replied truthfully.

"Goodbye, Colin. I'll find Catriona, and we'll go somewhere and have a good time with some Scottish lads who don't hate American girls."

As she walked away, he muttered to himself, "Damn you, Henry. Damn you for putting me through this."

TWENTY

JULY 1941

AT THE END OF June, Henry's wing commander told him he was giving him a 24-hour pass for the Fourth of July.

"Be nice if the rest of those damned Yankees joined the fight like you have," the wing commander groused. "Take the day off. Go see that knockout Yankee girl of yours."

Henry wished he could claim Gretchen really *was that knockout Yankee girl of his.*

At the end of May, Gretchen had moved in with Fiona's aunt and uncle. Soon after that, she'd started volunteering several evenings and every other weekend at the Red Cross canteen in Edinburgh's train station. All while putting in more hours at the office to cover for Fiona, now stationed in England. Henry thought it was good for Gretchen to stay busy, but regretted their limited time together, as their days off rarely coincided.

Then, much to his surprise, Gretchen also started volunteering at the military hospital, delivering mail, water, and good wishes to recuperating airmen and sailors. He was relieved that she wasn't out on the town with other men, though he imagined she was fawned over by the patients. *He'd* certainly be happy with her company if he was stuck in a hospital bed.

When he asked her why she was volunteering, she replied in a rather agitated voice, "I want to do something meaningful for the war effort. You know, do my bit. I'm not just some good-time girl!"

"Of course, you're not! Whoever said such a thing!" he replied, offended for her. "Was it one of those fliers that hang out at the canteen? Tell me who; I'll punch him out!"

She just shook her head. "Oh, Henry, you're so sweet," but didn't elaborate.

Gretchen was more like her old self when he called. "I already have the day off, and Fiona's coming home on leave," she said enthusiastically. "She'll be here Tuesday. Let's have a picnic. Fiona and I can put together a hamper of goodies."

"That's great! I'd love to see her," Henry said. "I'll bring Colin. It'll be a nice break for him. He's been doing a lot of flying. We can be a foursome, like old times."

Henry figured Fiona's presence would alleviate any awkwardness between Gretchen and Colin. He wasn't sure what had happened during the Holyrood visit. When pressed, Gretchen simply said, "Colin and I just don't hit it off. We went our separate ways after our tour of the palace." Colin claimed that Gretchen said she'd rather spend the evening with Catriona.

On July 3rd, Fiona called Henry and suggested they take their picnic to Traprain Law, the volcanic plateau halfway between Edinburgh and Drem. She had come by some gas rationing coupons and had the use of her cousin's roadster, stored away in the garage since he'd gone missing at Dunkirk. They'd learned in late 1940 that he was in a German POW camp.

"My uncle said the auto needs to be driven occasionally," Fiona said. "This is the perfect reason. We lassies will pick up you laddies at Drem with all the goodies. Let's all dress in civvies and no talk of the war, even to toast Uncle Joe Stalin for keeping the Nazis busy on the eastern front. It was very nice of Hitler to invade Russia and take the pressure off us."

Other than the Nazis hopefully using up their resources in a two-front war, the other news was grim. Crete was lost, with the RAF pulling all fighter aircraft out, though a combined British and Free French Force had invaded Syria and had taken it from the Vichy French before they could turn it over to Germany. But on the other hand, the Germans completed their conquest of Greece.

It took more than a few pints at the pub for Henry to convince Colin to join the picnic. "Colin, you've been down in the dumps for weeks. You're finally off ops for a couple of days. Come have some fun. We're going to have an old-fashioned Fourth of July picnic."

Colin snorted. "Thumbing your nose at the King? Planning on setting off fireworks?"

Henry figured the sniping between Colin and Gretchen would be fireworks enough but kept that thought to himself.

Colin released a huge sigh before quaffing half his ale. "I'm wasting my time here at Drem, Henry. I want to see some action."

"The Wing Commander says you're invaluable. You're training the new coastal command pilots," Henry protested.

"I could do more, and I'm bored with it, Henry. I hear the pilots on respite talk about their ops. I feel like a nyaff. I swear if they won't let me go south, I'll volunteer for Bomber Command. They're always recruiting."

"Yeah," Henry said, horrified, "that's because their chop rate is so high. You're just a sitting duck in one of those lumbering things. Besides, you aren't trained to fly bombers. It's a different kind of piloting."

"How different can it be? A pilot's a pilot. It's just a matter of a bigger plane." He took another large swallow of his drink.

"It's not up to you, Colin." Henry tried to be sympathetic.

"Aye, that's the shait of it," Colin muttered, practically slamming his glass on the bar.

"So forget all that for an afternoon. Come have a picnic on a summer day." Henry just wanted the four of them to be together again, doing something fun.

"I'd just be the dark cloud in your blue sky."

"Nonsense! The sky is way too beautiful at Traprain Law for you to ruin it."

Colin looked concerned. "I think some of the laws are off-limits. Besides, it's quite a hike up the hill."

"Some bomber pilot you'd make," grinned Henry. "Afraid of a picnic up on a hill."

After a moment's frowning concentration, Colin said, "Well, you'll be needin' an extra hand to carry a picnic basket and two lassies up the side 'o the mountain. I guess I can come."

Henry playfully drummed his hands on the tabletop before taking a sip of his barely-touched beer. He was spending his day off with the people most important to him.

——⊰✖⊱——

Gretchen was inordinately happy. Fiona was home on leave. They were having an adventure: a spin in a delicious roadster with the top down, her hair waving in the wind like a flag on a breezy day, a picnic basket packed to the hilt, and a planned hike to the top of a hill.

And Colin.

When Henry told her Colin would be making it a foursome, she agonized for days over what to wear. She wanted to look stunning yet act indifferently. Despite his obvious low opinion of her, Gretchen continually replayed her encounters with him in her mind: their dance at Drem, the trip to Stirling and the Wallace Monument, their day at Holyrood, and the few times they had been together with Henry and Fiona. She examined each word he'd said, each gesture he'd made, each possible meaning and nuance of his expression or the look in his eyes, certain that somewhere she would find the answer to what continued to puzzle her.

He was attracted to her. She knew that instinctively. Yet his reactions indicated just the opposite. Did he really think she only thought about having fun and making conquests? Because of him she started volunteering at the canteen and the hospital. Everyone's surprise at her volunteer work had her thinking about the way she was perceived by others.

But June had been the happiest she'd felt since Fiona left. The long evenings and weekends were finally filled with rewarding activity. She was a hit at the canteen—their Yankee Gal—and on her rounds at the rehabilitation hospital, delivering water, writing letters home or to sweethearts for the men who were too badly injured to do it themselves.

She saw men recuperating from devastating injuries, but she never let it crack her demeanor of flirtatious fun, which the men loved. She figured the nurses were there to do the work of changing bandages or giving medicine; she was there to brighten their day. Even in her subdued Red Cross outfit and her hair in a chignon, she attracted attention. But it wasn't the attention that made her feel good; it was proving that she could do something meaningful, no matter how small. She knew Colin would hear of it; Henry would certainly tell him.

She finally decided to wear a sleeveless sundress with a tight-fitting, low-cut bodice and flouncy skirt in a brilliantly pink flowered print. She showed off her figure. She left her hair loose and flowing and brought along a matching broad-brimmed hat.

"Gretchen, you look stunning, but we're not going to a garden party," Fiona scolded when she saw her outfit. "We're hiking up a hill and picnicking on a rabbity-holed field."

"Well, you told the boys no uniforms. That you wanted to forget the war. This is an outfit from before the war. I'm trying to help the cause. Besides, I have flats on."

"Well, certainly, one look at you, and the war will be the farthest thing from their minds," Fiona agreed. She was more sensibly dressed in light trousers, a camp shirt, and walking shoes. "I may not look like a fashion plate, but I'll be able to climb the path without help."

Then looking at Gretchen again, she burst out laughing. "Silly me, I see!"

Gretchen, feeling a rare blush on her cheeks, crossed her arms and pouted. "I don't know what you're talking about. There's no one coming but Henry and Colin."

Fiona simply raised her eyebrows in disbelief.

———— ⋈ ————

To Gretchen's surprise, Colin greeted her with a warm hello and a smile when he and Henry piled into the back seat of the car, challenging her resolve to be cool and aloof. But when they arrived at Traprain Law, it was Henry who helped Gretchen clamber around the "Off Limits" signs and over the wooden stile, then up the steeply-ascending, narrow dirt path, a trek that took nearly thirty minutes.

Colin and Fiona followed, with Colin carrying the heavy picnic basket and Fiona lugging the soft, plaid, woolen blankets.

"Let me carry something," Henry protested. Fiona declined. "You'll be too busy carrying Gretchen, who thinks we are invited to the Buckingham Palace."

Gretchen just laughed at her friend's good-natured kidding, repeating her earlier protests. "You said no uniforms. You said forget the war, so that's what I'm doing."

"Ach, now, you just reminded me of it by telling me I didn't want ta be reminded of it."

Gretchen thought the laborious climb was worth the effort, for when Henry pulled her up onto the plateau, she gasped at the startling vista. Pale wisps of cloud scurried across the intensely blue sky, almost low enough to touch. The surface of the law, barren of trees, seemed to undulate, as the ankle-high grass rippled before the breeze in ever-changing shades of green.

It felt fresh, alive, yet ancient. She could hear birds twittering everywhere and saw a rabbit or two hopping across the pockmarked ground. She had read that ancient peoples worshipped on the tops of these promontories, which stood out so profoundly on the flat terrain of the East Lothian countryside. Now she could understand why.

"Eat first, look later," Fiona called to Gretchen.

Sitting on their blankets, surrounded by verdant green grass, they unpacked the treasure trove of goodies assembled by Fiona and her aunt: cold, tangy meat pies that in crust that melted in their mouths; sharp cheddar cheese; herb scones that Fiona had baked that morning; crisp carrots; fresh strawberries; and a bottle of chilled, dry white wine.

"First, a toast," Colin said, uncorking the wine and standing after filling everyone's glasses.

Gretchen thought he looked trim and relaxed, dressed in khaki pants, a white button-down shirt, open at the collar with the sleeves rolled up, and a plaid linen vest.

"To America, home of the brave." He saluted Henry with his glass and turned to Gretchen, who had tilted her head back to see him. "And the beautiful," he concluded softly.

Gretchen felt her throat close with emotion, stunned by his sincere compliment. She could barely swallow the wine and saw the speculative look Henry gave Colin.

To cover her embarrassment, Gretchen stood up and said, "Well, that calls for a song. Come on Henry," and started a rousing rendition of *I'm a Yankee Doodle Dandy*. But it was Colin who joined in the song in a mellow tenor voice.

Not able to concentrate, Gretchen laughed herself to a halt. "Blimey, Colin, did you sing in a chorus?"

"As a matter of fact, I did." He grinned in return, his eyes warm. "At university."

"Well, golly gee and ah, shucks," Fiona said, American style. "Let's eat."

Which they did, with gusto. Gretchen was glad for the distraction, for she was thrown completely off balance by Colin's friendliness. All her efforts at being aloof were being waylaid rapidly, and her heart was beginning to hope that maybe her instincts were right after all.

At Fiona's insistence, Henry and Gretchen told alternating stories about their July Fourth memories as "a wee lad and lassie growing up across the Atlantic."

Colin's genuine interest in her stories further unnerved Gretchen.

Sometime later, Fiona, pulling something out of the hamper, said, "And for dessairt, Gretchen has gifted us with a chocolate bar! Hershey's, sent by her loving parents. I say here's for the good old U.S. of A!"

"And a wee dram, as the Scottish contribution to this Independence Day feast, supplied by my Da's locked liquor cabinet," Colin interjected, pulling out a small bottle. "Highland Park. Been saving it for a special occasion. I'm sure he would approve."

Once the day was blessed with the Scottish "water o' life," Gretchen jumped up. "Now I want to see the view," she said, heading toward the plateau edge.

———⊠———

Colin, watching Gretchen walk away, was startled when Henry said with a chuckle, "Would you make sure she doesn't fall off while I give Fiona a hand?"

Picking up his binoculars, Colin trailed behind Gretchen, admiring the swish of her skirt against her knees. He knew he had disconcerted her with his friendliness. But he was tired of fighting himself and decided for just one day he would enjoy her vibrant personality and not put a damper on his friends' festivities with his often-morose attitude.

When she stopped near the edge, he stood to one side slightly behind her, watching her breath catch as she took in the view. She apparently hadn't heard him come up behind her, for she started when he spoke. "Henry said you weren't to fall off."

Spinning around, she said with a laugh, "Such a dolt, Henry. I could always out-climb him in the rafters of the barn. He's the one who used to be scared of heights."

"Ach, is that so? That explains why he won't come up and see Scotland from the air."

She glanced at the sky. "I love the way the weather changes so quickly here. At home, it's a long time coming. You know hours ahead of time that it's going to rain or snow."

He laughed softly. "Well, it's what they say about Scottish weather. Wait a wee minute, and it'll change."

"Oh, yes." She laughed but shivered slightly in the dress that wasn't warm enough for a Scottish summer day, even in the lowlands. Then she smiled that brilliant smile that made her face glow and penetrated his heart like a long, thin blade, the pain so real he gasped involuntarily and put his palm against his chest.

She stepped closer. "What is it?" Her voice, filled with concern, wrapped itself around his mind like warm arms, the way her arms had felt when they'd danced. A delicious agony.

"What is it?" she asked again, laying her hand over his.

He could only look ahead over the farmland lying like a quilt of green and brown and yellow below the ancient plateau.

"Tell me what you see," she said in her charming American accent, removing her hand and turning to follow his gaze.

"I see a storm coming. You're likely to get wet if we stay."

"Really? That's enough to make you gasp? Must be some storm."

Colin laughed, handing her the binoculars. "Here, see for yourself." He watched her again, as she scanned the Scottish countryside. He still cringed to think of what he had said to her in May. "Henry says you've taken up volunteer work."

"Well," she said, her back to him, "I had to prove I'm not a good-time girl."

"Gretchen. I didn't really..."

"Why would you say it, if you didn't mean it?" She slowly turned, the binoculars still to her eyes, and looked at him through them. "If I look at you close up, will I understand you any better? Will I know why you despise me so?"

Her voice trembled. With a shock, he realized that beneath her sophisticated, flippant demeanor was a woman who cared deeply about what he thought.

She lowered the binoculars, holding them in front of her, like protection. Her face was tinged with pink, "Colin, what did I ever do to make you hate me?"

He looked into her eyes and saw what he didn't want to see—pleading, and something more. Something much more dangerous.

Longing.

Then he knew. What he never expected. What he both wanted and didn't want. What could only create havoc in his life. That this beautiful woman he found so attractive, so alluring, might fall in love with him. Might already be in love with him.

It wouldn't do. It couldn't. He mustn't let that happen. She was Henry's.

He looked back at her for an instant and knew his face revealed what his voice wouldn't. Her eyes widened, lips parting in an indrawn breath, and she took a step toward him just as he heard Henry shouting.

"Colin! Colin! I think it's German. Get her outta there. Gretchen! Run!"

Just as Colin heard Henry's panic, he caught the drone of the bomber. He grabbed Gretchen's hand and pulled her, racing toward the path that would take them down off the naked, exposed plateau. They sprinted across the open, uneven ground, Gretchen keeping pace. Ahead, Henry and Fiona stood by the half-packed hamper, staring in their direction.

"Go, Henry!" Colin shouted. "Get off this damn hill. Just go!"

Henry seemed paralyzed. He stared across the hundred yards between them. Oh no. He wouldn't leave without Gretchen.

"Fiona, get him out of here," Colin bellowed. Fiona grabbed Henry and pulled. Colin could hear her insistent voice. "Colin's got her. It's okay. We have to go so they can safely get down the hill behind us."

At that, Henry turned with Fiona and rushed toward the path. Overhead, Colin could hear the ominous low drone of an approaching Junker 88. He cursed his stupidity for allowing his friends to picnic on such a dangerous place. Then with a scream, Gretchen tripped on a rabbit hole and fell forward, sprawled across the ground.

Bending down, Colin said urgently, "Can you still run?"

Where was the feckin' Drem fighters? he screamed in his head. *Why hadn't they scrambled? Where was the goddamn coastal patrol?* Every fiber of him howled for a plane to climb into and blow the fuckers from his skies. But he had to stay calm and calculate the distance to the edge of the plateau. He could carry Gretchen if need be.

Gretchen moaned but got to her feet with his help. He put his arm around her waist to support her. They set off again, but at a slower pace, her wincing at each step.

"We're almost there," he encouraged her, relieved that Fiona and Henry had disappeared down the trail. He prayed they'd find cover on the hillside and not get strafed.

The time to reach the narrow descending path felt endless. His pounding heart and the approaching plane drowned out any other thoughts. Jumping down the first steep step, he reached up and helped Gretchen off the plateau. For one second, one excruciatingly delicious agonizing second, he crushed her to him and whispered, "I'll keep you safe." Then he commanded, "Get down. We have to crawl, and stay low. I'll be in front of you, helping."

They had just started slipping and sliding down the incline when he glanced up. The bomber was barely thirty feet overhead, the telltale swastika clearly visible on its wings, the bomb bay doors already open. He pushed Gretchen into the side of the hill and threw himself on top of her, bracing for impact.

"Colin?"

The fragrance of lilacs that grew in his mother's garden seemed out of place here. There was a Junker overhead, for crying out loud. Did she bring flowers for this picnic?

"Colin! What's happening? I felt a thud. But I didn't hear the bomb explode."

Lilacs. So sweet. But wait, who's speaking? That wasn't his mother.

Gretchen's voice dragged Colin back into awareness. He'd been so lost in the feel of her warm body, of the light scent of her perfume, he had forgotten for a fragment of time the very reason he was holding her.

To protect her. He lifted his head to scan the sky. Thank god the bomb had been a dud, but the Krauts might be circling back for another go.

"Gretchen? Colin?" He heard Henry's agonized voice drift up from below.

"Let's get the hell off this hill," Colin whispered into Gretchen's ear, her soft hair tickling his nose and for a disconcerting moment, tempting him to laugh. Instead, he rose to a crouch and shouted towards Henry's voice, "We're coming. Get to the car."

Keeping low, they scrambled and slid down the treacherous incline, Colin first, with Gretchen behind him, her hand on his shoulder for balance. Step by step they descended, Colin trying to go quickly but ever mindful of Gretchen's pained gasps. They rounded the last bend in the path, and there was Henry, pacing frantically beside the idling roadster, where Fiona sat in the driver's seat.

"Henry, she's fine," Colin assured, but Henry was already racing toward them. The two men helped Gretchen hobble to the stile and over it. Then Henry swept Gretchen up in his arms, carried her to the car, settled her in the back seat, and joined her there as Colin jumped into the front passenger seat, eyeing the sky for more German bombers. "Go, Fiona! To Edinburgh. Henry and I can find a ride back to Drem,"

Fiona pulled off in a roar. As the car raced down the macadam road, Colin turned around to check on Gretchen. Henry had his arms wrapped around her, soothing her as one would an injured child. "It's all right, Gretchen. We'll be home soon. You're just fine."

She lay still against Henry's chest, her eyes closed, sobbing silently.

Colin didn't know if it was from pain or shock. Seeing the fierce look on Henry's face, Colin felt a deep wrench inside. That moment between him and Gretchen on the plateau could never be repeated. The betrayal would destroy Henry.

He had to get away. If that meant volunteering to be a bomber pilot, that's what he would do. It would be torture to remain, knowing Gretchen's feelings. Glancing in Fiona's direction, he was startled to see the same look of despair on her face and realized she was as devastated by Henry's tender ministrations to Gretchen as he was. Why had he never seen it?

When Fiona looked his way, he smiled wanly and said softly, "What a fine feckin' Yankee Independence Day."

Fiona nodded, blinking away tears that had nothing to do with the wind in her eyes. "Aye, my laddie. Aye. A fine feckin' lot they are. Too bad we Scots will never be free."

Colin knew she wasn't talking about Scotland's longed-for independence from England.

Twenty-One

December 1941

As he always did, Henry started his letter to Fiona by writing the day, date, and time at the top: Sunday, December 7, 1941, 9:45 p.m. He had just added "Dear Fiona," when Theo, the newest ground crew member, burst into the barracks.

"Henry," he shouted, racing up to Henry's bunk, "Henry, the Japs. The Japs are bombing Pearl Harbor."

Henry looked up, frowning. "Theo, what are you talking about?"

"Henry! America! The Japs are attacking Hawaii!"

The few others who weren't on duty or out for the evening gathered around Henry as he slipped out of his lower bunk.

Theo was breathless with excitement. "They just said so on the wireless. Today. This morning, their time. Hawaii. Where is this Hawaii?"

His mind reeling from the news, Henry pulled a world map from one of his books. "It's a series of islands in the Pacific. See? Here. They're a territory of the United States. But how?"

Theo drew a deep breath. "It was a surprise, the BBC said. Complete surprise. Bloody awful. Ships sunk in the harbor. Dozens. And men lost. Oh, I'm sae sarry, Henry. I hope ye haven't got a brother in the Navy."

Then someone else came in yelling that the Japs had invaded Malaya and Hong Kong, both British colonies. That bit wasn't unexpected,

Henry knew, as the Japanese had been expanding their power in Indonesia and French Indo-China over the last year and been bombing Chungking in China for years. But no one had thought the Japanese would attack America.

In the morning, Henry learned that President Roosevelt was going to address Congress at 5:30 p.m. Edinburgh time and that the BBC would rebroadcast the speech at 7:30.

That evening, shortly before broadcast time, he stood in a corner of Edinburgh's unheated, Victorian train station, watching Gretchen pour tea for British servicemen at the Red Cross canteen. She looked so demure, with her wavy chestnut hair tied back in a neat chignon, topped by a white cap with a red cross, dressed in a conservative blue wool suit covered by her starched white apron, wearing a pair of flat, polished brogues.

She had been so somber in the months since their July Fourth picnic, even though she had suffered no more than a badly-sprained ankle. But then, so much had happened soon after that.

Within days, Colin got his transfer to Bomber Command. After a week's leave to visit his family in Achiltibuie, he was off to Canada for a six-month training course, for though he could pilot a Spitfire, there was a lot to learn about flying the four-engine Stirling. He'd asked Henry to give his regards to both girls.

Gretchen's face had drained of all color when he told her.

"Transferred? Bomber Command?" She said the words like a death sentence, sitting back in her chair at the restaurant he'd taken her to. "Henry, I'm sorry. I don't think I could eat anything." He called the waiter, canceled their order, and took her home. She looked ill.

Her shock puzzled Henry. She had repeatedly said she and Colin only tolerated each other for Henry's sake. Yet they had seemed to get along famously at the picnic, and Colin had been unusually cheerful. Until that scare with the German bomber.

As he joined the queue at the canteen, he longed to ask Colin about his current dilemma—go home to enlist, leaving Gretchen to fend for herself, or stay with the RAF and feel like a shirker. He missed Colin. The closest friend he'd ever had.

There was a throng of uniformed men, with a spattering of women in winter coats, sipping tea and munching sandwiches or Dundee Cake with rum-laced raisins served by Gretchen and four other women, two young and two older. Sounds of big band music from the wireless behind them echoed in the cavernous space.

"You heard about Pearl Harbor?" was the first thing he said to her when she looked up in surprise to see him.

"Of course!" She sounded offended.

"They're going to rebroadcast the President's address at 7:30. We should listen."

"Henry, I'm on duty."

"Gretchen, you're a volunteer," Henry snapped. "I'm sure they can spare you a few minutes to listen to your president talk about an attack on your country."

Gretchen was clearly startled, and he immediately apologized. "I'm sorry. I'm just... upset. I can't get it out of my mind. All those ships. Men. And us so far away from home."

One of the older women overheard and said sympathetically, "We'll all stop and listen, aye." In the meantime, Gretchen poured him a cup of scalding-hot tea the way he liked it. Strong and black, no milk. He munched a cucumber sandwich on day-old buttered bread.

Just before 7:30, a young naval officer shouted, "The American president is going to speak. Gather round." Brushing crumbs from her apron, Gretchen came out to stand next to Henry. Someone brought up chairs and insisted they sit.

A hush fell over the gathered crowd, which stood in a semi-circle around Gretchen and Henry, as the BBC announcer said in solemn tones, "We now rebroadcast for our BBC listeners here and abroad, the address to the American Congress made at twelve-thirty this afternoon, Eastern Standard Time, by the President of the United States."

To Henry, it felt like something out of a novel. A son of German immigrants, working for the British Royal Air Force, sitting in a Scottish train station, listening to Franklin D. Roosevelt, whom he had not voted for, talk about an attack on a Pacific island by the Imperial Navy of Japan.

He frowned in concentration as the distinctive voice of FDR drifted out of the wireless.

"Yesterday, December 7th, 1941, a date which will live in infamy, the United States of America was suddenly and deliberately attacked by naval and air forces of the Empire of Japan."

Henry felt Gretchen take his hand. He cradled their clasped hands on his thigh and listened as the President continued.

"The United States was at peace with that nation and, at the solicitation of Japan, was still in conversation with the government and its emperor looking toward the maintenance of peace in the Pacific. Indeed, one hour after Japanese air squadrons had commenced bombing in Oahu, the Japanese ambassador to the United States and his colleagues delivered to the Secretary of State a formal reply to a recent American message. While this reply stated that it seemed useless to continue the existing diplomatic negotiations, it contained no threat of war or armed attack."

Barely breathing, Henry listened as Roosevelt explained how the attack was obviously planned and that "very many American lives have been lost." Gretchen began to cry softly. He clutched her hand tighter.

When Roosevelt said the Japanese government had also launched an attack against the British colonies of Malaya and Hong Kong, an angry undertone of muttered voices rose among those around him. He had to lean in to hear the President say that the Japanese forces had also attacked the Philippine Islands, Wake Island, and Midway Island, all American protectorates.

Henry felt his heart constrict when Roosevelt said, "As commander in chief of the Army and the Navy, I have directed that all measures be taken for our defense."

At this point, thunderous applause from Congress interrupted the President's address. When the ovation died down, Roosevelt went on. "Always will we remember the character of the onslaught against us. No matter how long it may take us to overcome this premeditated invasion, the American people in their righteous might will win through to an absolute victory."

Once again, the members of Congress exploded in applause. Henry glanced at Gretchen. Tears were dampening her lovely cheeks. Taking his free hand, he gently wiped one away with his knuckle. Gretchen gave him a small, tremulous smile.

As the President continued solemnly, Henry thought of his older brothers, sure to enlist the very next day. "...with unbounded determination of our people," Roosevelt was saying, "we will gain the inevitable triumph, so help us, God."

A roar erupted from the wireless and the uniformed men around them.

In a stern, unshaken voice, Roosevelt finished his speech. "I ask that the Congress declare that since the unprovoked and dastardly attack by Japan on Sunday, December 7th, a state of war has existed between the United States and the Japanese empire."

Cries of "The Yanks are in it, the Yanks are in it!" echoed throughout the rafters of the railway station, and Henry felt enthusiastic claps on his shoulders.

"We're in it in the Pacific," he said to Gretchen over the uproar, "but I don't know about the Atlantic." The noise drowned out whatever analysis the BBC announcer was making about the speech, so Henry pulled Gretchen to her feet and led her through the throng to a table near the rear of the canteen.

"What should we do, Gretchen?" he asked, not even trying to check the frustration in his voice. "I should go home and enlist. I know my brothers will, and your brother too."

Gretchen gasped. "William? William in the service? Omigod!"

"He always said he was going to join the Navy, didn't he?"

"But he's a baby. He's only just started his freshman year at Dickinson."

"Gretchen, he's older than some of the pilots flying Spitfires and Stirlings."

Gretchen stared at him. He touched her still-damp face and blurted out, "Gretchen, marry me."

He didn't know who was more stunned, Gretchen or himself. But he knew it was the right thing to do, even if it was impulsive and unplanned.

"I know I didn't do it right the last time. I just assumed. I don't have a ring, but I'll do it right." He slipped off the chair onto one knee, and took her hands, trying to ignore Gretchen's agonized look.

From across the room, someone shouted, "He's proposing! The Yank is proposing. Righty-Hey. Three cheers for the Yank and his lassie."

Trying to ignore the tumult in the background, Henry went on. "Gretchen, you know that I love you. I don't think... I don't think I ever said that. I just thought... assumed... that you knew. I've never stopped loving you. That's why I'm here in Scotland. I came because of you."

Seeing the slow shaking of her head, Henry added in a voice he knew was pitifully begging, "Please," and then was still, staring up at her with longing.

Gretchen felt her already-torn heart rending. Over the cheers in the background and the shouts of "Get him while he's on his knees, lassie," and "I'll marry ye, lassie, if you'd rather have a good, stout Scot," Gretchen said in a trembling voice, "Henry, please get up. Please."

He slid back onto his seat but still held her hands, leaning forward, one foot jiggling nervously.

"Henry, my dear, dear Henry, you know I can't marry you," she said at last, knowing she had to speak these hope-killing words out loud to this man waiting for a different answer.

"Why, Gretchen? Why? I know I'm not worthy of..."

"Stop it. Stop saying that. Henry, you are the most loyal, kind, generous, decent man I know. I'm the one who doesn't deserve you..."

"Gretchen, I..."

"No, Henry, listen. Please listen. I was so awful to you back then, in '39 in that restaurant in Harrisburg. So full of myself and my plans. So cruel and thoughtless. I didn't really understand what it was like to love somebody who..." She stopped, choking, thinking of Colin.

"...doesn't love you back," Henry finished for her in a flat voice. "There *is* someone else. But that can't be! Anyone you loved would surely love you back. They'd be mad not to. And why would you keep

THE BOMBER JACKET   271

on hoping if you knew they didn't..." He trailed off. "Yeah, right," he muttered after a pause.

Gretchen wanted to weep with regret. "You know I've never wanted to hurt you. You have always been there for me. Always watching out for me, even when you introduced me to other guys..."

She blinked, realization dawning. *Of course. How could I be so stupid? Of course, Colin must have known how Henry felt. They were best mates. And no matter how Colin felt, he wouldn't betray his friendship with Henry.*

Gretchen let herself be transported back to July Fourth on Traprain Law. Let herself see, for one split second, Colin's feelings clearly reflected in his eyes. Let herself feel his arms around her, his warm, protective presence sheltering her on that hillside. Longing for nothing more than to turn in his arms and kiss him with abandon.

She recalled that it was Henry who had taken charge when they'd gotten to the car. Henry who had consoled her, tried to ease her pain. At the time, she had been stunned, confused, and lightheaded, half sobbing from shock and half from unfathomable joy. Colin loved her! On that drive back to Edinburgh, she waited for him to turn around and put into words what his eyes and actions had told her.

Instead, he spent the ride talking in undertones to Fiona in the front seat while scanning the sky. Instead of clearly staking his claim, he allowed Henry to help her into Fiona's aunt's house, hanging back, barely looking at her. As if he were sorry. As if he regretted his momentary lapse of control. And then, proving her right, he vanished from her life, volunteering to fly over German territory on bombing missions from which half the crews never returned.

With an indrawn breath, she looked at Henry seated across from her, who still held her hands in his strong, calloused ones. Her heart bled for him. Of course, she knew how he felt. Of course, she understood the hopelessness of loving someone who is beyond reach. Someone who can never be yours.

I could tell Henry I was in love with Colin. He would want me to be happy. He would tell Colin it was okay, that he gave us his blessing. As soon as the thought flitted through her mind, she recognized with disgust how selfish it was. It was bad enough to break Henry's heart by once again refusing his proposal. She would not destroy him with the knowledge that she was in love with his dearest friend.

Who was in love with her.

A betrayal Colin had clearly decided was untenable, answering at last the question of why he had taken himself out of her life so abruptly.

Henry had been sitting quietly, waiting, watching with his vividly blue, guileless eyes.

Gretchen looked directly at him and said softly, tender regret in her voice, "Henry, I cherish you with all my heart. I just can't love you." Leaning forward, she gave him a gentle, sorrowful kiss on his lips. And walked away.

Henry had been unable to eat, sleep, or concentrate since that night. He looked so haggard that the commander finally said, "Smith, it's pretty clear this Pearl Harbor thing has you torn up. I'm giving you a 72-hour pass. Get the hell off this aerodrome."

The only place off the aerodrome that Henry could think of other than Edinburgh was London. To see Fiona. Not knowing how to reach her by phone, he sent her a telegram: *Coming to London. Stop. Take you to dinner. Stop. Name the place. Stop. Staying with Alice.* Then he called Alice, and yes, he was welcome.

Friday morning he caught the London train, sitting immobile as the miles flew by, Gretchen's refusal tumbling in his head: "Henry, I cherish you with all my heart. I just can't love you." Feeling over and over the touch of her lips on his. The only time she had ever kissed him.

He was fussed over and pampered by Alice, whom he hadn't seen since the summer of 1940. Her husband was a fire warden and gone many evenings, so she was delighted to have company. She fretted about how tired he looked and asked after the Yankee girl. He replied that he had come to London to visit Fiona, who called to tell him where and when to meet.

"Ah, so it's the Scottish one you settled on then, right-o," Alice said with a wink. "Quite a posh place you're taking her to, The Savoy. Hope you saved your pounds and pence."

Henry didn't have the desire to lay out his tale of woe for Alice, so he simply said, "She's just a friend," to which Alice laughed uproariously.

"And they say the Brits keep it close to the chest. 'enry me boy, you are a hoot. I'll not expect you then, Saturday night?"

Confused, Henry replied, "Aren't I welcome?"

Alice simply shook her head, "You silly goose."

It was a rainy, miserable evening when Henry sat down across from Fiona in the Savoy's upscale restaurant. The weather was as grey as his mood. He felt jittery and distracted. The soft candlelight, the muted conversations and laughter, the orchestra playing soothing music did nothing to settle his nerves. He barely touched the savory chops, buttery parsleyed potatoes, or the sugary beets, all special treats in rationed London that Fiona had ordered for him because he was too unfocused to even read the menu.

When he rejected the idea of wine, she ordered him a pint of lager, which he drank mindlessly. Still not a drinker, it was already making his head buzz as he finished the story of his impulsive, rejected proposal. To his surprise, Fiona was less than sympathetic.

"Henry, as usual, it was sweet and romantic of you to propose in such an impulsive way. I'm sure Gretchen was just as shocked as she was the first time you asked her to marry you. But what would make you think you had any better chance now than two-and-a-half years ago?"

"She's been... she's never been... she always seemed..." Henry fumbled for an answer.

"She's always been warm. Enjoyed your company. Led you on..."

"Fiona! That's not true."

Fiona softened her tone and leaned across the table, laying one hand on his, rubbing it tenderly. "Did she tell you she was in love with someone else?"

Henry nodded miserably.

"Before you proposed?"

"Of course not," Henry said, startled. "I might be a fool, but I'm not an idiot. Why would I have proposed if I knew she was in love with someone else?"

A waiter in a pristine white dinner jacket came by to check on them. "Another lager for the gentleman," Fiona said. "He's going to need it. Aye, and another glass of wine for me."

Looking around at the other guests, Henry noticed a lot of glittering jewelry and high-ranking officers. It occurred to him he might not have enough cash to pay the bill. "Fiona, this is a pretty swanky restaurant you chose. I'm only a grease monkey."

"A what?"

"Oh, sorry. It's American slang for mechanic."

"Na worry your wee little haid about it," she said. "It's my treat."

He was horrified. "Of course not, I didn't mean to imply..."

She sighed in frustration. "Henry, shut up. When you said you were coming to town, I called a business colleague of my da's and asked for a favor. We're always putting him up, so he was happy to arrange the night out on the town for me."

Henry was a bit scandalized. It seemed... forward of a girl to ask such a thing.

She laughed at his expression. "Henry, you remain a dear. And an innocent. You worry about a lassie treating you to dinner, while the world's gone to hell, and your country is finally in this with us against the Nazis."

"It was a stunner when Hitler declared war on us. Pearl Harbor was enough of a shock. Like the Brits, we'll be fighting a two-front war."

"What will you do, Henry?"

Henry again felt flooded with confusion. "I should go home and enlist."

"But you are helping your country, Henry."

"How?"

"Why, you're like that Eagle Squadron, those flyboys from America who came over in '39 and '40. You've been here for a year and a half, helping us Brits hold out against Hitler. The rest of the Yanks will show up after a while. Why not just wait till then and see about joinin' up."

Taking another swig of his lager, Henry considered Fiona's suggestion.

"Besides, I doubt you could leave Gretchen," Fiona added, with sarcasm.

"Fiona, I thought you and Gretchen were friends."

"We are friends. She's like the sister I never had. And better. She's practically part of the family. I think my aunt and uncle have adopted her. It's just, I hate to see you bash your haid against a door that will never come open."

Henry took a couple more swallows of his lager. He thought the stuff got better the more he drank, though he still preferred chilled American beer.

"I just wish I knew who the guy was who's breaking her heart."

Fiona made an odd noise and started coughing.

"Are you all right?" He leaned forward in alarm.

She nodded yes, and sipped some water, "Swallowed my wine wrong. Sorry. So Gretchen didn't tell you who this guy was?"

"No."

"And you have no idea?"

Her stare was intense, almost as if she didn't believe him. He shook his head. "I even asked Colin before he left for Canada if he thought Gretchen was in love with someone."

"And what did Colin say?" Her voice was tentative, hesitant.

"He said he wouldn't hazard a guess."

"Aye, 'twas a right smart answer." She sighed again. "Henry, I am so happy you came to see me, even if it is to pour your heart out about another girl. I'm happy to listen. But, can we dance? You're such a good dancer, and you'd be surprised at what a clumsy lot these Brits are. Guess the lads in Scotland learn from their highland dances not to trod on a lassie's toes."

She stood up, extending her hand. It was the first he had noticed her outfit, a soft green sateen suit, pencil-thin skirt, and form-fitting, low-cut jacket. A strand of pearls circled her neck.

Henry said, "I thought you'd be in uniform. I've never seen you in uniform."

She smiled. "Henry, I'm not sure you've *ever* seen me."

He tossed back the rest of his lager. Was that his third? He had lost count. Standing up, he said, "I see you now. You look smashing."

She smiled even more. "I'm glad you noticed." She took his hand and led him to the dance floor. Her reddish-blonde hair swayed, flashing. What a pretty color. "If you keep looking, laddie, you might see more than you can imagine."

A knock sounded at a door and a male voice called, "Room service."

Henry stirred. His head pulsed. Those flyboys would do anything to get a rise out of him, he grumbled, sinking back into sleep. He was almost unconscious when the knock became more insistent.

"Room service!"

A nearby female voice called, "Coming! Just a moment."

Instantly wide awake, three facts struck him like bullets: he had a splitting headache, he was completely naked under the bedclothes, and he was in a room he'd never seen before. Closing his eyes, he struggled to remember where he was and how he got there. Certainly not a barracks, not with the soft sheets, thick mattress, and warm, downy comforter.

And a woman. At that last thought, Henry sunk under the bedclothes.

He heard a door open and a soft female voice with a Scots accent say, "Put it on the coffee table." There came the sound of heavy steps, some rattling china, a female "Thanks," the tread of retreating steps, and a closing door. He heard a spoon clink against china and light footsteps padding around to his side of the bed, which sank slightly as someone sat next to him.

Henry laid perfectly still, hoping it was just a dream.

"I know you're awake, Henry. Don't play at being a wee bairn. Sit up; have some tea."

Fiona! What had he done? All he could think to say was, "My head is killing me."

Her soft laughter was sympathetic. "Poor wee darlin'. You'll be feelin' better once you have some tea and something to nibble."

Brief flashes of smooth naked skin, round fleshy curves, luscious lips, and intertwined bodies made him shake his head no. And then groan from the pain.

"I haven't much time, Henry, and you said you wanted to see me in my uniform."

Awkwardly, he sat up, pulled the sheets up around his armpits, and slowly opened his eyes. The dull, rainy Sunday light filtered in drips and drabs through gauzy sheers.

Fiona laughed again. "Henry, you are so sweet. You have no idea how wonderful you are. I'd like to stay and remind you, but I've a bus to catch. I'm on duty at noon." She sat on the edge of the bed, holding out a cup of tea, gazing at him with a wry smile and a tilt of her head, looking polished, pristine, and very much in control.

Henry, on the other hand, felt disheveled, rumpled, and at a complete loss for what to do. Or say. He managed to mumble, "You said you didn't think I noticed you," as he took the cup of tea from her hands.

She stood up and smiled at him, a glow of happiness about her that he never remembered seeing before. But then, had he ever really paid attention?

"I certainly do think you noticed this time, ye daft Yankee. And you certainly have a lovely doodle."

At which Henry spat his tea across the bedclothes, sending Fiona into merry laughter as she took his cup, "Let me get you a refill."

She walked serenely to the coffee table and poured him more tea, brought it back to him, then poured herself one. Sitting on an ottoman, she scraped some marmalade across some toast.

"Would you like a piece?" she asked like the proper hostess.

He muttered, "No, thank you," and sipped the soothing hot tea. Earl Grey. Not his favorite, but anything to chase the taste of alcohol and cigarettes from his mouth.

"But I don't smoke!" he protested out loud, astonished that he had.

"You did last night. We smoked and drank and danced. And danced and smoked and drank. And then came up here and..."

"Stop!" he nearly shouted. "I'm so sorry I...

But she walked quickly around the bed and stopped his words with a lingering kiss. As she stepped away, he heard himself say, "Are you sure you can't stay for a while?"

She grinned, her pert Scottish face aglow. "Now that's more like it!"

But just as quickly, he felt ashamed at what he had done and looked away.

"Henry," she said softly, standing nearby. "No regrets. Really. I know you love Gretchen. You will till the day you die. She wishes you'd find love somewhere else because she loves someone else. But I'm content with being second best. I'm here, Henry, if you ever need or want me. Or want someone who wants you. No chains. No obligations. Just good company."

He could find no words to respond to that amazing statement, spoken lightly, but shot through with feeling.

"There's toast and fruit and a wee bit of marmalade." As she talked, she picked up her overcoat, service hat, purse, and air raid helmet in its drab brown shoulder bag. "Checkout time's noon, so you've time to wash up, and relax. Tab is all taken care of."

"Fiona..."

"It's all right, Henry. I won't tell Gretchen. I know *you* won't. She'd be happy for you, though, I think. And she'd be happy for me. Well, maybe. She's more possessive of you than she realizes. I know you always thought Colin and I would be a good match. You were wrong."

She came back to the bedside for one more lingering kiss. "Don't be a stranger, Yank. Come see me when you need some London life. This certainly isn't staid Old Edinburgh."

He simply looked at her somberly.

"A smile, Yank."

He obliged her with one.

"Maybe when the war's over, all of us will get our haids on straight. You. Me. Gretchen. Colin. Till then, Henry, it's live and let live while we have life."

And with that, she was gone.

On the day she turned down Henry's second marriage proposal, Gretchen decided that if she wasn't going back to the States to support the war effort there, she would do more where she was. Something besides just volunteering. Something that would take her mind off Colin.

She just wasn't sure what *she* could do.

The following Saturday, while making her volunteer rounds at the hospital, she had the answer. She could become a nurse. Edinburgh's Royal Hospital had a two-year course starting in January, with the option for a one-year assistant program. Once she was certified, she could work in an RAF hospital in England.

Closer to Colin, once he was permanently assigned to a bomber base.

Enrolling in the nursing school was more difficult than she had thought. No one knew quite what to do with her. She was an American, to start with. And though she had been living in Scotland for two-and-a-half years, and the United States was now in the war, her idea was greeted with skepticism. First, by Fiona's Aunt Margaret, who was practically a surrogate mother, and next, by Fiona's uncle, whom she worked for. When she told Henry in late December over drinks in an Edinburgh pub, he looked at her oddly and then said tersely, "You're doing it for this chap. It's a flyboy, isn't it?"

Gretchen nearly blurted the truth, but the pain on Henry's face stopped her. "Henry, I'm not going to talk about this... this... other person. He can't, he won't ever be... mine."

In a voice laced with censure, he replied, "Is he married? That's it. You've fallen in love with a married man. Gretchen, how..."

"Henry, stop! Stop now!" Gretchen was stunned. She had never heard Henry speak so savagely. Pulling her thoughts together, she said firmly, "I am not going to talk about it. Ever again. And if you can't... if we can't just be friends, well, then we can't spend time together."

She finished in a bluster, realizing immediately how empty her life would be without Henry. She needed him as her companion, her pillar. But he needed someone else to love.

Henry's nod seemed reluctant, his voice clipped. "You're right. I'm sorry. It's not my business." He sighed, and his voice softened. "I guess, more than anything, I'm worried about you... seeing... well... those boys can be quite a mess when they come back."

The most surprising objection came from Fiona, who stopped off in Edinburgh on her way for a Christmas visit with her parents in Inverness. "Gretchen, my uncle needs you more than ever in the office. Why, look, you practically run the secretarial pool," Fiona protested. "Besides, you're not the nursing type."

That infuriated Gretchen. "That's exactly what Henry said when I first volunteered as a Red Cross visitor. And I proved him wrong."

"It's a hell of a lot different to be a nurse than to be a visitor. What does Henry say now?" Fiona replied in her irritatingly calm Scottish manner.

"I don't care what he says. He's got no say in my choices." At Fiona's raised eyebrows, Gretchen glared back. "Yes, he proposed again. I wrote you all about it. He probably did too. The two of you write enough letters to fill a book."

"Henry looks out for you," Fiona said mildly, but the flush on her face made Gretchen wonder if there wasn't something more than letters between her and Henry. Not that she cared. Or should care?

But that didn't stop Gretchen from blurting out, "What did he do, come cry on your shoulder?" She hated the way she sounded, petty and peevish. She knew Henry needed someone, but was she willing for that someone to be Fiona? No, he and Fiona were just friends. When did they ever see each other except with her?

But the biggest hurdle to her plan was the hospital matron.

"It's just so, unusual, you see," the tall, soft-spoken woman in her mid-forties said. "It's not that I don't admire ye, and I see that ye've been workin' as a volunteer visitor and at a Red Cross canteen. Aye, and ye've got fine recommendations. But Miss Dunst, the work ye're doin' now is important. It's vital to the war effort, everah bit as much as nursin'."

Gretchen worked hard to stay calm and charming, but apparently, charm wasn't what was needed here.

"Ma'am, here's the story. It's too dangerous to go home. The Atlantic is filled with Nazi U-boats. My brother's joined up, you see. The Navy. He'll be shipped out to the Pacific after training. To fight the Japs. If there were some Scottish girl in America stranded there because of the war, I would hope she'd be welcome to do her bit."

She leaned forward and added softly, "Ma'am, I've been in your country since May of 1939. I've been in this war with you since the beginning. Your war has been my war. I've seen the brothers and cousins of my Scottish friends go off to war and not come back or be terribly injured. I've gotten to know RAF pilots and crew myself, and I've lost..."

Her voice broke at that moment, knowing the terrible danger Colin had put himself in. Knowing he *was* lost to her. She wasn't playing it for drama, and it wasn't taken as such, for the Matron sighed and said gently, "Aye. I see. It's as you say; we all have to do our bit. And it's in working that we heal our wounds."

And with that, Gretchen was on her way to becoming a nurse.

Twenty-Two

April 1942

Going home. Aye, we're headed home. Another night spent. Another night survived.

The chill of the plane penetrated the leather and wool of Colin's bomber jacket. Even with spring on the ground, it was never warm in the clouds. The only warmth came from the fear in the pit of his stomach, though as he got closer to home, different sensations took over, starting with awareness of the intense cold.

And with it, his other senses. There's engine oil, a smell that feels thick; the sharp, bitter odor of cold metal, a smell he can taste; and the sweet, musty smell of leather and slightly damp wool of the bomber jacket.

3:53 a.m.

The crew were quiet; they always were on the return. The nervous chatter that accompanied their trip out in the heavy four-engine Stirling was replaced on the way back by exhaustion, hunger, and the anticipation of home. Ahead was the barely discernible outline of the English coastline. Somewhere below was the English Channel. He could not see it, only sense it. It was always there, a kind of being: churning, roiling, heaving. Like his stomach.

His stomach always clenched on the way back. On the way out he was calm, focused, steady, even when flak exploded around them, or the plane next to him erupted in a fireball of death. But on the way back, that's when the odds began playing in his mind. His eyes constantly darted between the fuel gauge, the altimeter, and the speedometer. Then ahead, to the right, to the left. His ears constantly listened for a change in the sound of the engine, a warning sputter, a hint of a cough.

They depended on him, the men. To get them home.

After six months of bomber training in Canada, there was a month at an Advanced Flying Unit on the east coast of England and another month at an Operational Training Unit in the Midlands. It was there, in early April, that he had been "crewed up," that bizarre RAF ritual of eyeballing each other and choosing the six other men on whose skill and guts his life depended.

For him that meant the navigator, the bomb aimer, the front gunner/wireless operator, two air gunners, and the flight engineer. Counting himself as the pilot, a crew of seven. Once crewed up, they received their first Bomber Command assignment—Bomber Squadron 115 at RAF Marham in Norfolk, in the east of England.

Only five missions in, he and his crew were still new to each other. Soon they would stand down for a week's leave. But then they'd have to come back and keep up the routine, night after night, with a few breaks between, until they'd completed their thirty missions.

Would Lady Luck hold? He didn't trust her. Just when you thought she was on your side, she'd bugger you. Couldn't afford to get cocky. Lots of planes limped back to base only to wreck at the end of an airfield: out of fuel or missing the landing gear. Each nighttime bombing raid only raised the probability of not returning. It didn't bear thinking of.

The plane hit an air pocket and dipped. The sting of acid rose to his throat. Thickening clouds warned of turbulence.

"Look sharp," he told his crew. "We're heading up to get out of this cloud cover. It might get a wee bit rough."

If Colin closed his eyes and tuned out his hearing, he could almost imagine he was still at University, eighteen years old and learning to fly in a Tiger Moth over the low rolling Pentland hills south of Edinburgh. He could recall the exhilarating freedom of soaring off into the sky, the sheer joy of defeating the gravitational pull of the earth, and leaving behind the uncertainty of a future in the midst of war.

But also, in the silence of their flight, amidst his vigilant attention to the plane, there was a lot of time to think.

About Gretchen.

It was the only time he allowed himself that indulgence. The rest of the time he focused on getting his crew to the night's target and keeping them attuned to their jobs. On the ground, he was washing away the possibility of getting the chop with long nights drinking at the pub near the aerodrome or having an occasional fling with a willing WAAF.

Civilian girls were too messy to get involved with. He learned that lesson after that girl in Canada.

He felt so disconnected from the war, being in Canada, in spite of learning to fly a Stirling Bomber. Maybe the Canadians, like the Americans, felt safer due to oceans on two sides of them. It was from that distance he'd read the stunning news of Singapore's fall, the seemingly impregnable British stronghold at the tip of Malaya. Then there was the ongoing fight in North Africa against the Desert Rat, Rommel, and the Russian defense of Moscow against the Nazis.

A bit of a romance was a welcome distraction. Molly was lovely. Sweet. Her parents didn't like him and he didn't blame them one bit.

"Navigator to pilot. Of course, captain. Steady as she goes." The voice in his headphones interrupted his thoughts of the Canadian girl.

"Right oh." He said automatically, his mind already drifting back to last fall.

He tried to avoid Molly's open pursuit. But after a while, he decided if she was willing, he was too. He had done his best to be honorable. Hadn't taken more than she was willing to give, which was time and lots of intense petting in a borrowed car or on a wooded walk.

He never heard from Gretchen. Hadn't expected to. But of course, he heard of her from Henry, the ever-faithful correspondent.

Colin dropped Henry a few lines, mostly about training, about Canada, about Molly, knowing he would tell Gretchen. It was a heartless way to say, "Look, you and I can never be."

The shocking events of Pearl Harbor occurred while he was in Canada, followed shortly by Henry's revelation that he had proposed to

Gretchen. Colin's initial reaction to Henry's news had been a gasping, breathless pain in his stomach as if he had been sucker punched.

She turned me down. Again, Henry had written. *But you know me, Colin, I'm not giving up. She hinted that there was someone else. But he must be a worthless piece of shit not to love her back. I told her so myself. I'll back off for a while, but I'm not going away. She needs me. I know it. I'll prove to her that I'm more worthy than that nameless bastard who's trampled her heart.*

Though Henry's proposal was not unexpected, it reinforced that it was all a bloody mess. He might love Gretchen. Gretchen might love him. He cringed to imagine how she must have felt when she heard about Molly. And there was also Henry. Faithful, loyal Henry, his best friend.

In the end, he'd tried to ease away from Molly, but she confronted him one weekend. "Colin McAuley, I know you are leaving this place sooner than later, and I know you're going off to war, and even when the war's over you don't be back, but I have you *now.* So..."

So for one long weekend in a country inn, he put Gretchen completely out of his mind. Well, almost. There was that moment in the middle of the night when he ached to be holding a different woman from North America. Molly wrote after he left. He replied only once, after he was sure he hadn't left her with an unwelcome gift from their weekend together. Told her to find a nice Canadian bloke.

Back in England, he swore off civilians. The girls in the service understood a wartime relationship. Lots of laughter. Liquor. Love that wasn't love. Just the distraction of kisses in the back alley or a quick roll in the sack. And see you around, flyboy.

It kept his mind off of Gretchen, though somehow in that cold, dark bomber, he could feel her touch. They were dancing. She was laughing. He was holding onto his self-control with a grip of iron, or was he clutching the throttle? And that flowery tingle of her perfume mixed with the acrid scent of fuel. The softness of her skin and the feel of her hand on his neck during their first dance were like the warmth of the wool on the collar of his bomber jacket.

So long ago. Time had a way of dissolving in the endless drudgery of wartime routine. New Year's Eve. Just as the calendar turned over to

1941. Now it was spring of 1942. More than ten months since he last saw her, at Traprain Law.

He remembered the gut-wrenching terror that she would be injured, the rush of protectiveness, the incongruous heat of desire as he'd sheltered her in his arms on that steep path, just below the exposed plateau. Covering her with his body.

Ready to give his life for her.

But not to her.

Though Colin had been back in England for a month, Henry had not yet seen him. After only a couple ops on his Stirling, Colin and his crew were sent to a month-long training at a Heavy Conversion Unit to learn to fly the much-anticipated Lancaster Bomber.

Henry tried unsuccessfully to get a seventy-two-hour pass to visit Colin. And since Gretchen had started nursing school, he'd barely seen her. She continued to volunteer weekends at the canteen, so their visits were limited to a few snatched hours.

He did his best to stuff his feelings deep inside his mind, knowing she'd refuse to see him if he talked anymore about love. But he dropped her regular notes and called if he didn't see her.

Fiona wrote, as faithfully as ever. Only more personal, more teasing. She addressed them, *To my Yank* and signed them, *Your Scottish Lassie*.

In early March he got a long weekend leave and, needing a break, took up her invitation. Once again, they went to dinner, danced a long time, drank, and ended up in her hotel room. This time, Henry knew what choices he was making but still could not shake the sense of betrayal. This was Gretchen's friend. He was in love with Gretchen. What was he doing?

"Henry," Fiona said the next morning, "The last thing I want is for you to eat yourself alive with guilt. I don't expect anything of you, Henry dearest. It's just... we dance well together. And I know I can trust you; you know you can trust me to keep this a secret between us. The war is a long way from ending, even with you Yanks joining in. Can't we just enjoy the dance?"

So, he developed a type of deliberate amnesia. When he was with Fiona, he didn't think about Gretchen. But the rest of the time, in spite of Fiona's weekly letters and his faithful responses, it was Gretchen he thought about, not Fiona.

Gretchen was grateful that the nursing course filled her time and her mind. The days were long, the studies demanding, and the instructors unforgiving. The theory of medicine taught in the morning classes from eight to noon was undergirded by afternoons and evenings of practical, hands-on duties, which for Gretchen, as a beginning nurse, consisted of changing sheets, giving baths, and dealing with bedpans. Routine checks came next. And then wound care.

She was officially on duty Monday through Friday, 8 a.m. to 8 p.m. and circulated through the wards, including the children's ward and maternity. One day a week was spent at the rehabilitation hospital at the edge of the city, where Scottish servicemen were sent to finish their recovery nearer home. This included a few pilots, but Bomber Command had its own network of hospitals and rehab centers in England.

She was neither queasy nor shocked by anything she had to deal with, unlike some of her fellow trainees. Her childhood on the farm and her volunteer work had been good preparation. Besides, she had a strong stomach.

Henry gave her updates about Colin. When he said Colin was seeing some Canadian girl named Molly, it took all of Gretchen's self-control not to weep in front of him. Months later, when he told her Colin was back in the UK, she had to keep herself from doing a dance of joy. *At least he's back home,* she thought. Then acknowledged that *back home* meant England and a bomber station. And missions.

To her, the devastating wounds of each RAF crew member she nursed represented some terrible thing that could happen to Colin.

She no longer frequented nightclubs, only going out when Henry came into Edinburgh, and often only to see a movie or take a walk or catch a show. Evenings and weekends were spent studying for exams, and she continued to volunteer at the canteen on Saturdays. She found the routine surprisingly soothing and finally felt that she was doing something worthwhile.

Something that would make Colin proud of her.

Twenty-Three

June 1942

HE AND GRETCHEN STOOD hand-in-hand in the Achiltibuie churchyard *some distance from his family home. It was bitter cold.*

She spoke urgently, a desperate, intense look on her face.

"When I die, I want to be buried next to you in this graveyard. I don't ever want to leave you or this place. This is my home now. Will you promise me that? Colin? Promise me that?"

He was practically shaking from the cold.

"Gretchen, we need to get you home. If it makes you feel better, of course, we'll be side by side in this graveyard. But you're not going to die anytime soon. Besides, it's cold. You're nearly frozen. Let's get out of this graveyard. Come. I'll get you home safely. I promise you <u>that</u>."

"Cap'n, Cap'n, remember what you always promise?" came the panicked voice of his navigator, Tack, in his headset.

"I'll get you home safely. I promise you that," Colin replied groggily.

Intense cold filled the bomber cabin as it flew through the predawn June morning at cruising altitude. Colin's eyes were closed. They shouldn't be. He was flying a plane. He forced them open.

The cockpit was choked with the smell of engine oil, gasoline, and cold leather. A strangely metallic taste lingered in Colin's mouth. Blood.

Then it came rushing back. He could see the blinding flashes of flak, feel the concussion of the exploding incendiary as it destroyed his far port engine, and hear the whiz of bullets tearing through the cabin. Over his headset came the agonizing screams of Ox, the tail gunner who'd been strafed by a pursuing Messerschmitt.

"Stay awake Cap'n, you've got to keep awake. We're almost home." He heard the pleading in the young Aussie's voice and the roar of the rattling plane limping home on three engines across the English Channel.

Colin strained to remember. Where was that damn Messerschmitt?

Oh, right. He had taken evasive action, and the German fighter, attempting to line up another shot, had banked directly into a Lancaster flying slightly below to his left. Both planes had fallen out of the sky in a tangled mass of metal.

Bloody hell for the other RAF crew. And those Krauts too.

The sense of Gretchen's presence faded slowly as excruciating pain surged through his left jaw and thigh. He realized he'd been hit.

Fitz sat slumped over next to him. With shaking hands, Tack was trying to staunch the flow of blood from the flight engineer's stomach.

"He's bad, Cap," Tack shouted over the noise, his voice shaking. "He's bad."

"What about Ox?"

"Don't ask."

The rest of the crew checked in, one by one. Rattled, but uninjured. And counting on him to get them home. Safely.

It was a promise he always made to himself and them as they set out into the night to Germany or Belgium or France, wherever their briefing revealed. Always. "We're heading out, now, men. I promise that I'll get you home safely."

A foolish promise, one beyond his power to keep, but one that he made, nevertheless. He would do everything within *his* power to get his crew back to base. Even bargaining with God.

I won't think of her ever again, I promise, if you just let me get these lads home safely, Lord. Please. I'll give her up. Completely. Just let me get these lads home. They're depending on me.

What if the hit which disabled the engine and filled the cabin with shrapnel also damaged the landing gear? Should he tell the crew to bail out? Should he ditch in the drink and hope they don't drown in the sinking plane? Or risk a belly landing on the tarmac that could kill them all?

It was too risky to test the gear yet. The drag on the damaged plane would use up even more of their limited fuel. And then there was his wandering mind and alternating periods of sweating and shivering.

He tried to ignore the pain in his jaw, the blood in his throat. Other places in his body had begun to scream.

Ox's moans had gone ominously silent, and though Fitz might have been able to take the plane in, he was slumped across his controls, seemingly lifeless. There was no one else who could fly, which he was now attempting by dead reckoning, by the stars, and by the shape of the land miles below. His squadron had scattered in an effort to evade the pursuing Messerschmitts. There was no one else to follow.

True, flying by starlight was his favorite way to skim the sky. Just him and a plane and the night. He shook his head to clear it, staring into the darkness. Ironically, it was a perfect night to fly. And to drop bombs. No moon. Just the pinpricks of light to float among.

Only it wasn't just him in the Lancaster Bomber floating among the stars.

Were there stars in the sky when he and Gretchen were standing in the churchyard? Was it night? Was that why it was so cold? And when had that happened? Had he taken her home to visit his family?

"Cap'n, Cap'n?" Tack's worried voice brought him back to the present. Again. He'd rather have stayed with Gretchen.

Churchyard? It was a graveyard.

He'd told her she wasn't going to die anytime soon. He hadn't promised that he wouldn't die. Was it a premonition? Was that why she had been crying?

He had to concentrate. "Pilot to bomb aimer, any sign of Jerry?" Even to his own ears, his voice sounded slurred, thick.

"Bomb aimer to pilot, Cap'n. Haven't seen any Jerries in the last hour."

The crew had been together since early April. Ten ops. Only four on the Stirling before being switched to the Lancaster. A few close calls. But they'd managed by some sheer dumb luck to return to England safely night after night in the early hours of dawn.

"How long till we're home, Cap'n?" the wireless operator asked, his voice showing the strain. How long had they been in the air? Colin's brain was too fuzzy.

"Not long now," Colin replied, trying to sound assured. "We're over the Channel," though he didn't say, *what part of the Channel is anyone's guess.* And then, in the predawn twilight, he saw the outline of land.

Home!

Or was it? More than one pilot flying without instruments and evading enemy aircraft had ended up in the wrong country. Gathering all his energy and wits, he said in a strong voice. "There's land, boys. It won't be long now."

A cheer echoed in his earphones and throughout the metal fuselage. It was then the far starboard engine coughed, choked, and sputtered out. The cheering abruptly stopped.

Down to two engines.

Fine, Colin thought. *I can land with two engines. It's the landing gear I need now.* And he began the slow descent.

"Pilot to navigator, I need you up front."

Colin felt the pain in his leg increase. Sweat began running down his face, despite the frigid cold of the cabin.

When the young Aussie crouched next to him, Colin pushed his headset from his ears, "Tack, the instrument panel is useless. Can you tell where we are?"

Together they stared into the gradually lightening landscape. They had already left the water behind. He saw light in the sky to his right, East, and made a slight adjustment in the plane's heading. Slightly northeast. In the direction he hoped the airbase lay.

At this point, any airbase. And he was close enough to home to break radio silence.

"Pilot to wireless operator. Can you get us a contact?"

There were agonizing moments of static, and then the crackling voice of a control tower operator, "Control Tower. We have you on radar. Report in, Lancaster Bomber."

He responded, "Lancaster AVR1074 reporting in. Visual only. Instruments gone. Two injured crew. Down to two engines. Not sure about the landing gear."

He ignored Tack's sharp look.

"You're about two miles out. Adjust your heading east northeast by three degrees."

Colin made a mental calculation, having no instruments to rely on, and eased the lumbering bomber ever so slightly to the east.

"Pilot to crew. Strap yourselves in. This could be a rough one." To the navigator, he said, "Tack, the moment we touch down, I need you here to help. I'm afraid I might pass out."

"Sure thing, Cap'n," the Aussie replied, his voice shaky, but solid. "You bet."

In moments, he saw the aerodrome in the distance, glistening in the early morning sun, which had just peeked over the horizon. Even with his confused brain, he had somehow managed to bring them to their base. Colin wanted to weep for joy. He adjusted his heading, eased up on the throttle, and pushed on the hydraulic landing gear control.

The welcome sound of descending wheels brought a rousing cheer from the crew.

The first bounce of the wheels on the grass runway sent shards of pain up Colin's leg, into his back, exploding like fireworks in his brain. Holding on to what little consciousness he had, with Tack yelling commands in his ear, he managed to keep control of the bomber as it made a skidding, erratic landing, coming to rest feet from another plane which had also just landed.

"You did it, Cap'n," his young navigator said, slapping him on the back. "You brought us back safely, just like you promised."

He nodded and let the pain carry him off into unconsciousness.

———◅✕▻———

The screech of wheels woke him. They needed oil. Must tell Henry about that.

No, wait. There weren't tires on a grassy field at dawn. No landing tires squealed like that.

There was the warmth of the sun on his face, but it was a daytime sun. Intensified. Reflected.

He sensed movement. Heard solid, heavy footsteps. A muttered male voice with a heavy Cockney accent. "There you go, sir." A garbled reply. Was that his own voice?

Heaviness encased him. It was a struggle to pay attention to what was happening around him, but he could tell that things were clean. White. He felt wrapped in white. White light. White linen.

Even the air smelled white. Starch, antiseptic. Yet beyond that, there was a light touch of air on his face. And the smell of violets. Honeysuckle. Lilacs.

Lilacs. Gretchen's perfume.

His eyes flew open and shut again immediately against the blinding brightness of the afternoon sun, beaming into the enclosed portico through the floor-to-ceiling window. He's seen enough to remember, which made him want to forget.

The hospital. It was his wheelchair that made that godawful screech. He'd have to tell the orderly to oil it. It was enough to wake the dead.

The dead. *His crew.*

They were dead. The flight engineer. The tail gunner. He had promised to get them home. That he had done. But not alive. Not all of them.

He had a vague memory of the others standing by his bed. Tack's voice soft and breaking in his down-under accent, "Ox and Fitz didn't make it, Cap'n. I'm sorry."

Grief tore at Colin's mind, and then the pain pressed in pesteringly. And that he has been constantly drugged against it.

"The air'll do you good, sir," the orderly said with his Cockney lilt. Just like Ox's. His tail gunner.

A breeze seeped in through the open casement windows. It was a perfect English summer afternoon, with everything abloom: pink and red flowers, trees fully leafed out, the lawn an intense shade of green. Patients were being wheeled about in the garden by orderlies, or walking, accompanied by nurses in starched uniforms and caps. In some places, the men sat on benches chatting to family members.

Tea cups clinked. It sounded like a regular English garden party. But all he could taste was a lingering metallic flavor, distasteful and confusing.

His wheelchair was more of an upright bed than a seat. He was dressed in a striped cotton pajama top, which felt too big for him, and not much else underneath the crisp starched sheet and cotton blanket. A long tube running from a bag hanging from a metal pole next to his wheelchair dripping something cold into his arm. His legs were propped up. He could move his right one. His left was throbbing, heavy. Wrapped in a solid mass. They had laid him back at an irritating forty-five-degree angle. He wanted to sit up.

But the moment he tried, he screamed in pain. But it came out like a squelched moan, though loud enough to get the orderly hurrying over.

"Don't do that, sir; you're not ready yet, sir," a voice cautioned as the pain carried him off into memories he'd rather forget. And into unsettling dreams, one he had over and over since that dawn when he landed the battered plane, however long ago that was.

In the dream, he is flying the bright red biplane from the aerodrome on Lewis, the first plane he'd ever sat in. He's dressed in his pilot's uniform, jacket, and flight helmet, but he can't see out over the controls. Because he's only seven. Like he was when he first saw the plane.

In the dream, he's flying above home, above Coignach and Achiltibuie, in the shiny red plane, and it is a hot summer day, and the sun is blazing down, and the paint on the wings begins to soften and then, to his horror, begins to melt and run off the wings and drip, red drops falling from the wings, like blood.

Below, the mountains, touched by the drops of red paint that look like blood, come alive. They wake like angry old men disturbed from a thousand years of peaceful sleep and roar with rage that sounds like the roar of an engine on a Lancaster Bomber, the bomber he sits in night after night flying over Belgium and Germany. But he's only seven. He's too young to be a pilot.

The mountains rear back and reach up, grabbing for his biplane that roars like a bomber, that drips blood from its wings. He rolls the plane, dives, weaves, mounts up, and spins down, trying to avoid the mountains which try to pull him out of the sky, back to the earth, and he can't let them. He won't let them.

But his gas gauge is blinking red, red like the drops of blood dripping from the wings, warning him it's too far to go back to Lewis, it's too far to go ahead to Inverness, and there's no safe, flat land in between. Then the plane's engine ceases to roar and just sputters and chokes, and he stares at the blinking red gas gauge. He's only seven and doesn't know what to do.

And then he woke up, heart racing, head throbbing, his mind filled with the color red. Like the blood spattered on Fitz's face. And then he realized it was his own blood that had painted the flight engineer's cheeks and forehead like an American Indian war chief.

On another day, he drifted in and out of a drugged sleep, though it hardly felt like sleep, for he's never rested. Someone brought him a thick liquid in a glass with a straw he didn't touch and left him books he didn't read. Sometimes when he woke, it was day; other times, it was night. Sometimes, he was on the porch; other times, he was in a ward, one of many beds.

The men next to him came and went. Some made conversation. He wanted to reply, but he couldn't seem to form the words in his head, or if he did, he couldn't make his mouth work. He sensed someone changing bandages on his neck, probing painfully at his jaw.

Was that his oldest sister floating by? Catriona? No, he's hallucinating. She's in Achiltibuie. Not here. Wherever *here* was. And when he tried to ask, his mouth didn't work.

Then one day he woke up. Truly woke up, for the first time.

It was her perfume that did it, with its hint of lilacs.

This time, it wasn't a hallucination because he heard her voice too. "Colin? Colin!"

"He never seems to pay me any mind." This one was Catriona. "The doctor says he's narra in a coma but more of a pain-induced and drug-induced sleep. They took wee pieces of shrapnel out of his jaw, his leg, his hip, and his lower back. And some weren't so wee."

He heard Gretchen's indrawn breath and wanted to comfort her.

But no words come, only a strangled sound.

"He's awake. Henry, he's awake!"

He opened his eyes, and there, standing by his wheelchair, were three people he'd been sure he'd never see again.

Gretchen. Henry. Fiona.

"Mind ye, don't try to talk, Colin," Catriona said. "You can't anyway. Your wee jaw is wired shut. But it's almost healed, now. Soon ye'll be able to talk all ye want. Even order me about, aye." She grinned at him in her usual teasing manner.

Henry stood slightly to one side, but not looking at Colin. He was watching Gretchen. Colin thought he looked protective, wary of how Gretchen would react. Or what she might reveal. Ironically, Fiona was watching Henry. It was so ridiculous, it almost made him laugh.

He turned his head in Gretchen's direction, half afraid to see her face.

But Gretchen was calm, cheerful, in the bright, flowery sundress she'd worn on the day they'd gone to Traprain Law. It instantly brought back the feel of her body beneath his on that sloped, dirt path. Today she was dressed to the nines, with a dashing red hat, gloves, and purse. She was like a walking garden among the conservatively-dressed British visitors drifting past in their grey serge suits or ration-issued clothing.

She smiled at him casually, as if it were an everyday occurrence for her to see someone all bandaged up and unable to talk. Then he realized that it was. She'd been studying to be a nurse now for... *What day is it? What month?* He could only make sounds that had no meaning to anyone but him. But his hands were free.

He made a writing gesture, and they brought him a pad and pencil.

"What day is it?" His handwriting was scrawled, shaky. He could barely read it himself.

It was Gretchen who replied, perching herself on a stool next to his wheelchair. "You've been asleep! Like Rip Van Winkle!"

"Gretchen, that's an *American* fairy tale," Henry pointed out.

"No, it's by the Brothers Grimm, Fiona corrected, with a voice that implied it was important, but Colin didn't care.

"Oh. Well then," said Gretchen. "Sleeping Beauty. But just a few weeks."

He raised his eyebrows in a question. It hurt, and he winced. Gretchen ignored his grimace. "Today is July third, Colin. Henry and I didn't want to celebrate our American holiday without you. We both managed to get a few days' leave and come down here to southern England to see you."

Fiona, dressed in her WAAF uniform, commented to no one in particular, "We've had quite a year, haven't we?"

Colin noticed Henry glancing at Fiona, who simply crossed her arms and shrugged. He wondered what that was all about, but his sister cut in.

"Ye've been fadin' in and out since ye returned from that mission in mid-June," Catriona explained. "I've been here for nigh onto two weeks."

At Colin's surprised look, she said, "Mother and Father thought it best we have one of the family nearby in case... ah, well, ye know, these places are so short-staffed, they do let family help out with some simple chores."

Colin figured she was going to say, "In case you didn't make it."

Like Ox and Fitz. The thought of them filled his mind with anguish, and he closed his eyes so it wouldn't show.

"Oh, he's tired. We should let him rest." It was Gretchen, in her best nurse voice. "He's over the worst of it and will be up and about before you know it."

But he wasn't.

They came to see him later that day, and the next day they brought a picnic lunch to celebrate the Fourth of July. He found their cheerful, healthy presence exhausting. Especially Gretchen's. Her nearness filled him with longing and despair. Since he couldn't keep his eyes off her and knew he would betray how he felt, he listened to their conversations with his eyes closed. Perhaps they would think he was asleep and leave him alone.

It was mostly Gretchen and Fiona who chatted, talking about what they were doing, Gretchen in her nursing course, Fiona at Biggin Hill. They swapped information about people they knew from Edinburgh.

Henry was quiet, even for him. When Colin opened his eyes, he saw that Henry sat and twirled his fedora between his hands, round and round. Something was making him edgy and uncomfortable. Every time Fiona came near, Henry seemed to stiffen. There was something between them, something more than the surface gave away.

He knew it was uncharitable but was glad when Catriona said, "I'm going home tomorrow for a spell, Colin." Fiona will look in on you and let us know how you're doing. You should be home on leave soon. The good highland air will help you recuperate," she said in her broad Scots accent. "This Anglish air is just so stifflin'.'"

That afternoon the others came to say goodbye. He was relieved. Their visits had made him feel useless. Trapped. He shrugged off the news that the cast was coming off in a week or two and the wiring on his jaw soon after that.

He couldn't seem to get himself to care.

"I'll be checking in every week, Colin," Fiona said as she kissed his forehead, one place that wasn't swathed in bandages. He nodded in reply.

Henry told him in a quiet voice, just for his ears, "I know you don't think so, but try to remember that you're lucky, Colin." He seemed to read Colin's mind.

Colin could barely look at Gretchen, whose air of lightheartedness pained him. Only at the last minute did she falter and look at him from behind the shelter of her broad-brimmed hat, which hid the anguish in her eyes from the others.

"Colin..." she began in a strained voice, but she stopped when he shook his head.

She bent over, filling his senses with her presence, her hand resting on his wrist, her touch scalding like fire. Wincing momentarily, he hid his heart behind dull, expressionless eyes.

Feigning indifference. Rending his heart in two.

Twenty-Four

August 1942

"He's sinking, Henry. He's not healing. At least in his mind," Fiona said when she called Henry in early August. "He has a smaller cast, but he won't use his crutches. And though his jaw is finally free of wires, he has trouble making himself understood, so he says nothing."

Henry felt his own spirits sinking. "What do the doctors say?"

Fiona's sigh carried her sadness through the telephone wires. "The doctors say the only thing they can do is send him home in hopes that will cure him. I was there when the doctor told him he was being awarded the Distinguished Flying Cross, and the look he gave the doctor would have knocked over a weaker man."

"Is he well enough to get home?" Henry wondered at the wisdom of sending Colin to a very isolated part of Scotland.

"First they're sending him to the rehab hospital in Edinburgh where he'll stay a few days," Fiona replied. "But I can't imagine how he'd make his own way home to Achiltibuie, Henry. And I can't take any more leave. If you can't, maybe Gretchen can escort him. I think she's on a short summer break."

Once apprised of this scheme, Gretchen said she'd meet Colin's arriving train, but Henry talked her out of it. "He's not going to want us fussing over him. Once he's gained some strength, we can make plans for getting him home."

"We have to go with him even if he won't want us, Henry. You know that. He's a damned stubborn Scot."

"Gretchen, I think we should ask him first. He has the right to decide if he wants or needs company on his trip home."

She wasn't having it. "I could help if he needs attention on the train."

"Gretchen," Henry said, more firmly, "I'm sure the RAF has it figured out."

Gretchen made a disparaging sound, but after more argument, finally agreed Henry should visit Colin alone.

Henry wondered at Gretchen's emotional response. Her attitude toward Colin seemed different from their July visit. He thought they didn't like each other, though at Traprain Law, they had been at ease with each other.

By the time he got to Edinburgh, Colin had been three days in the rehab hospital, a converted boarding school on the fringes of the city.

On the ward, Henry approached a group of pajama-clad men playing or observing an intense poker game. Some had bandages or plaster casts around arms or legs or heads, leaned on crutches, or sat with propped-up legs. Some were missing a limb. Amazingly, most were joking and laughing.

When he asked for Captain McAuley, someone pointed to the far end of the large room, where Colin sat next to a bed, in a wheelchair, staring out a window, a pair of crutches nearby. Colin looked horribly thin and pallid.

"Colin."

Colin, unresponsive, continued staring at a green lawn surrounded by tall hedges.

"Colin," Henry said louder, stepping closer. Colin looked up slowly, his face haggard, his eyes dull and unfocused. For one terrible moment, Henry thought his friend was blind, but then recognition seeped into Colin's face.

"Henry." His voice rasped. His breath was tinged with a suspicious wheeze.

"You're looking better than the last time I saw you," Henry said with false cheerfulness. He sat on the bed so Colin wouldn't have to look up.

Colin gave a slight shrug. "Suppose," he muttered.

"Well, the good thing is, you're out of the hospital."

Colin raised his eyebrows.

"Or you will be in a day or two and on your way home. Your mother and sisters to look after you. All that fresh highland air."

Colin looked back out the window.

"Do you want to walk outside? Your crutches are here."

Colin shook his head. "Tired."

"Gretchen's on school break; otherwise she'd be at this hospital one day a week."

Colin shook his head slowly but firmly from side to side. "No. Practicing. On me."

Henry thought he was joking and laughed, but Colin didn't break a smile. "Well, Gretchen and I will travel with you to Achiltibuie, to get you home safe and sound."

Colin suddenly pounded his fists against the arms of his wheelchair. "No! I won't! Have it!" he said in slow, jumbled words. Like he had marbles in his mouth.

"Why are you so angry?" Henry said softly. "We're your friends."

"Save leave for. Something... important." Colin spoke in short spurts with each exhale, struggling to form words, occasionally missing one, clearly a source of great frustration for his articulate friend.

"You're important," Henry protested.

"Won't have... Gretchen... treat me... like... basket case... Going home... mistake. Why not... get better... where I... was."

"Because you *haven't* been getting better where you were," Henry replied in a quiet but insistent voice, which got Colin's attention. Henry drew a deep breath and then plunged into the speech he had mentally prepared for days.

"I know you've had it rough. And don't give me some shit about not understanding. I helped pull dozens of battered men out of Spitfires in September of 1940. They were my friends, like you are my friend."

Henry didn't look away from Colin's stare. "I won't let you rot away in some hospital, killing yourself with guilt. Because that's what it is, Colin. You survived, and some of your crew didn't. But you brought the others home, in spite of being shot up yourself. Don't their lives mean something?"

Colin looked away. He was silent for the longest time, then, turned his face toward Henry. "Longest... goddamn... speech ever... you... make."

Henry chuckled. It was good to see a hint of the Colin he knew. "Well, we're getting on the train with you in four days, whether you like it or not," he said affectionately.

"You. Yes... Gretchen... don't want... her."

"Well, you might not want her, but she'll be good company for me," Henry retorted in a joking manner then stopped at Colin's pained look.

"Not good. Idea." Colin said loudly.

Henry shrugged. "I'll tell her you don't want her to come. Oh, and Catriona will be waiting for us at the other end."

Colin let out a slow, grunting sigh. "Don't... let her bring... bloody... amb... lance."

When Henry told Gretchen that Colin didn't want her to escort him to Achiltibuie, she shrugged. "I don't care what he says. I have some nursing skills, and if I can help your friend... well, I'm going to do it."

"He's your friend, too, Gretchen."

She stared into her tea. "It's clear he doesn't think of me as a friend."

Henry sighed. "Are you going to go visit him in the hospital?"

"No, it'll just get him riled up. I'll meet you both at the train station. He won't be able to do anything about it then."

The following Wednesday Henry met Colin in the hospital lobby at seven a.m. An orderly wheeled him to the waiting taxi, helped Colin get up from the wheelchair into the cab, and told Henry, "They'll have a Red Cross lady there with a wheelchair." Henry was pretty sure who the Red Cross lady would be.

"But what about when we get on the train?"

"He's to be using his crutches."

Henry cringed. What Colin was to be doing and what he was capable or willing to do was the whole point.

"You don't... have... to do this," Colin said as the taxi headed to downtown Edinburgh.

"It's a... verra... long way... to go... for... haggis," he slurred.

It took a few seconds for Henry to recognize the joke, and when he started laughing, Colin smiled wryly, the first smile Henry had seen from his friend in a very long time.

The journey ahead was daunting: a six-hour ride north to Inverness; another two hours on the local train to cover fifty-seven miles to the western port of Ullapool to meet Colin's sister Catriona; ten miles on a narrow, two-lane thoroughfare; and finally, a torturous fourteen miles over the twisting, single-track road to Colin's tiny seaside hometown of Achiltibuie.

Colin was immediately infuriated when he saw Gretchen in her nurse's outfit. He pushed away her helping hand as he got out of the cab into the wheelchair and said loudly when she began steering him to the platform, "I'm not... helpless." But he let Henry support him out of the wheelchair and assist him into their train compartment.

When Gretchen tried to help Colin get settled, he muttered fiercely, "Don't. Fuss." After the train got underway, Gretchen asked Colin if he wanted something from the club car.

Colin snapped, "Gretchen. Don't. Hover. Leave me... be." The flash of pain on Gretchen's face gave Henry pause.

As the train rattled north, Henry glanced surreptitiously between Colin and Gretchen, lost in their own thoughts.

Colin never seemed to warm to Gretchen, he mused, *though there had been that day at Traprain Law...*

Since his last failed proposal, Henry had been perseverating on who the "unavailable man" she was in love with might be. He tried unsuccessfully to picture the many pilots and ground crew he had introduced her to for a night of dancing and dining, with Fiona making up the foursome.

She had flirted in her usual manner but never asked after any of them. Never spoke of the other men who squired her and Fiona about town. It was only Colin that she encountered repeatedly. Yet they had an inexplicably uneasy relationship.

Something must have happened on those trips to Holyrood and Stirling. When it had been just the two of them. Alone.

Henry recalled that day on Traprain Law. Gretchen had been glowing, Colin uncharacteristically relaxed. He had jokingly told Colin to keep Gretchen from falling off the precipice. Gretchen had placed her hand on Colin's chest. They had been looking at each other...

Henry felt his chest growing tight. He'd had many rivals for Gretchen's affection, but Colin had never been competition. He only stepped out on the town when he was with Henry, Fiona, and Gretchen. Nothing had come of Fiona and Colin as a couple. Yes, there was that Canadian girl, but she was surely a passing thing...

He looked across at Gretchen, who sat with her eyes closed, her head resting on the seat. *Who wouldn't be in love with her?* He shot a glance at his friend then stopped breathing as icy shards of suspicion pierced his mind. *Could the flyboy who didn't love Gretchen... be Colin?*

When they changed trains at Inverness, there was time for a bite to eat. Colin sulked at a table, his face pasty gray, while Henry and Gretchen stood in line for sandwiches and coffee.

"Gretchen, why did you bring such a large suitcase?" Henry said. He had noticed a porter pull out an enormous leather portmanteau for her. "We're only going and coming back."

"I'm going to stay through the autumn."

Henry nearly choked on unexpected fury. "You have school. And volunteer obligations. People are counting on you."

"I've arranged a leave of absence from school," she looked oddly guilty.

"When did you decide this?" He lowered his voice but didn't remove the anger.

Gretchen still did not meet his eyes. "Once Colin's family knew he was coming home to recuperate, Catriona wrote me and asked me to stay for a while. She thought he'd need a nurse, and they are so isolated..."

"Why is this the first I've heard of all this?" he interrupted, struggling to smother his jealousy.

"Fiona was the one who talked to Catriona and suggested they contact the nursing school to see if I had the skills needed."

"Fiona? She didn't say anything to me, either."

"Henry, what's wrong with you?" Gretchen snapped. "Since when do either of us have to report to you? You didn't tell me last week you're being transferred to England. Who is going to keep me company in Edinburgh with you gone?" Then she added, with a touch of sarcasm, "At least you'll be much nearer Fiona to keep *her* company."

"And why would I do that?" he said louder than he intended. A sick feeling invaded his stomach. Could Fiona have told Gretchen about their secret liaisons?

"Oh, Henry." Gretchen was suddenly teary-eyed. Her hands on his arm immediately quenched his anger. "Please, don't let's argue. Who knows when I'll be able to see you again, and you've been my bedrock. And Colin is really ill, and you and I both want him to get better."

Struck with a maelstrom of conflicting emotions, Henry could say nothing. The three of them continued the journey in strained silence.

When they arrived at Ullapool, Catriona greeted her brother effusively and suggested they have tea before setting out on the last leg of their journey.

But Colin said, "Tired. Let's get... home."

"Ah, well. No worry. Cook packed a thermos of hot tea and some wee cold pork pies, so we can stop along the way and have a bit o' a picnic tea," she responded brightly, ignoring her brother's gruffness.

Their trip took them ten miles along the main road, then onto a single-track road on the north side of a loch, under the foot of the mountain Stac Pollaidh. They drove most of the length of a peninsula, then headed southeast before meeting the sea, and finally headed south along the coast of a bay to Achiltibuie.

Henry sat with Colin in the back of the roomy two-toned, high-roofed station wagon while the two girls chattered away up front. He was glad to hear their bright voices and laughter, trying to bury his suspicions about Gretchen's feelings for Colin.

Henry caught an occasional glance that Colin gave Gretchen and thought he recognized... longing.

Henry swallowed acid bile rising in his throat. Could it be possible, at all possible, that Colin was in love with Gretchen? That all his gruff aloofness and cold demeanor with Gretchen was to cover his true feelings? Who would Colin want to hide his feelings from?

From me. Colin knows I'm in love with Gretchen. That I've proposed twice.

Colin would never deliberately come between him and Gretchen. *Would he?* And Gretchen would never put Colin in a position to sneak around behind his best friend's back. *Would she?*

Maybe he had been reading the relationship between them all wrong. Maybe Colin didn't *dislike* Gretchen; maybe he simply refused to *like* her.

"We're pretty isolated here," Catriona was saying. "We only see the postman twice a week, and most supplies arrive by boat, as well as most people comin' our way. But we knew Colin hates boats," She added teasingly. Colin kept stone-silent.

"How long can you stay, Henry?" Catriona continued.

"Only a few days."

"They need you at Drem?"

"No, actually, the Wing Commander called me in a week ago and told me I'm to report to the U.S. 8th Army Air Force headquarters in Bushey Park.

"About fifteen... miles south... west of... London." Colin put in. He stared at Henry, his face emotionless. Henry had not mentioned his reassignment.

"Why?" Catriona said. "They canna tell ye what to do. Aren't you a volunteer?"

"Well, actually, they can," Henry replied, trying to keep his voice light. "Seems that with the arrival of our Eighth Army Air Force, the long arm of the draft has finally caught up to me."

"I don't understand." Catriona looked at him in the rearview mirror.

" I'd originally been given a deferment because I was in England working for the RAF. The Wing Commander said I'll be sworn into the U.S. Air Corps, but attached to an RAF unit and be a kind of liaison, or as he said it, 'helping the Yanks understand how we do things.'"

"Will you... get... credit for... work with... RAF?" Colin asked.

"My work as a civilian with the RAF will give me two years' time in grade. And Harrington said he'd convinced the powers that be that my knowledge of RAF methods was needed right here, right now, so I won't have to go back to the States for basic training."

Henry reflected on what else Harrington had conveyed.

"You apparently have friends in high places," he'd said. At the commander's questioning pause, Henry remained silent. The only person who came to mind was Fiona's father, with his hush-hush work in Whitehall.

"I'm sorry you can't stay longer," Catriona chimed into the quiet, "but I'm happy Gretchen will be with us for several months."

"Several... months?" Colin's voice was full of astonishment.

"Oh, I thought you knew," Catriona said with unnatural brightness.

"Didn't," Colin replied sullenly.

"Well, we'll give her a real Highland welcome, aye?"

Conversation died out, interrupted by Catriona's occasional explanations of the view, including the Summer Isles lying in waters off Achiltibuie in the Badentarbat Bay. They had acquired that name because crofters would transport their sheep for the summer grazing.

"Tanera Mor, the largest of the Summer Isles, once had over 100 inhabitants but now is almost deserted," she explained.

The magnificent sight of the coast and the distant Summer Isles in the fading August sunlight made it momentarily possible to forget the war, its deprivations and devastating losses. The wild beauty of the place could be healing.

Henry hoped Colin would feel its effects.

"Not that's there much of an estate left," Colin had explained when he first met Henry. "It was the seat of the original clan lands, but many emigrated to North Carolina during the clearances in the late 1700s, after the defeat at Culloden. We live in the estate house, which takes summer visitors to make ends meet, or used to till the war started. Losing that income was difficult. It's too isolated to be requisitioned as a hospital or officers' quarters, as so many large houses have been."

Colin said those who didn't make their living by fishing were tenant farmers who lived in rented crofts, but the soil was more suited for gorse than grain. With the younger men off at war, things were difficult. "It takes a lot of physical labor to maintain the farm. With Alistair and I in the services, my sisters Catriona and Mairi help out a lot. My other sister Margret is married and lives in Aberdeen."

Their destination was a village spread on a hillside hugging the gently curving bay, set against the mountain backdrop. Henry spotted whitewashed houses, a shop, a store, a church, and a small building with a post office sign hanging above the door.

Set slightly up and away from the village's northern end was a very large white house with two shorter wings at either end, making an elongated "I" shape. It was certainly grander than the homes he'd seen in villages around Drem and Edinburgh. It drove home the fact that Colin came from a different world than Henry and Gretchen, as Henry pictured the narrow brick row house where he had grown up and Gretchen's run-down farm.

He suddenly felt nervous. Would dinner be formal? Was he dressed properly?

The driveway led off the main road and rose with the hillside then split, one branch circling around to the front of the house with its covered portico and the other, which Catriona took, leading to the rear of the house. Cultivated farmland behind outbuildings and several barns stretched out toward the mountains. Catriona parked next to a multi-bay garage which looked like it had once been stable. A pathway led to the rear of the house, where he could see a flagstone patio and a series of wall-to-ceiling windows.

The next few moments were a flurry of introductions to Colin's parents, Donald and Elspeth, and his younger sister Mairi. Then came the laborious task of getting Colin into the house and up to his bedroom after he refused to stay in the room they had prepared at the back of the house.

After Colin was settled, Catriona showed Henry and Gretchen to their rooms in the guest wing. Henry took a few minutes to wash up then joined Gretchen, who had changed out of her nurse's uniform and the family in the dining room, where Mrs. McDougal, the cook/housekeeper, had laid out a light supper of salmon filets and fried potatoes.

Someone took dinner up to Colin on a tray.

Conversation at the table was casual small talk. Catriona did most of the talking, asking Henry and Gretchen about life in the States. Though invited to sit with the family in the parlor after dinner, Henry agreed with Colin's mother that after such a long day, he might prefer to turn in. He didn't know how long Gretchen lingered with the family.

On Thursday, Catriona showed them around the estate, village, and quaint white clapboard church with its gated graveyard and family plot. Sitting on a stone bench, staring into the distance at the lapping waves on the pebbled beach, Henry longed to stay and let the sound of the sea and the wind in the scotch pines fill up his soul with the ease and peace of the place.

Away from the war. Away from the world.

Colin did not come out of his room; his sisters took his meals to him. Henry and Gretchen stopped in for a few minutes, making idle chatter, but Colin was uncommunicative.

On Friday, Henry readied himself to leave, not knowing when he'd be seeing Gretchen or Colin again. He found his friend in bed, propped up with several pillows, his face flushed, his breathing shallow. Colin struggled to sit up as Henry entered but quickly lay back when the effort was too much.

The marked decline in Colin's health alarmed Henry. Making his voice cheerful, he said, "I've got to go, Colin. I'm taking the weekly boat to Ullapool. Your sister said it'll be much faster than driving."

"Just... you?"

"Gretchen is staying on." Henry worked hard to keep his face devoid of envy.

"Wasn't my idea... mate," Colin said, his face grim. "Didn't ask her... to."

Henry said lightly, "She'll take good care of you. If you let her. Don't be unkind, Colin, even if she isn't your favorite person. I've never understood this animosity between you."

He waited to see if Colin would contradict him, but Colin only said, "Good luck... Yank. See you... at... Bomber Command."

"Right oh, Colin. Right oh. You get better." He walked out the door before Colin could see his anguish, tormented more than ever over what might lie between the woman he loved and his best friend.

Twenty-Five

December 1942

It was Christmas until Henry could get back to Achiltibuie. He
was able to hitch a ride in a transport plane to a base near Inverness,
where he took the local train to Ullapool and then caught a ride with
postal delivery. He had written Colin and Gretchen regularly in the four
months he had been gone. Colin never wrote back. Gretchen dropped a
brief letter now and then.

I'm practically a member of the Women's Land Army, she said in
her letter in early October. *I got tired of playing nursemaid. Since Colin
recovered from that scary bout with pneumonia, he doesn't need nursing;
he won't let* me *tend him. His sisters wait on him hand and foot. I think
that's half the problem. He's been spoiled by all this catering and pity. It
was weeks until he would leave his room and then only sit on the front porch
staring at the sea for an hour.*

*I finally convinced Colin's parents that I grew up on a farm and could
hoe and plow and milk like the rest of them. They found some extra
gumshoes, and I got to work. Colin's father can't do a lot, and most of the
farmhands are off to war. I actually shocked them.*

*I've thought about just going back to Edinburgh, but I already arranged
a semester's leave from school, so I'll be starting again in January. In the
meantime, I'm being useful here on the farm, and I've become great friends*

with Mairi. She is so much fun, and I am learning Gaelic. You'll think I'm a highland girl when you see me, but I'd do anything for a new lipstick.

Henry managed to find tubes of lipstick for Gretchen and Colin's sisters, as well as whiskey for the men and oranges for Colin's mother. His unused cigarette rations were as good as cash in the airfield black market.

It was mid-afternoon, but growing onto dusk at this northern latitude, when the postal van dropped Henry off at Achiltibuie's tiny post office, housed in one corner of the village store. Henry waited until the mail for the manor house was sorted and took it along with him as he trundled up the long driveway.

Mairi opened the front door with a broad smile. "Henry, we wondered when ye'd arrive. Come in, come in, and we'll get ye settled. We're puttin' you in the same room. Let's take your things up, and then you can come have a cup of tea in the kitchen."

He followed her up the ever-impressive wide, curving staircase with its polished railing twined with ivy for the holiday. "Is Colin resting in his room?"

"Nay." Mairi laughed in a delightful way that reminded him of tinkling bells. "He and Gretchen are down at the bay," she said, leading him to the guest wing.

"The bay? Doing what? It's December. And the sun's soon to set." Henry had not realized how early night fell in December in the northern realms of Scotland.

"Ach, it's a bloomin' miracle. Gretchen won't take no from my brother, the twit. She got him so fired up, calling him a bloody layby, sayin' he was using his home as a funk hole." Mairi struck a match to some peat in the fireplace, filling the room with its pungent fragrance. The mantle above was decorated with sprays of spruce, pinecones, and red ribbon.

"And what did Colin say at that?" Henry asked as he placed his suitcase on a colorful rug beside the four-poster bed.

She stood up and wiped her sooty hands on her apron. "Ah, Colin was nigh beside himself with rage. The next mornin' he was fully dressed and at the breakfast table at ha' past six." She laughed. But Henry thought it was a laugh tinged with sadness.

"When was that?"

"'Twas only the beginnin' of the month. But since, he's been up every mornin' doing hand chores that he can sittin' in the kitchen, on the patio, or by the garage. He wears out after lunch and sleeps the afternoon till dinner, but it's clear he's on the mend now. Fer a while there..."

She raised her deep brown eyes to Henry.

"I know," he replied. "I'm glad Fiona convinced the doctors to let him come home. Otherwise, he would have stayed in that hospital and just..."

"Aye," Mairi said softly. She placed her hand on his arm, her face troubled. "But it's not just bein' home that has helped him turn the corner, Henry. It's being around Gretchen..."

Henry met her concerned eyes. "She doesn't belong to me, Mairi. I don't have any claim on her."

"Aye, I know. But it was easy enough to see how it was, Henry, when you were here in August. The way you looked at her. Gretchen told me ye'd asked her ta be yer wife."

Henry felt his face grow red. How could Gretchen be so indiscreet with such a personal thing? "That was years ago." He tried to cover his embarrassment. "We were younger. Before the war. It seems a century ago now."

"But ye asked her agin, since then, haven't ye? Ye havena given up hope, nay?" Her slightly rounded face was flushed a pretty pink.

Henry sighed. He may as well be truthful. "I can't say I'll ever be able to give up hope."

"Ye're a one-woman man, Henry Schmidt. That's a high compliment. A woman would be happy to have such a man love her."

"Apparently not Gretchen," Henry said, looking away.

"Colin 'tis a hard man to know," Mairi said in a confusing change of subject. "He'd be a hard man ta love. I say this as his sister. He's so inward. Always thinkin', dreamin'. He's not quick to show how he feels, not at all like da; they used to have such words. And you're his friend."

"What are you saying, Mairi?"

Mairi walked to the double casement window. Henry followed her. He could see two figures in the distance, sitting next to a small fire. He hadn't noticed them when they drove into town.

"She convinced him to go on a picnic. Nearly Christmas, and they go ta the beach! Only Gretchen could get him to do that. Mrs. MacDougal packed them a wee lunch. It's the furthest he's walked since he started getting 'round. Still uses a cane. Goes slowly. But goes."

She lifted her eyes to Henry, soft and understanding. "He'd ne'er do anything to stand in your way. To come between you and Gretchen."

"Mairi..."

"Henry, I think she's saved his life. She thinks we just think she's a paid nurse; fer sure she's gettin' a stipend. My da would have it no other way. But she's made herself part of the family, you see. Workin' on the farm and all. And it's clear, though she tries to hide it, it's clear that..."

Henry closed his eyes, unwilling to see the truth in Mairi's. After a deep shuttering breath, he said, his voice strangled, "You're saying she's in love with him."

"You said yourself that ye didn't have a claim on her. Though ye were still hopeful?"

"Yes." Henry barely said the word, as he opened his eyes and looked at his friend's sister, so much like Colin in coloring and facial features.

"They love ye, Henry. And fer the world, would ne'er go agin' ye. Ne'er do anything ta trample on that heart o' yorn. That's all I'm sayin'. Now go on down to the beach and tell them we'll be havin' supper in an hour. Colin will be too worn out to make the trip up the hill, so I'll send Catriona with the car to fetch ye."

Henry nodded, his throat constricted, heart clenched into a fist.

The distant blue-grey hills of the mountains of Stac Polly, Cul Moor, and Cul Beag lay behind him as he walked down to the beach. Ahead, he saw the low-lying rocky Summer Isles and far away, sixty miles to the south, visible at the edge of the sea, the Cuillen Hills of Skye. The sound of the incoming tide made a constant backdrop to the wild beauty of the isolated cove.

He could hear Gretchen's laughter long before he reached them. They were sitting on a woolen blanket. Though it was late December, the day was touched with warmth, as the area benefitted from the warm Gulf Stream. Yet the cool ocean breeze made him glad for his heavy coat.

As he drew closer, he saw Gretchen lying back, propped up on her elbows, one leg bent, her foot resting on the pebbly sand. Wrapped in a tartan shawl, she also wore corduroy trousers and a heavy sweater. Next to her in a camp chair, Colin braced himself on a cane, one leg extended straight out. Even from the back, Henry thought he looked frail.

The crunch of his boots caught their attention. Gretchen leaped up with a squeal, running the few paces to fling her arms around him in a tight squeeze. Henry struggled to keep Mairi's gentle plea in the front of his mind as he held Gretchen in his arms for just a moment.

"Henry," she said, "you are a sight for sore eyes. We've missed you!"

She was bronzed, and her longer hair, pulled back in a ponytail, was still lightened by fall days spent in the fields.She looked like a farm girl dressed up in sophisticated clothes. Colin was struggling to get to his feet, and Henry moved quickly to give him a hand.

Though he was leaning heavily on his cane, Colin looked considerably better than he had in August. The scars on his neck and jaw had lost their ugly reddishness, and his hair had grown out, covering the deep groove cut by shrapnel. But his face was still gaunt, his eyes hinting at pain. In their depths, Henry glimpsed unwanted memories that he had seen too often in shell-shocked crews returning in a ravaged cockpit, or pulled from a plane that limped back to base only to skid in on its undercarriage because the landing gear was gone.

He was obviously far from well, but he was healing, and for that, Henry said a silent prayer of thanks to whatever god still cared about this war-ravaged world. And a prayer of gratitude for Gretchen, who had played a major part in this near-miracle. Though at what cost to Henry's heart, he wasn't ready to acknowledge.

"Henry! God, it's good to see you." Colin's voice was edged with fatigue but hearty. "How long can you stay?"

"Colin. You're looking great." They all knew it was something to say. "I've got to be back at my base by midnight December twenty-eighth. To cover for the New Year's holiday. Five days. I'll be heading out the twenty-sixth and visit Fiona on my way through Edinburgh, and then head south. She's up with her aunt and uncle."

Colin nodded. "Here, have some tea. A Mrs. McDougal special. She says it heals anything." He sat back down, pulled a thermos from the picnic basket, and poured hot liquid into a mug.

Henry took a sip of the hot, sweet, whiskey-laced tea. A peaty aroma flooded his nose. "Whoa! That's got a kick. I've been sent down to tell you it's almost time for supper, but maybe you won't need it after this."

"Well, Mrs. McDougal's been giving me a dose nearly every day."

Henry laughed. "You'll never get whiskey like this back at base," he joked, then could have kicked himself for the look that passed over Colin.

Gretchen intercepted before the mood could change. "Hey, McAuley, help me get some driftwood, the fire needs some fuel."

"I'll stir the fire," Henry said, sitting on the striped woolen blanket. He took a stick and pushed the coals around, watching Gretchen and Colin's slow progress to the edge of the water. Gretchen played tag with the waves while she gathered driftwood, and Colin, leaning on his cane, shook his head at her antics.

From his angle, Henry could see Colin's unmistakable admiration. But who wouldn't admire Gretchen? She was beautiful, slim, athletic, and full of endless energy.

Colin carried back several pieces of driftwood precariously in his free arm then tossed them in the fire all at once, sending sparks and heat skyward.

They drank tea and watched the fading afternoon light play on the surface of the sea.

"I hear Gretchen's become quite the farmhand," Henry teased, for something to say.

"Aye." Colin nodded, looking at Gretchen out of the corner of his eye. "She's been pretty amazing. Everyone's been surprised."

"Ha." Gretchen crossed her arms, pretending to be angry. "You're the only one who thought I couldn't do it. Never believed me when I told you I grew up doing farm work."

"Aye, but to see you at Drem, who would have guessed," Colin retorted.

Henry watched the interplay silently.

"And what does that mean, your lordship?"

"You were always dressed to kill, and cut out that lordship stuff."

"Did you know his father is a lord?" Gretchen looked at Henry with a wide-eyed smile. "I wasn't sure if I should bow or what."

"That would be a curtsey, Miss American," Colin retorted.

Henry looked at Colin in surprise, at the information as well as his teasing manner.

Colin shrugged. "It's an ancient family title. 'Laird,' to be proper. It means nothing to the Brits. They don't honor Scots titles. It belongs to Alistair as the oldest. And the farm."

"That doesn't seem fair." Gretchen's voice held a frown.

"Does na matter, as I wouldn't have wanted it anyway. I was always plannin' to leave, see the world you know, someday. Before the war came, that is." Heaviness descended on Colin.

"Yeah," Gretchen replied quickly in a teasing voice. "I wanted to see the world, and look where it got me.. To some isolated farm in the Scottish Highlands."

"It's rather spectacular," Henry interjected. "Nothing like York County, Pennsylvania."

Gretchen laughed. "What I would have given to have the beach at my front door. Wow."

"Talking of beaches," Henry said, "I think I'll take a bit of a walk along this one. I've been shut up too long in various forms of transportation and need to stretch my legs. I'll be back in a bit and help you pack up."

"Tis a fair day for a stroll along the bay," Colin said wistfully, once again making Henry feel like shit for being so insensitive.

Gretchen said, "Won't be long, Colin, till you're able to do it too."

Henry nearly winced at the tenderness in Gretchen's voice and the smile on Colin's face.

"Go on, Henry. We'll be holding down the sand," Gretchen teased. Colin's laughter made Henry smile. They exchanged glances. He saw the question in Colin's eyes. And the anguish.

"Don't let some silkie carry you off into the sea, Henry," Colin called after him as he walked away. "They're mighty pretty."

"The prettiest one is yours," Henry called back with a wave and a forced smile, turning quickly before his face would show the pain. As he walked toward the surf, Henry heard Colin laughing at something Gretchen said.

It's good to hear Colin laugh, he told himself. *I'm glad Gretchen is bringing him around.* And he meant it.

It became quickly clear to Henry that there was a real spark between Gretchen and Colin. He had not seen them look so happy since that Fourth of July on Traprain Law before the German Junker 88 terrified them all.

Though Colin had made enormous progress since August, there were times, in spite of the cheer of holiday decorations and festive meals, he slipped into some deep void at the center of his soul, turning him glum and bitter. It was usually Gretchen who would pull him out of it.

But at Christmas Day dinner, some remark unexpectedly enraged Colin, who suddenly limped off to his room, yelling at Mairi when she brought him dessert on a tray. Mairi, not one to bend to her brother's rages, gave it back as good as she got. Temporarily alone, Henry and Gretchen could hear the shouts in the sitting room at the back of the house.

"Does this happen often?" Henry said quietly to Gretchen, who sat next to him on the flowered sofa, her face a study of forced composure. He was rattled by Colin's lack of control with guests in the house, and on a family holiday.

"Not as often as it used to, actually," she answered, looking at him. "I'm sorry, Henry..."

"Don't apologize for Colin. He's got his own demons. You've worked in the hospitals..."

"I know." Her voice was pained and hollow. "I just... it's just by this time, I thought... I mean, I didn't ever picture Colin..."

Henry knew exactly how to end all of her sentences, but instead, he said, "Colin will be forever scarred by losing two of his crew. He was their captain. Their pilot. It's a burden of responsibility that is nearly impossible to explain."

"But it wasn't his fault!" Her distressed look knifed tiny slices in his heart.

Henry drew a breath. He longed to take her in his arms and comfort her. "Gretchen, just because something isn't your fault doesn't mean you don't blame yourself for it."

"Henry, that's completely illogical, and you're a very logical man."

"I'm not talking about logic. Sometimes people just need time and space." He thought it an ironic description of how he would need to deal with Gretchen and Colin becoming lovers, which he knew wouldn't happen if he didn't give his permission. The idea that he had such power over the happiness of these two people made it difficult to think clearly.

The next morning, Colin didn't come down to say goodbye to Henry. After everyone left the breakfast room, Henry stood staring out at the distant mountains, almost obscured by low-hanging clouds. The day looked dreary. The way he felt.

Gretchen came in from the kitchen.

"I want to say my goodbyes now, Henry," she said in a soft voice. "While we're alone." Her eyes were full of a sadness he couldn't define.

Was she sad that they had not talked about her feelings for Colin? But it wasn't something he could talk to Gretchen about. It was Colin who needed to know Henry would not stand in the way, and more importantly, would encourage Colin to make Gretchen happy.

He sighed. "When are you going back to Edinburgh?"

"In another week. The new session starts mid-January." She kissed him lightly on the cheek and ran her fingers tenderly down his arm. "Henry, please take care of yourself. I'll miss you. You are my rock. My link to the world we came from. If anything ever happened to you..."

She turned and reentered the kitchen through the swinging door, leaving him standing there, dizzy as always when she was tender toward him.

He went upstairs to see Colin, who was sitting in an armchair facing the ocean.

"Colin, I'm off soon. Mairi is giving me a ride to Ullapool."

Colin nodded, not turning from his view. "Sorry, I didn't come down to breakfast..."

Time to say the very thing he didn't want to say.

"About Gretchen..."

"Gretchen?" Colin's voice was wary, hesitant.

"Colin, I know... how she feels about you," Henry couldn't manage, "She loves you."

Colin made a strangled sound. "God, Henry, I've never encouraged her. Tried to keep her at arm's length. It's just..." He turned in Henry's direction, confusion and pleading in his eyes.

Henry said, "It's clear what's between you."

"Honest, I swear I dinna touch her. I know you've always..."

"I've always wished," Henry said softly, looking at the floor. "But wishes are just that. She's only ever seen me as a friend. But it's clear she loves you." There, he said it. And couldn't say much more without breaking down, so he said the rest all in a jumble.

"Colin, only you can make her happy. Please do. Tell her I said so. That I give my... blessing. That I want only for her, for you... to be happy. With each other."

And with that, he hurried from the room, Colin's words following him out the door. "I am sae sorry, Henry. I never meant it to happen."

Colin knew he should be ecstatic. But he felt like crap. His lungs burned. His leg ached. His jaw throbbed. His head pounded. His future had nothing for Gretchen. He was a cripple. A man the war had chewed up and spit out. And Henry was clearly crushed.

Just then Gretchen stuck her head around the edge of the door. "Colin, you didn't say goodbye to Henry. He's leaving soon."

"He came up. We talked. About you."

"About me?" Her face flushed. "What do you mean?"

"He's not stupid, Gretchen."

Her face flushed even more. "Of course, he's not stupid. But I've done nothing to be ashamed of. Nothing to betray any trust. And it's not as if you've given me any encouragement!"

That was true enough. Their camaraderie on the beach was rare. Mostly, Colin had remained distant and cool.Though she had been unbelievably patient while prodding him to do more. She had been the one who could ease him out of that place of darkness he fell into all too often. A place that would always be there to trip him up.

"What did he say?" Gretchen finally asked, sitting on the edge of the bed across from him. He stared across the space separating them, overwhelmed by her beauty and the thought that she was willing to share her future with him. But what could that future be? Stuck here in this remote highland farm. She wasn't meant to be some farmer's wife. That's why she had left that life. She belonged in a city where she could glow, sparkle, dazzle.

Back home. In the States. After the war.

"To put it bluntly, he gave us his blessing." Colin heard the bitterness in his voice and saw Gretchen's confusion.

"You don't sound happy about it."

"He's my best friend, Gretchen. I know it's eating him up inside."

"We can't help who we love," Gretchen protested, the tenderness she'd hidden from him now shining through her eyes. "And he knows that."

"It's not just about Henry."

She sat up straighter, her eyes growing wary. "Who is it about?"

"You and me."

"And?"

"It takes two."

"What are you saying? You're not making sense."

"It's making a lot of sense. The first sense I've made in months. I have nothing to offer you. No future. No hope. I'm just a cripple who wonders why he's even alive."

"But that's just it. You're alive! You're mending. And not only that, Henry has removed the last barrier between us!" She knelt in front of him and placed her hands on the armrests so he was locked into his seat, surrounded by her alluring presence, drowning in her pleading eyes.

"Colin. I love you. There. I've said it at last. And I know you love me, though you've never said. We knew, that day at Traprain Law. I saw it in your face. You can't deny it."

"I'm not that man anymore. The war has changed me."

"Hell, it's changed us all! Which is all the more reason we need to hold onto what love we can find in the middle of it."

He closed his eyes to shut out the sight of the one thing he wanted more than anything. That one thing which could be his if only he would say what they both knew.

That he loved her. Wanted her. And needed her.

But he refused to let his need be the reason. He wouldn't let her tend him the rest of his days. He shook his head, "No. No. It won't happen. Not anymore."

He could sense her trembling, but he kept his hands clasped in his lap. He would not touch her. He would not give in. And then he said, flatly, "It's time for you to go home. Henry hasn't left yet. You can get a ride with Mairi and give him some company back to Edinburgh."

"I'm not leaving."

He opened his eyes and stared, willing himself into that fathomless space of despair. "Go, Gretchen. I don't want you here anymore. You're planning to leave in a week anyway. Why wait. You've overstayed your welcome."

He could see how each sentence landed like a blow. He felt like a coward, a cad, a soulless abuser. *But I am soulless,* he thought to himself.

She stood up, visibly shaken. Breathing as if she had been running uphill.

He refused to look up at her and said once more. "Go. You've overstayed your welcome."

He didn't say, *I don't want you.* Because he did. With every breath, every thought, every cell in his body.

"If that's how you want it." Her words were strangled, begging him to contradict them.

He simply turned his head and looked at the wall.

———⫘———

Henry's reaction to the news she was leaving with him and why stunned Gretchen. He stormed down the hall from his room to Colin's. She could hear them shouting at each other as Mairi helped her pack. She caught only a few words, and those made her cringe, as though they were poison darts aimed directly at her. She had never heard such language from Henry, nor heard Colin speak with such venom.

"Bloody fool."

"Fucking asshole."

"Prick."

Mairi put an end to it, flinging Colin's door open. Outshouting them both in Gaelic, of which Gretchen understood more than she let on. A chill descended on the house, pervaded the apologetic goodbyes from Colin's family, and followed Gretchen, Henry, and Mairi to Ullapool.

Each was utterly silent on the long ride.

At the train station, Mairi finally broke down in tears. She hugged Gretchen and begged her to come in the summer when Colin was sure to be himself.

"There's no sense in it, Mairi," she replied, giving in to tears as well. "It's clear he has no use for me, and I'm just a thorn in his side. I'll miss you. You're like a sister to me."

Gretchen followed Henry onto the train, her head muddled, her heart shredded. It had happened so unexpectedly. One moment, Henry gave her what she longed for, and in the next, Colin savagely ripped it away. And almost worse, the very thing she had tried so hard to prevent had occurred. Henry and Colin had fallen out. Over her.

Henry offered no consolation, no sympathy, no words of comfort on the endless train ride. She didn't know what to say. They sat in icy silence for hours. Though Henry, always a gentleman, occasionally asked if she was warm enough, or needed something from the club car, to which she replied with a simple "yes" or "no."

They separated in Edinburgh. He told her he needed to get back to base and would have to skip the visit he had planned with Fiona and her aunt and uncle, catching the next train south.

"They'll be disappointed, Henry. Especially Fiona. Don't change your plans because of me."

"It's not about you, Gretchen. I just need to... I just need some time alone."

He looked at her with a face so stricken she nearly grabbed onto him, pleading for him to stay. Riddled with guilt, she whispered goodbye, feeling she had lost Colin and Henry too.

———⟫⟪———

Fiona stared at her over her wine, surprisingly unsympathetic. "It's about time that Henry realized the truth." They were out for a night before Fiona headed back to Biggin Hill.

"But I feel like I betrayed him."

"How? You never said yes when he asked you to marry him. You always made it plain that you didn't love him. Other than hitting him on the head, this was the best way to wake him up."

"But it's not like it has a happy ending."

"This isn't one of your fairy tales, lassie. Colin and Henry will have to sort it out for themselves. As for you and Colin..."

"What?" Gretchen tried to read the emotionless face of her friend.

"That's really for Colin to decide, nay?" Fiona responded coldly. "There's nary a thing you can do but wait for him to come around, or..."

"Or what?!" Gretchen felt as if she were losing Fiona as well.

"Or realize that we can't always have what we want. And besides..." Fiona drained her glass and signaled the waiter for another. "...truth be told, I dinna think that Henry will ever give up on you, Gretchen, not even if you do end up with his best friend."

"I don't think they're best friends anymore," Gretchen replied, a catch in her voice.

"Well, all's fair in love and war, aye?"

"Fiona, sometimes I don't understand you."

Fiona shrugged. "I don't understand myself sometimes, so join the crowd. Besides," she added with an acrimonious sigh, "Henry'll love you till the day he dies, Gretchen."

"Fiona, what are you so riled up about? It's not like I ever led him on. And you can't force someone to love you, or for that matter, not love you."

"Oh, aye, I well know that," her friend replied, surprising bitterness in her eyes. "Don't mind me. I just wish I had someone who loved me the way Henry loves you."

Gretchen shook her head silently. Henry would never want to be a part of her life again.

TWENTY-SIX

JULY 1943

UPON RETURNING FROM ACHILTIBUIE, Gretchen threw herself into her studies. On completing her training in May, she found a position at the RAF hospital near the West Wickham Aerodrome in the Cambridge area and moved south. Day after day, she treated injured airmen, many wounded in the most horrendous ways, mourning the loss of their companions yet fiercely determined to get back in the fight. As the weeks went on, her sympathy for Colin began to leach away.

This feeling persisted, despite Mairi's letters she had received throughout the spring and summer. One said, *I despair of him, Gretchen. I think he's wishing himself into the grave. The doctor says he's mostly healed. But that he'll always have a bad limp and pain in his back, especially in cold weather. As if you can escape the cold in the Highlands.*

Then came the stunning letter in mid-May with the news that Alastair had been killed in mid-April when his destroyer, the *HMS Beverly*, was torpedoed in the North Atlantic. Only four of the 155 crew survived. She had never met Alastair but had heard so many stories about how he and Colin, growing up, bedeviled their sisters or got up to some outrageous prank.

Gretchen sent her short, heartfelt condolences to the family and received a brief reply from Colin's mother, thanking her for her kind thoughts and saying how much all of them appreciated what she had done for Colin, "*who is taking his brother's death very hard.*"

She worried about her own brother, William, serving aboard a naval destroyer escort in the Pacific, where the battle raged endlessly. Islands she had never heard of became familiar names: Corregidor, and Guadalcanal. Letters from her mother—Naomi had stopped writing—were full of news clippings as if Gretchen, in Scotland, wouldn't know what the American navy was doing.

When she was settled at the aerodrome, she sent a note to Henry, stationed nearby at the U.S. Eighth Air Force Base from where the American B29 crews flew their daytime missions over Germany, with the British continuing their nighttime raids.

No response. She had not heard from him since they parted at the Edinburgh train station, though Fiona kept Gretchen informed of Henry's whereabouts. Gretchen missed his reliable, non-intrusive presence. She occasionally thought it would have been so much easier if she had loved Henry, not Colin.

On a mid-July afternoon, Gretchen was wheeling a slightly battered bike into the stand at her quarters, a metal Quonset hut shared by twenty nurses and WAAFs who boiled in the summer and froze in the winter, to see Henry standing near the telephone kiosk.

The look on his face sent shards of terror into her heart.

Henry strode over quickly, put an arm around her shoulders, and led her to a nearby wooden bench. "You've heard then?" His voice was soft, sympathetic.

Gretchen was unable to form words but shook her head. Colin. Mairi said he seemed to be wishing himself into his grave.

"Your father sent me a telegram. He asked me to tell you."

Gretchen put her fingertips to her throat, where she was trying to force enough breath through to stay conscious then stared in confusion at Henry.

"My father?" she was finally able to force out in a hoarse voice.

"I'm so sorry, Gretchen. It's William."

For a moment a treacherous flood of joy surged through her body. It wasn't Colin!

Then she gasped. "William? What?" She could only articulate one-word questions.

Henry took her hands, his face conveying concern and sorrow. "Gretchen, William's ship was sunk in the Pacific. He's believed lost at sea."

Gretchen stared at Henry, trying to comprehend his words, but her thoughts were on Colin.

"Are you listening, Gretchen? Do you understand? It's still possible they will find him. Lots of men are rescued at sea days after their ship goes down."

"Alistair wasn't," she countered bluntly. "Do you know about Alistair?"

Henry simply nodded.

As the mid-afternoon sun blazed down, Henry's news crystallized in her mind. He was talking about William. Her little brother. And she was thinking about Colin. *Well, now we have something in common,* the bitter thought passed through her mind. *We both lost a brother at sea.*

"But he's so young," she managed, at last, trying to picture the brother she hadn't seen in four years. He had been barely sixteen and so full of himself.

"He took me for a ride in his brand-new Ford Roadster when I went to see your family in the fall of '39. He loved that car. Terrified the living daylights out of me with his driving."

Henry's voice seemed to be drifting across the years. To a time that no longer existed, that was nothing but a gossamer thread of memory. She had never even seen William in his roadster. Now he was dead. Yet she could barely conjure up the grief she should be feeling, grief she would have felt if it had been Colin. The guilt at such a realization made her nauseous.

She had to ask. "Have you heard from Colin?"

"No." She shouldn't have, but she couldn't help but persist.

"Or of him?"

"Mairi drops me a line now and then."

"Mairi?" Gretchen didn't know why that surprised her.

Last week, when Gretchen complained that Henry had dropped off the face of the earth, Fiona's words had stung. "Henry's not yours, Gretchen. You've made that clear enough times. Maybe he's found somebody who actually appreciates him."

Gretchen knew Henry wasn't "hers," but she had never reconciled herself to a life without him and found herself inordinately comforted by his presence.

She stared off at the lush, flat farmland of southeastern England, paved over by ugly, oil-strewn concrete runways. The sound of returning American bombers echoed far off.

Gretchen, what is wrong with you? Your brother may be dead, and all you can think about is that Colin is still living and breathing. Or that Henry might finally have found someone else to set his sights on. Naomi would be so disgusted.

Thinking of Naomi brought her back to reality. "Henry, should I go home?" She could picture the letter from her sister: *Mother and Daddy need you, especially now.*

"You don't know that he's gone, Gretchen. There's always hope. And there's no passenger service between England and home. Even if there were, it'd be too dangerous with the U-boats."

"Yes, you're right." She stared down at Henry's rough, oil-stained hands, still holding hers tenderly. "About both things. William could very well turn up in a prisoner of war camp, though thinking of him in a Jap prison camp..." she shuddered. Her little brother.

"You're doing valuable work here, Gretchen. As a nurse." Then he added in a lighter tone, "I heard you picked up on your duties right away."

"How could you hear?"

Henry smiled wryly. "I've got my sources."

"I bet you have!" Should she be indignant or flattered? She might not have heard from him, but he apparently was keeping tabs on her. Maybe through Fiona. "Heard anything else?"

"Yeah."

"Like what?"

"Like there's this pretty Yank nurse at the RAF hospital who turns down all the guys."

Gretchen gently removed her hands from his. "You do have your sources." Then she looked at Henry, who watched her warily. He looked thinner, fatigued.

"I'd only go out with one guy."

"At a time?" His voice was flat.

"Henry!"

"Well, we know that one guy is nowhere in the neighborhood." His voice was resigned.

Gretchen's heart lurched to think about Colin, but she said without emotion, "Not that guy."

She saw Henry stiffen. "Gretchen, I..."

"Henry, listen. I don't want to say this at all, so I'll only say it once. I never meant to fall in love with Colin. And he was always honorable. He never told me how he felt. I only guessed it. And he tried to stay away. I'm the one who spent those months at Achiltibuie, hoping he would come around. And in the end, he did not. He just wants to live in that dark cloud of his."

"Gretchen..."

"Please, Henry. Hear me out. Given all that, I have no desire to go out with any more flyboys. RAF or US. But there is *one* guy I would spend time with..." She looked at him straight on, noticing how pale he had become. "...as a friend. If he is able to be that person. That loyal companion. Knowing I could never love him as I've..."

The grief struck her then, like a blow to the head, stunning her with its intensity. She dropped her face into her hands and wept. For William. For Alistair. For Colin. For all the young men... boys, most of them... that she nursed day after day so they could go back into the air and risk their lives all over again; and the others who didn't ever rise from their beds, but were sent home in wooden coffins to families trying to comprehend the incomprehensive.

Henry put his arm around her, and she let him comfort her, hold her, and whisper soothing sounds and gentle words. Like that day he held her in the back seat of Fiona's car at Traprain Law. When it was Colin she wanted holding her. But it wasn't to be then.

Or now.

———⬥———

For all intents and purposes, Colin knew he was healed. But he still needed a cane, and he could always feel the change of weather in his jaw, right forearm, thighbone, and lower back, like an unwelcome internal barometer.

On a muggy afternoon in early August, not yet dimmed by storm clouds that were still out to sea, but which he could feel in his body, he sat on the beach glumly staring out into the bay, swatting away the pesky midges that buzzed around him.

It was there Mairi found him. "You've got a letter."

He shrugged. Letters came from time to time. From Fiona. From an old school chum. And occasionally from Tack, his former navigator. Tack and the other surviving crew had managed to stick together and found themselves a pilot, flight engineer, and rear gunner and were only a few missions from the magic thirty.

"It's from Gretchen."

Gritting his teeth, he shrugged again. What could she want? She had never written after that awful December day when he cruelly sent her away. But he'd recognized her decorative handwriting on letters addressed to Mairi. Full of curves and curlicues. Suited her, he thought.

He'd asked once, "What's she say?" when he saw his sister reading a letter from Gretchen.

"It's not your goddamn business," Mairi had replied in a pleasant tone, as if she'd just said, *nice to see you*. He had glowered back at her.

Mairi had laughed unpleasantly. "Well, you told her to be gone, and so she was. Yew can just live with yourself, ye daft bamstick, seeing as ye got yer wish."

Only Fiona kept him up to date on Gretchen's life, not that he wanted to know. He sometimes thought Fiona wrote just to torment him. He learned Gretchen had finished her nursing program and had taken up a post in the south of England.

He also learned that Gretchen's brother was declared missing in action in the South Pacific when his ship was sunk, but was not among the 732 survivors later rescued from a small island on which they had taken refuge. William was among the 168 who had perished.

He thought of Alastair and returned to his familiar place of darkness.

Purgatory, he thought, remembering his catechism. Father MacQuarrie told him that suffering on earth, if accepted in the right spirit, would shorten one's time in Purgatory in the afterlife, as time there cleansed the soul for admission into heaven. But Father MacQuarrie had told him on a recent visit that making his life on earth a deliberate Purgatory was not something God would approve of. And might actually get you a longer stint there.

He thought that a rather unconventional piece of theology for a Catholic priest. Colin had come to find his Purgatory a comforting place. It suited his state of mind. And he told his rector just that, to which the gray-haired priest simply sighed and walked away.

Henry had not written either. No surprise, considering the awful things they'd said to each other that day when, in trying to save Gretchen from himself, he had demolished their friendship.

Fiona also said that Henry was once again escorting Gretchen places. *I haven't had the time to spare to visit them, and Henry's not come to visit me in London since Gretchen moved south.*

Colin thought she really meant, "I'm back to playing second fiddle." He wondered how much "fiddling" had gone on between them. Henry would be too much the gentleman to even hint he was shagging his one true love's best friend while moping around after that true love who wouldn't give him the time of day... or night.

That was unkind, even for you, Colin chastised himself. *This is wartime. Love the one you're with. It's just shait if the one you're with isn't your true love.*

Mairi stood blocking Colin's sea view. "She's not written you once. It must be important."

"How do you know?"

"I'm the one who fetches the mail from the post office."

"So did you read it, too? Tell me what she said. It'll save me the trouble."

He heard his sister's sharp intake of breath but refused to look at her.

"Colin, I do believe you've lost your soul." With those searing words, she tossed the envelope in his direction and walked away.

The letter fluttered in the air and landed at his feet, face up. He saw Gretchen's lovely handwriting, as lovely as her face. With a grunt, he bent over and retrieved it. "May as well get this over with," he said to the sea, his daily companion, which he preferred to human company.

There was just one piece of paper in the envelope. He pulled it out and unfolded it. It didn't even cover half the page. But it covered all of the truth.

Colin, I assume you've heard about my brother William. His ship sank, and he was lost at sea. Most of the men survived. William didn't. How horribly sad that both of our brothers died the same way. Not even tombstones to mark their graves. Yet there you are hiding in your mountain lair, ignoring the world and the war. Even you, with your injuries, could do something for the war effort. Are you even a man anymore? Certainly not the man I loved. Just a blob of self-pity. Others continue to fight on. I tend them day after day. Some make it. Some don't. The ones who do can't wait to get back into the fight. To do their bit in ending this godawful war.

She didn't even sign her name.

As he reread it, he could hear each word, distinct and precise, echoing in the hollow chamber of his heart. Tiny scorching flames of letters.

Hiding. Ignoring. A man? Blob. Self-pity.

When he finished, Gretchen's voice played over and over in his head. *"Are you even a man anymore? Certainly not the man I loved."*

It was nearly dark when Mairi returned. He was sitting exactly as she had left him, staring out to sea, but with Gretchen's letter clutched in his hand.

"Colin, it's near nightfall. Ye've missed your supper."

Had he lost his soul? It would be so easy to just walk out into the ocean and let it take him like it had taken Alistair. And Gretchen's brother.

Only when his sister gasped and knelt on the sand in front of him, did he realize he had spoken those last thoughts out loud.

"I'm sae sorry," she sobbed. "I dinna mean it. I was just so riled at ye."

He handed her the letter and saw the anguish in his heart reflected on her face as she read it. She stood and touched his shoulder. "She loves ye, Colin."

He shook his head.

"If she dinna love you, she wouldna write to ye at all, or be so courageous as to tell ye the truth. Do ye love her still, Colin?"

He could not speak the words. They seared his throat, but he nodded, finding to his great astonishment that he was weeping.

"Aye, brother, aye," his little sister soothed, holding his head against her chest, and rocking him gently like a babe in distress. "It's time ye did some cryin'."

Twenty-Seven

December 1943

As summer turned into autumn and then winter, Henry saw Gretchen whenever their time off coincided, which wasn't often. Neither ever mentioned Colin.

He knew from Mairi that Colin had finally emerged from his black hole and was working regularly around the farm, withdrawn but showing signs of his old self. *It's near a miracle*, she had written. Gretchen probably knew this too, but he never asked. Colin was the ghost haunting both their lives, and Henry didn't want to enflesh that spirit by mentioning his name.

When he wrote to Fiona that he was keeping an eye on Gretchen, she replied in her usual forthright manner.

Henry, I have always known you'd never give up on Gretchen. That all she has to do is call your name, and you'd swim through a shark-infested ocean to get to her. After all, you crossed that U-boat-infested North Atlantic for her. I do admire your loyalty. Or do I pity your self-deception? Oh well, we all have to endure this war in whatever way we can. Try not to feel guilty about our rendezvous. They were delightful, and I like to think you were equally entertained.

I know you so much better than Gretchen does or ever will. With me, you were never trying to impress. You were just yourself. There's a lot more depth to you than Gretchen can ever imagine. If she could, she would love you, as you are immensely lovable. But you put her on a pedestal and make her an object of worship. A woman finds it hard to love a man who worships her. She's afraid of falling off that pedestal.

Try not to get your heart broken. More useless advice. In the end, you'll probably give Colin and Gretchen your blessing. But look at the mess they made of it the last time you did. Maybe we're all better off if we just continue to lie to ourselves and others about who we really love.

I won't be writing anymore, Henry. Stay safe.

Her letter gave him pause. Despite Fiona's nonchalance, he never felt right about their relationship, flogging himself mentally after each weekend he had spent with her in London. What kind of man claims to love one woman and sleeps with her best friend?

Did Fiona care for him more than he thought? Was he being as cruel to Fiona as Colin was to Gretchen? If only he could either love Fiona or let go of Gretchen... it was all so fucked up. And here he was again, squiring Gretchen about. Though he did very little of that, with their leave time so limited. The air war had intensified, with hints everywhere of a buildup to an invasion.

Everyone knew the Allies would be taking the war to France at some point since the Brits and the Yanks had begun an invasion of Italy. The British Eighth Army, under Field Marshal Montgomery, crossed the Strait of Messina from Sicily and landed at Calabria, the "toe" of Italy, on September 3, right as the Italians agreed to an armistice with the Allies.

The U.S. Fifth Army, under Lt. General Mark W. Clark, went ashore at Salerno on September 9, facing unexpected German resistance. By now, December, the allies had bogged down in their attempts to reach Rome, due to difficult terrain and ongoing German defenses.

Meanwhile, for Henry, the war consisted of living in his strange limbo of "liaison." He spent a lot of time carrying messages, explaining the Brits and the Yanks to each other, soothing ruffled feathers, and teaching the ground crews more efficient ways to do things. He would have preferred being a mechanic, but this way he could see more of Gretchen.

True to his word, he never mentioned his feelings and was never obtrusive or overbearing. Others took it for granted they were a couple. Any newcomer who didn't was quickly set straight. "Oh, that one's not available." As the only American nurse at the RAF hospital, she was well known. The Yankee nurses, increasingly more of them, worked on the US airbase.

If Fiona had been with them, it would have been like old times, Henry sometimes thought. And yet he knew that was a futile wish. Instead, he hoped the future could be different. Gretchen would gradually come to forget Colin, though Henry missed both Fiona and Colin with a sadness he couldn't erase.

On New Year's Eve, the Yanks were hosting their neighboring RAF partners in a big celebration. Perhaps a night of dancing on a holiday marking a new beginning could mark his and Gretchen's own new beginning. The end of the war wasn't in sight, but there was finally a sense that it might end. In a year. Maybe two. The tide had turned in 1943.

It was time to look once again to the future.

Colin's climb out of his physical and emotional purgatory took months of concerted effort. He barely passed the doctor's exam, but through the powerful influence that Fiona seemed to have, he was reinstated in the RAF as an air commodore's adjunct. After all, he was a "hero." He had been awarded the DFC—Distinguished Flying Cross.

He still had a pronounced limp, and at the end of a long day, he needed a cane to keep him steady. His intention was to get back in the air; he wouldn't be able to fly again, but he could be a navigator. He could "do his bit" that Gretchen had so scathingly said he was shirking.

Though his parents and sisters were happy to see him functional, his mother asked him, just once, to consider accepting the medical discharge he so rightly earned and remain on the farm where he was needed. The sadness in her eyes almost broke his resolve.

"I can't, Mother. I know this is very hard for you, but it'd be harder for me to stay when I can still do something..."

She merely nodded, touched his face with her hand, and walked away. His father said only, "Colin you must do what your conscience tells you to do. I will respect your decision and love you, no matter what you decide."

It was the most emotional statement he'd ever heard from his father in his entire life.

His sisters both wept openly, but neither said, "Don't go," only, "Be safe." It was Mairi who said, "I think there's still happiness out there for ye, Colin, even in the midst of all this war. Don't deny yourself that, ye ken?"

"But what if my happiness comes at the expense of someone else's?" he replied softly.

"Colin, Henry would never be happy if he knew Gretchen missed a chance for happiness with you. I know that sounds like so much bosh, but he knows it's you Gretchen loves."

"I don't think so, Mairi. Not after all this. Not after I treated her like so much shait."

Mairi just sighed. "Colin, I'm a woman. I understand a woman's heart. And believe me, it takes a lot more than some stubborn ass of a lad to turn away the love that a lassie has for him."

He arrived at the RAF aerodrome in mid-December, knowing that Gretchen worked at the nearby hospital and that Henry was often at the aerodrome. He decided to leave their inevitable encounter to fate, though he knew an honorable man would have looked Henry up and asked his forgiveness for the awful things he'd said to him last year.

Colin wasn't really sure he believed Mairi about Gretchen still loving him, especially since Henry was "squiring" Gretchen again. He had no doubt that Henry was hoping Gretchen would finally love him back. But can you choose who you're going to love?

I certainly didn't choose to fall in love with Gretchen, he thought to himself.

So it was with both heart-fluttering hope and gut-wrenching dread that he walked into the American hangar on New Year's Eve. What more ironic twist of fate would there be than to see her tonight, sparkling and breathtaking as ever in the light of a dimly lit hangar, three years after that night at Drem?

The long buffet tables of food and drink supplied by the American hosts amazed him. It certainly marked the difference between the United States, a country with its vast resources of industrial might and agricultural riches, and England, a country entering its fifth year of bombed cities, rigid rationing, and a generation being depleted of young, vibrant men. Though cigarettes weren't rationed, they were in short supply. But the arrival of the Yanks made them once again obtainable, often through the black market. Seems the Yanks smoked as much as the Brits.

The representatives of the two allied air forces mingled with no apparent concern for their differences. All levels of brass and enlisted personnel were present, as were lots of young women, many in uniform, others arrayed in their party finest. In the soft glow of the strung lights and votive table candles, no one would see frayed collars or threadbare sweaters.

Colin had deliberately left his cane in the officer's quarters. As an adjunct, he was now entitled to a private room in the nearby estate house the RAF had requisitioned. He also had access to a driver. Such luxuries made him self-conscious, but he knew they were a deliberate demarcation between the rank and file, which included the pilots and the brass.

He had consciously conserved his strength in the hopes of staving off the inevitable end-of-day pain that required a cane, though lately, he had managed to go longer without it. The first thing he needed was a bracing dram of whiskey, which he indulged in from a flask he carried in an inner pocket. It was another way to stave off the pain.

It didn't take long to spot her. She was on the dance floor, being spun about by some RAF flyboy to the full orchestration of the latest Benny Goodman tune, *Taking a Chance on Love,* sung by a sultry-voiced girl in a glittery gown, fronting the white-tuxedoed musicians. It could have been a Hollywood stage set with Gretchen as the star. She had on a simple but sleek gown that showed off all her assets, ones her partner was trying to get a little too familiar with.

Colin felt his blood rise, affronted at a crass countryman. He began to make his way over, with no real plan about what he would do when he got to her. Punch the guy's lights out would be his preference. But Gretchen knew how to handle an overzealous dance partner. She firmly but laughingly pulled herself out of his lecherous grip, slapping him gently on the cheek.

"That won't do, Captain. Don't want to offend the allies." He could hear her words and ironic laughter above the music as he approached. The RAF Captain didn't seem to understand the word "no" and roughly pulled Gretchen back in his arms.

Colin wasn't the only one keeping a protective eye on her, for he and Henry grabbed the overzealous flyboy at the same time, one on each side, allowing Gretchen to step back.

"Thank you, my two knights in shining armor," she said over the Captain's loud protests. "Both a Yank and a Brit to my rescue at the same..."

Gretchen's eyes widened, visible shock passing over her face. Henry, who had been looking at Gretchen, did a double-take when he glanced at his fellow "knight." Sensing something brewing, Gretchen's dance partner vanished into the crowd.

Colin felt a wrench in his innards, a torturous longing and a dreadful desire to simply turn into smoke and join the lingering tobacco mists floating overhead. Finally, he turned to look at Henry, who stared back at him steadily, his face a study of neutrality. But Henry's eyes held emotions Colin knew all too well—wariness and an underlying layer of despair.

At last, Gretchen said with a shaky laugh, "So, here we are. Together again."

Henry spoke, his voice guarded. "I heard you were back in the service, Colin. I'm pleased to see you looking so well."

"I'm pleased to be looking so well," Colin responded, trying to inject a note of humor.

"Why don't we sit down," Gretchen said brightly, stepping between them and linking her arms in theirs, leading them across the emptying dance floor.

To Colin, the trip across the dance floor seemed as long as the trip across the English Channel on a return flight from a bombing raid. His senses were on high alert, just as they had been then, though instead of dreaming about her, he was beside her, his arm linked in hers, feeling her slight tremble, hearing her taxed breathing, as if she were winded from an enthusiastic spin on the dance floor.

He could sense Henry on her other side, providing a steady arm, a sure foot and a dependable, but unobtrusive presence. As he always did. Two men. Loving the same woman.

Colin thought it so trite, so passé, so stale—if it had been someone else's life, he would have laughed sarcastically. But by coming here, he had once again inserted himself between Henry and Gretchen. He could have stayed away. He *should* have stayed away, he chided himself as he simultaneously reveled in her presence.

Gretchen could barely breathe. She felt dizzy and disoriented. What year was this? New Year's Eve. A hangar dance. Henry. And Colin.

She longed for Fiona's sardonic, flippant, yet calming presence. A foursome was doable. She could talk to Colin or Henry while Fiona talked to the other. Not be stuck in the middle.

Something had changed in Fiona, who had become distant and cool since Gretchen had come south to England. She didn't come visit, rarely dropped her a line, and almost never responded to her phone calls. Henry said she had stopped writing him as well.

It was all wrong.

"I think the two of you need to talk," she said when they reached the table. She pulled her arms away and did her best not to tremble. "I have an early shift. It's time I left."

She refused to listen to Colin's protest or Henry's "I'll take you back right now."

"No. I'm quite capable of arranging my own transportation, Henry. I am a grown woman. You don't have to do everything for me." She said it in a harsher tone than she meant to, from the pain on Henry's face and Colin's look of disapproval.

Good, she thought to herself. *Good. Get them both angry. At me.*

Waving to an older RAF officer at the next table, she deliberately avoided looking at them. "Colonel Smithers, might I trouble you for a ride to the barracks? I've a really early morning shift, and I don't want to deprive these fine gentlemen of a New Year's Eve bash."

A surprised, pleased look came over the middle-aged RAF wing commander's face, who gave both Colin and Henry a speculative look. "Be delighted, by all means."

Gretchen nodded at Colin and Henry, her color high and her face set in a falsely cheerful smile. "Cheerio, and happy 1944. See you around."

She linked her arm with the senior officer's and headed through the crowds, not looking back.

Twenty-Eight

February 1944

WHEN HENRY WENT BY the hospital on New Year's Day at the end of Gretchen's shift, he was told she was working overtime. Over the next week, he called the pay phone near her Quonset hut, but after three attempts on three different days, a nurse answered, saying Gretchen was out.

He sent several notes to her at the hospital, against regulations, each growing more pleading, but got no response. Three days after his fourth note, the courier appeared at Henry's desk with a letter in his hand. The private winked conspiratorially at him. They were both from Lancaster, Pennsylvania, and the private enjoyed flaunting authority.

Henry told the unit clerk he had to run an errand, flagged down a driver, and got a ride to his quarters. In his room, he sank shakily to the edge of the bed. The letter was short. And very clear.

Dear Henry,

I'm sorry, but I won't stand in the way of a friendship between the two people I love most in this world. I'd rather have neither of you, as friend or lover, if it means an end to your friendship. For years, you have been my rock. However, it's time I stand on my own. As Naomi would say, it's time I grew up. I only hope that you and Colin find a way to repair the damage I did to your friendship. I wish you well, and I wish you safe. *Please don't*

*call or visit. We'll have to get through the rest of this godforsaken war on
our own.*

All during this wretched war, Gretchen had been his reason for going
on. In these recent months, he had allowed the tendrils of possibility to
burrow into the very core of him. Having them yanked out felt like some
clueless gardener was mistaking flowers for weeds. The result, he knew,
would be a shriveled heart in a life that was a decaying garden.

An unexpected rage surged through Henry as his mind turned to
Colin. Pacing in short, agitated steps around the room, he thought *what
kind of friend steals the woman you love*? No amount of rational thought
cooled his anger. He contemplated a trip to the RAF base, to confront
Colin. But then a turn of phrase from Gretchen's letter echoed in his
mind.

Wait, what was that she said about loving...? He picked up the letter,
looking for the words she had written... *The two people I love most in this
world.*

She does love me! For a moment, a sense of breathless joy overcame him.
She does love me! She says so right there in the letter.

And then the bitter reality of her rejection struck. *She loves me but she
won't choose me. As friend or lover. So now I have nothing of her. Not even
her friendship.*

Crumpling her letter in his fist, he bowed his head and rocked in silent
mourning.

For a long moment, Colin stared at the envelope addressed to him in
Gretchen's lovely handwriting. With a deep breath, he slit it open.

Colin,

*I don't know what you hoped for by coming back into my life, but I
haven't forgotten or forgiven the things you said that day in Achiltibuie.
The only thing I ask of you is to mend your friendship with Henry. If not
for your sake, then Henry's.*

Colin hadn't known what to expect from arranging, with Fiona's
connections, to be stationed near Gretchen, and coincidentally, near

Henry. He didn't blame her for not forgiving him. His conduct had been appalling.

He heard Gretchen's plea to repair his friendship with Henry, but there wasn't any way to make it happen. *We've all paid a price for this deception*, he thought. He wondered once again if it wouldn't have been better if he had perished with his crew members.

On a biting, frigid afternoon in early February, Colin was at the officers' mess on the RAF base heading for a table with a cup of tea and sweet roll in hand, when he looked up to see Henry a few feet in front of him. Colin was surprised it had taken so long for their paths to cross.

"Henry."

"Colin."

"Coming or going?" Colin kept his voice neutral, noticing Henry's gray pallor of exhaustion.

"Coming for tea. I see you have yours," Henry replied, in a flat tone.

"Yes." Colin hesitated a moment, then added, "Care to join me?"

Something flashed in Henry's eyes. Anger? Bitterness? But he shrugged. "I have a few moments."

Colin nodded to a nearby table.

"I'll get my tea and join you," Henry walked to the service area.

Colin tried to fathom how he might begin what Gretchen had asked: *Mend your friendship with Henry. Do it for Henry's sake.* But what words could start that process? There were only three that mattered. The three he said once Henry returned with his tea and scone.

"Henry, I'm sorry."

Henry froze, his teacup halfway to his lips, then set the cup down on the saucer without a sip. Colin continued with words he had mentally rehearsed. "I don't ever expect we can mend our friendship, given all that's happened. And all I said."

Henry sat expressionless. Motionless. Looking at Colin, who didn't look away.

Colin took a breath and said, haltingly, "But I need you to know that I'm sorry. For everything. For this awful mess."

Henry continued to stare at him warily, his hands motionless next to his untasted tea.

Finally, Colin said in a terse voice, "Well, don't just sit there, you daft Yank. At least beat the shait out of me!"

Henry's silent eyes conveyed an emotion Colin knew all too well: a man's grief at an unspeakable loss.

Henry carefully brought his cup to his mouth and took a large gulp. Then he stood, his cup making a clunk on the saucer. "It wouldn't help," he finally said in a tone of such resigned despair Colin almost cringed. He had never seen Henry like this. Like something was eating him from the inside.

Colin quickly rose to his feet as Henry turned. "Don't go. Please." He tried to keep the pleading from his voice. "I know you don't want to have this conversation. But here it is. Gretchen sent me a letter..."

Turning back, Henry interrupted with a sarcasm foreign to his voice. "Oh, you too?"

Colin ignored this. "...and told me, basically, that she wouldn't be seeing me or having anything to do with me, but she asked... she *pleaded*, Henry... that I try to mend our friendship. She said to do it for her sake." No way would he say "for your sake."

"She asked you that?"

They stood on either side of the table, talking in low tones. But they were attracting attention. "Let's go outside, Henry, where we can talk privately."

"I have nothing to say to you, Colin, in private or in public. Gretchen wrote to me, too. To let me know that she refuses to stand in the way of our friendship, that since choosing one of us as a lover and the other as a friend would always come between us, she won't do either. So she will just erase us both from her life."

Henry's voice had grown deeper and angrier, but beneath, Colin heard the suffering. *Oh Gretchen, how could you do this to Henry?*

Colin saw increasing perked-up interest from airmen nearby. They were both well-known in this small world. Colin, a decorated pilot, returned to active service in spite of horrendous injuries. Henry, a liaison between two allies, well-liked by enlisted and officers alike. And known to be the constant companion of the Yank nurse who worked at the aerodrome.

"Henry, let's go outside."

"Colin, I am outside. I couldn't be more outside if I tried. I'm neither fish nor fowl. I'm not a Yank, and I'm not a Brit. I'm not an officer, and I'm not enlisted. I don't fit in anywhere. And I'm neither a friend nor a lover." With that remark, he turned and headed toward the exit.

It would be best to let him go. The breach was too wide, the wounds too deep, the passage of time too long. If he followed Henry, Henry was likely to knock his lights out. But that would feel good. It would be a way to put a final blow to their friendship. Literally.

He caught up to Henry just outside the door. Light, icy rain had begun falling, and the wind had picked up. It was as bitter and miserable a day as one could want in southern England. It certainly fit his mood.

"Henry. Wait!"

Henry turned around, angry desperation across his face.

"What do you want, Colin? Really, I've heard about the stubbornness of the Scots, but this is ridiculous. Why can't you just let it go?"

"So why don't you just stop being so self-righteous and hit me one? It would make us both feel better."

"Oh, for God's sake."

"Henry, I don't know anything anymore. The reason I'm here, back in the RAF, is because of a different letter Gretchen wrote to me, making me realize what a useless, self-pitying blob I was, sulking in the Highlands while her brother and mine both gave their life for a cause I'm not sure I even believe in anymore. I didn't have the guts to do what I constantly longed to do—walk into that bay and just let the ocean take me. Like it had taken my brother. And Gretchen's."

Henry had gone very still.

"She told me off in no uncertain terms, both in that letter and this most recent one. She told me there's no going back. There's nothing left between us. Henry, you're the one who followed the woman you loved into a foreign country and took up a war when it was not yet your own fight. You're the one who deserves her."

"Apparently not," Henry said, looking across the distance to the B17s returning to the neighboring American base from their daily raid on Germany.

Colin tried once again to get through to his old friend. "I just want you to believe that I did nothing to make Gretchen fall in love with me. I don't know why she did. I did everything to discourage her. I was cold to her, cruel even at times, and said heartless things."

"I guess that's it," Henry said with a shaky sigh. "I did nothing to *discourage* her. I made it clear how I felt and waited for her to feel the same. But it didn't happen in the States, and it didn't happen in Scotland or here in England."

The rain was growing heavier.

"Henry, it's after four. The bar's open. Let's go get a drink."

"We could be thrown in the brig for neglecting our duty."

"I don't give a bloody feckin' shait."

"You know, Colin, when you're upset, your accent gets worse."

Colin looked at Henry, taken aback, and then burst out laughing. "Aye, ye damn Yankee, and you still can't tell the difference between a lowland and highland brogue."

"I'm not much of a drinker, you know," Henry replied.

"And I am. So let's compromise and just get *slightly* smashed."

"Aye. Let's," Henry shrugged, with an exaggerated Scottish accent.

Over the next several weeks, Colin and Henry met occasionally, sometimes over a hurriedly-grabbed lunch or a bit of afternoon tea, but mostly at the pub for a warm ale and the company of the Brits and Yanks.

The atmosphere had grown more charged on both bases. Thousands of Yanks were pouring into the country. Soldiers. Marines. An invasion was pending. No one was supposed to know, yet everyone did. How could you not help but know, Henry thought, even if you didn't already because of your job? Everyone had a friend, who had a friend, who said there were all these secret maneuvers in the west of Scotland...

All very hush-hush. All very expected.

With the coming of late winter and better weather, the bombing campaign heated up. The USAAF and the RAF were throwing everything they had at the Germans. Softening them up. And as a consequence, the casualty rate mounted exponentially, and the sense of *live today or not at all* pervaded every free moment.

Henry and Colin gradually grew more comfortable with each other, talking about everything under the sun except for the one topic—the one person—who was most on their minds.

Henry missed Gretchen in the way one would miss a limb. No longer capable of certain mental postures. Though he had gone through other times of separation, either physically or emotionally, he had always been able to eventually bridge the gap, even if it was not the intimate connection he craved. He had settled for whatever he could get. He hadn't figured out how to settle for nothing.

Henry knew there was only one way to get Gretchen back in his life. He would have found a way to make Colin and Gretchen see they were miserable without each other, and that *he* was miserable because *they* were. He'd come to the anguished conclusion that he'd rather have Gretchen as a part of his life, loving someone else, than completely gone from it.

And it couldn't be done subtly or softly, only by laying out the harsh facts. It was wartime. Anything could happen to any of them. Especially Colin, getting ready to head out for a refresher course in navigation so he could go back into the skies on a Lancaster bomber. He would be away for nearly six weeks and then assigned who knows where.

"I can't be a pilot, Henry," Colin explained. "They won't let me. But I finally convinced them, with some help from our well-connected friend Fiona, that I could handle the job of navigator. And as a trained pilot, I could be a backup if…"

Henry was well aware of the "ifs." He had been heartsick at Colin's news, even knowing that for Colin this was necessary. And even more necessary was seeing Colin and Gretchen together before Colin left, having some joy in what few spare moments could be had.

After a night of watching Colin get plastered, Henry laid it out for him. "Colin, here's the thing. You love Gretchen."

"Henry," Colin protested, his eyes hazed from drink, "we're not going to talk about this, ye ken? It's over."

"No, it isn't. It hasn't even begun, and it has to. Because Gretchen loves you. And we both know how I feel about her. I've always wanted only the best for her. I always thought that that was me..."

"Aye, 'tis. But, please, I can't..."

"Shut up. And listen. I know that the only thing that will make Gretchen happy is you. And I'm tired of us all moping about. Though I don't see her, I hear about her. She's miserable."

"Henry, for the love of God, can we please..."

"I said shut up, Colin. You know there's a push-on. It's clear the target is France or Belgium. It's only a matter of when. And you're going back to flying ops."

"Not flying." There was bitterness in Colin's voice.

"You'll be in the air in a bomber visiting Germany. That's flying enough. And putting yourself back on the block. You could get the chop..."

"Thanks for the encouragement."

"I'm just telling the truth. Because I don't want any of us to leave this world regretting that we passed up a chance for happiness. If Gretchen isn't happy, I never will be." He paused for effect. "But I want to be the best man at the wedding."

Colin involuntarily spit a large mouthful of ale all over the unfortunate Yank who happened to be walking by.

The Yank pulled Colin to his feet. "What the hell, you bloody British piece of shit!"

Colin was coughing so hard he could hardly breathe.

"Ah, leave him alone, Michaels," Henry yelled at the flyer over the din of the pub. "He's about to get married."

"Get married?!" the Yank replied. "God damn it to hell. To whom?"

"That Yankee nurse who works at the RAF hospital," Henry shouted, sending Colin into another coughing fit.

"Well, bloody hell, let's celebrate." Climbing on top of the table, Michaels bellowed, "Hey everybody, listen up. This here damn piece of British riff-raff is getting married to one of our Yank gals. The one who works at the RAF hospital."

Then he looked down at Henry and the intended groom and asked, "When?"

"Pretty soon," Henry pushed Colin back on his chair before he collapsed.

A huge hurrah swelled up from the crowd, and Brits and Yanks alike pounded Colin on the back in congratulations. Someone handed a dram of whiskey to him and Henry. Colin stood up shakily, stunned disbelief on his face, looking his friend in the eye.

Henry smiled wryly, then pronounced at the top of his lungs, "Here's to the groom, my best friend, and damn fine Scottish pilot, Domnhall Cailean MacAmhlaigh!"

With a clink of his glass against Colin's, Henry added quietly to his friend, "Your fate is sealed," and in one swallow poured the burning liquor down his throat.

When Louise, Abagail, and Edith, three nurses Gretchen worked closely with, began making odd comments to her during the morning shift, Gretchen thought they had all gone daft.

"Well, you sly one, you. Congratulations!" Louise jibbed.

"Yeah, and we thought all this time that it was that Yank," Edith chimed in.

"No, instead you have to go and steal one of ours," Abagail added.

Gretchen frowned at them and went about her work. The next time she encountered the group, they started up again.

"Go on, then, tell us," Louise said. "Secret's out. The guy Edith is walking out with said they were all celebrating it down at the pub."

Edith explained. "The whole lot of them apparently got rip-roaring drunk, including, I'm sorry to say, your intended and that Yankee friend of yours."

Gretchen was growing angry. "What in the name of Sam Hill are you talking about?"

The other nurses frowned at each other. "Who's Sam Hill?" Edith asked.

"Go on, Gretchen," Abagail forged on. "You can't keep anything a secret here that hasn't been signed off on the Official Secrets Act. Did they make you sign it? You being a Yank?"

Gretchen tried again. "Really, girls, I haven't a clue. What, where, and who was celebrating and what's that got to do with me?"

"Are you kidding?" Louise looked stunned. "You're engaged, and you don't even know it?"

Gretchen clutched the clipboard to her chest so hard it hurt.

"Engaged?" She could barely get the word out.

"Omigod, it's a secret even to her? Isn't that romantic?" Edith squealed.

"Romantic?" Louise snorted. "I say it's bloody cheek of that Scottish flyboy."

"Edith's beau said it was your Yankee mechanic turned officer who made the big announcement," Abagail explained. "Then he bought a round of drinks for the whole pub."

"Henry announced it? That I was getting married?"

"Well," Abagail said, "Edith told us he announced that Captain Mc..."

"MacAuley. Colin."

"Yeah, that one. That he was getting married to the Yank nurse who worked at the RAF hospital. Everyone knows that's you, Gretchen. You're the only Yank nurse here."

One of them got her a chair when she looked like she would collapse.

"I'm not even speaking to either of them," she said, dazed.

"Well, no wonder, if they make the announcement before you're even asked." Louise mused.

"I still think it's romantic," Abagail piped up, sighing. "Who wouldn't want the whole world to be drinking to your impending marriage?"

"'Twasn't the whole world, you ninny, it was a bunch of drunken Brit and Yank flyboys."

"What's going on here?" The ward Matron's voice brought them all to stiff attention, except for Gretchen, who simply stared ahead, trying to fathom this news. Henry and Colin celebrating Colin's engagement... to her! Apparently, they had mended their friendship. Maybe just a little too well!

"I'm sorry, Matron," Abagail babbled. "We were just congratulating Nurse Dunst on her recent engagement."

"It appears Nurse Dunst needs consoling, not congratulating," the older woman countered stiffly. "Back to work, and keep your personal business to yourself while on duty."

The other three nurses scurried off to their rounds as Gretchen slowly rose to her feet.

"That order goes to you as well, Nurse Dunst," she said, but gentler.

Gretchen realized she must've looked ill, for the Matron said, "Perhaps you need to take an early lunch?"

"No, no, Matron," Gretchen said, working to bring her scattered thoughts to the job she was supposed to be doing. "I'm sorry."

As Gretchen walked off, she muttered under her breath, "I'll deal with them later."

Later came much sooner than she was prepared for. That afternoon, at the end of her shift, she walked out the staff entry door, and there stood Colin, looking fit and trim, though a bit bleary-eyed. It was the sight of his cane that made her heart ache, though.

She hardly knew what to say or where to begin, so decided to say or do nothing.

"Ah, hello Gretchen." His voice was tentative. "I was wondering if you'd like to get a spot of tea."

Gretchen shrugged. She wasn't going to make this easy. "Is that to make up for all the whiskey you were drinking last night?" She smiled inwardly to see him cringe.

"Well, aye, tea would be a better choice right now. My haid does smart a wee bit."

"Fine." She turned towards a nearby tea shop, bound to be overcrowded at this time of day, but one that would require the least amount of walking. She noticed his heavy reliance on his cane, something she did not remember from New Year's Eve.

He apparently saw her glance at his cane and said sheepishly, "I sort of... tripped on my way home and, ah... banged up my bad leg a bit. I'm usually pretty good without... with walking and only need it at the end of the day if it's been a long one."

"I hear yesterday was. A long one, that is." She was beginning to enjoy this.

On entering the café, the hostess saw the decorated pilot with the cane and seated them quickly, ahead of others already waiting. Gretchen said nothing while they got settled and ordered tea and scones.

"Would you like something more substantial?" asked the waitress. "Cheese toast?"

Gretchen shook her head. "A scone is fine. With some jam," she added. The waitress nodded and left.

Colin sat stiffly in his chair. If he thought she was going to talk first, he had something coming, she mused.

With a sigh, he folded his hands on the table and leaned forward slightly.

"Gretchen, I honestly don't know where to begin. It appears you've heard a bit of what went on at the pub last night."

"A bit?" she said with a harrumph in her throat. "It's all I heard at work today. Everyone congratulated me, and I hadn't the foggiest idea what they were talking about. Some drunken flyboy and his Yank friend telling everyone there was an upcoming wedding."

"Ah, I guess that was a bit awkward."

Gretchen felt as if she were watching this scene in a movie. What was supposed to happen next? Oh, yes. The girl was supposed to say, "Oh, darling, the only thing that matters is that I know now you truly love me." But this wasn't a movie; this was her life, even if it was, in a most stunning and unexpected way, offering her just what she had longed for these past years.

Colin.

Yet she couldn't shake those memories of the last days at Achiltibuie, more than a year ago now, and all the pain and torment she had gone through since then. Waiting for their order gave her time to compose her thoughts, which she did while she moved her spoon in endless circles in her cup, half mesmerized by the swirls it created.

"Gretchen," Colin's gravelly voice interrupted her thoughts. "First of all, I need to tell you that I'm sorry for those months in Achiltibuie, the way I acted, the way I was. There's no excuse for what a bloody ass I was."

Though his voice was low, his crude language got him a frown from the elderly couple at the table next to them.

Gretchen sighed and met the eyes of the man she had ached, mourned, and despaired for. "Colin, you did have an excuse. You were horribly injured, and we—your parents, sisters and I—couldn't be there in that dark place with you. We just wanted you to be well. We couldn't understand what you had experienced."

She paused as her mind filled with unwanted images of bandaged stumps, disfigured faces, and nightmarish screams. Shuddering slightly, she added, "But I can tell you, now I understand it so much more."

When Colin started to speak again, Gretchen held up her hand.

"I can't tell you what joy it gives me to see you recover. Yes, I know you have to use a cane from time to time, but from the letters Mairi wrote after I left, I really thought there was no..." Here, for the first time, emotion choked her voice.

She swallowed and continued shakily. "...no hope for you. And that's why I wrote those awful things to you after my brother was... lost...in the Pacific. I'm sorry Colin. I'm sorry for your family losing your brother. I'm sorry for my family losing mine."

She hadn't wanted to, but she was crying now. Tears moistened her face, quiet, silent tears. Colin reached across the table with a napkin, and gently wiped the dampness from her cheeks, breaking her heart with his look of sympathy.

There were so many words that lay unspoken between them, Gretchen thought. So many things that could be said. Recriminations. Regrets. And the knowledge that their happiness meant Henry would never be truly happy. And yet, once again, had he not given his blessing?

"Colin," she said as she took the napkin from his hand and crumpled it in hers. "I heard... that... that Henry was the one who made the announcement."

Colin broke into a coughing fit, which he eased with a swallow of tea.

"Had you discussed this ahead of time?" She was stern again.

"Discussed... hell, no. He took me completely by surprise. I mean, we were just trying to... do... you know... do what you had asked us to do."

"Mend your bridges."

"Something like that."

"Well, then, Colin, I have just one question."

Colin's face was wary now, watchful.

"When's the wedding?"

For a long moment, Colin did not react. He looked at her across the table, his brow wrinkled in what she thought was a very attractive frown. She finally let herself smile, let all of the happiness inside her show.

"Oh, God, Gretchen! Is that a yes?" He stood and pulled her to his feet, crushing her to his chest.

"She said yes!" he yelled to the startled onlookers, who erupted in a thunder of applause.

"Well, kiss her!" the elderly lady at the next table demanded loudly. "There's not a moment to waste while there's a war on."

"Oh, aye," Colin replied, then did a very good job of following directions.

TWENTY-NINE

MARCH 1944

THE NEWS THAT COLIN was leaving in two days for six weeks of training in Scotland nearly dashed Gretchen's happiness. But she chose to think only of the delirious truth that at last they were a couple.

The first thing Colin said they must do was see Henry.

"I mean, honestly, if not for Henry forcing me, I wouldn't have come near you. You did command me to stay away. And your wish is my command." He promptly kissed her on the spot, ignoring the fact they were walking slowly down the sidewalk.

The taste of tea and cigarettes on his kiss sent her head swimming, her heart drumming. It nearly overshadowed her concern at his words. "Forced you?"

"What I mean is I thought *he* should talk to you first, but he was tired of running interference, and I needed to say my own piece."

"What piece is that, Colin?" Gretchen teased as they walked on toward the pub.

Colin stopped, pulled her into an alley they were passing, and faced her. He tossed his cane down and put his hands firmly on her arms. "This piece, Gretchen. That I love you. That I've wasted an entire year feeling sorry for myself when I could have spent that year showing you how much I love you. And I intend to do that now, in whatever way I can, in whatever hours and days I can squeeze out of this war."

And tucked away behind a stack of boxes for the next few minutes Gretchen savored the sweetness of being shown, as Colin thoroughly kissed her, pressing the hard warmth of his body against her.

The sound of someone clearing his throat startled Gretchen. Looking around, she saw an older man in a cook's hat and apron, smoking a cigarette, leaning casually against the back door of a restaurant.

"Don't mean to interrupt," the gray-haired man chuckled, "but I need to get into those boxes if I'm to start on tonight's dinner. Are you needing something to eat?"

When Colin simply stared at the man, pulling himself away from Gretchen, the cook said with a shrug, "Guess not." He walked around them, pulled a box off the stack, and then said respectfully, "Would you mind doing your loving on the other side of the door?"

Gretchen felt herself blush, but Colin merely laughed. "No problem, mate," he said and was about to do as the cook suggested, but Gretchen protested. "Colin, we have to go."

"We have some time. I told Henry I'd meet him about seven."

"Well, then," the cook said, "you've time for dinner. Got some fresh tinned ham here."

Gretchen couldn't contemplate eating, wondering how to face Henry without flaunting their happiness. "No, thank you. But I could use a drink."

Colin sighed but nodded and picked up his cane. They walked to the pub, arm in arm. His nearness made her breathless as if she had risen rapidly from the crushing ocean depths into a sparkling light-blue sky. She ignored the fact that he would be leaving in less than two days.

"You are coming back, after your training? I mean, coming back to this aerodrome?" She needed to get her feet on the ground.

"Aye," he said, looking at her with such open adoration she nearly stumbled.

"Don't look at me that way!" she said, half joking.

"What way?" He was clearly clueless.

"Like a puppy."

"A puppy?"

"Oh, a really cute puppy who wants all of my attention."

"But I do."

"Colin, I can barely take this in. I... it's... so sudden."

He stopped her in the middle of the sidewalk, forcing others behind them to walk around. "Gretchen, I don't expect you to fall at my feet. Hell, with my leg, I'm the one most likely to do the falling. I just can't hide the way I feel."

"But..."

"And we have a day, not even that. Only this evening. Tomorrow, I've got duty I can't get out of, and I leave at first light on Wednesday. I'd like to spend every minute of those few hours kissing you madly, but I'll refrain."

Gretchen felt a slow, burning warmth seep through her body at that idea. But it was quickly doused when Colin added, "I don't want to flaunt my happiness in front of Henry."

Gretchen said softly, "Yes, but we will have some time... to... to be alone?"

"As you Yanks would say, you can bet your bottom dollar." But all bets were off when Colin was suddenly summoned to headquarters.

So it was she and Henry who spent the evening in the corner of the rowdy pub, talking as they had done so often over the years. But not about the war, not about their life in England and Scotland, but of home. Pennsylvania. It was the best kind of reminiscence, laced with laughter, steeped in family stories. And Henry was his usual attentive, cheerful self as if it were years ago.

She wished Colin had been there to hear all this about herself and Henry. Things neither of them had probably ever told him. By midnight, it was clear that Colin wasn't coming back, so Henry escorted Gretchen to her quarters and bid her a casual goodbye, just as in the past.

"Goodnight, Gretchen," he said in a cheerful voice that was laced with checked emotion.

"Henry, I don't know how I can thank you. I never ever meant to..."

"It's all going to be alright, Gretchen. Colin will be fine. You'll be fine. We'll all be fine. I'm just so damn happy we're all sorted out. All but Fiona."

She kissed him on the cheek. "Someday, Henry, I will do something wonderful for you."

She fell asleep wondering if she had imagined it all in some fevered daydream.

In the morning, as she readied for work before dawn, she answered a knock on the door of the Quonset hut to see a sober-faced teenager in a postal uniform holding a telegram.

"I'm looking for Gretchen Dunst."

Gretchen began to tremble. A nurse behind her said, "I'll take it," and put out her hand for the sealed envelope.

"It came late last night, after delivery hours," the boy said, his eyes begging forgiveness, for always delivering the worst of news.

Someone led her to a seat, and another opened the envelope. All of them gathered around, an arm around her shoulder, a hand on her. *Gretchen. It's Father. A heart attack. In the barn. Saturday. Funeral was yesterday. Naomi.*

Once again, it was Henry who consoled her. For Colin had been sent that morning, a day early, to western Scotland.

Fiona came to see Gretchen a week later. "I couldn't just send a sympathy card."

Gretchen thought her friend looked worn and thin.

"Your father was such a genuinely honest and kind man," Fiona continued.

They were sitting in the same tearoom where Gretchen had said yes to Colin. "Besides, I thought if Henry and Colin could make up the tear in their friendship, we could do the same."

Astonished, Gretchen stared across the table with its white starched linens and polished silver. "There's a rent in our friendship? I know there's been a tear in the friendship between you and Henry. He said you stopped writing."

"Gretchen..."

"Look, Fiona, I know that you think I've been terribly selfish, the way I treated Henry..."

"Ah, yes, Henry. So, is he finally out of the picture?"

"Fiona, you know he was never *in* the picture."

"That's not what *he* thought, no matter how much I..."

Gretchen frowned at the odd look on Fiona's face. "No matter how much you what?"

Fiona shrugged. "Tried to convince him otherwise." She stirred her tea, looking down.

Gretchen grunted. "Well, he's convinced now. Have you seen him? Did he tell you that he's the one who persuaded Colin to tell me how he felt?"

"Well, actually, I haven't seen him, so he couldn't have told me, but I'm not surprised. Colin never would have crossed that line without Henry's blessing."

"And are you giving me your blessing?" Gretchen said, longing for the former closeness of their foursome.

"Oh, yes. More than that. I'm here to give you a weekend with Colin."

"Fiona, what are you talking about? Colin's already shipped out to his navigator's training."

"I know that. It so happens my cousin owns a hotel on Skye near Colin's duty station. Though it's primarily used by RAF officers on temporary duty, they do take guests by special arrangement."

Gretchen frowned. "I thought all the western isles were restricted territory."

"They are. Even residents need passes to travel about the islands. But there's always an exception to every rule." She chuckled.

"Fiona, you're sounding more American than British."

"Well, we Brits have learned a bit from you Yanks. And this Scottish lassie wants to see her best friend have some happiness before..." She stopped, her face troubled.

"Before? Before the big push, you mean. We all know it's coming..."

"Don't you want to spend time with Colin?" Fiona sounded genuinely astonished.

"Don't be daft, Fiona, of course I do."

A flash of anger crossed Fiona's face. "Gretchen, are you living in a fairy tale? This is war, and it's going to get horribly worse once we start fighting the Krauts on their own territory..." She looked at Gretchen sternly. "I can get you four days. That's all. You leave Friday. Colin has four days' break before his course starts. I can book you into the hotel."

"Fiona, are you some sort of sorceress who makes things happen with a wave of her magic wand? Does Colin know any of this?" Gretchen was trying to keep her mind from envisioning the possibility of being alone with Colin.

Fiona interrupted her thoughts. "He knows I can arrange a visit."

There seemed to be something more to Fiona's plan. "So you're planning to see Henry?

Fiona nodded. "We have plans for dinner tonight."

"What do you think he'll say?"

"Bloody feckin' hell, Gretchen," Fiona hissed across the table under her breath. "Why should it matter what Henry says? Why can't you just leave him alone?" Her face flushed, Fiona turned quickly to look out the window as if something had suddenly caught her attention.

The truth left Gretchen speechless. Of course! Fiona was in love with Henry. Had been, for a very long time. But Henry had never been available to Fiona as long as he thought Gretchen might come around. Such an entangled mess.

"Fiona," she said softly, "have you ever told Henry how you feel?"

Fiona looked back at Gretchen with an irritated noise. "I've never come right out and said it, but I'm pretty sure he knows."

"And?"

"And what, you lunkhead? You know Henry's loyalties."

"But Colin and I are engaged... well, I guess we are."

"You guess? You don't know?"

"I mean, he... I... we agreed. But I don't have a ring. It's not official."

"Gretchen, you drive me to the brink! So you won't go see the man you love because you're not officially engaged? Have you completely lost your mind? You've no time to be waiting for some romantic scene in a gothic church with a long white dress and a handful of posies."

"Well," Gretchen said, beginning to tremble at the idea of having Colin to herself for a whole weekend, "I've always wanted to see Skye." She choked back tears as she clasped her friend's hands. "Once you turn your sights on Henry, he won't be able to resist you."

Fiona smiled wanly. "Well, the lad's done a good job of it 'til now."

———⋈———

The rising sun streaming through the window woke her. The room was cold. The peat on the grate had burned out in the night, though Gretchen's skin still felt the heat of Colin's touch like liquid fire, leaving trails of desire across her body. He lay so still next to her that for a moment panic gripped her throat. Then his breath came, quiet and easy. She had never seen him so at ease or so completely vulnerable. So open and accessible. To her. Her alone.

The sheer power of that intimacy filled her with an odd grief. They had shared three days of exquisite delight, learning the pleasure of both tenderness and heated passion. Examining how to please each other, how to tease, and yes, torment, with tongue and touch and joined flesh. They had barely left the room. Years of pent-up desire had melted whatever hesitation she had.

What little of Skye she had seen was the ten-mile trip from the aerodrome to the lodging, located in the town of Sligachan, the Black Cuillins glimpsed out the window of her hotel room.

And now she was leaving. Colin would take her to the aerodrome for a late morning flight back to southern England, and he would begin his navigator course.

On that first night, he had knelt painfully before her on the floor and taken her hands in his. "Gretchen Elizabeth Dunst, I love you. I love you so much I think I could die of it sometimes."

"Don't say that..."

"Gretchen, will you marry me? I never actually asked you. Everyone else decided for us, but thank goodness they did. I don't have a ring yet. The first I can get leave, I'll buy you a sparkling one and make it official. I promise."

She had stood up and began unbuttoning her blouse with trembling hands.

His eyes were the soft brown of a Scottish hillside at sunrise. "Gretchen, what are you doing?"

"Yes, Colin. Of course, I will marry you. Whenever you say. But I will not let you leave me without loving you completely."

He'd tried to protest. But she stopped his words with her lips and his objections with her touch and his reluctance with her body. She followed her instincts, and he guided her on the way, for she had never known a man physically and had waited patiently for the one who she would love forever, no matter how long they would wait to be together.

THIRTY

PART 3: PAST AND PRESENT

MAY 1997

AFTER HER TRIP TO Skye with Robbie, Beth completely immersed herself in her dreams, her journal, and her research, to the point she could fall in and out of Colin's presence by merely closing her eyes. Sometimes it didn't even require that effort.

Some days she couldn't tell what decade she was inhabiting.

She began missing lectures and tutorials and was barely present at the ones she did attend, her mind adrift in a constantly shifting terrain of time.

"What happened to that scholar I met?" Iain teased, as he noticed her increasing lack of focus and introspective moods.

Their relationship had morphed into a comfortable friendship. He had become like a big brother, in spite of being younger. He came by her room, walking her to the cafeteria or taking her to the pub with his friends.

He finally asked, tentatively, "Is this about that professor guy?"

Beth said flatly, "Don't go there, Iain, okay? I don't want to talk about him."

Iain nodded. "So it's like that, is it? He dumped you? I can go knock his lights out. Beat him with my hockey stick."

Touched by Iain's quirky version of chivalry, Beth shook her head slowly. "It's okay, Iain."

Yet only by immersing herself in Colin's story could she forget those days and nights with Robbie and her deliciously sensuous introduction to intimacy. Or the stunning, heart-wrenching revelation that Robbie was a distraction and an impediment in her efforts to learn why a spectral Scottish bomber pilot needed something from her.

But yesterday, when she encountered Robbie in the Student Center, she had fought her intense desire to wrap her arms around him and beg him for help in discerning what was real and what was fevered imagination.

Robbie's anger and dejection nearly crushed her. That his behavior might arise from loving her was unfathomable and almost terrifying. How could she could engender such emotion in a man? But there was no ability to wonder.

For Colin was the past and the present. And the immediate future.

Seeing Robbie did spur her to action, casting off the lethargy weighing her down for weeks. In her dorm room, she stuffed her backpack with a pair of jeans, two shirts, socks, underthings, pjs, journal, and research notes, plus her wallet, passport, and camera. And credit card.

She left Anja a brief note and taped one for Iain on his dorm door. She had this unexpected trip out of town, didn't know when she would be back, and wished them well if the semester ended before she returned. She told them not to worry. Just something she had to take care of.

Then she grabbed her bomber jacket, took a taxi to the train station, and bought a ticket for London. She had to find out what Colin meant in those brief seconds on Skye when he stepped out of the past and into her present. Living. Breathing. Speaking.

Telling her she needed to know the truth. Implying he needed her to discover it.

But how do you help a ghost? she thought as she sat on a bench in the huge Victorian train station then desperately contradicted herself. *But he could still be alive. He must still be alive.* After all she'd been through, she had to find him, talk to him in person. He'd be about her grandfather's age by now, but at least he'd survived the war. Right?

Maybe that was what he wanted. Maybe just to return his bomber jacket. Maybe it was just as simple as that.

Endless questions and doubts tormented her on the six-hour journey, so different from her trip five months ago when she met Robbie. She arrived in London near midnight. Too tired to worry about expense, she took a hotel room near the train station and spent the night tossing and turning.

In the morning, she took a hot shower, changed clothes, and had a cup of tea and a scone in the hotel's restaurant. At the nearby tourist information booth, she asked how to get to the British War Museum.

"Oh, you mean the Imperial War Museum. There are three locations here in London," the gray-haired attendant said pleasantly. "Do you want the Churchill War Rooms, the HMS Belfast, or the main museum on Lambeth Road?"

"Where would I do research about... pilots?"

He eyed her coat. "RAF World War II by the looks of things, miss. You're American. Looking up a relative? There are some nice displays about the Yanks there. Or was your grandma one of ours that your Yank grandpa stole away? My aunt was a war bride. Visited her many times. The whole way to California it was. Are you from California?"

"No, no, Pennsylvania." Beth was having a hard time concentrating. "Just some research for... a college project."

"Well, there's the restored RAF airfield at Duxford out in Cambridgeshire, but if you're doing research, you might want to start first at the main building on Lambeth Road. Take the tube to Waterloo, and it's about a fifteen-minute walk from there."

She hoped she didn't encounter Robbie's friend who had sent the original list of pilots. She was directed to the research department where, as coherently as she could, Beth explained what she knew of Colin's story to a friendly young woman, who explained she was an intern.

"Are you a college student?"

"Yes," Beth replied curtly, growing frantic at being so close to concrete information about Colin. "At the University of Edinburgh. For a semester."

"Oh, I love Edinburgh. I spent a whole year there. Did you..."

"I'm sorry. I don't mean to be rude, but I've come a long way today, and I'm rather short on time. Can I research his war records?"

"Oh," the intern replied, frowning. "Are you a relative? Information about a specific person's record is usually restricted to a relative."

Beth froze. All this way, and she would be denied the truth? Then she remembered how she convinced her college counselor to let her switch her semester abroad destination.

She had lied.

"Yes. I am. I mean, he is. A... great uncle. Ah, married my, ah, grandfather's sister." She could feel sweat behind her neck as she kept inventing. What if she needed proof? A birth certificate or something. "I know he spent some time stationed at Drem. Near Edinburgh."

The young woman paused. "Well, I..."

"I'm doing it for my granddad, my PopPop. They met in the war. My PopPop is a veteran, you see. Served here in England. I promised him when I left home in January... to... find out what I could of the... family... ah... history."

She wasn't making any sense. If Colin had married the made-up sister of her grandfather, and they'd met in the war, of course, the family would know all about him.

But her intensity must have overridden her jumbled story, for the research assistant nodded. "Well, everyone in the department is out today at a conference, and this being the middle of the week, we're slow. So, right. It should be okay. Follow me."

She was led to a computer terminal in a windowless room and asked for Colin's full name. Beth gave both Gaelic and English versions. The intern called up some records, reviewed what was on the screen, and said, "You're in luck. He's the only one with that first, middle, and last name. Here you go. I'll be at the desk if you need me."

Beth sat trembling, barely able to manipulate the mouse and call up his record of service. Breathing harshly, she read the details. Every place he'd been stationed. A Distinguished Flying Cross. A medical discharge. A reinstatement. Work as an adjunct. Training as a navigator. And his final duty station. It was all there in computer records. Newspaper articles. Sterile. Straightforward. Stark.

They filled in all the gaps. They told the story of his life.

And his death. *July 4, 1944.*

She gagged, bent over, head in her hands, the date seared into her brain and onto her heart like a hot iron. The world spun in a slow, sickening motion, as if gravity had ceased, and she was beginning to float away.

Before she forced herself to read on and wrap her brain around the details of his horrid, ironic death, she imagined it this way:

His Lancaster Bomber, flying daylight missions in support of the massive Allied landing on the beaches of Normandy that began June 6, had been badly shot up. The plane, riddled with bullets and filled with bloodied airmen, made a sloppy, nearly disastrous landing under the guidance of a desperate pilot focused on getting his crew home safely. And himself back to that American girl. He'd made it home. Brought the crew back. Some of them badly injured, but home. Colin, though, died shortly afterward in a nearby hospital.

But reality begged to differ.

Not a bombing mission. He was driving near his aerodrome. The car had been smashed into by a drunken Yank.

One of her own had killed him.

She saw him on a hospital gurney, a sheet covering over his head. Waves of nausea surged through her stomach.

Of course, he was dead. Would she have been haunted by someone who was alive? Would she have seen him at all those places on her grandfather's list? Why was Colin always there? What did her grandfather have to do with her bomber pilot?

Now what was she do? What did he want of her, across the years? Fifty-three years. Whatever it was he wanted, the answer wasn't here on the digital display in front of her.

In sudden frantic motion, she grabbed her backpack and rushed from the staid, academic atmosphere of the research room, past the startled intern who called after her, "Miss? Miss! Wait, wait, I'm sorry, I didn't realize it might be a shock. Come back..."

The final facts on the computer screen were embedded into her retinas. She blinked constantly trying to wipe them away.

Buried in his hometown. Achiltibuie. Scotland.

July 1944

To Henry, it would always be the most gut-wrenching irony of the war that Colin survived his return to the air, lived through D-Day and the month following, only to be killed by a drunken Yankee driving on the wrong side of the road on the American 4th of July holiday.

Leaving Henry to break the news to Gretchen. And tell her the emergency room nurse found an engagement ring in Colin's pocket. The nurse who told the MPs to give Henry the task of ripping Gretchen's soul apart.

How much easier if Colin had been shot down on a mission. That ending would have made more sense, if any death made sense.

This goddamn war.

He had given his blessing on their union. Outwardly. In words. Inside, it crushed him, tore at his very being that the woman he loved preferred his best friend.

Now, his best friend and Gretchen's Scottish flyboy was dead.

At first, Henry refused to believe it. The MPs almost had to drag him to the morgue to identify Colin's bashed-up body. And see the truth with his eyes. Then he went to Colin's room, where he carefully organized and packed his trunk because he wasn't going to let anyone else touch Colin's things. It wasn't his duty or right to do so. But nobody stopped him.

Against all regulations, he took a few of Colin's things. He had to have something. His bomber jacket because it was such a part of him.. The picture of Gretchen he kept by his bed, the one of her wearing the jacket on Skye. The notes Gretchen had written. He had saved every one of them, even the scathing ones.

And the letter. The letter every airman, every serviceman wrote and placed with his things. To whom it may concern. Or to his sweetheart. Or mother. In this case, it was to Henry. And it was recent, dated June 5, 1944. Written in Colin's neat, educated hand.

Dear Henry,

If you're reading this letter, it's because I didn't make it back one night. It could happen. It certainly almost has many times. Some luck or fate or mercy of God has been with me.

Henry, you've been the most decent man I've ever had the fortune to know. And I have no right to your friendship because I've taken the one thing you care about more than anything in the world—Gretchen. I haven't been fooled by your declaration that "She loves you. She's yours." I've never forgotten the incredible grace and generosity of heart you showed when you brought us together because Gretchen's happiness matters to you more than your own.

Henry, if you're reading this letter, then you know what I need you to do. Not that I have to ask you, for you'd do it anyway. Take care of her, the woman we both love. I'm terribly afraid of what this will do to her. She hasn't been well lately, and I'm worried about her. In time, she will turn to you. She always does. And it will be okay, Henry. Really. I give you my blessing.

I don't know if she will go home. She said she never would. She may decide to live with my family. They would love that. It's her family now too. And you're one of them as well.

I had a dream that night back in April 1942, the night I was shot up, where she made me promise to bury her next to me. In the family graveyard in Achiltibuie. It was an odd dream, but I've never forgotten it. If she does go back to the States with you, remember my promise to her. Remember that when the time comes, she wants to lie beside me for all eternity in a small Scottish graveyard in the Highlands.

God bless you, Henry. I know you'll take care of her.

Your friend,

Domnhall Cailean MacAmhlaigh.

May 1997

From the moment Beth realized Colin had died, he vanished from her dreams, disappeared from her presence. Thrown out of the 1940s like some unwanted child into a cold night, she went in search of him.

Somehow she managed to catch a train from London to West Wickham, near Cambridge, Colin's last duty station. It was nearly dark when she found the only thing remaining of the airbase—a memorial plaque dedicated "to all who served on the units of this station, 1943-1945."

She stood in front of the bronze panel until she could stand no more.

In a fog of grief, she checked into a neighborhood guest house. The next day she located what had been the hospital he'd been taken to after the accident. Where he'd breathed his last. For an entire day she kept vigil on a nearby bench. Waiting fruitlessly for him to appear.

The following day she headed to the far northern highlands. London to Edinburgh, Edinburgh to Inverness, Inverness to Ullapool, Ullapool to Achiltibuie.

The journey was a whirl of disorientation: trains and busses, missed connections, hours in stations and terminals, one overnight on a hard bench. She dozed occasionally but mostly stared out the window of whatever conveyance she was on, seeing nothing of the brilliant May weather or the gorgeous countryside.

She saw only that date on the computer screen and a wrecked jeep, wheels spinning in the air, a man tossed into the road, broken and bloodied.

She had come to understand his thoughts, to feel his emotions, certain she would meet him in person. Now she was depleted, directionless. Why had he left her with nights devoid of dreams and days denied of his presence? And what of this American girl he loved? Was she the reason Colin had haunted Beth? Maybe the girl never knew what happened to Colin.

It must be that she had to visit his grave. That she'd learn the answer there.

Beth arrived in Achiltibuie late on a Friday afternoon by bus, exhausted, bedraggled, days in the same clothes. Thankfully, there were two B&Bs in the village.

"Try tha Sea View, up yonder on the heel," the post office clerk said in a thick Highland brogue.

"Aye, I've got a room," the woman at the door said, unsurprisingly hesitantly. Anyone would be put off by her appearance. She hadn't showered in days. Plus, the bomber jacket often drew curious or resentful stares.

But the woman, a Mrs. McIntyre, made no comment on her attire, and simply said, " 'Tis early in the season, so ye're in luck. Come the end of next month, ye'd not had such luck. We fill up in the summer holidays, especially for the Gathering and the piping school."

Mrs. McIntyre was a fortyish, slender woman in a stylish apron and flowered housedress, friendly and chatty as she escorted her into the wide entryway.

"Hae ye had your dinner then, miss? It's a long, windin' way ye've come, I would guess, and in the late of the day, no less. Come by bus, did you then? From Ullapool? I didn't hear a car. Car park is in the back, and guests generally arrive at the back entrance. American are ye? You can get a nice bit of supper at the pub down in the village. The hotel dining room doesn't put out dinner till the beginning of June, and we sarve only breakfast."

Beth's stomach gurgled at the mention of food, something else besides sleep she'd had very little of since she left the University. Still, she said, "I'm not very hungry. I'll just get some rest," as she filled out the registration card at a small polished table.

"Wael, let me show you to your room then. There's a kettle and makings for tea and some crisps and crackers thar if ye want a wee snack. Won't be a supper though. But first, do ye mind if we step into the parlor so ye can meet my mam? She likes to say hello to anyone that stays. My husband and I run the B & B, but this was her house growin' up."

Too tired to put words together for a reply, Beth reluctantly followed Mrs. McIntyre through a doorway. Seated by French doors leading onto a flagstone patio, was a petite, gray-haired woman quietly knitting in an overstuffed saffron yellow easy chair, feet resting on a matching ottoman, her lap full of brilliant cerulean blue and scarlet red yarns.

"Mam, this is our unexpected guest. Miss Beth. She's from the States. This is my mother, Mrs. Mairi Gordon."

An eerie sense of familiarity crept over Beth as she looked at the woman, who finished the two remaining stitches in her row then glanced up, staring at her through thick glasses that did not hide deep brown, penetrating eyes. Mrs. Gordon looked at her with a puzzled expression, taking in Beth's face and the bomber jacket.

Mrs. McIntyre broke the stillness by saying, "Mam, welcome our guest now," as if she were talking to a child who needed instruction then said as an aside to Beth, "You'll have to forgive my muther. She gets a bit befuddled at times."

"I am not befuddled, Clara Catriona! Don't ye treat me like some dotterin' ault fool. I've not yet reached my seventy-sixth year and am not ready to be carried out to the boneyard. I am trying to figure out why the wee lassie looks so familiar," Mrs. Gordon said in a scolding voice.

Beth, momentarily distracted by the fact that this woman and her own mother had the same middle name, responded hesitantly, "I can't imagine why."

Mrs. Gordon scrunched her face, closed her eyes as if concentrating and muttered something in Gaelic.

Perhaps the flight jacket triggered memories of the war.

Mrs. Gordon sighed then looked up again. "It'll come to me. Aye, 'twill. Why, it seems as if I met ye afore. I'll recall, mind ye, afore ye leave us." She smiled in a welcoming manner that lifted Beth's weary spirit.

"Wael, then," her daughter said, "Come this way, and I'll show you to your room."

Beth followed Mrs. McIntyre into the hallway and up the wide stairs, then right, down a spacious hall. It was a large house, and she wondered if the owners had once been landed gentry. The room toward the end of the hall was cozy, but knowing she wasn't far from Colin's grave nearly overwhelmed her. She sat on the bed with a small gasp.

"Miss, miss? Are ye ailing? You're probably famished. Let me make you that tea."

Beth protested, but Mrs. McIntyre pooh-poohed her and bustled about plugging in the electric teakettle and laying out a snack for her on a tiny table tucked into the corner of the room.

"I've nary a guest this weekend, so you'll get to be pampered and looked after when I'm not tending my mam. Don't have the summer help in yet. Don't expect we'll have another stray guest come wandering in. Achiltibuie is hard to get to. You have to want to come. Can't stumble on it by accident, like some of the places along the main highway."

She crossed the bright, airy room and cracked the window, letting in the chill sea air. "You can see the Isle of Skye from your window, miss."

"Please, call me Beth," she replied then said dreamily, "I've been to the Misty Isle."

"Oh, aye. Ye ken it then, Miss Beth?" the woman nodded.

"Yes, it was beautiful. We..." She stopped suddenly. "I will take that cup of tea..."

"Come sit here by the table, and I'll get it for ye."

"Oh, please, I can manage on my own."

"Aye, I'm sure ye can, being a modern young American lassie. You're all very independent, you young girls. Mind ye, my youngest daughter is in her last year at the University, so I know how you push yourselves."

"Actually, I'm a student this semester at Edinburgh." *Was,* she said to herself. Having skipped two of her three exams, she was pretty sure she had blown the entire semester. *A silly waste of money,* her grandmother would be saying right about now.

"Tis a lovely place, Edinburgh. A bit too bustly for me, I must say. My daughter's at school in Inverness. A local college."

Beth thought *local* was a bit of a misnomer. Achiltibuie was a good eighty miles to Inverness by way of Ullapool.

"So, are ye on vacation? The school term's over, aye?"

"A bit of research, really."

"Genealogy, is it? Well, we do get a lot of Americans trying to trace their roots here. A lot of Scots left these parts after the war in '45 and crossed the seas."

Beth knew she was referring to the Jacobite rebellion against the English that began in 1745 and not the 1945 from World War II.

"Schmidt. That's your surname? That's nay Scots. On your mother's side, mayhap?"

"Hmm," Beth said.

"You can check with the church registry. I can call Maggie, the church secretary, if ye want to take a peek. She's my cousin. Maybe Sunday after church? And then there's the cemetery. You might want to take a look in there."

Beth nodded, distracted by echoes of voices which might be coming from outside or maybe from inside her head. She just wanted to lie down on the inviting bed with its flowered, downy comforter and crisp linens.

"Who knows; we could be related," the hostess chuckled. "As Mam said, you do seem oddly familiar, even with your German name."

"Mrs. McIntyre, I don't mean to be rude..."

"Oh, dearie, I'm sae sorry. And call me Clara. I can see ye're fallin' down from weariness, and here I am yammering away. My husband tells me I just don't know when to stop. He says it's my Irish ancestors that gave me the gift of the gab. Well, then, I'm away. You sleep as late as you want, dearie. I'll just make you something whenever you come downstairs in the mornin'. Don't be worrying about being down at any time special. You're welcome to use the lounge downstairs if you get bored up here in your room. There's a television set there. We're a bit old-fashioned and don't put them in the rooms. Guests come here for an escape from the world. There's another blanket in the chest if you get cold. It can be a bit nippy at night in the spring."

Beth nodded, wishing her hostess away. As soon as Mrs. McIntyre shut the door, Beth slipped off her shoes and rose. She tossed her bomber jacket on a nearby chair and lay down on the bed. In an instant, she was asleep.

"Colin what a beautiful view!" the American girl exclaimed, waking him from dozing.

"*Yes,*" he mumbled. *Not that he could get up to see it, lying here on the bed, pain wracking his jaw and his back, his leg still swathed in bandages, his lungs burning.*

"*If I had a view like this, I never would have left home. All I ever saw from my bedroom window was tobacco, wheat, and corn.*"

He loved her warm, sultry laugh, as much as he tried to ignore it.

"*Uhmm,*" he grunted, *unwilling to be drawn in by her vibrancy.*

"*And a beach! There are no beaches in Pennsylvania except at Lake Erie. But just imagine! Every morning to look over at a beach and a bay and, oh, what's that in the distance?*"

He hadn't wanted her here at his home.

A male voice chimed in, "*The Summer Isles, they're called. In the distance is Skye.*"

"*Oh, marvelous! When you're all better, we'll take you to Skye, Colin, won't we, Henry?*"

Beth jerked awake, shocked out of her dream by the familiar name. Or maybe it was another waking vision. The woman said Pennsylvania. This American girl was from a Pennsylvania farm? Someone named Henry, another American by his accent, had also been in the room. Uncanny that it was her grandfather's name.

Beth had decided on her long, exhausting journey from London that Colin wanted her to find this American woman, who'd now be as old as her own grandmother. Tell her Colin had loved her. If any of Colin's family remained in his hometown, they might know about her.

"That's what you want, right Colin?" she whispered to the air.

Where had this conversation occurred? Probably at home, convalescing from the first time he had been shot down. When he had won the Distinguished Flying Cross for bringing the plane and the crew home, though not all of them were alive. It was all there in the record she had read. His home must be nearby.

Suddenly cold, she got up to shut the window, pausing to gaze at the distant Isle of Skye.

She thought of seeing Colin there, when he said so urgently, "*I want you to find out the truth. You need to find the truth.*"

Beth drew a deep, rattling breath and crawled back into the bed.

I did what you wanted. I found out the truth about how your life ended, and the truth is breaking my heart. Is that the truth you wanted me to find?

But what was it *she* wanted? What was her desire at this time in her life?

It didn't take long to name it. She wanted someone who desired *her*, longed for *her*, loved *her*. Someone in whom she could completely lose herself. With whom she could be completely vulnerable, open, giving.

Was that someone Robbie? Did sleeping with someone mean that you loved that person?

Beth laughed bitterly. This was 1997, almost a new century. Weren't such ideas long outmoded? Yet hadn't they been on the verge of something wonderful?

She had deeply wounded Robbie by the way she'd suddenly shut him out. And now wasn't the time to explore her feelings about him. Or his feelings toward her.

If his look of angry hurt was any indication, it already was too late to ask for a second chance. But she'd have been leaving in May anyway, returning to the States. What could have become of a relationship separated by an ocean?

Beth shook her head, trying to clear all the confusing thoughts and emotions. She was incredibly exhausted and horribly grimy, but the bed was too inviting to consider a shower.

Whispering, "Sorry, Mrs. McIntyre," she pulled off her socks and jeans and crawled into the bed between the fresh, crisp sheets which smelled of pine and salt.

July 1944

The morning after Henry had identified Colin's body and sorted through his locker, he went to the Quonset hut to catch Gretchen before her seven a.m. shift. She hadn't been expecting Colin the night before; he had told Henry he was going to surprise Gretchen. Henry didn't even think Gretchen was aware that Colin had finally been stood down, off ops permanently.

His news must have been written on his face, for she just stood in the doorway and stared at him, her eyes glazing over with grief. He took her hand, leading her to the bench where he had told her about her brother William nearly a year ago.

She was there for a very long time, motionless. Frozen.

"Oh, God," she finally said. "What will we do without him, Henry?" She began to rock slightly, keening softly under her breath, like a Celtic woman wailing for her lost loved one.

He didn't have the heart to tell her how it had happened. Not then. He would tell her later, but she insisted he take her to him now.

"I have to see him, Henry. What am I going to do otherwise? I will go mad."

Her strength astonished him. He thought he was the strong one. He drove her to the hospital and told the head nurse that her fiancé had just been killed. The other nurses surrounded Gretchen with a wall of sympathy, subtly shutting him out. They seemed to know how to take care of her, though that was Henry's job.

Especially now. Especially after what Gretchen had told him as they were sitting there on that bench. What she hadn't yet told Colin.

"I'm pregnant, Henry. Only about six weeks. I just found out for sure yesterday. I was going to tell him when he got off ops."

Then Henry did something he had never done before in his life and never did again.

He drove to the American airbase, went to the lockup, claimed to be a friend of the man who had been driving the jeep that hit Colin's car, and then beat the living daylights out of him. The guy never put up one hand in defense, and the MPs never intervened.

For the story of Colin, Henry, and Gretchen was known by them all.

May 1997

After a deep, dreamless sleep and breakfast with her friendly hosts, Beth set out to explore the area. The walk from the bed and breakfast took her through the small village, whose buildings were strung out for two miles along the bay like white beads on a brown string necklace. She passed a tiny post office, a grocer's, a two-story youth hostel, the other B&B, some cottages, a garage, and the rather grand Summer Isles Hotel, all splashed with the same brilliantly white stucco that made her think of a Mediterranean village, except the signs were in Gaelic.

It was a sapphire day. The sun sparkled on the bay, which swept in a semicircle along the edge of the land. The tide was working its way out, leaving pungent seaweed and broken shells. The air was cool, and the breeze stirred her hair, its fashionable bob something she wasn't yet used to. She had showered and changed into her last clean clothes.

As Beth walked through the late May morning, she gathered wildflowers, creating a bouquet of soft pink, brilliant yellow, and baby blue, clutching them tightly in her fist, knowing their destination. She trudged up a path toward the whitewashed church and its small cemetery enclosed by an ancient dry-stone wall.

The ironwork gate to the burial ground swung open with a groan. A pebble walkway followed the perimeter of the wall and also divided the cemetery into four quadrants. In the center rose a high stone cross carved with the distinctive Celtic curves and swirls. In the far corner, a wooden bench offered a place of shelter beneath a tall, solitary Scotch pine.

The gate clunked shut behind her, and Beth was suddenly aware of her isolation. As she walked toward the bench, she found herself growing short of breath. Waves of vertigo began to sweep over her. She stumbled quickly to the seat, sitting, bent over, her head in her hands, as she fought the disorienting sensation of floating, soaring, turning upside down, like a pilot in a one-seater plane doing loop-de-loops.

"Who-ee!"

The exultant voice of a young pilot discovering the joy of flight was in the air, in her heart.

Above her, the wind, filled with pine and sea salt, breathed through the long, delicate branches of the tree as she struggled to regain her equilibrium. She realized she had dropped her bouquet of wildflowers. Bending over to pick them up, she sensed movement out of the corner of her right eye. Yet when she looked, there was nothing. Not even a bird or a rabbit.

She turned right and walked on the path along the edge of the wall, her feet crunching on the small stones. After a half-dozen steps, her feet dragged, as though mired in muck. She stopped and turned to her left, facing a simple white gravestone, as blindingly white as the computer screen in the Imperial War Museum.

Domnhall Cailean (Colin) MacAmhlaigh. Nov. 27, 1920–July 4, 1944. RAF. In the service of his country.

She had convinced herself she was ready, though she was stunned to learn she had been born on his birthday, fifty-four years later.

What she wasn't prepared for was the grave next to Colin's.

THIRTY-ONE

AUGUST 1944

THEY HADN'T LET HER see Colin's body, so Gretchen could almost convince herself he was still somewhere soaring in the skies, floating through the clouds. Since neither she nor Henry could get to Achiltibuie for the funeral, it helped support her delusion. Even sending the letter telling Colin's family how much she loved him, what a wonderful man he was, felt like a part in a play.

Colin's unborn child was part of this other reality. She hugged it like a secret, whispering nothing of it in her letter. Nor did she read their replies, putting the unopened letters in her trunk.

Each morning she got up, drank tea, ate toast, and went to work. Work enabled her to pretend Colin would be back. He always came back, eventually.

She wore the engagement ring on a chain around her neck. It was closer to her heart that way. Off duty hours, she lay on her bunk or took long walks, reliving her moments with Colin: dancing on New Year's Eve, touring Holyrood, climbing the Wallace Monument, picnicking on Traprain Law, the months with his family at Achiltibuie, that incredible day at the tea shop.

Thinking of their wondrous weekend on Skye and the few days robbed from the war after his return to base in late March made breathing difficult. Nights, numbered on one hand, hiding in a guest house on weekend leave. Moments of exquisite joy, of sensual delight, of something almost spiritual, feeling no guilt, no shame, for Colin loved her. That they would soon be married.

The nurses tip-toed around at first. She didn't mention Colin, and neither did they. She was just one more woman who'd lost her sweetheart, husband, or fiancé. Everyone had lost someone. Hers was a story all too common

Henry checked on her as much as he could, but he was often on twelve, even eighteen hours of duty, sometimes days in a row. The U.S. Army Air Force was in high gear supporting the painfully slow push against the Germans, who were fighting back ferociously. It was a bloody war, both on the ground and in the air.

Henry's solicitous presence was cloying, like a thick, damp blanket. Yes, Colin asked him to take care of her. But she didn't want *Henry*. She wanted *Colin*.

By early October Gretchen could no longer hide her pregnancy. The matron said it was an exception for married women to be nurses, but a single, pregnant one was a scandal. She lost both her job and her housing in the nurses' quarters. Taking pity on her, the RAF quartermaster gave her a week to pack.

The end of her job was the beginning of her rage.

How dare Colin leave her like this? Alone. Pregnant. He didn't have to return to the air. Or even to the RAF. Be a hero. He'd had his discharge.

Yes, her scathing letter had sent him on a path back to active duty. Yes, without returning to the war, he wouldn't have come back to her. If only he had been content to be a laird, like his father.

"My God," Henry said when he found out that she'd lost her job. "I'm sorry. I know what your work means to you. Don't worry about a place to live. I'll think of something."

Henry found a tiny, furnished efficiency apartment in the village. When he wasn't working, he came by and cooked meals, repaired things, and did chores. He never asked about her plans.

One day in late October, they sat eating dinner in the apartment. Playing with his fork in a way that annoyed Gretchen, Henry said in a hesitant voice, "I've been... thinking... well... maybe... well, perhaps...do you think..."

In spite of her obvious indifference, he rushed on, not looking at her.

"For appearance's sake, we could get married. So no one would point fingers. I wouldn't expect... I mean it wouldn't have to be... a real marriage."

He continued to play with his fork, making patterns on the tablecloth, one he had bought for her at a village jumble sale. One of many little gifts he brought regularly. It was the first time Henry mentioned the baby. When she said nothing, he looked up.

"Marry... you?" She said the question in a slow, drawn-out manner.

His face flushing, Henry stumbled through his explanation. "Colin told me... he made me promise to take care of you, Gretchen."

"I saw the letter, remember, though you tried to hide it. Said it would upset me. I know what he told you to do. He also said to bury me next to him in Achiltibuie."

She heard the sarcasm in her voice, saw him go white, but couldn't stop. "I thought you were being kind. I didn't know you were trying to worm your way into marriage. Is that why you're always bringing gifts?"

"Gretchen, I'm sorry. I didn't..."

"No, you didn't, and you won't. Marry you? How could I? It would be all wrong." She cruelly ignored Henry's stricken face. "I think it's time I left."

"Left? Go where?" His voice was panicked.

"Goddammit, Henry, I don't know!" It felt incredibly good to unleash her fury. She picked up some dishes and walked to the sink, slamming them onto the counter. She was disappointed they didn't break.

"Gretchen?" She couldn't stand his pleading tone.

"I can't take any more of it, Henry. You're always nice. Always calm. Never angry."

"Maybe you should go to Colin's family. They would be...they look at you as..."

"No!" It was almost a scream.

"Gretchen, don't get upset..."

She spun around, glaring. "Stop telling me not to get upset. Because of the baby? Is that what you mean? I could never go to Colin's family. They'd be so fawning. And there would be his gravestone in the churchyard. I don't want this baby. It can never, ever replace Colin."

There, she'd said it. What she never voiced even to herself. Henry looked stunned and grief-stricken, but it felt so good to speak the truth.

He said, pained, "I'll pay the rent on the apartment as long as you stay... until you decide what to do. But I won't bother you."

Gretchen turned back to the sink. "It doesn't matter. Maybe after the baby is born, I'll give it to Colin's family and just go."

But where?

The door opened, but she didn't stop Henry. Her rage was slowly draining away. Pooling into a puddle of despair. The days ahead were empty, endless, meaningless. But she refused to cry. If she started, she would drown in her tears.

———◄✕►———

She went for long, rambling walks. Stood for hours at the edge of the airfields, watching the American B57s and the British Lancasters roar off into the sky. Slept late. Took naps. Went to bed early. She ate only out of obligation to the child she was carrying.

Henry dropped off groceries, leaving them by the door if she wasn't home, carrying them to the table without a word if she was. She did nothing to ease the bitter silence, in spite of the sorrow seeping off him, like a bitter perfume. In a perverse way, it felt good to punish someone. After all, Henry had introduced her to Colin.

She preferred not to think about what Henry had lost.

One afternoon in mid-November, she opened the door to a knock. There stood Fiona, whom she had not seen in eight months. She'd never replied to the letter Fiona sent after Colin died.

"Well, now I understand what Henry meant when he said you were doing poorly," Fiona said as she looked at Gretchen, whose condition was clearly evident.

Her friend's face was written with tenderness and sorrow. Gretchen felt her frozen, angry heart suddenly thawing and began to sob softly. Fiona led her to the faded, flowered couch.

"What a bloody, feckin' mess, this whole goddamn war," she muttered as she held Gretchen and, together, they cried for themselves, for each other, and for those they had lost. After the tears ran out, they drank endless cups of tea and told each other all their secrets.

"I've been a terrible friend," Fiona confessed.

"Henry can sure keep a secret," Gretchen replied.. still astounded at the things Fiona spilled. "But I think he's treated you badly." She got up to put another kettle of hot water on the burner. "Still, it's nice to know Henry's not a saint," Gretchen added, hiding her unreasonable twinge of jealousy over Henry and Fiona's relationship.

"Well," Fiona said, with a chuckle, "he may not be a saint, but he can be heavenly in bed."

"Fiona!" Gretchen nearly dropped the kettle, genuinely shocked.

Fiona joined her at the sink, taking the kettle and filling it at the tap. "He'd be mortified if he knew I was confessing to this."

Gretchen wondered who had taken advantage of whom. "Yet he's carried through on the promise Colin..." Gretchen's voice caught, and she choked back more tears then continued. "Henry found this apartment, brings me groceries."

"Henry wouldna done anything else. I'm surprised he didn't ask you to marry him."

Gretchen felt her face grow warm.

Fiona shook her head slowly. "Silly me, of course he did. For your sake, right?"

Gretchen heard Fiona's desolation. "I said no, Fiona. And I'll continue to say no. I just couldn't do that to Henry. It would be wrong."

"So, what are you going to do?"

She told Fiona the plan she'd devised. Take the baby to Colin's family after it was born then go back to the States. Surely the war would be over, and travel would be easier.

"Oh, Gretchen. Are ye sure? Won't you regret it someday? I'm sure Colin's family would be thrilled to raise his wee bairn, but they'd probably rather you did it with them. Would you go back home? To Pennsylvania?"

"Oh, no, I don't think so," Gretchen replied, pouring the now boiling water into the teapot and putting the lid on to brew. She closed the blackout curtains, as dusk was settling in. "That's not home anymore. I would probably move to a city. Philadelphia. Maybe New York."

"And what about your mother? Wouldn't she want to know about her grandchild?"

"You mean her bastard grandchild."

"Gretchen, it happens all the time. Especially now."

Gretchen thought of her quiet, conservative mother. "She wouldn't understand. She isn't here. She doesn't know what it's like to have someone you love fly off every night and..."

Fiona interrupted. "There's still someone else to consider."

"Who?" Gretchen asked as she carried the teapot back to the table.

"Henry."

"Oh, God, Fiona, I am considering him. By *not* marrying him. So he's free for *you*."

Fiona made a snort. "Gretchen, you're as much of an idget as you were when I first met you. Colin gave Henry a charge to take care of you, like a last will and testament. He's yours. Wrapped up and tied with a string. Whether you want him or not."

The guilt of being unable to love Henry weighed like a millstone around her neck. As did the horrible way she'd treated him.

"Well, Gretchen, you've got time to decide. Henry'll never leave on his own unless he's sent to France with the Air Force."

"Will Henry have to go?"

"Who knows? He's in a very odd situation as a liaison."

"But Fiona, what about you?" For the first time in months, Gretchen began to think about someone else.

"I'll always be your friend, Gretchen. And if you need anything, you know I've got connections in high places. It's just, you see, I can't be Henry's friend anymore. He wrote me and asked me to visit you. But I haven't seen him and don't plan to."

When Gretchen protested, Fiona said, "No, listen. I went into this with my eyes open. I knew from the start that you were and are Henry's first and only love. It's not that he hasn't been sweet, and dear, and more than adequate as a lover."

Gretchen covered her ears. "Fiona, stop."

"You're such a Yankee prude, Gretch, for all your fallen state. And we Scots are supposed to be all uptight and holy. I know Henry has always felt guilty about our relationship. I was more than willing to take Henry, guilt or not. But I knew he could never really be mine."

"I'm not some delicate flower of womanhood," Gretchen replied, feeling defensive. "You don't all need to shelter me or save me from the truth."

"Aye, Gretchen, but we all love ye and never wanted to see ye be hurt. Like I said before, it's this goddamn bloody feckin' war."

———— ✠ ————

Henry wasn't sure if he was relieved or regretful that Fiona didn't look him up when she came to see Gretchen, but he was deeply grateful for her visit, and told her so in a letter, because it made a change in Gretchen. She started inviting him to stay when he dropped off groceries and to come to dinner whenever he was off duty.

She was becoming surprisingly domestic, cooking and cleaning. Whether from sheer boredom or a need to feel useful, she experimented with baking. Since he had access to the American base and its well-stocked store, she had flour and sugar and other things her British neighbors would have given their eyeteeth for. He often found her up to her elbows in flour, the very picture of a mother-to-be basking in contented domesticity.

Yet she was making no effort to find baby clothes, diapers, or other baby things. And she made no mention of it. She did finally start going to the maternity clinic, something he insisted on, as her time drew near.

"Gretchen, don't you think we should be looking for a crib? There was a notice on the duty station bulletin board. I can check at the base furniture exchange."

She only replied, "Don't worry, Henry. It'll all work out."

He couldn't imagine what she meant. Was she planning on leaving right after the baby was born? It was too unnerving to contemplate. Then one afternoon near her due date in early February, as they were having a late supper at the kitchen table, Gretchen terrified him by saying, "Henry, you need to make me a promise."

He broke out into a cold sweat at her intense tone and forced himself to keep his tone light. "Sure, Gretchen. What is it?"

"If anything should happen to me..." She held up her hand at his instantaneous protest. "Listen, please, Henry. You know it can be dangerous having a baby. So if anything happens to me, take the baby to Colin's family. See that I'm laid to rest beside him. Up there, on that hill. In the highlands." Her voice had grown dreamy, as if she were already imagining herself there.

Henry was incapable of a reply.

She laid her hands on his cheeks remorsefully, "Oh, Henry, darling. I'm so sorry to upset you. I just need to say this and know that you hear me. I've written Mairi and told them about the baby and that I'll come to them once the baby is born and stay until I decide what to do."

She took his hand and laid it on her rounded stomach, something he had longed to do but never dared ask. Looking at him solemnly, she said in a tender voice, "I've come to terms with it all now, during these last months. Time to think about what I've lost. What all of us have lost."

Henry wished against all sense that it was his baby. That she wasn't taking herself and the baby away from him.

She said, as if she had read his thoughts, "This is Colin's baby, Henry dear. It's a McAuley and needs to be raised by a McAuley. Promise me you'll see it happens, if I can't make it happen myself. If it's a boy, name him after his father. If it's a girl, call her Susanna Catriona."

If she had intended to tear out his heart, she couldn't have chosen a better way.

And he told her so, slamming out the door before walking miles in the bitter English winter. Consoling himself with a warm ale at a pub. Coming back hours later to find a note on the door. *Dearest Henry, I'm sorry I've never been able to make you happy. Please, when this is all over, go home and find yourself someone to love.*

February 1945

She was drowning in waves of pain. Sweat drenched her. Exhaustion swamped her. Someone kept wiping her forehead. Someone kept saying, "Just one more push. Just one more."

With what little strength she had left, she did as commanded. And with that last effort, she felt a wondrous release and an odd sense of something letting loose.

"It's a girl. You've got a wee baby girl. A bonny baby girl."

She felt them lay the wailing child on her chest, but she hadn't the strength to lift her arms or open her eyes. The pain was subsiding. In its place was a comforting sensation of being wrapped in a light gray mist. And what was that?

Through the mist she could see a shape. A form. A silhouette. In a bomber jacket.

"Colin?" *she asked, afraid to believe.* "Colin," *she called,* "come see our daughter."

He seemed to materialize before her eyes. Her mind recognized the drug-induced dream, for Colin was dead, buried in his family's cemetery far to the north, but her heart knew it was love taking the form of the man she had lost.

"Colin!" *she said with joy, then stopped, realizing what she'd be leaving behind.*

Their child.

"It'll be all right, Gretchen," Colin said tenderly. "My family will take care of her. She'll be well loved and looked after."

With a sigh, Gretchen rested her hands on the tiny life that lay upon her chest.

"Be well, my little love, my wee little girl," she whispered.

And then stretched her arms out to the young man in the bomber jacket.

———◄━━►———

In the end, Henry tried to convince himself he'd done everything possible to prevent any harm coming to Gretchen. What he couldn't do was prevent the long and difficult labor, the treacherous delivery, the ruptured artery.

He was barely able to write the letter to Colin's family explaining that Gretchen had died in childbirth and the child along with her. That she had wanted nothing more than to be buried next to her bomber pilot, in a quiet churchyard in the Scottish highlands. Something she had made him promise a few days before she died.

And sealed in the coffin with her, to be buried alongside her father, was the baby girl she had borne to their son and brother. That was what he told them.

Thus, he carried out one part of his promise to Gretchen.

However, when he held Gretchen and Colin's tiny baby girl in his arms and baptized her with his tears, sobs racking his body so he could barely stand, Henry knew he could not carry out the other part of her request. The baby was all he had left of her. And of Colin. And he would not give her away, not even to her rightful family.

Instead, he put his name on the birth certificate as the father. Half out of his mind with grief, he called Fiona and told her the awful end of Gretchen's life and the lie that he had begun to perpetrate. He asked if she would come with him to the States, be his wife, and raise their friends' daughter as their own, knowing he would never stop loving Gretchen. Her voice tear-filled, she told Henry that Gretchen and Colin would haunt them both, but she would do as he asked. She'd always liked living in America.

Fiona once again used her father to pull strings, this time with the American military, and got Henry a compassionate discharge. It would take at least a month.

He would then take Susanna home, and Fiona would follow when she could. It might take months to arrange her discharge, if that was even possible. She might have to wait out the war and join him afterward.

There was a limit to how much her father could manipulate.

But two days later, on a sunny afternoon in London, while Fiona was walking to the marriage registry office, a V1 unmanned rocket struck the street she was walking, one of the many parting shots from the collapsing empire of the Third Reich.

Just as he hadn't attended Colin's or Gretchen's funerals, he did not attend Fiona's. In an incoherent letter to her father, he thanked him for all he had done, blaming himself for Fiona's fate, for if he hadn't involved her in his plans, she wouldn't have been on that street on that day.

Then Henry swore to never love another person. Except the baby he had claimed as his own.

Barely functioning in the face of wrenching grief, Henry took the newborn to London—to Alice, the only woman he knew who might be able to find a temporary home for Susanna Catriona. Alice was full of tearful sympathy and pragmatic assistance. From her acquaintances, she gathered a bassinet, baby clothes, blankets, and all the paraphernalia needed to tend an infant.With the help of her married daughter, she offered to keep Henry's daughter, as he presented her, until his discharge and arrangements to travel home were finalized.

In the few days he could travel to London, Alice taught him to change diapers, prepare bottles, feed and burp little Susanna Catriona, and rock her to sleep.

She asked him how he would tend the baby alone once he got home.

Not for the first time, Gretchen's voice floated back... *This is Colin's baby, Henry dear. Colin's. It's a McAuley and needs to be raised by a*

McAuley. Promise me you'll see that happens, if I can't make it happen myself.

Henry would stare at the baby each time, taking in her delicate fair skin, tufts of chestnut hair, and hazel eyes—Gretchen's eyes. *No, Gretchen, I'm sorry. I have to have something of you, and she is all that's left. I did love you first, you know. And probably best.*

Still, Alice had a point. What would he do alone? He couldn't imagine his parents, especially his conservative mother, welcoming a baby born out of wedlock, though he could lie and say they were married. That he'd never told them.

That was when Naomi came to mind.

September 1945

The mid-September Saturday was still very much summer, as Henry straightened his tie in the mirror of what had been William's bedroom at Naomi's farmhouse. Too warm for the shirt he had bought for his visit to the farm in May. Now his wedding shirt.

Through the window, the decaying barn reminded him how much Naomi and her mother had suffered during the war, though the now-rented fields were showcases of American bounty that helped win the bloody battles in the Atlantic and Pacific. Time for 'happier' days now.

In March he had written Naomi a long letter, not his usual single page. Nor the usual apology, "I should be ashamed for taking so long to write after all your faithful correspondence."

He was sure she'd be stunned, possibly repulsed by his words: *Naomi, I'd like you to consider the possibility of marriage.* It wasn't the first thing he wrote, or the last, but it was the most important.

I don't know how to say this, to make it easy, or to soften the blow. There is no way but to tell you outright. I couldn't bear to put it in a telegram. I thought you'd rather get the news in a letter. Gretchen is dead. I can't believe it. I can hardly write it, or put it down on paper, and even then it seems like a horrible mistake. There is a child, you see. We had planned to marry, but we couldn't. It's too complicated to explain.

And the last paragraph...

I would like you to be the mother this child needs. Without you, I will not be able to raise her properly. By the time you get this letter, I'll most likely be home in Lancaster. My parents will help out while I look for a job. If it's okay with you, I'll come by with her so you can see her. Write to me at my parents' home, and let me know what you think.

She'll be more than a niece to you. She'll be your daughter. And she'll be my daughter.

He never said, *she is my daughter.*

In Naomi's letter he found waiting at his parents' house when he arrived from England, she had been sweetly delighted at his proposal--well, more of a proposition. He hadn't mentioned love, and he was relieved when she hadn't either. He knew she wanted a house and a home of her own. A marriage. He was offering all that, though she practically had a farm of her own.

But he didn't want to be a farmer, and living there would continually remind him of Gretchen. Even now... he glanced at the window. Out there were painful remnants of days with Gretchen when they were younger... the tire swing that still hung by the huge oak tree near the faded barn; the basketball hoop where he and Gretchen and William had practiced free throws.

He twisted his cuff links, a gift from his parents, making sure they were secure. He had delayed setting a wedding date as long as he could after his mother proclaimed there was something not quite right about rushing into a marriage with the sister of the woman he claimed he loved. That she was fine looking after the baby and could do so if he found a job in Lancaster.

The revelation left him flummoxed. He hadn't expected his parents, especially his mother, to be excited about a daughter born out of wedlock. But at this point he could hardly tell Naomi he'd changed his mind, that he had written to her in a haze of grief, not thinking he could raise Susanna without a wife, not knowing of his parents' warm reception. But he had a good job offer in Carlisle and wanted to have Susanna in his life every day, something he couldn't do with his parents tending her in Lancaster.

And so it was that he brought her to Naomi's farm in May, when the fields were showing the first signs of corn, wheat, and tobacco, and the large kitchen garden was freshly weeded.

Ada was warmly welcoming, all oohs and ahhs with her baby granddaughter, looking as perky as the pink and blue pansies in the flower boxes along the freshly painted front porch. But he could see she was as faded around the edges as the house with its second-story peeling window frames and missing roof slates.

Naomi, however, was uncomfortably awkward and stiff, though he noticed tears when he first arrived. Whether she was touched by his bouquet of carnations or saddened by thoughts of Gretchen on seeing the baby, he wasn't sure.

When Susanna got fussy, she didn't reach out for her, instead just stood clenching and unclenching her hands. "I'm not... I haven't been around... babies... much..." was her excuse. Still, she did go and get the bottle ready.

Henry checked the mirror again. At least Naomi had a decent amount of practice these few months. He dusted off his suit jacket, hanging on a chair. Not long now.

The wedding was taking place at the Lutheran church Naomi's family had attended for generations. He and Naomi would travel from the farm to the church and walk down the aisle together. None of the "who gives this bride in marriage" tradition, with her father buried in the graveyard, and a stone marking William's empty plot, his body forever lost in a watery grave.

Henry shrugged on his jacket, sighing as he looked around the room still filled with trophies and trinkets. A cheeky, cheerful boy grew up here. A cheeky, cheerful young man took him for a spin in 1939. Was he cheeky and cheerful in the navy? Henry forced away the thought.

The guest list was very small. Besides the minister and his wife, the organist, there would be Naomi's mother, her mother's sister Orpha, several neighbors, and two of Fiona's women friends from the Women's Missionary Society at church.

On Henry's side, there were only his parents and his mother's cousin from Carlisle, with whom he had been living. Both of his brothers were still in the military in some far-flung place. When Naomi asked him about friends, he said in a strangled voice, "I lost them all in the war."

Afterward, they were having a small reception at the farm.

He thanked her for planning a low-key wedding. "We're too old for all that fuss and bother." When he asked Naomi if she wanted a wedding trip, she said, "No, it's not practical. We'd be best saving the money for furniture."

"I figured you'd say that," he said, relieved. "You're a very practical lady." He'd suggested an overnight trip to Harrisburg for a nice dinner and maybe a show, while Ada kept the baby. To that, she had said little.

Two months after Henry returned in May, Ada had stunned them by announcing she was selling the farm and moving in with her sister Orpha, another widow living in New Freedom, at the Maryland border. And she was giving a wedding gift to Naomi and Henry—a cash down payment for a house in Carlisle.

Henry picked out the house, a roomy three-story Victorian with a turret on a quiet street. It was a bit run down but had potential.

When Naomi pointed out the house's condition, he'd replied enthusiastically, "Oh, don't you worry. I'll fix it up right nice. And it's got such a big kitchen. I thought you would really like that. And we can make a room for Susanna in the attic when she's older. It'll be like living in a castle. She'll love that."

She seemed disconcerted when he suggested she contribute her saved inheritance to further reduce the mortgage but finally agreed. Henry tried not to think of the days and years ahead, living with Gretchen's sister, being a husband to a woman he didn't love. Keeping a secret. What would happen if Naomi found out that this wasn't his child after all? At least the birth certificate had his name on it. Anyone who could contradict that lived on the other side of the Atlantic. Or was dead. Like Fiona.

Worse yet, what if Naomi learned that he might not be able to give her children? He had discovered during his military physical that his bout with childhood mumps might have left him infertile. By marrying her, he might be denying her the right to have children of her own.

It was unfair, maybe even cruel... but... it was for the best. Naomi couldn't stay unmarried forever. He needed Susanna, who needed more than just him. In the end, they all benefited. As for Gretchen and Colin... he would do right by them. Make sure their daughter had a good life.

His decision would haunt him all his life.

THIRTY-TWO

MAY 1997

GRETCHEN SUSANNA DUNST. OCT. 15, 1920—February 4, 1945. Beloved of Colin. And their daughter, Susanna Catriona, February 4, 1945—February 4, 1945.

Confusion swirled like clouds in Beth's mind as she stared at the simple white grave next to Colin's. Gretchen Dunst? The Gretchen Dunst she knew of was her grandmother's sister. The one who had died during the war in England. The one Naomi never spoke of. Was it possible this was the American girl Colin loved?

But clearly *this* Gretchen knew Colin loved her. And clearly, she loved him in return, for they had a child. A child that was born and died on the same day. And her mother with her.

A baby named Susanna Catriona.

Why did this daughter of Colin and Gretchen have the same name as her own mother? It made no sense.

"Then what did you want from me, Colin?" Beth demanded of the air. "Wasn't I supposed to find your American girl and tell her you loved her? But if this is her, she's dead. So why did you put me through this? Why did you bring me to this place? There's nothing left for me to do! There's no one left for me to know! Everyone's gone!"

The grief overcame her like a tidal wave. Blinded by tears, she sank to her knees, shoulders shaking. For a very long time, she was lost in a tsunami of sorrow.

A gentle hand on Beth's shoulder and a soothing voice by her ear brought her to awareness.

"Aie, my dearie, come, come. I should hae never let ye come alone. Mam kept saying, there's something so familiar about that lassie. But I never knew them, you see. But Mam talked about them so many times, and we have the pictures, you see, from the time they brought Colin home to heal with his injuries—Colin's two American friends."

"Beautiful girl, my mam said, was Gretchen," Mrs. McIntrye was saying. "I never knew Henry's last name was Schmidt. Mam asked this morning what your whole name was, and when I told her, she about had a conniption. She always said there was something not right about the whole story and how Henry just disappeared, never came to see the family."

Beth struggled to hear, to make sense of Mrs. McIntyre's words. Why would Mrs. Gordon find anything familiar in her, unless it was her resemblance to Henry?

But when Mrs. McIntyre knelt beside her and began to rock her gently, crooning a soft Gaelic lament, Beth lost herself in that ancient keening of the soul. Long after the song had dissolved into the wind, they sat beside the graves. As they finally stood to go, Beth unloosed the flowers she was still clutching. They floated to the ground in a puddle of color, gracing the graves with a benediction.

Beth spent the next days in a haze, sleeping hours at a stretch. Mrs. McIntyre, who insisted she call her Clara, occasionally woke her with a tray of broth or a cup of tea and a scone. In what had been Colin's bedroom, she slept and dreamt, while his grandniece tended to her, and his youngest sister fretted downstairs.

But none of her dreams were of Colin. Or of the American girl he loved. Instead, they were about her own childhood, memories dredged up from forgotten corners in her mind.

It was a summer Sunday drive. Sitting in the back seat of the big Chrysler Imperial, she could barely see out the window. The tops of buildings, the sky, and telephone poles flashed by.

Flip. Flip. Flip.

The faster Grandpa drove, the faster the poles zipped by.

She sat up on her knees and rested her chin on her folded arms along the edge of the window sill. Her hair, just starting to lose its baby blonde color, waved in the breeze from Grandma's front passenger window.

"Susanna Elizabeth Schmidt, sit down this minute. You're mucking up the upholstery with your shoes. And I don't want you arriving looking all mussed."

"What if I take my shoes off, Grandma?"

"Don't you argue with me, young lady."

"Pumpkin." Grandpa always intervened. "It's not safe for you to kneel up on the seat. Sit down, honey." Grandpa had lots of pet names for Beth. Sometimes he called her Betsey, or Pumpkin, or Little Bits.

"Where are we going?" Beth said as she sat back down, reducing her view to blue skies, white puffy clouds, and zipping telephone poles.

"We're going to see Nana Dunst," Grandpa said.

Beth frowned. "Do we have to?" to which Grandma snapped, "Mind your mouth, missy."

When they got to the old people's home, Nana Dunst was sitting outside on the patio, where the nurse's aide was having a cigarette. Beth wanted to go to the duck pond, a short walk away, and was reaching for Grandpa's hand, when Nana Dunst said, "There you are. Where have you been? I've been looking and looking for you. Come here, girl."

Nana Dunst's ancient face was pasty and full of wrinkles. Her skin sagged, and her hair was frizzy white with bald spots. With surprisingly strong hands, she grabbed Beth's arm, pulling her in front of her wheelchair and banging Beth's shins on the footrest.

Beth whimpered, "Ow."

"Gretchen, where have you been?" Her voice trembled.

"This is not Gretchen, Mother," Grandma protested loudly.

Beth was also contradicting her great-grandmother. "I'm Beth. Susanna Elizabeth Schmidt," proudly reciting her whole name as she had learned to say it in kindergarten.

"No, no, that's not right," Nana Dunst scolded her. "Don't you know your own name?"

"I'm named for my mother. Her name is Susanna," Beth said, confused. The old woman's eyes filled with tears. Beth watched with fascination as they rolled, one by one, from the rheumy, red corners of her eyes, diagonally across the valleys of wrinkles, and then dropped down onto Beth's hands. The tears were warm.

"Gretchen," the old woman whispered in a trembling rasp, using the grip on Beth's upper arms to pull herself closer. "Gretchen, my little girl. I knew you'd come back home. You should never have gone. I told you there was going to be a war. Why didn't you listen?"

Beth tried to back away. The old woman's breath smelled of her tuna fish lunch and rarely brushed teeth. At the same time, Naomi pulled Beth out of Nana Dunst's tight grip so that her yellowed, broken nails scraped painfully across Beth's upper arms, exposed in her short-sleeved Sunday dress.

Naomi gave Beth a shake with each word she spat out at her mother. "This... is... not ... Gretchen. This... is... not... Gretchen. This... is... Beth."

Beth began to cry. Grandma's harsh voice and her rough treatment were frightening. Grandpa took Beth out of Grandma's hands and up into his arms. He enveloped her in his warm, comforting embrace and let her sob on his shoulder.

In the background, she heard Nana Dunst say over and over again, "It has to be my Gretchen. She looks just like Gretchen. I knew she would come back," and her Grandma futilely shouting in return, "It's not Gretchen. It's Beth. For God's sake, Mother, Gretchen's dead. She's been dead for more than thirty years."

After that October day, they never again took Beth to see Nana Dunst.

Beth sat in bed, staring out the window at the ceaseless movement of the waves on the beach, remembering snippets of other odd scenes and overheard conversations from her childhood. She tried to tie those together with what she had learned recently.

Gretchen and Colin had a daughter. Susanna Catriona. All three of them lay in a graveyard at the other end of this small Scottish village. Yet Beth's mother's name was Susanna Catriona. Did Naomi and Henry name their daughter after Gretchen and Colin's tiny baby who lived only one day? As a way to honor Gretchen? But why wouldn't Naomi have told her that? Was it too painful? She'd never even seen a picture of Gretchen. When she asked one time, Naomi said that Nana Dunst had all the old family pictures, and they were probably lost in the move to the nursing home.

Naomi also rarely spoke about Beth's mother, as if Naomi had wiped away memories of the people she'd lost. Her daughter. Her sister. Her brother. Her father. What Beth knew of them, she had learned over the years from Henry, who had occasionally told her stories about Beth's mother and Naomi's family. But he, too, rarely spoke about Gretchen. It was the war, she had always thought. Wasn't it?

Beth knew her Grandfather Henry had spent many of his teenage summers at his uncle's homestead, next to Naomi's family farm. In junior high school, she went with him once without Naomi. The farms were gone. Rows of suburban houses were planted where corn used to grow. Henry had said, "I first met Naomi and her sister Gretchen here," his voice oddly quiet and sad, for a memory Beth would have thought was happy.

Gretchen's name wasn't listed as McAuley on the tombstone. They must not have been married. And Colin... he couldn't have known he had a daughter. He died in July of 1944. His daughter was born in February 1945. Did he even *know* he was going to be a father?

Colin said he wanted her to know the truth. What was that truth? That her grandmother's sister had been the love of his life? That his daughter would have been her second cousin? The link to it all was Henry, who had been in this room more than fifty years ago, and whose life was somehow entwined with Gretchen's and Colin's.

"I knew a Scottish pilot once," Henry had muttered one day last fall. What other secrets had Naomi and Henry kept hidden from her? And why?

—————⋈—————

After several days, she began to join Clara and Mairi for meals. She took walks and spent time in the cemetery sitting next to Colin and Gretchen's graves, hoping, wishing, longing for Colin's presence. But he was gone. That door had been closed forever.

She didn't tell Clara and Mairi about the dreams and visions of Colin. They were politely non-curious, asking no questions, though it was apparent she was grieving for someone. She asked no questions either, though she would often stare at the old family photos hanging in the upstairs hallway.

Pictures of a family. Mother, father, two girls, two boys. As youngsters. And grown. A young man in a naval uniform. Another young man in a bomber jacket. It was comforting to see an actual likeness of Colin, to confirm the man in her dreams and visions had been real. Had actually worn her bomber jacket.

When she made noises about imposing, Mairi said gently, "No, child, you've had a long journey. This sea air will do you good. We loved Henry. He was like family. You can stay as long as you want," and then she told stories about the time Gretchen stayed at the farm to help Colin recover from his war injuries. About Henry coming to visit at Christmas.

"I wouldn't mind seeing Henry again," Mairi said in a soft voice.

One afternoon, a week later, Clara appeared at her bedroom door. "Beth," she said quietly, "you have a visitor. He's talking to Mam in the sitting room."

Beth felt suddenly short of breath. It could only be one person. Robbie.

He must have tracked her here. Gone through the records of those twenty-seven bomber pilots with Colin in their names and found those born in Scotland then narrowed it down by those stationed at Drem.

From there he would have discovered where Colin was buried. Realized she would come here.

Beth managed to say, "Give me a minute; I'll be down."

Hands shaking, Beth tried to freshen herself up, washing her face, combing her hair, and changing into a fresh shirt. Recently Clara had sorted through clothes her daughter had left behind and found some that fit Beth, telling her to wear them. "She won't mind a bit," Clara said.

Beth made her way down the now-familiar hallway and stairs and paused outside the sunny sitting room where Mairi sat every day, knitting or reading or more recently, chatting with Beth. She steeled her nerves for the unexpected encounter. But when she turned the corner and walked into the bright room, it wasn't Robbie sitting on the couch next to Clara and across from Mairi.

It was her grandfather. Henry.

Beth stood in the doorway, stunned. She must have made some noise, because Henry looked up, his face anguished, a sight that made Beth's heart melt. With a catch in her voice, she exclaimed, "Grandpa!" and dashed across the room, throwing her arms around him as he stood up to envelop her in a fierce embrace. Beth felt his silent sobs, heard his broken pleas for forgiveness, for what she couldn't fathom, but knew only joy to have him here.

Early that evening, Beth and Henry sat on the sturdy wooden bench beneath the towering Scottish pine tree which stood like an austere guard over the cemetery. Beth snuggled into the warmth of Colin's bomber jacket, glad for its protection against the brisk breeze that blew off the bay. In late May, days stayed light well past nine, though the evenings could be quite chilly.

On the pebbly beach below, the waves played like children, their lapping echoing in the quiet cove. Beyond the bay, the distant Cuillen Hills of the misty Isle of Skye, sixty miles south, were a hazy purple mass at the edge of the world.

Henry took out the thermos Clara had packed for them and poured its contents into two mugs. Beth sipped the scalding, darkly brewed tea. The acrid taste lingered on her tongue and, mixed with the salt air, felt like a mouthful of tears, tears that lingered at the back of her eyes since the moment she saw Henry in Colin's childhood home.

Alone in the parlor with Beth, Henry had explained the call from Robbie, his own trip to England, and their search for Beth.

She asked, "He did all this for you?"

"For you, Beth." Henry smiled gently.

"Where is he now?"

"He had to go back to Edinburgh, get ready to teach a summer seminar, but said anytime you want to talk, he'll come."

Beth's stomach twisted. "I'm glad that... he's helped you."

"He wanted to give us time together. Not interfere." Henry looked at Beth then added, "He's a fine young man, that Robbie. I think he cares for you deeply."

"I can't really think about that yet, Grandpa. Maybe in a bit."

"Of course. There's time enough for all that."

Now, sitting in the quiet cemetery, Henry's voice turned dreamy. "I always envied Colin his homestead. The sea. The sky. It would be... wonderful... peaceful to just stay here."

She saw him glance at the gravestones before he added wistfully, "To be buried here."

Beth was horrified. "Grandpa, don't, don't talk about... about being... buried." She couldn't face any more losses. "And besides, you can't stay here. There's Grandma..."

"Mairi invited me to stay as long as I wanted."

"Yes, yes, that's wonderful. She's wonderful. But Grandma..."

"Yes. Grandma. She told me if I came after you, here to Scotland, that I didn't need to come home again."

Beth looked with shock at her grandfather's exhausted, pale face, noticing for the first time that he seemed to have aged tremendously in the five months she'd been away. This trip had obviously been too much for him.

"Robbie shouldn't have called you. He shouldn't have worried you this way." She was growing angry. What gave him the right to interfere? Look at the results. "I'm sure Grandma didn't mean what she said. She was just upset. You know how she gets when she's angry."

Henry shook his head in contradiction. "Oh, no, she meant it. And after I tell you the story, you'll know why. And probably understand." His tone had changed from dreamy to hesitant.

"Grandpa," Beth interrupted, "You don't have to explain. I think I've figured it out. Mairi told me you and Colin were great friends, and Gretchen and Colin fell in love, but that he was killed during the war before they could marry."

Henry patted Beth's hand gently. "Yes, yes that is right. But that's not all of it." His voice held a tremble.

"Oh, Grandpa, you don't have to say any more. I'm not sure I understand why you or Grandma never told me the story. It's very romantic and sad. And sad to think they had a child who didn't live. But it seems right that they are all buried together here. Right here."

Beth sighed deeply as she looked in the direction of their graves. She was still at a loss to know what truth Colin wanted her to learn. That he and her grandfather were friends? Perhaps that was it. And the story of him and his sweetheart, Gretchen. Their lives celebrated, not hushed up like some disgraceful family secret.

Henry interrupted her thoughts. "I was never fair to your grandmother. When she found out the truth years ago, well, she didn't let me forget it. That's why she's been... hard on me. And you. All this time."

"But what's her sister's story got to do with you Grandpa? Other than you were here with Colin and Gretchen during the war?"

Henry took the cup of tea from Beth's hand and put it on the bench beside him then took both her hands in his.

"There's a story you need to hear, an explanation that you deserve, before you decide whether there's forgiveness for a stubborn, arrogant old man at the end. I deliberately chose not to follow Gretchen's last wishes and stole something so precious from Colin's family." His hands were icy cold, even with the tea he had been drinking. "That decision impacted many lives—Naomi's, your mother's, and yours, and others here in Scotland."

Beth felt her throat thickening. "It wasn't your fault their daughter died," she protested.

"Hear me out. It's going to take a long time to tell this story. And I need you to listen the whole way through. Not ask questions 'til the end. Then I'll answer any you have."

He poured her a fresh hot mug of tea. "You'll need this."

By the time Henry finished his story, the sun had dropped closer to the sea, and the mug of tea had long gone cold. She barely remembered holding it, this foreign object. She put it back on the bench and clenched her hands in her lap.

"Now you know the truth," Henry said. "The whole truth. I don't know how much of it you ever suspected. But the truth is, I lied. To everyone. To Colin's family and to Naomi. To your mother, Susanna. She never knew her heritage. She thought Naomi and I were her parents."

Beth tried to take in the enormity of her grandfather's story. Henry let out a deep sigh as if expelling the burden of a lifetime then looked at her with teary eyes, waiting for her questions.

"Why would Grandma suspect that Susanna wasn't your daughter?" Beth felt like a book editor, analyzing some novel, puzzling out the character's motives and actions, and looking for clear explanations. It felt unconnected to her. Someone else's tale.

"She didn't until, well, until time went on, and we didn't have children. She thought it was her fault, but the doctor said she was fine and asked if I had ever had mumps as a child."

"Mumps?"

"They can make you... sterile."

Beth stared at the distant ocean, her mind coming and going over the same territory like the tide. This convoluted story of two men who loved the same woman, one who ended up dying and the other who ended up marrying her sister. She struggled to put it all together, a tale too overwhelming to comprehend.

Though logic told her the truth, she still had to ask, and fought to form the words, because they would change everything. "So you mean, so what all this means, is that you're not... my... that Gretchen and... Colin are my..."

As Henry slowly nodded his head, Beth felt the foundations of her life crumbling. Where she had come from. Who she was in the world. Naomi and Henry weren't the people they claimed to be. More than just grandparents, they had raised her. But in reality, only Naomi was *related* to her mother and to her *real* grandparents. None of Henry's blood ran in her veins.

This was what Colin had wanted her to discover. The reason that he, her grandfather, her *real* grandfather, had traveled through space and time into her dreams, into her life. A truth that seemed more fantasy than fact. A truth that felt like a black hole slowly sucking her into its destructive core.

Henry took Beth's hands in his trembling ones. "I loved Gretchen with every ounce of my being. I thought I... deserved to raise her daughter." His voice shook. "Then when Naomi realized who our daughter really was, that I had tricked her into thinking this... was my baby as well as Gretchen's, she began to take her anger out on Susanna, and I... I... countered by what I thought was protecting Susanna, countering Naomi's anger by giving Susanna whatever she wanted. I made terrible choices. So many times."

His voice had grown so quiet Beth had to strain to hear him over the sloughing of the wind in the pine tree above them. She gently extricated her hands from Henry's and crossed her arms in front of her, staring ahead, ignoring his ravaged face. Neither spoke.

After a long time, Henry said, "I don't know what to do, Beth. Whether to go back to Carlisle to someone who resents me bitterly or to stay here in Scotland and try to earn back the trust of Colin's family."

Beth stood up suddenly.

"I can't... I can't answer that question for you, Grandpa." She found herself stumbling over that last word. *Henry. He is Henry.* "You have too many debts to pay, and I can't be telling you which matters more. Why does it have to be one or the other? Can't you do both? Oh, I don't... I... can't think right now. Can we... just go back, and it's late, and Clara and Mairi will be worried, and..."

She began to gather the thermos and cups.

"Suzy Q..."

"Don't!" she said harshly, startling her grandfather. "I, please..."

Henry nodded, his eyes awash with sadness. "Of course."

They walked back silently, with the sound of the sea for company. Endlessly washing the beach. Erasing the tracks of those who had walked there today. And more than fifty years ago.

Beth went right to her room, pleading exhaustion. "I'll make a cup of tea in my room."

Thirty minutes later, Clara brought scones slathered with jam and clotted crème, as well as slices of cold ham and cheese.

"You barely ate dinner. You need your nourishment, Beth. Ye've had... a shock. It's been a shock for all of us, now that we know the whole story. But my darlin' Beth..." Clara's voice caught. "I can't tell you how happy my mam is. Her Colin's granddaughter..."

Clara's heartfelt words touched Beth's shattered heart. She had been lovingly enveloped by Colin's family, though with none of them knowing the truth that she *was* family.

But it was all too new, too sudden, too overwhelming. Bitterness was seeping into her thoughts. How different things might have been, had it not been for choices her grandfather...

No, he isn't my grandfather, she chided herself.

The person who had been her anchor, her protector, her compass was not at all the man she thought he was. What other secrets had he kept from her? About the circumstances of her own birth. Maybe they did know who her father was. With all of Henry's lies and the way he imposed her mother on Naomi, no wonder Naomi resented Beth.

Though she had claimed exhaustion, sleep eluded her. Only the moon kept her company in Colin's room while she watched the play of silver light on the churning, inky waters as hours ticked by, demarcated by the distant gong of the grandfather clock in the downstairs entry.

By the time the stars faded, well before five, she had made up her mind to leave.

Though her journey for the truth was finished, she needed time to digest it. To rethink her relationship with Henry and Naomi. She couldn't do it with him here or surrounded by Colin's remaining family.

She felt a restless urge to keep traveling. Somewhere. Anywhere.

She could catch a ride with the postal van, which doubled as an informal taxi, if she got to the post office by six. Jamming her belongings in her backpack, she scribbled an apologetic note saying she needed to be on her own a bit. That she would be in touch.

There was just one thing to leave behind. Laying the bomber jacket on the bed, she gently brushed the wool collar and whispered a quiet goodbye to the man who had once worn it.

Then she crept down the stairs, shoes in hand. The house was flooded with early morning sunshine, and, to her relief, no one was yet stirring. Laying her note on the hallway table, she picked up a brochure listing the B&B's telephone and email address. Padding softly to the kitchen, she took some scones from a tin, a bottle of water, and several apples.

Leaving without saying goodbye in person, resorting to a hastily-penned apologetic missive was a habit becoming all too familiar. A habit she would say was cowardly in someone else.

Were she truthful with herself, she'd admit it was just as cowardly in herself.

Thirty-Three

June 1997

In Ullapool she withdrew the max advance available on her credit card—a thousand dollars, dispensed in pounds. She decided to get on the first bus that arrived and get off at the last stop it made. Then do that again. And again. Until she ran out of buses or towns. Or money.

It was the first journey she'd ever taken without a destination. Long, exhausting bus rides, some on motorways near towns and cities, others on winding highland roads through pristine villages and hamlets. In all directions, but never the whole way to Edinburgh. Hours in clean, brightly-lit waiting rooms, huddled over her backpack, or standing in line for fish and chips or a cup of tea. Sometimes wandering aimlessly through streets and neighborhoods.

She bought a novel but never opened it. She opened her journal but never wrote in it. She bought postcards but never sent them. If she arrived in the evening, she stayed at a guest house and stood in the shower until the metered hot water tank ran cold.

It's not about the destination; it's about the journey. Isn't that what some philosophers said once? But she had never been without a destination or acted without a plan. That is, before her impulsive decision to spend her semester abroad in Scotland. But even that had a purpose.

Four days into a trek from Elgin to Aberdeen, she caught a reflection of a haggard girl in the rain-splattered bus window.

Do people who love you lie to you? she mouthed fiercely to her reflection. "It's better to tell the truth than not, Beth," Henry always told her. Hypocrite! Who was there left to believe?

At the end of a week, she found herself at Mallaig and a ferry ride away from Skye. *What will I do in Skye but remember Robbie and long to see Colin?* She stood a long while then sighed. Her breath misted, phantom-like. *But then, what else is there to do?*

As the sun set, she got off the bus at the northeast tip of Skye on the Trotternish Peninsula in an isolated, scattered settlement called Flodigarry. The bus driver said there was a small hotel, a hostel, a post office, and a small grocer. He told her there was also a memorial to the famous Flora MacDonald, who had smuggled Bonnie Prince Charlie across the sea to Skye.

The hostel seemed clean and well-kept. She was greeted by a thirtyish white guy with dreadlocks, a face badly in need of a shave, and a surprisingly posh English accent. He showed her the shared kitchen, laundry facilities, lockers, and communal bathroom, adding that the least expensive accommodation was a bunk available in a four-bedroom.

The thought of sharing her sleeping space with strangers, coed in true hostel tradition, wasn't attractive, but tonight she was the only guest.

"You'll be just a night?" He eyed her backpack. "There's an outfitter back in Portree."

"Not sure," she said, realizing she was finally ready to be anchored somewhere. "Just looking to do some... ah... quiet. You know. Recover from school."

He handed her a registration form. "Been here awhile? In Scotland?"

"Since January."

"What school might that be?"

She saw no reason to lie. Who would track her here? "Edinburgh."

"Indeed. Great pubs. But here's the place to breathe."

She nodded, blurting on impulse, "If I wanted to stay a bit, is there anywhere to work?"

He pursed his lips and scrunched his face thoughtfully. "Can you brew a proper pot of tea? Whip up a batch of scones? Do a bit of cleaning? Rise early? Get breakfast ready by six?"

"Yes. I'm an early riser," she replied to his last question.

"The girl who was supposed to be here for the whole summer up and left last week without notice. I could use some help around the place."

"Do you own this place?"

"No, just run it with part-time staff." He smiled in a friendly way. "Been here about two years. Chucked the city life. Bernard's the name, by the way. Bernie for short."

Beth knew she was staring at him.

"Yah, I know." He shook his head, rattling the beads on his dreadlocks. "Well, can you make scones or the like?"

"With a recipe. I used to help my grandma..." She stopped, suddenly stricken with the thought of Naomi, alone in the kitchen, making pies on a Saturday night or biscuits with gravy on a Sunday morning. With no one to eat them.

Some sense of her unanchored state must have shown on her face, for Bernie said softly, "A lovely place to recollect yourself, Skye is. Places to walk, sit, think. Though the midges can be a nuisance on a still day. I need a hand till the end of August when the high season ends."

A place to recollect myself. A place where my money would stretch a bit further. A plan, at least for the next ten weeks.

"Sure, I'll do it."

"Then the rent is free, and the job comes with a tiny private room in the back. Have to use the communal loo, but you've got a grand view, a desk, and your own closet. Meals included, plus seventy-five pounds a week. We split the shifts and days. Someone always needs to be here to take reservations, greet visitors, cook. You don't mind scrubbing toilets, do you?"

She didn't.

He asked for no references and no next of kin.

With the immediate future settled, Beth adapted quickly to the routine.

The daily work of making breakfast for guests, cleaning the bathroom and kitchen, mopping the floors, and washing towels and sheets occupied her mornings, leaving her afternoons free, often to take a nap, except when she was assigned to "mind the store."

On those days she also took phone calls and reservations, registered guests, dealt with walk-ins, and handed out flyers or information. But there was always downtime in the afternoons or evenings to sit on the porch.

One afternoon when Bernie was out, she impulsively jotted a note to Naomi.

You probably know that Henry caught up with me on Achiltibuie. I assume he wrote you that he told me the whole story. In case he didn't, I want you to know I now know the truth. About Gretchen and Colin. How my mother was theirs, not the child of your marriage to Henry. How Henry stole my mother from her rightful family and lied to you about being her father.

I wanted you to know I understand so much more now than I ever did. And I realize why you were so bitter all those years, how you tried in your own way to love me even though I was not your granddaughter, but your sister's granddaughter. I understand how seeing me in that bomber jacket just brought it all back to you, as if it was ever far from your memory.

I don't know how you managed to stay with Henry all those years once you knew he had lied to you. Used you, really. I'm sorry if I've been the cause of grief and sorrow for you.

At some point, I will probably come back to the States. Right now, I'm working a summer job in a hostel on a Scottish island and just trying to come to grips with this new reality of who I am. I hope you are doing okay, and I'm really sorry that you are on your own now. I don't think it's at all fair of Henry to leave you after all these years.

But who am I to say what is right or wrong?

I hope it will be okay to come home when the time comes. Maybe then, you and I can make a new start. Find a new way to relate.

Before she could change her mind, she addressed an envelope she found in the living room desk, but put no return address on it, not wanting word to get back to Henry where she was. She knew she was being unfair to Naomi, denying her an opportunity to write if she chose to, but she couldn't bear the thought of Henry or Robbie finding her.

———⊠———

Despite her seven-day bus journey around Scotland, her mind was still in a whirl, a maelstrom of anger and agony as she paged through the mental book of her life, searching each scene for possible lies that Henry told her.

When that effort grew too exhausting, she'd review each detail of her search for Colin, rereading her journal. That inevitably led to thoughts of Robbie. But each time Robbie came to mind, she closed her mind to those thoughts.

There was someone completely new to think about instead. Gretchen. Her grandmother. How beautiful she must have been to inspire two men to love her ferociously. How alluring that Henry had never stopped loving her.

Finally, there was her own mother. Colin and Gretchen's daughter.

She wracked her brain for mental images of the pictures of Susanna that Henry had given her, trying to connect her mother's looks to her Scottish father. And to herself.

On her free afternoons, she explored the stunning scenery, including the long walk up to a series of pinnacles and grassy platforms known as the Quiraing. Other days, she took the gentle ramble down to the stony beach, where she sat on an old blanket, armed with a thermos of tea.

As time passed, the sigh of the wind on the tall grasses or the swish of the waves kissing the shore began to soothe her thoughts. The days meandered by like the clouds floating across the stunning blue dome of space above her. There, on what seemed like the edge of the world, she spent mindless hours simply watching the sea and the sky, both ever changeable, both ever dramatic, both ever surprisingly soothing, like a mind-numbing drug.

The routine of the hostel provided a helpful structure. The through hikers generally arrived at dinnertime and left right after breakfast.

Bernie always cooked a pot of soup or stew and threw together a salad, which guests could purchase for a small fee. It also served as dinner for her and Bernie. Oddly, the weekend hikers who had less time often lingered longer at the hostel, sharing hiking horror stories and swapping hints and tips. Occasionally a non-hiking tourist or two arrived to spend several days, exploring Skye on foot and by car.

When guests asked for her story, she said she was taking a break after a semester at Edinburgh University before heading back to the States.

On her third Wednesday, Bernie put up a "be back at 4" sign on the front door and said, "Let's play tourist." He took her to see the dramatic, cliff-hugging ruins of Duntulm Castle, once the stronghold of the Chiefs of Clan Donald. A week later, he invited her to go whale watching on Rubha Hunish, Skye's most northerly point.

"Get us out of the hostel. Good mental break," he explained, though Beth hadn't asked. True enough, she found the adventure a welcome change of pace.

"Shouldn't we lock up?" she questioned the following week when Bernie proposed another escape to the Museum of Island Life in the village of Kilmuir.

"Nah. Hikers have a code of honor," Bernie replied. Beth must have made a face, because he said with a sideways glance, "Honor's something you're not too sure of?"

"No, I believe in it."

"But you don't think others do?"

"Some people."

"Some people you know? You can lock any valuables... money, your passport... in the office safe if it'd make you feel better than leaving them in your room, which does have a key."

Beth nodded and followed Bernie silently to his beat-up green Peugeot. He had been an undemanding companion so far. Respectful of her privacy and her space. Asked no probing questions.

"You know, Beth, there are generally two kinds of people who end up here for extended periods of time." Beth climbed into Bernie's patched passenger seat. "There are the people who are running away from themselves..."

When the silence stretched for a bit, Beth probed, "And..."

"The people running toward themselves."

She glanced at him briefly then looked out the window. "Which are you, Bernie?"

He chuckled. "Started out I was trying to escape a future in finance. What a rat race."

"Where were you?"

"London. Sometimes New York. Sometimes Dubai. It was the high life. Lots of adrenaline. And coke."

"I take it you don't mean Coca-Cola." They both laughed. The sensation felt unfamiliar after so long.

"And then I took up photography."

"Ah, I see."

"Do you?" He put the car in gear and pulled away from the hostel.

"What did photography do for you?" Beth was genuinely curious.

"It taught me to see what I was looking at."

Beth let this bit of philosophy hang in the air. "I don't really want to talk about my life," she finally said.

"Didn't ask you to."

"No?"

"But if you'd want to, I'm a good listener. You learn to listen out here—to the wind, to the rain, to the hills."

"Going all ethereal on me, are you?"

"Spent a little time as a Rastafarian on my journey to Skye, by way of Jamaica."

"Don't worry, be happy?" She heard her own bitterness.

"I kept the dreadlocks. It took so damn long to grow them, I wasn't going to give them up easily. The philosophy kept some of it. Like to be tuned into nature. I'm not a Celt, but the locals here know how to commune with nature spirits."

"And you, Bernie?"

"I prefer to commune with malted spirits."

Beth laughed easily this time. "You're a piece of work, Bernie."

"Ah, thanks, Beth."

———— ✖ ————

She began to try her hand at making soup and bread and throwing together different combinations of salads, tasks she found comforting. Naomi had never let her do much in the kitchen. As a thank you, Bernie continued his weekly Wednesday "Skye education" ventures, taking Beth to his favorite overlook or up a mountain path. She had accumulated hiking gear, forgotten or discarded at the hostel, and purchased herself a good pair of boots. In her free time, she often brought a towel and a thermos of tea to the stony beach, letting the sound of waves wash away her sorrow, which throbbed like a raw wound.

He told her what Skye's place names meant. "The Gaelic cill means church," he explained. "That makes Kilmuir translate to the Church of Mary. Kilmaluag is related to St. Malaug and Monkstadt means Monks' farm in Norse."

He never told her the destination of their Wednesday trips, but she should have expected that one day she'd see the familiar sight of the Talisker Distillery. As he was pulling into the car park on a day in the middle of July, it was Robbie's voice, not Bernie's, that she heard explaining that Talisker came from the Gallic word meaning 'land of the cliff,' which came from the Norse word for "rock."

The heady scent of hops and barley reinforced the dizzying attack of déjà vu. She zoned out on the tour and begged off the tasting room, saying she'd meet Bernie in the gift shop.

She wandered to the display of amber liquid in various-sized containers and cartons. As she held a bottle of the famous single malt in her hands, she could hear Robbie extolling the special flavor of Talisker compared to highland blends.

The memory of the evening after their distillery trip swooped in like a punch to her stomach, and the feverish sensation of heated, intertwined bodies flushed through her. With a strangled groan, she thrust the bottle back on the shelf and rushed toward the door. Bernie found her hunched down by the passenger door of the car, her face buried in her hands.

"You've been here before," he said, almost an accusation.

Beth looked up at him, alarmed. He seemed almost put out.

"Yes." She replied hesitantly. He sat down beside her and muttered, "You never said."

She shrugged. "You never asked."

"No, I didn't. But I am now. You've been to Skye before, apparently."

"You said I didn't have to talk about my life. Besides, it was over long ago."

"You're not old enough for it to be long ago," he countered. "Besides, you've only been in Scotland since January, so it has to have been since then."

She looked away. "It's all so tangled up, all of it. Him. My family. Being here. Scotland. I wouldn't even know where to begin."

"Begin at the beginning and go until you get to the end." He jostled her gently.

"Not now, not here."

They sat in silence a few moments before he stood and reached down to take one of her hands. "Come, get in the car. We're going back. I'll order takeaway from the hotel. We have no one booked tonight."

She was too lost in her unexpected surge of grief to protest.

That evening, watching the sun sink into the west from the deck, she told Bernie the whole convoluted, messy story, beginning with the day she bought the bomber jacket. He let her tell it in her own way, handing her tissues when she broke down, waiting patiently for her to gather herself together. He interrupted only to ask the occasional question or get her a glass of water.

As she spun out her story, he cleared away the plates, fed the fire in the built-in pit, and brought her a warm throw. She left nothing out. Not the early dreams or the later visions, not the convoluted relationship with Robbie, nor the utter sense of devastation and betrayal she felt when she learned the truth of who Colin was and Henry's part in concealing it.

It took a very long time. The stars were out by the time she finished, and it didn't grow dark in Scotland at that point in the summer until nearly eleven. When she finished, Bernie said nothing for a while then, excusing himself, went inside. A few minutes later he returned with two glasses of amber liquid.

"Now it's time for a wee dram," he said, handing her a tumbler. "I added some water to yours because I know you're not a regular drinker." Even watered down, the whiskey was intensely warming. They sat in a long silence.

Beth let her eyes wander over the spectacle of a moonless night by the ocean in a place without light pollution. She felt as if she could reach up and grab a handful of stars.

"You could, and you should," Bernie said, startling Beth. Apparently, she had spoken aloud.

"And what about you, Bernie? Have you grabbed a handful of stars here on Skye?"

He let out a deep sigh. "Let's just say I've actually started seeing the stars again."

"You've been on a journey too."

He replied with a soft, "Yes."

"There's a universe down here as well as up there," Beth remarked, staring into the tiny twinkling bits of burning wood, all that was left of their fire.

"Ah, did you hear yourself, Beth?" His voice was gently probing, quietly supportive.

She pondered his question then asked one of her own. "You haven't asked me, like Robbie did early on, if I was doing drugs, hallucinating."

"I did not."

"Why not?"

"You didn't give Robbie the benefit of the entire story like you've given me. How the dreams crept up on you. How they began to expand and take on dimension. How you were able to inhabit them. Some people might think that was a drug-induced experience, but not me."

"Why not?"

"I've seen and lived more than my share of drug-induced experiences, and I've had a lot of interactions with people." You've been given a gift."

The rage that tore through Beth astounded her. She jumped up. "What the fuck are you talking about? A gift? I've been dragged through hell. How in God's name is that a gift?"

Bernie calmly sipped his dram. "It's about time you said it out loud."

She took a steadying breath then said quietly, "Bernie, you are so full of contradictions."

He laughed, then drank the rest of his Talisker in one swallow. "Who said a gift is always wanted or appreciated?"

After that day, Beth returned to her journal. She hadn't written a thing in it since early May. It took her several weeks and another whole journal to write the tale she had related to Bernie in one evening. She found that putting the last eight months of her life on paper in one continuous story was both excruciating and clarifying.

Her thoughts inevitably strayed to Naomi. She pondered a phone call for several days. Then when Bernie was out one afternoon, Beth sat next to the phone at the living room desk. It'd be about nine in the morning in Carlisle right now. Using her calling card, she dialed the number, feeling an ache in her stomach as the phone on the other side of the Atlantic began to ring.

"Yes?" Naomi's voice was abrupt. Unwelcoming. Beth found herself speechless.

"Who's there? Hello?"

"Ah, it's ah, me. Beth. Grandma, it's Beth."

There was a sharp intake of breath and the sound of chair legs scraping across the kitchen linoleum. Naomi must have sat down at the table.

"Grandma? Are you there?"

"Beth." Naomi's voice was tentative.

"Did you get my letter? I'm sorry I'd not written for a while. I've been... working."

"Yes. Yes, I did. So you know then," Naomi said, sounding more like herself to Beth. A tinge of bitterness. A sarcastic undertone.

"I know about your sister, my... who she is to me."

Naomi's sigh floated out. Then after a long pause, she replied more gently, "There's too much to tell you over the phone. Beth, when are you coming home? You know, I haven't... well, I haven't been well."

Beth gasped. "What do you mean? Not well in what way?"

Naomi grunted. "Damn heart, you see. I had a spell."

"When?! Oh, Grandma, I feel so bad. You all alone." Beth lowered her head onto the desk, overwhelmed. But the next bit had her sitting up straight.

"Alone?"

"I mean, with Gran... Henry in Scotland."

"Henry's here, Beth. He came home in late June when I told him I was in the hospital."

"Oh, my God! Grandma, the hospital!"

"I'm sorry, Beth. I read him your letter. So he would know you were in a safe place, and it was okay for him to come home."

Beth shook her head to clear it. "You... you wanted him to come home? I thought..."

"I know. I know what I said. I know he told you. But he also said you helped him make up his mind."

"I did?" Beth strained her mind to remember her conversation with Henry that day in May in the parlor, at dinner, in the cemetery.

"You said, why does it have to be one or the other? Paying his debts. Making amends."

"Oh," Beth replied, not even remembering. "And has he? Made amends."

Naomi's voice grew suddenly weary. "Beth, there's so much to say. I'm plumb worn out. Have to take it easy these days."

Her mind swirled. "Is Grandpa taking care of you? Is he there?"

"He's running errands. And yes, he's taking care of me. Like he always has tried to do."

Beth was astonished at this bit of praise for Henry from the always bitter Naomi. Maybe there was hope for them.

"When are you coming home, Beth? We can talk then."

"I don't know yet," Beth responded. Hurt tugged her one way, hope, fluttering hope, another way. "I'm obligated here till the end of August. Then, then I'll... I'll come home. In early September. After I go back to school and get my things and settle up my grades."

There. She made another plan. Another decision. Another forward step.

To her shock, Naomi said, sadly, "Beth, I... I miss you."

Beth felt her heart constrict. "I miss you too, Grandma," she said, and found to her surprise it was true. "I'll send you a postcard with my return address if you want to write me a letter. Tell me your story. I've only heard Henry's."

"Thank you, Beth. You're being very fair. And you sound so... grown up."

Beth smiled at Naomi's backhanded compliment. "I've sort of had to whether I wanted to or not. Gotta go, Naomi. Bye. You take care of yourself, please. And... tell Henry... Grandpa... I'm thinking about him too."

She thought she heard a quiet sob as she disconnected the call.

THIRTY-FOUR

AUGUST 1997

WITH HER NEXT STEP mapped out, Beth felt she could finally turn her mind to Robbie.

She started hiking for hours at a time, and during those hikes, she began to mentally relive both the delightful and the difficult interactions they'd had. How totally unprepared she had been for such an intense relationship. Sure, she'd had male acquaintances in college—mostly literary geeks who went with her to foreign films and art shows. It wasn't till last summer that she had ever dated seriously. And it was only four months ago she'd tasted the delights of lovemaking.

Oh, Robbie. History-loving Robbie. Considerate Robbie. Vulnerable Robbie. She had been terribly unfair and selfish to him. Cruel, really, the way she had suddenly shut the door on him just when their relationship had become intimate. At least Jason had carefully pushed past her hurt, angry walls and explained why he didn't return her kiss. Even now, she could still remember him gently pushing her on a swing as he told her in halting, stumbling words about his struggle to come to terms with his sexuality. The summer night air was thick with the threat of rain.

It was well after one in the morning when he walked her to her house and gave her a hug. "Don't worry, you're gonna blow some guy away someday. He'll fall head over heels in love with you."

Was that what Robbie had done? Fallen head over heels with her? What about Iain? No, she had just been a distraction for him, so far away from his Canadian girlfriend. Something to keep her mind off Robbie. But Robbie had never said he loved her. At least in words. But then, she hadn't either. She hadn't given him, or them, enough time to explore that possibility once their relationship turned physical.

She had used Colin as an excuse. A need to concentrate on the search for him. But would Colin have wanted her to give up the possibility of loving someone? Yet hadn't he, from Henry's story, given up twice on Gretchen?

And it was Henry who made it possible for Colin to be with Gretchen. No matter how sad their ending, Henry had in reality made it possible for her, Beth, to exist.

Love and life were just so complicated. She cared deeply for Robbie, but didn't love mean a commitment? Would she be willing to stay in Scotland for him? Not that he had asked. She still had things to do in her life. School to finish. And there were her grandparents in the States.

As she pondered her relationship with Robbie, she continued to take her weekly discovery tours with Bernie, who began telling her more about his life, although she was sure he edited the more lurid bits. His tales of life as a Rastafarian on Jamaica were hilarious. But he stunned her when he told her something she never suspected—he had been a member of the RAF ground crew that supported the 1991 Gulf War operations.

"You're a veteran? An RAF veteran? I thought you were a financier."

"I was. The war came at the end of my term of enlistment. It was my last deployment."

It was Wednesday of the third week of August, and they had taken a boat ride from Elgol to Loch Coruisk, tucked in between the Cuillen Hills. They were sitting on a dock bench after an hour of hiking, eating a hot pork pasty from the small store.

"Had you been in finance before?"

"Sort of. I had studied finance at the University of Oxford."

"Oxford?"

"I'm smarter than I look."

"Uh-huh. Then what?"

"I spent a couple years working in my dad's wealth management company in London, learning the ropes, being groomed for a climb up the corporate ladder, with a few steps skipped because I was the owner's son. But I hated it. And I decided to tick him off."

"By joining the Air Force?"

Bernie winked. "Yep. Told him I wanted to do something for God and King."

"And did you?"

"If you call loading cruise missiles onto fighter jets in the middle of Saudi Arabia giving God and King their due."

"So, you were ground crew?" Beth tried picturing Bernie in an RAF uniform.

"Like your grandfather."

Beth grew suddenly still. "He's not my grandfather."

"He was up until June."

"You make it sound like I fired him. Henry was never my grandfather... in truth. Our whole relationship is built on a lie. On a lot of lies."

Bernie looked at her intently then said, "I didn't see the kind of action your grandfather did. The Gulf War was brief. But I saw friends fly off and some of them didn't come back."

"So what? That's what war means, doesn't it?"

"You're very cavalier about losing your friends in combat," he said quietly.

Beth was ashamed of her remark but said defensively, "I'm sorry... I... but what's this got to do with Henry?"

"Has it ever occurred to you that war changes a man?"

Beth looked away. She didn't want to hear any more of Bernie's story.

Bernie told more regardless. "My grandfather was in the RAF in World War II. Ground crew. He was too old to fly but not too old to send 'em off night after night."

"Oh," Beth replied softly as she stared at the loch, a deep mysterious blue-green color.

"He never talked about the war much, though I asked. Except for one time. I was visiting him in the old folks' home. He was pretty feeble, though his mind was still sharp. We were sitting on the veranda, and he began talking. Almost to himself. He began listing the names of every member of bomber crews he worked with who hadn't come back."

Bernie took a swig of his Irn-Bru, the ubiquitous Scottish orange soda that Beth thought tasted like bubblegum.

"My grandfather said, 'I wrote them down, you see. In my diary. I thought that was the least I could do, to record their names. Everyone else tried to forget. Or at least pretend it didn't matter. *Got the chop, they did. Oh well.* Have another bloody drink. Kiss another pretty girl. We did lots of reckless and sometimes illegal things to forget that it could be us tomorrow.' " Bernie sighed.

"Then he went over to his dresser, opened a drawer, and returned with a small, battered, leather-bound journal and handed it to me. He said to me, 'Every day of my life, I've read every single name in this book. And I wonder, why did I survive? Why did I live through the war? Lots of bombs were dropped on airfields and cities. My cousin died in the London Blitz, and my aunt and uncle died in Coventry.'"

Beth felt herself grow chill despite the August sun on her face

"He gave me the book, Beth. And said, 'Bernie, I need you to honor these men. I need you to read their names every day. I know you didn't know them, but because they've impacted my life, they've impacted yours.'"

Beth turned now and looked at Bernie. He was sitting with his hands folded in his lap, his eyes closed, as if remembering. Or praying.

"He died a week later, and I joined up, the day after his funeral. Actually, it wasn't really to tick off my dad; it was to honor my grandfather, which I'm not sure it actually did in the end."

After some moments, he opened his eyes and looked at her. "Maybe your Grandfather Henry has a list of his own."

Several mornings later Bernie came into the kitchen where Beth was just taking freshly-baked scones from the oven. As she stood up with the cookie sheet, she glanced his way and spilled the doughy confections on the counter.

Bernie was sitting on a barstool at the breakfast island between the kitchen and living room. Completely bald.

Beth was stunned speechless. When the silence drew out for a minute, Bernie grinned. "It'll grow out."

Beth simply stared. He looked a bit like Bruce Willis. Certainly nothing like the Bernie she had come to know. He looked younger. More vulnerable.

Bernie picked up the scones from the counter and put them in a basket then poured himself a cup of coffee. "I'm hungry," he said, finishing off a scone in three quick bites then asked, "I assume you're still leaving next week, at the beginning of September?"

Beth nodded.

"Then what?"

She laid out plates, jam, and butter on the counter and filled her mug with the Darjeeling she had just brewed, giving herself a moment to formulate her answer. She sat next to him. "Well, I've given it a lot of thought. I decided I'd go back to Edinburgh, retrieve any of my things that might still be there, and then head to the States. I didn't tell you, but I called my grandmother."

"I figured as much. You got a letter from someone named Schmidt in Pennsylvania some weeks back."

She tutted. "Bernie. You snoop."

"Hey, it was right there on the envelope. I couldn't help seeing it. So I figured you either wrote her or called her and gave her your address."

Beth nodded. Naomi's letter had been short, but full of details about her hospital stay and her diagnosis of congestive heart failure, which Naomi said sounded worse than it was. Apparently, she just wore out sooner than she used to. She also said Henry was relieved to hear she was fine and that she'd be home in September.

"What will you do when you go back home?" Bernie prodded gently.

"Find a job, enroll in school for January, and finish my degree."

"And will you stay with your grandmother?"

"Grandparents. Apparently, Henry went back at the end of June."

"Ah, I see. So you'll be needing to reconcile with him after all."

Pointedly silent, Beth carefully slit open a warm scone, slathered each half with butter and topped them with a dollop of blackberry jam she had made last week.

"I'll give you a ride to Edinburgh, Beth."

She looked up in surprise. "You don't have to do that, Bernie. I'm quite capable..."

"I know you're quite capable," he interrupted, making short shrift of another scone, not bothering with any toppings. "You're quite capable of many things, including forgiveness."

Beth felt her jaw tighten. "I don't want a lecture."

"I'm not giving you one." Bernie snagged a third breakfast treat from the basket. "I'm simply stating a fact."

Beth sighed.

"I'm heading back south to London, stopping in Edinburgh to see some friends."

"That account for the... scalping?"

"Guess it looks like a scalping. Just needed to get a head start. Get it...?" He chortled, spewing a couple of crumbs.

Beth shook her head at his pun. "Taking a break from the hostel life?"

"Not a break. I'm not coming back."

"Oh?" It was hard to imagine the hostel without him.

He took a swallow of his coffee. "This was never intended to be a lifestyle, only a stop on the road. It's time I reintegrated into society. It's been arranged. One of the staff at the hotel will be taking over. It's something she's been wanting to do for a while."

"But isn't this a life? That girl thinks it's a life, apparently. Lots of people live on Skye."

"It's not *my* life. Besides, I need to go see my parents, my brother, and my sister. I haven't spoken to any of them since the day I returned from Saudi Arabia."

Beth mentally calculated the years, but he got there first.

"Six years."

"Have you written..."

"Nope. Not a call, card, or communication of any kind."

"And they had no idea where you were?"

"I kept in touch with a cousin. She must've let them know because I always get a card from my mother on my birthday."

"But..." Beth felt a bit guilty about not communicating with her grandmother, but it hadn't been six years.

"My father was furious when I quit the firm to join the Air Force and then even more furious when I refused to be treated like a hero when I came home. They had arranged this big party, and I wouldn't go. Great publicity for the firm, you see." He picked at a scone. "I couldn't be a hypocrite. I didn't feel like a hero. I had done nothing heroic."

"Bernie, I..."

"And neither was it heroic to disappear out of their life. I know that. And now it's time to make amends. I hope you won't take six years to make amends with your grandfather."

Beth struggled to keep the tears from her eyes.

"Beth, I'm the one that lost out. I missed my sister's wedding, the birth of two nephews, my father's very serious illness, and an Air Force buddy's funeral. He died of a drug overdose."

He retrieved another cup of coffee then leaned on the counter across from her. "I was nearly twenty-nine when I came back from the service, but I wasn't really grown up. Just messed up. Wound up. Bitter, too. And too much of a coward to face my own questions. So I ran away. *Don't worry; be happy.* But it was all a lie. Just a way to avoid being a man. It didn't have to be all or nothing, but I made it so. It's time for me to stop running away. I need to start running *toward* again. See what's next."

He stared into the dark liquid. "It's really been these two years on Skye that have helped me get my head on straight. I'm not sure I'll ever go back to living in London, but I'm thinking about teaching photography. Working with veterans."

Beth could think of nothing to say. There was so little she knew or understood about this man she had spent nearly three months with.

"I have a favor to ask of you, though," he added, looking up. Beth looked at him warily. "What is it?"

Bernie laid his hand over hers. "Go see Robbie before you leave for the States."

—✵—

Edinburgh in early September felt like October in Pennsylvania, Beth thought. The days were in the high fifties, but at night it grew quite chilly. She declined Bernie's offer to stay with his friends, instead making reservations at a hotel near the University. She stood next to Bernie's car at the hotel entrance, holding her backpack.

"I'm only going to say goodbye one time, Beth," he said. "I don't believe in dragging it out, either. But I don't mind staying in touch if you want to." He handed her a card with a London address. "This is my parents' address. They'll know where I am. I've been in touch with them." He grinned.

At her skeptical look, he smiled wryly. "Honest. I'm done running away from myself. And from them." He gave her a quick kiss on the cheek.

"Wait," she said, reaching into her backpack. "I have a present for you."

"Ah, damn it, Beth, I..."

"No, it's something practical." She handed him a driving cap in herringbone tweed.

"Oh, God..." He laughed in a way she hadn't heard before, settling it on his bald head.

"Winters in London get a mite bit chilly, I understand," she said.

"They do, indeed." With a tip of his hat and a courtly bow, he was gone.

And Beth was back in Edinburgh, trying to think of ways to arrange an unemotional goodbye to Robbie. For to leave without seeing Robbie would have been an uncalled-for act of heartlessness, and it hadn't taken Bernie's request to make up her mind.

But then maybe Robbie didn't want to see her. Things had ended so badly between them. Maybe he'd put it all behind him. Well, one way or the other, *she* needed to see him and thank him for all he did for her grandfather.

The next morning she went shopping. She bought new jeans; a soft blouse; a fitted sweater; a classy, fall, padded jacket; and a pair of ankle-height boots then went to the hairdresser to restore her bob. After months in grungy clothes or hiking gear, it felt good to be dressed up.

Then she bought her plane ticket. Surprisingly, she was excited about going home. Even with the emotional challenges that faced her there.

By early afternoon she was walking across campus toward the registrar's office, praying she would not run into Robbie on her quest for her possessions and a formal withdrawal from the University. She wasn't ready to see him yet.

It was a prayer not answered.

Thirty-Five

September 1997

As Robbie made his way across campus that afternoon, he had every hope of seeing Beth. Henry had called recently from Pennsylvania to tell him that Beth was planning a trip to the University to formally withdraw from college. Henry had also called in mid-July to inform him Beth was safe and working at a hostel on Skye.

That Beth was spending the summer on Skye was a punch in the gut. That was where their relationship had become something solid. Real. Beautiful, until the last day. He'd racked his brain trying to determine what he had done to make her slam the door in his face. She had been a willing participant, in fact, the initiator of their lovemaking.

She must have cared for him. Maybe even loved him.

But after meeting Henry and hearing the whole convoluted, heartbreaking story of lies and deception, of love lost and promises betrayed, he realized that Beth was caught up in something beyond him. That the RAF pilot whose bomber jacket she'd been wearing was her real grandfather more than unnerved him. It was a supernatural connection he didn't understand and wasn't sure he wanted to.

No wonder Beth had been distant and distracted half the time. There was probably much about her ghost story that she hadn't told him. As it was, he had accused her of being on drugs when she had tried to explain it during their encounter at Holyrood. No wonder she'd rarely confided more, other than at the Wallace Monument when she claimed to have seen the pilot... that the pilot saw *her*.

Maybe Beth would prefer not to see *him*. He was probably just one more complication in her already knotted life, made all the messier by her suddenly disappearing without a trace, not once, but twice. He hated the damn drama of it. But at least he'd met Henry, the man who meant so much to Beth.

Though Henry had done an unbelievably despicable thing in stealing Colin's daughter from his family, he had liked Henry from the moment they met. Who could explain what love would drive a man to?

Love, if that was what it was, had driven him nearly mad these last four months, first as he helped Henry track down Beth to Achiltibuie then doing the noble thing by not staying to see her so he didn't distract her from their reunion. And next, finding out she'd vanished again, agonizing for weeks about where she was, what she was doing, if she was safe. Until Henry, in his weekly call from Achiltibuie, said Beth had been in touch with Naomi, and she was working in a hostel on some Scottish island.

For some reason, the idea of Skye never crossed his mind.

Until then he had constantly watched for her around Edinburgh, around the campus, sure she'd return for her things or retake her exams.

"You've gone off the deep end, mate," Andrew told him after two weeks of trekking daily to the places she hung out with that Canadian kid.

As he reminisced about the events of May, Robbie ducked into the student union building for a cup of coffee, still mulling over his encounter with Beth's grandfather.

He had picked Henry up at London Heathrow, finding other professors to cover his office hours and tutorials, explaining to the department head that he had a family emergency, without going into details. It didn't go down well, and he was already on thin ice with the dean.

His original idea of researching Scottish pilots named Colin at the London War Museum proved unnecessary, for Henry told him Colin's full name and where he was buried. However, Robbie suggested they check at the Museum to see if anyone remembered her visiting. That would confirm his hunch about her ultimate destination.

By luck, they'd encountered the same intern who'd shown Beth Colin's service record. She was all apologetic about how Beth had taken the information, running out of the building. Like she was freaked out. Made her feel terrible, the intern said.

Robbie thought Henry would collapse when this thoughtless girl started blabbering on about Beth's reaction to reading Colin's record. The old man looked like he hadn't slept a wink on his overnight flight from Philadelphia. Though he'd tried to get Henry to check into a hotel, Henry had insisted they start the search for Beth immediately.

On the long trek to Edinburgh, Henry told him the whole agonizing story about Gretchen, Colin, and Fiona and then the unbelievable tale of how he'd lied to Naomi about Susanna's parentage. By the time they reached Robbie's apartment, he was truly worried about Henry, who was ashen and short of breath.

They ate a hearty takeaway dinner; then he settled Henry in for the night. Andrew had graciously bunked in with a friend so Henry could have his bed. After Henry had retired, Robbie researched Achiltibuie and found two B&Bs and a hotel. He called the first B&B, telling them he was a history professor researching World War II pilots and was looking for the family of Colin McAuley. The first B&B referred him to the other, where he struck gold.

When the woman who answered hesitantly said she was Colin's niece, Robbie cautiously told her he was with an American friend, Henry Schmidt, and did they have room at the B&B if they arrived tomorrow. The woman was silent for a long moment then said, hold on, she'd have to ask her mam.

In a few moments, she was on the phone again. In a tentative, Highland voice she asked, "Professor McLeod, is Mr. Schmidt aware that his granddaughter Beth is staying here?"

For a moment, Robbie couldn't draw a breath then with a deep inhale replied, "I, ah, I had hoped she would be. You see, that is, he's been looking for her. I don't want to say too much; it's not my place, but she left campus early, and I was... well... very concerned. She'd been... upset lately. She was researching... a pilot."

"Aye, I see. Yes. That does make sense and explains a lot. How she knew to come here. She's been quite upset but hasn't really explained why. We sort of wondered, you see. My mam says she looks so much like her brother Colin."

Struggling with words, Robbie finally managed, "I knew she was very focused on finding out about him. I think she's probably had a bit of a shock. Does she know that Colin..."

"Nay, nay. She doesn't seem to have made the connection. And it t'weren't our place to say so. I'm verra happy Henry is coming. It'll be him who needs to tell her the story, but it won't be easy for her to hear. Till then, we'll na say a thing."

"Good," Robbie sighed in relief, both to know Beth was somewhere safe and that she'd be surrounded by family when she learned the truth of her heritage. "I'll be bringing Henry tomorrow; it'll be mid to late afternoon till we get there, but I'll not stay. I don't... I... that is, I think it's best not to distract Beth."

Robbie could almost hear the speculation in the silence.

"Verra well, Professor. I'll let my mam know to expect Henry tomorrow. If you dinna want to stay here, there's another B&B along the road."

"Thank you," he replied, "but I'll need to get back to campus."

It had been torture to drop Henry off at the B&B entrance, knowing Beth was either inside or nearby. He'd driven the whole six-hour return trip home, pumping up his adrenaline with endless cups of high-octane coffee and sugary treats.

"Professor McLeod," a young feminine voice with a decided English accent interrupted his reverie. "Oh please, I have some questions for you about yesterday's lecture."

Robbie sighed, slowing down, forcing his mind off a different student.

She spotted him first, heading toward her, holding his ubiquitous cup of takeaway coffee. He was chatting with a pert blonde who appeared to be hanging on his every word. At least she wasn't hanging onto him. She assumed it was a student.

The encounter wasn't unexpected; the surge of jealousy was.

She half-heartedly hoped he'd walk by without noticing her but felt herself slowing down, studying his familiar face, his hair curling at the collar, his neat beard, his trim physique. Feeling her heartbeat in her head. They were only a few feet away when he looked up from his conversation and came to a sudden halt. Clearly, she had caught him off guard.

"Beth?" his voice was raspy.

The girl's pouty look almost made Beth laugh. "Robbie."

They stared at each other in silence until the blonde interrupted. "Ah, Professor, about that question on the history..."

"I'm sorry, Miss Matthews, we'll have to take that up later." There was no mistaking his dismissive tone. The girl glared at Beth, walking on.

When she was out of earshot, Robbie said fiercely, "You could have let someone know where you've been. Your grandfather..."

Beth was having none of it. "He's not my grandfather, Robbie. I'm sure he's told you the whole story by now."

"Can we get a cup of..."

"No, really. I've not much time. I came to see if I can get my things from the..."

"I have them."

Now it was Beth who was taken aback. "You what?"

"When the semester ended and you weren't here, I asked Anja to pack your things, and I stored them at my flat. I figured once you were back in touch with your... with Henry... he'd tell you how to get your things."

"Well, that didn't happen. So, you're holding them hostage?" Beth wasn't sure if she was angry or touched. It was easier to be angry, recalling how Robbie's interference had prompted Henry's exhausting transatlantic trip, the argument between Henry and Naomi, and maybe even Naomi's heart condition. "If I hadn't run into you, I'd be leaving without my things."

"Are you leaving?"

"Of course, I'm leaving." She was trying to stay angry. She knew she was being unfair because, despite the negative repercussions of Henry's trip, it had been the beginning of a healing process for many people. But being angry might prevent making a fool of herself.

"Where are you leaving to?" His voice was curt.

"Home, of course."

Suddenly his tone altered. "Where's home, Beth?" he asked tenderly.

Without warning, tears flooded her eyes. She had to blink fiercely to keep them from slipping down her cheeks. The last thing she wanted to do was cry in front of Robbie.

"Please, come have a cup of coffee with me. Tell me what I can do to help you."

"Help me do what?" Her voice cracked. It was hard to ignore the subtle pleading in his voice. Or deal with his question about home.

"With whatever you need. Petitioning to take your finals. Officially withdrawing from the University. Getting a ride to the airport."

Her mind awhirl, she focused on the first thing he said. "Finals? I can still take them?"

"It'll take a bit of doing, but it's quite possible. Then you can get your courses officially transferred to your American college and get credit for your semester here."

Beth felt sudden excitement. "I can take my exams? It won't have been a wasted semester."

When she saw Robbie flinch, she realized how he had taken her words. She wanted to correct herself and say, *It wasn't a wasted semester, Robbie. It was the most life-altering months of my entire existence, and you were a major part of that.*

Instead, she kept to something safe, "How do I go about making that happen?"

"We can go to the Chair of the Visiting Students Department and..." Robbie began but stopped when he saw her frown.

"Is it something I can do on my own? And if so, how much time will it take?"

"On your own?" She heard disappointment in his voice.

For the first time, she let her face soften. "Robbie, I'm not trying to be ungrateful…"

"I know. But it's okay to let someone help if they can get it done quicker. And you said you're under a time frame?"

"I have tickets for next Thursday," she replied.

"It's Tuesday, so a little over a week. Please let me see what I can do to help you."

Beth pictured Bernie standing next to her, arms crossed, his head tilted. He still had dreadlocks in her imagination.

"You're right. That makes sense."

Robbie visibly relaxed. "Great. Let's start in the administration building."

She found his air of determined capability both familiar and acceptable. She could deal with this Robbie. By four-thirty, she had filled out all the necessary paperwork, and Robbie had taken her to see both professors whose finals she had missed. It was all taken care of. She could take her exams on Friday morning.

As they left the second professor's office, Beth said, "Friday. Wow! I haven't thought about school and tests since early May. I'll need to cram…"

"I have your books and materials at my apartment," Robbie interrupted. "I can arrange a tutor…"

Beth shook her head. "I have my own system of studying, Robbie, I'll need to hunker down."

"Where are you staying?"

She named the hotel. "I can arrange…" he began, but she shook her head again. "I already turned down Bernie's offer to stay with him and his friends."

Robbie's face turned stony. "Bernie?" He dragged out the name in a sarcastic tone.

"Yes. Bernie. A friend. We worked together…" Beth stopped, suddenly reluctant to tell Robbie she had been on Skye for the last three months.

"Worked together? On Skye?"

She glared at him. "How did you know I was on Skye?"

"Henry called me after you sent the first letter to Naomi, so I didn't know you were on Skye until a few weeks ago."

"You've been in touch with Henry this whole time?"

"Of course, Beth. He was worried about you."

"And you?"

Robbie grunted. "If you have to ask, why bother talking about it." When she didn't respond, he added in a strained voice, "How about if you come by my flat and pick up your things."

"Yes, that would be good. When would it be convenient?"

"I'm done for the day now. And the flat's within walking distance. We can borrow Andrew's car to get your things to the hotel if we need to."

She nodded.

As they walked the blocks to Robbie's flat, he was uncharacteristically silent. Beth longed for him to be his professorial self and give her a lecture about the area of Edinburgh they were walking through. Though she ached to tell him everything she had gone through since May, she wasn't ready to open that door. Besides, she had little more than a week left in Scotland.

Back to the States. Home. If it still was one.

They loaded the bag of books, her laptop, and her suitcases into Andrew's car. She was glad Robbie's roommate was nowhere in sight. She didn't want to meet him under these circumstances. At the hotel, Robbie parked in the drop-off and retrieved a luggage trolley. She politely but pleasantly declined his offer of help taking her things upstairs, as well as his suggestion they have dinner.

"I have two days to get my brain wrapped around material I haven't thought about since spring. I'm just going to get take away and study as much as I can for two days."

He was standing next to the car. "And after Friday? What will you do until you leave next Thursday?"

"I'm going to Achiltibuie to see my family."

He looked at her intently. "Your family," he said softly.

She nodded. "Yes, my family."

"I can drive you. I'm done with lectures by two on Friday."

Beth longed to say yes. Ached to spend hours in a car telling Robbie about these last months, but she wanted time to prepare herself for a return trip to Achiltibuie. She shook her head slowly.

His defeated look nearly broke her heart. "Will I see you again? Before you leave? Can I take you to the airport Thursday? What time's your flight?"

"How about if I call you Wednesday? I'll make sure I'm back by Wednesday night."

He looked at her, unsmiling. "Right-oh. Wednesday. Good luck on your exams, Beth, and with... your visit."

He got in the car but rolled down the window.

"If you need anything Beth..."

"I know, Robbie. Thank you. For everything." When he pulled away, she realized how final it sounded.

The first thing she did was send an email to Clara using the B&B's website. "I'm in Edinburgh now making up the finals I missed. I'm leaving next Thursday for the States, but I'd like to come visit this weekend. I'll be there Saturday, late in the day. Then I'll need to leave Tuesday."

Clara wrote back, "Of course, my dear! We anxiously await your visit. Mam will be so pleased you are coming."

The final bit of business was composing an airmail letter to Naomi, explaining her plans and arrangements for transportation from the airport. Not to have Henry pick her up. With all that taken care of, she once again locked Robbie in a corner of her mind and got down to studying. It felt good to concentrate on something so intensely.

Friday morning was taken up with her two exams, proctored in a classroom. She wasn't the only student, so it probably wasn't an uncommon event. By Friday at two, she was on a train to Inverness.

The hotel stored her luggage, and she took only her backpack, packed for the weekend.

———— ※ ————

It was early afternoon when she rang the doorbell at the B&B. Clara answered, her face wreathed in smiles. "Oh. Oh. Oh, my dearie, oh. Come in. Come in. 'Tis quite the chill blowing out there, aye, on this drizzly day. Your cheeks are a bloomin' with pink. Come have some tea."

As she led the way, she said, "Put your things here by the guest registry table. We'll go into the parlor. Mam is there."

Beth tried not to flinch, but Clara caught the look.

She lowered her voice and put her arm around Beth. "I know you've had a difficult time of it. It can't 'ave been easy to learn the truth of your family the way ye did. And I know that Henry isn't your blood grandfather. That he made some terrible choices. But Beth dearie, he raised you. He was father and grandfather to ye. And he loves you terribly."

Unbidden, Bernie's words flitted across her mind. "Maybe your Grandfather Henry has a list of his own." She couldn't begin to imagine the losses Henry had suffered, of losing the woman he had followed across the ocean and the pilot who had become his best friend. And then on top of that, their friend Fiona. All those losses had driven him to make the choices he had. Who knew what choices she might have made in those circumstances?

As she followed Clara into the parlor, a shaft of sunshine suddenly burst through the gray, overhanging clouds and shot into the room. With it, a sense of Colin's presence filled the space. Then she knew. She hadn't lost Colin. He was right here. Reflected in the faces of his sister and niece. Carried in the heart of the man who had been his closest friend, the man who had raised her and loved her as if she were his own daughter. The man waiting for her to come home. On the other side of the Atlantic.

———— ※ ————

The four days were filled with stories, memories, and laughter. Learning about her Scottish lineage through food, through folklore, and even meeting several local relatives warmed her heart in a way she didn't know she needed. More than that, she got to know Colin as a boy and a young man through pictures that Mairi showed her. She saw Colin with Henry and Gretchen on their visit to Achiltibuie in December of 1942.

Mairi shared more about the three friends' complicated relationship from her perspective as Colin's sister. "Remember, time and distance dinna change love. Your Grandfather Henry never stopped loving Gretchen, and he loved her enough to give her what she most wanted. Colin." During these long talks, Beth felt the pain of these last months fading.

On Tuesday after breakfast, Beth brought the bomber jacket down. She found it in the closet of Colin's old room, where they had put her up again. "Mairi," she said when she laid it in her lap, "this is for you. This was Colin's, and I think it belongs here."

Mairi's aged face grew moist from tears. "Ah, ye blessed child. Ayre ye sure? It looks so right on ye."

Beth nodded, feeling stronger than she had in months. "It brought me to you. But it needs to be here with his other things. Taken out and shown to his family."

"To your children, Beth. That means you'll be needin' to bring 'em home to Scotland when that time comes."

Beth nodded, unable to speak.

"And 'ye're to be comin' back often, nay?"

"Often," Beth smiled, then laid her head in Mairi's lap, atop of the bomber jacket which smelled of old leather, damp wool, and the faintest ancient lingering odor of airplane fuel.

It was early evening when she reached her hotel. She had only to repack one suitcase, and then she'd be ready for tomorrow's plane trip. As she did, she found notes inside from both Anja and Iain, which included their home addresses and phone numbers and a request to let them know she was okay. And an invitation from Iain to come visit Canada. It made her smile.

At nine, after a shower and a room service dinner, she climbed into bed and picked up the phone to call Robbie. He answered on the first ring.

"Hi there," she said, working hard to infuse cheer in her voice. The realization that she was finally leaving Scotland had begun to sink in.

"Hi there, yourself," he replied tentatively.

"I'm sorry it's so late. I hope it's not too late to call."

"It's never too late, Beth."

She let his statement hang in the air.

"Are you still leaving tomorrow?" he asked.

"Yes."

The silence was heavy. There was so much Beth wanted to say, but there wasn't time. In less than twelve hours, she'd be on a plane. Once again, her plans seemed to leave no room for Robbie. The realization intensified the ache in her heart. But she was too much of a coward to share it with him.

"You know, it might be easier if I just got a taxi. I mean I'd hate to put you out."

"Is that what you think you've done?" His voice was suddenly angry.

"I just thought maybe..."

"Oh, for crying out loud, Beth. These months, you think you've been an inconvenience?"

Beth felt his fury battering against the strong walls she had built around her heart. Like a cartoon drawing, she saw a vision of Robbie in knight's armor, battering ram in hand, racing toward a castle wall she was hiding behind.

"No, Robbie. It's just, I... I'm... I can't find the words to explain. To say how I feel. What you've meant...."

The silence stretched out uncomfortably. He finally said, "Meant? As in past tense?"

Beth left his question unanswered, and after a pause, he sighed. "Fine. Just tell me what time I should pick you up." His words sounded slow, weary.

She didn't want to fight anymore. "Six. Can you pick me up at six?" "I'll be in front of the hotel at six." The phone clicked down. She had heard him angry, shocked, bitter. But never resigned. Well deserved. But at this point, what was there to say?

She had a terrible night's sleep, filled with dreams of knights storming castles and of her throwing rose petals out a tower window. But never the whole rose.

She was out front well before six, shivering in the cold air, working up the courage to say the things he deserved to hear.

Robbie was prompt and uncommunicative on most of the thirty-minute ride to the airport through the dark streets and countryside of Edinburgh. When he greeted her, his voice was low and polite, his face calm but drawn. There was no anger in his eyes but no smile either. In the uncomfortable stillness, Beth mentally flipped through mental photographs of their time together. Their amusing meeting on the train where he showered her with lined yellow tablet notes about WWII airplanes; the next awkward encounter at Holyrood and his well-intended yet clumsy insults about her unnerving experience of hearing Colin's voice being drug-induced. His sweet way of making up by offering to take her places on her grandfather's list.

She shot a furtive glance his way. He was staring ahead, a grim expression on his face. She longed to reach over and soothe away the lines of tension. So much of her relationship with Robbie was intertwined with her search for Colin; they both grew unnervingly complicated and intense at the same time. She thought of Traprain Law and the Wallace Monument.

She took a deep breath, clearing her thoughts of Colin. Robbie looked over and then away. Her heart twinged at his distance.

This isn't about Colin, she reminded herself. This is about Robbie. From the very beginning, he was someone she was attracted to. Someone whose company she enjoyed immensely. The night at the movies, dinner at the Indian restaurant. Their conversations. His thoughtfulness. His increasing tenderness. Their shared joy on Skye.

After all that, she owed him an explanation. An apology. Finally, as they approached the International Terminal, brightly lit in the predawn September morning, she screwed up her nerve and plunged in. "Robbie?"

He glanced sideways at her.

"I'm thinking... I think... there's things... I need to... say to you. That I should have... said months ago."

He grunted but said nothing else, clearly waiting. Shit, this was hard.

"I think, I think... I owe you an apology. Wait, no—" she wrung her hands. "Th-There's more, but that's where... where I need to start."

He pulled a short distance from the drop-off point and put on the blinkers, then turned in his seat to face her, his expression flat. "Well... start then."

"I don't want to make excuses. I was horribly rude... no, cruel. Stupid. Just Naïve. Confused."

He continued to stare at her wordlessly.

"I... my visions..." No, definitely not that, he never understood. She took another breath. "Robbie, by now... you know. You know... everything. I had to leave... you. I had to. But..." She gripped her hands tighter. "But I shouldn't have left like that. Cutting you off so suddenly... Going silent like that... I should have tried to explain..."

Beth forced herself to meet Robbie's gaze, even as she trembled a little. "You didn't deserve that." She closed her eyes, remembering his stunned confusion and anguished voice when he dropped her at her dorm. "You didn't deserve that." She whispered.

Robbie's hand lighted gently on her arm. "Are you all right?"

His soft voice crumbled all the walls she had built around her heart. She had so not wanted to cry in front of him. But she did now, her hands covering her eyes. How she ached for a different ending to their story.

"I owe you an apology too, Beth," he said, his hand a comforting presence on her shoulder. "For misjudging you. For not listening. For not believing that you had this uncanny gift to see into the past. To be a... I don't know... a medium... that sounds too weird... a vehicle for bringing about healing for a wound from fifty years ago." He shook his head. "I won't pretend I understand it now, but... I should've taken you more seriously."

Beth lifted her damp face and took in the tenderness in the eyes of this man she could so easily come to love. Or maybe already loved. But they were out of time.

A knock on the driver's side window startled them both.

"You can't park here, sir," a uniformed security officer said sternly. "This is a drop-off area."

"Yes, sir, yes, will be moving in a moment," Robbie said, then turned to Beth. They stared at each other silently for a minute before he nodded and pulled the car ahead in front of the British Air terminal.

"Can you pop the trunk?" She jumped out of the passenger side and retrieved her backpack from the back seat. Robbie walked around to the rear of the car. She drew in deep breaths to calm herself.

She snagged a luggage trolley from nearby. Robbie lifted the suitcases one at a time onto the waiting cart. Then, slamming the trunk shut, he stood looking at her. Waiting. He was always waiting. But how long would he continue to wait?

"So then, what are your plans on going back?"

She cleared her thick throat. "I'm going to finish up my undergrad at Shippensburg, and then, well, I'm thinking of a master's in history."

Quietly, he added, "And *where* might you be taking this master's?"

"Well, let's see. Probably not Shippensburg." She laughed nervously. "Probably, probably somewhere in... Scotland?" She looked at him solemnly. "What would you think of that?"

"I think..." He gently touched her arm. "I think your Scottish family would like it very much if you came back here for your master's. And your American family would miss you."

Her voice was shaky, "And... you?"

He shrugged. "I'll probably still be teaching a bunch of bamstick freshmen." He jammed his hands into his coat pockets.

"But you didn't answer my question."

She thought of his answer later, as the airplane climbed into the sky, over the city she had come to love, heading away from the country that felt so much like home.

"Nae, I suppose I haven't," he had replied, cupping her face, wet with her tears, in his warm hands, kissing her tenderly on her eyes, on her cheeks, and then on her mouth. Telling her with his lips what he wouldn't say with his words. Words she herself couldn't admit to.

Leaving her standing there, watching him drive away into the brightening morning. Knowing her heart would always be torn between two places on either side of the Atlantic.

THE END

ABOUT K.M. KING

K.M. King has lived countless lives—member of the United States Army, legal secretary, editor of a community newspaper, junior high school English and history teacher, staff development specialist in the disabilities field, personal coach, corporate trainer, and author.

She and her husband Dana reside in Lancaster County, Pennsylvania. They have two children and four grandchildren. She enjoys playing scrabble, dabbling in abstract art, writing poetry and fiction, and engaging in philosophical discussions. Her K-drama obsession intensifies through her blog *Kdrama for Life*.

The Bomber Jacket is her first published novel.

Learn about K.M. King's upcoming works, explore a book club discussion guide to The Bomber Jacket, and connect to her blogs at her website: www.kmkingauthor.com.

ACKNOWLEDGEMENTS FOR THE BOMBER JACKET

Many people supported me in my long journey to publication, and I am forever grateful. Thank you to the many beta readers who gave feedback on the many versions the book took to its final form.

My husband Dana always encouraged my passion for writing and provided time and space for me by doing more than his share of the daily tasks involved in raising children and maintaining a home. He never objected when I went away to write for extended weekends or even a whole week.

Special and heartfelt thanks to my friend, Dani Church, who lent hands-on editing expertise in shaping the story and honing the characters, then helped search for agents even as her cancer relapsed. It is a bittersweet part of this journey that she did not live to see *The Bomber Jacket* in print.

It may seem odd to acknowledge a country, but were it not for the beauty and allure of Scotland that transfixed me over many trips, this novel may never have come to be. I'm thankful for the curiosity and questions of my grandchildren Zoe, Owen, and Lola that shaped the story on our visits to the UK. (Olive, your trip is coming soon!)

And many, many thanks to my sister, Riley Kilmore, whose middle grade novel, *Shay the Bray*, was recently published by Wild Ink Publishing. Riley asked Abigail Wild to look at one of my manuscripts. Though I had several to choose from, I decided I'd give *The Bomber Jacket* one last chance after a string of rejections over a number of years. Abby not only accepted my book for publication but also designed the cover, which perfectly captures my vision of the story. Sometimes, it takes a long time for an author to meet the right publisher. So, if you're a writer, don't give up. Believe in your story. And thanks, too, to Brittany McMunn and the other Wild Ink staff for so much behind-the-scenes work.

Special credit to Ian Tan, my editor at Wild Ink. He championed my story and characters while being an exacting craftsman. He gave me the creative freedom to work within his editorial guidance, never demanding or insisting, but always encouraging and explaining, serving as much as an instructor of writing as a shaper of sentences, all while being so diplomatic—I told him he could have a career at the United Nations. Because of his sense of story, eye for detail, and way with words, my first published novel is polished and primed to be released to the world.

In the process of writing the novel, I had the privilege of meeting Richard Boyd, a highly decorated WWII Royal Air Force pilot who flew a Lancaster bomber on 33 missions in the European theater. His belief that his greatest success was getting his crew home safely became the foundation of my Scottish pilot character.

This novel is dedicated to all the courageous men and women of "The Greatest Generation," including my father Earl Whiskeyman, who waged a desperate struggle to preserve democracy for my generation and my children and grandchildren's generations. It's a gift many gave their lives for, and one we must not take for granted.

Made in United States
North Haven, CT
18 August 2024

56238769R00274